MICHELLE SAGARA

and The Chronicles of Elantra series

"No one provides an emotional payoff like Michelle Sagara.
Combine that with a fast-paced police procedural, deadly magics,
five very different races and a wickedly dry sense of humor—
well, it doesn't get any better than this."
—Bestselling author Tanya Huff

Cast in Shadow

"Intense, fast-paced, intriguing,
compelling and hard to put down...unforgettable."
—*In the Library Reviews*

"The fast-paced plot and intriguing characters beguile."
—*Romantic Times BOOKreviews*

Cast in Courtlight

"Readers will embrace this compelling,
strong-willed heroine with her often sarcastic voice."
—*Publishers Weekly*

"A fast-paced novel, packed with action and adventure...
integrating the conventions of police procedurals
with more fantastic elements."
—*Romantic Times BOOKreviews*

MICHELLE SAGARA

CAST IN SECRET

LUNA™
www.LUNA-Books.com

LUNA™

First trade printing August 2007

CAST IN SECRET

ISBN-13: 978-0-373-80280-7
ISBN-10:   0-373-80280-3

www.LUNA-Books.com

Printed in U.S.A.

Author Note

I always wonder at people who tell other people to get a life, because for all accounts and purposes we all *have* one. For me it's a good life, but there are times when it's overwhelming, and when it is, I seek a little bit of escape and a little bit of something that's larger. I find it in different places—I adored *Buffy*, especially the first two seasons, adored beyond reason *Firefly*; I read novels, manga, and I play video games.

I do all these things because they entertain me, and when I decided to write THE CHRONICLES OF ELANTRA books, I wanted to return some of that entertainment, to capture some of its essence. It was a bit of a departure for me—the stories are structured a little bit more like the beloved television shows mentioned above; each volume has some hint of a larger arc, but should be self-contained in the events. I went for a modern sensibility, because the world itself is strange enough. I wanted to be able to make other people laugh, or to move them, because that's what I want when I seek escape.

Cast in Shadow introduced Kaylin Neya, a young officer of the law, who's still trying to sort out who she is and where she fits in. *Cast in Courtlight* threw her headfirst into politics, which is not one of her strengths, and in *Cast in Secret*, she's very much looking forward to business as usual. Given the circumstances, this may very well *be* business as usual—but only in the City of Elantra, where very little is what it seems to be....

This one is for my kids—and peers—in Makaveli, on Shadowsong

/bonk
/hug
/love

ACKNOWLEDGMENTS

My long-suffering husband, Thomas, kept home, household and the peculiar space authors often need safe, as always, but also found time to read the work in progress, even when the progress was agonizingly slow. My parents, Ken and Tami; my children, Daniel and Ross; John and Kristen Chew and their children, Jamie and Liam, kept my house lively. Terry Pearson read this in all stages, and offered the usual commentary and the incentive to keep going.

Mary-Theresa Hussey proved saintly in her patience and invaluable in the way editors are when the author is still too much *in* the book to see it *as* a book. (And Adam Wilson sent helpful and cheerful reminders, which were, as it turns out, entirely necessary.)

CHAPTER 1

Private Kaylin Neya studied the duty roster, and given how little she studied anything that wasn't somehow involved with a corpse, this said something.

The official roster was like a dartboard, except that people threw pencils at it instead. Sometimes they hit a bull's-eye anyway. Lined up in columns by day, and color-coded for the more moronic—or hungover—by district, it told the various members of the branch of law enforcement known as the Hawks where, exactly, they were meant to either find trouble or stay out of it. Kaylin could easily make out her name, although some clod with lousy aim had managed to make a giant hole in it.

If it was true that the roster could never make everyone happy, it was somehow *also* true that it could make everyone *un*happy. Sergeant Marcus Kassan, in charge of assigning duties on a monthly basis, had a strong sense of fairness; if someone was going to suffer, everyone might as well keep them company.

As the Hawks' *only* Leontine officer—in fact, the only Leontine to *be* an officer of the Halls of Law—he presided over the men and women under his command with a hooded set of fangs in a face that was fur, large eyes and peaked ears—in that order. He also boasted a set of claws that made daggers superfluous and did a good job against swords, as well.

Kaylin had no pencil with which to puncture the paper, or she'd have thrown more at it than liberal curses.

Swearing at one's assignment wasn't unusual in the office; as far as office pastimes went, it was one that most of the Hawks indulged in. Kaylin's partner, Corporal Severn Handred, looked easily over her shoulder, but waited until she turned to raise a dark brow in her general direction. That brow was bisected by a slender, white line, a scar that didn't so much mar his face as hint at secret histories.

Secret, at least, to Kaylin; she hadn't seen him take that one.

"What will you be missing?" he asked, when her impressive spate of cursing—in four official languages—had died down enough that he could be heard without shouting. Severn rarely raised his voice.

"Game," she said curtly. "Ball," she added.

"Playing?"

She grimaced. "Betting." Which, for Kaylin, was synonymous with *watching*.

"Figures. Who were you betting on?"

She shrugged. "Sharks."

"So you'll save some money."

This caused an entirely different spate of swearing, and she punctuated this by punching his shoulder, which he thoughtfully turned in her direction. "You'd be betting on the Tigers, I suppose?"

"Already have," he replied. "Our shift?" He glanced at the window. It told the time. Literally. Mages had been allowed to go mad when they'd been asked to encourage punctuality, and it showed. The urge to tell the window to shut the hell up came and went several times a day.

The fact that mages had been allowed to perform the spell or series of spells seemed almost a direct criticism of Kaylin, who wasn't exactly punctual on the best of days.

"Private Neya and Corporal Handred, report to the Quartermaster before active duty." Some sweet young voice had been used to capture the words. Kaylin seriously wanted to meet the person behind it. And was pretty sure the person behind it seriously didn't want to meet her.

"Quartermaster?" Severn said, with the barest hint of a sympathetic grimace.

Kaylin said, "Can I break the window first?"

"Won't help. He's probably responsible for having the glass replaced, and you're in enough trouble with him as is."

It was true. She had barely managed to crawl up the ladder from thing-scraped-off-the-bottom-of-a-shoe-after-a-dog-fight in the unspoken ranks the Quartermaster gave the Hawks; she was now merely in the person-I-can't-see category, which was a distinct improvement, although it usually meant she was the last to get kitted out. The Quartermaster was officious enough, however, to make last and late two entirely different domains—if only, in Kaylin's case, by seconds.

"It was just a stupid dress," she muttered. "*One* dress, and I'm in the doghouse."

"I doubt it. You know how much he loves those dogs."

"Yeah. A lot more than he likes the rest of us."

"It was an *expensive* dress, Kaylin."

"I didn't choose it!"

"No. But you did give it back with a few bloodstains, a dozen knife tears, and about a pound less fabric."

"It's not like it could have been used by anyone else—"

"Not in that condition, no. And," he added, lifting a hand, "I'm not the Quartermaster, I didn't have to haggle with the Seamstresses Guild, and I don't really care."

"Yeah, but his life doesn't depend on me, so he doesn't have to listen to me whine."

Severn chuckled. "No. Your career depends on him, however. Good job, Kaylin."

They walked down the long hall that led to Marcus's desk, which just happened to be situated so that it crossed almost any indoor path a Hawk could take in the line of duty. He liked to keep an eye on things. Or a claw across the throat, as the Leontine saying went.

As the Hawks' sergeant, assignments came from him, and reports—which involved the paperwork he so hated—went to him. Caitlin, his assistant, and for all purposes, his second in command, was the one who would actually *read* the submissions, and she wisely chose to pass on only those that she felt were important. The rest, she fudged.

And since the Festival season was, as of two days past, officially over, most of those reports involved a lot of cleanup, a lot of official fines—which helped the coffers of the Halls of Law immensely—and a lot of petty bickering, which would be referred to the unofficial courts in the various racial enclaves for mediation.

Ceding that bickering to the racial courts, rather than the Imperial Courts, took *more* paperwork. But the Emperor was short on time and very, very short on patience, so only cases of real import—or those that involved the Elantran nobility—ever went to him directly. Given that he was Immortal, being a dragon and all, this struck Kaylin as unfair. After all, he *had* forever.

"Lord Kaylin," Marcus said, as they approached his desk. The title, granted her by the Lord of the Barrani High Court, caused a round of snickers and an unfortunate echo in the office that set Kaylin's teeth on edge. The deep sarcasm that only a Leontine throat could produce didn't help much. "So good of you to join us."

She snapped him a salute—which, given his rank didn't demand it, was only meant to annoy—and stood at attention in front of his desk. Severn's short sigh, she ignored; he offered Marcus neither of these gestures.

"There's been a slight change in your beat today."

The official roster changed at the blink of an eye. A Leontine eye, with its golden iris. "You're to go to Elani Street," he told them.

"What, mage central?"

"Or Charlatan central, if you prefer," Marcus snapped back. Elani Street was both. There was the real stuff, if you weren't naive and you knew what to look for, and then there was love potion number nine, and tell your fortune, and meet the right mate, all of which booths—usually with much finer names—saw a steady stream of traffic, day in and day out.

Kaylin was always torn between contempt for the people who had such blind dreams and contempt for the people who could exploit them so callously. Elani Street was not her favorite street, mostly because she couldn't decide which of the two she wanted to strangle more.

She flipped an invisible coin. It landed, after a moment in the mental ether, on the side of people who made money, rather than people who lost it.

"Who's fleecing people this time?" Kaylin muttered. "It's only two days past Festival—you'd think people would be tired enough to give it a rest. Or," she added darkly, "in jail."

"Many are both," Marcus replied, and something in his tone made her give up her sullen and almost perfect stance to lean slightly into the desk. Slightly was safe; he still hadn't cleared half the paperwork the Festival produced annually, and knocking any of the less than meticulous piles over was—well, the furrows in the desk didn't get there by magic.

"What's happened?"

"There's been a disturbance," he replied. "I believe you know the shop. Evanton's. You may have given him some business over the years."

She knew the shop; she had had her knives enchanted there so that they left their sheaths without a sound. Teela had been the Hawk who had both introduced her to Evanton and also made clear to Evanton that anything he offered *for money* had better damn well work. Given that Teela was one of a dozen or so Barrani—also all Hawks—who had made their pledge of allegiance to the Imperial Halls of Law, her word tended to carry weight. After all, she was, like the dragon Emperor and the rest of her kind, immortal—and the Barrani loved nothing better than a grudge, at least judging by the way they held on to the damn things so tightly. Startlingly beautiful to the eye, they were cold as crackling ice to the ear, and their tall, slender bodies radiated that I-can-kill-you-before-you-can-blink confidence that was, in fact, no act.

Evanton, to his credit, had been neither offended nor frightened. In fact, his first words had been, "Yes, yes, I know the drill, Officer." And his second: "You're on the young side for a Hawk. So take my advice, for what it's worth. You should pay more attention to the company you keep. People will judge you by it, mark my words."

He generally had a lot of words he wanted marked.

Which had caused Teela to grimace. And Tain, her beat partner, to laugh.

As for the enchantment, he'd approved of it. "Most people who come here want something to make them look prettier," he'd said, with obvious contempt. "Or younger. Or smarter. This, *this* is practical."

She had never asked Evanton if he had ever belonged to the Imperial Order of Mages; there wasn't much point. If he had, he'd managed to get out the unusual way—he wasn't in a coffin. Although to Kaylin's youthful eye, he looked as if he should have been. His hair was the color of blinding light off still water, and his skin was like wrinkled leather; he was almost skeletal, and his work—or so he said—demanded so much attention he was continuously bent over in a stoop. She had been certain, the first time she saw him, that he would break if she forced him to straighten up.

But still…she liked him. So she frowned. "What kind of a disturbance?"

"That, I think, is what you're there to ascertain." He paused. "Are you waiting for something?"

"No, sir."

"Good. Get lost."

"Yes, sir."

"Corporal?"

Severn nodded.

"Make sure that she understands that 'get lost' in this case isn't literal."

"Yes, sir."

"What I want to know," Private Kaylin Neya said, not quite stomping her feet as she marched down the streets, "is why no one calls *you* Lord Severn."

The corporal—which rank still annoyed Kaylin, and yes, she knew it was petty—shrugged. "Because it doesn't bother *me*," he replied.

"It didn't bother me when the Barrani called me Lord Kaylin," she said sourly.

He laughed. He kept an easy pace with her march, given the difference in the length of their strides, and her mood—which could charitably be described as not very good—seemed to cheer him immensely.

"What's so funny?"

"It bothered you enough to cause you to point out that no one called Teela Lord."

She waved a hand dismissively. "It wasn't the Barrani," she insisted. "But when Marcus started—"

"The entire office, you mean?"

"The entire office follows Marcus's lead, except when he's chewing through his desk." Which was only partly a figurative description of an angry Leontine officer. Leontine fur, when it stood on end, was impressive; Leontine jaws, massive, boasted teeth that were easily capable of rendering most throats not quite useful for things like breathing—but most of the danger they could offer came from their massive, and usually sheathed, claws.

Marcus's desk was a testament to how often he lost his temper.

"If you give it a few days," Severn told her, "it'll pass."

She snorted. "Sanabalis started it."

"Lord Sanabalis."

"That's not what I call him."

"It is, however, what everyone *else* calls him, and what you'd like to call him at the moment would be…ill advised. You're his student, he has graciously agreed to continue to tutor you, and you both know that your career depends on whether or not he decides to actually *pass* you." He didn't add that in this case career and life were the same thing. He didn't need to. Kaylin had a magic that not even the most august of the Imperial scholars understood, and if it had been a weak magic, it wouldn't have mattered—much. But it was strong enough to withstand the full breath of a dragon in his true form. Strong enough to make a hole in a thick stone wall that was wider across than Severn. Strong enough to heal the dying.

And the Emperor was in possession of all these facts, and more. Kaylin's glance strayed a moment to her arms; the length of her sleeves all but hid the dark marks that were tattooed there, in whirls and strokes, as if she were parchment, and they were the scattered telling of a story that was ancient before history began.

Her powers and these marks had arrived almost at the same time, in the winter world of the fiefs, where only the desperate and the criminals lived. Funny, that the fiefs should lie so precisely at the heart of the city.

"Kaylin."

She looked up, and realized that Severn had been speaking. Dragged her eyes from sleeves that weren't all that interesting, anyway, and nodded.

"Lord Sanabalis might be unusual for a Dragon, but he *is* a Dragon." He paused a moment, and as Kaylin realized she was losing him and pulled up short, he added, "He meant it as a gesture of respect, Kaylin."

"I don't need that kind of respect. And anyway, no one *else* means it that way."

"Well, no. But they're Hawks. You expected different?"

She started walking again. "What are the odds?"

"Which betting pool?"

"Mine."

"Four days," he said cheerfully, "before you lose your temper and try to break something over someone's head."

"Any bets as to whose?"

"Some."

"Name names."

He laughed. "I've got money riding on it."

"Figures." She almost paused at the stall of a baker who was known to be friendly to the Hawks or the Swords. Almost. The coin in her pocket would probably last her another three days if she didn't bother with food. And less than the afternoon if she did; if the baker was friendly, she wasn't stupid.

"If you're betting on the Sharks," Severn said, stopping by her side, "it's no big surprise you're always so broke. Good morning, Mrs. Whitmore. We'd like a half-dozen of the buns."

Hunger versus pride wasn't much of a struggle; she let Severn buy breakfast, because that was what it was. She'd been keeping company with the midwives the past two nights and it showed. The circles under her eyes accentuated her mood. But it was a good sort of bad—no one had died, no mothers, and no babies. And she had spent time helping to lick the fur of a sole Leontine cub clean.

She still had hair in her mouth. But she was aware of the singular honor offered her by the mother: the willingness to let a stranger near the helpless, mewling cub. It was a gesture not only of trust, but of respect, and it was also a request that Leontine women seldom made.

The mother had watched as Kaylin's entirely inadequate human tongue had, in a ritual way, licked some of the birthing fluid from the cubling's closed, delicately veined lids. Kaylin's stomach was not up to the task of more, but more wasn't required; she handled the infant with care, marveling at the fine, fine hair that covered him. It was a pale gray, with a spattering of white streaks—these would fade into the Leontine gold she best knew with time. But the birth colors were considered important to the Leontine. And these were not bad colors.

It wasn't all that often that she was called into a Leontine birthing—because there were no Leontine midwives in the guild, and the Leontines defined the word suspicious when it came to outsiders. She had expected the birth to be difficult, and by Leontine standards, it was—but it was also unusual. There was one cub, and only one. The pregnancy, she had been *very* quietly told, had been labored and difficult, and it was thought—many times—that Arlan would lose the cubs.

Losing the cubs and not losing her life were not things that Kaylin would normally be consulted about. This time was different, but she wasn't certain why, or how.

"It's important," an exhausted Arlan had deigned to inform her, "that I be able to bear cubs." She did not say why, and Kaylin, seeing the almost subconscious flick of claws at the end of the pale golden fur of Arlan's hands, had known better than to ask.

"I will name him Roshan," his mother had said, and then added, "Roshan Kaylarr." She'd nodded, then, to Kaylin, and Kaylin had understood that, in as much as a Leontine *could* be named after her, this child was.

If she had been human, this indomitable and ferocious Leontine woman, Kaylin would have asked what the father thought of the name; in the case of the Leontine males, this was pointless. They loved their kitlings—but they knew when to stay out of the way.

They had wives, plural, and the wives could fight like, well, cats when the need arose—but the pridlea was also a unit unto itself, and where husbands were concerned, they formed a wall of solidarity when it came to protecting their own.

"Kaylin?" Severn said, and she hastily swallowed a mouthful of pastry that thankfully tasted nothing like the salty skin of newborn cub. Shook her head. He backed off, but with a slight smile.

"Where are we?"

"Almost there. Pay attention?"

"I was."

He nodded with the ease of long practice. "Pay attention to where we actually are, hmm?"

"Trouble?"

"No."

"Then what's the problem?"

"You're going to trip over your own feet, and stone isn't the best cushion." He paused, and then said quietly, "And I have something for you."

She grimaced. "The bracer?"

"It was on my breakfast table in the morning. I thought you'd been with the midwives, and I kept it for you." He took it out of the satchel he carried by his side. It gleamed gold and sparkled with the caught light of sapphire, ruby and diamond. It was her cage.

And it was, in its fashion, her haven. This, this cold, gleaming artifact, could contain the magic that Sanabalis, the heartless bastard, was trying to teach her to control. It was the only thing that could, and without it—without its existence—she would probably be dead by Imperial order.

It had come from the personal hoard of the Emperor, and it was ancient, although it looked as if it had been newly made. It took no dents or scratches, and no blood remained across its golden surface for long. Its gems didn't break or scratch, either.

"Put it on," he said.

She nodded, her fingers keying the sequence that would open it. Sliding it over her wrist, she thought of making some feeble protest—but she was with Severn, not Marcus, and Severn understood.

"You think I'll need it?" she asked softly, as it clicked shut.

"I don't know," he said at last, but after a pause that was evasive. "You know you're not supposed to take it off." As she opened her mouth, he added, "By the Hawklord's orders."

She bit back the words for a moment, and when they came, they came more smoothly. "You know I can't help the midwives if I wear it."

"I know."

"I can't heal—"

"I know. I told you, I thought you might have been with the midwives when I saw it this morning."

The other property of the bracer that would have been the envy of the stupid because it looked so very expensive was that it was impossible *to* lose. She could take it off if need be, drop it in the nearest trash heap, and it would find its way back to its keeper—that keeper *not* being Kaylin. For seven years, the keeper had been the Hawklord.

And for a month now, it had been Severn. He never asked why it came to his hand—which was good, because no one, as far as Kaylin could tell, had an explanation—and he never asked, except obliquely, why it wasn't on *hers*. He simply gathered it and brought it back to her. And waited.

As a Keeper, he was a lot less onerous than the Hawklord.

"Severn—"

"It's Elani Street," he replied with a shrug, "and if you hunt long enough, you'll find magic here."

"I know where to find—" But she stopped, catching her words before she tripped over them with her tongue. "I hate magic."

He stopped walking, turned suddenly, and looked down at her from an uncomfortable height. His hands caught both of her shoulders, and slid up them, trailing the sides of her neck to cup her face, and she met his eyes, brown and simple, dark with a past that she was part of, and a past that she didn't know at all.

"Don't," he told her quietly. "Don't hate it. It's part of what you are, now, and nothing will change that. It's a gift."

She thought of the ways in which she had killed in a blind fury; thought of the stone walls that had parted like curtains of dust when the magic overwhelmed her. "A gift," she said bitterly.

And he said, "You have fur on your tongue." In almost perfect Leontine.

And a baby's name—did race really matter?—like an echo in the same language, waiting to be said in affection and wonder, even if she were never again there to hear it.

He let his hands fall slowly away from her face as if they had belonged there, as if they were drawn there by gravity.

"Severn—"

He touched her open mouth with a single finger. But he didn't smile, and he didn't say anything else.

Elani Street opened up before them like any other merchant street in the district. If you didn't know the city, you might have mistaken it *for* any other merchant street. It was not in the high-rent district—Kaylin's patrols were somehow always designed to keep her away from the rich and prosperous—but it was not in the low-rent district, either. It hovered somewhere in the center. Clearly the buildings were old, and as much wood as stone had gone into their making, but they were well kept, and if paint flaked from signboards and windows had thinned with time, they were solid and functional.

The waterfront was well away, and the merchant authority didn't technically govern the men and women who worked here for some complicated legalistic reason that had a lot to do with history and nothing to do with the *law,* so the Hawks and the Swords were the sole force that policed the area. And everyone was happy that way. Except for the Merchants' Guild, which sent on its annual weasel report in an attempt to bring Elani under its jurisdiction.

Once or twice things had gotten ugly between the Merchants' Guild and the Elani Streeters, and blood had been shed across more than just this part of town. This was practical history, to Kaylin, so she remembered it better than the codicils on top of codicils that kept the Merchants' Guild at bay.

They had—the Guild—even tried to set up trade sanctions against this small part of town, and while everyone in theory agreed with it, in practice, they'd come anyway, because there *wasn't* any actual evidence that they'd been here. You didn't exactly bear a brand saying Fortunes Have Been Read Across My Palm, Look Here when you left. The sale of love potions may have dropped a tad during that embargo, however.

No, the rents weren't high here, but the take was high *enough* that the vendors could usually fend off the more powerful guild with effective political sleight of hand. Or so Teela said; if she admired it, it had to be underhanded.

She was, after all, Barrani.

Severn's expression was so carefully neutral, Kaylin laughed. He raised a brow.

"You don't like Elani Street?"

"Not much, no. You?"

She shrugged. "It's a street."

He stopped in front of a placard that was leaning haphazardly against a grimy window. "Love potions?" he said. The sneer was entirely in his tone. "Meet your perfect mate? Find out what your future holds?"

As she'd said more or less the same thing—well, more and more heated—she shrugged again. "It's a living."

"So is theft."

"Yeah, but people come here to empty their pockets. There's no knife at their throat."

"Dreams are their own knife, Kaylin. Dreams, what-ifs, desires. We all have to have hope."

"This isn't hope," she replied quietly. "It's just another way of lying to yourself."

"Almost everything is, in the end." He glanced at the board again, and then continued to walk down the street. He walked slowly enough that she could catch up to him; on patrol he usually did. But there was distance in his expression, some thought she couldn't read—not that he'd ever been transparent.

Still, the street itself was quiet; the Festival season had passed over and around it, and the merchants who had, enterprising hucksters all, taken stalls near the Ablayne had returned home to the nest to find it, as it so often was after festival celebrations—and the cost of those—empty.

Evanton was not above taking a stall—or so he said—but his age prevented him from doing so so close to water. It made his bones ache. Kaylin expected that it was his jaw that ached, because he had some idea of what customer service was supposed to be, and fixing a smile across lines that were worn in perpetual frown taxed his strength.

Still, she smiled when she saw his store. Touching the hilts of her daggers for both luck and memory, she walked up the three flat steps that led to his door, and frowned slightly.

"Is it late?"

"You just had breakfast. You answer." But Severn's frown echoed hers; the curtains were drawn. In the door's window and also, across the shop's wider front. Gold leaf had flecked in places, and glass was scratched atop those letters—some thief attempting to remove what was on the other side had no doubt had too much to drink that night.

She knocked. Waited a minute, counting slowly, before she knocked again; Evanton never moved quickly, and his temper soured greatly if the visitor was too stupid to realize this.

But before she could be *really* annoying, the curtains flipped back, and she saw a wizened face peering through glass. He didn't look much older than he had the first time she'd met him—but then again, she doubted that was possible. The curtains fell back into place, black drape that was almost gray with sun. No stars on it, no moons, no fancy—and fake—arcane symbols.

The door opened slowly; she heard keys twisting a rusty lock, followed by creaking hinges.

"You really should get some help around here," she muttered.

"Good help," he said coolly, "is hard to find in this city."

"You've tried?"

He grimaced. "Don't force me to be rude, girl. You're wearing the Hawk."

She smiled. It wasn't the forced smile of an officer of the law, either; she had walked back into his dusty parlor, with its long counter, its rows of shelves—a city, no doubt, for spiders—its odd books stacked here and there like so much garbage so many times she couldn't feel uncomfortable here. If it was an odd place, it *felt* like someone's home, and she was welcome in it.

"I don't believe we've met," Evanton added pointedly, looking up at Severn. As Evanton, bent, was about Kaylin's height, he had to look up.

"No, sir," Severn said, in a much politer—and cooler—voice. "But I am aware of your establishment."

"Fame gets me every time," the old man replied. "Who are you?"

"He's Severn," Kaylin answered quickly. "Corporal Handred is also—as you can see—a Hawk."

"Aye, I can see that," Evanton said. "I would have called him a Wolf, if you'd asked me."

Severn raised a brow. It went half as high as Kaylin's. "He was a Wolf—" she began, but stopped as Severn stepped neatly, and heavily, on her foot. "What do you know about the Wolves?"

"Meaning what dealings have I had with them?"

"Meaning that."

Evanton snorted. "You haven't spent enough time with those Barrani, girl."

"What?"

"That's no way to get an answer."

"I could threaten to break your arms if you want."

He laughed his dry, low chuckle. "Aye, but they're more subtle than that. I'm of use to them. It's important in this business to be of use to people."

Severn said, quietly, "We're here on official business."

"Dressed like that, you'd have to be. Although the uniform suits you."

"You sent a message to the Hawks."

Evanton shrugged. "I? I sent no message to the Hawks. I believe a message *was* sent, on the other hand. I know my own business," he said at last, "and I know Hawk business when I see it. I prefer to keep them entirely separate, you understand, but we can't always get what we want. You'll want to follow me," he added.

Kaylin was already behind him, because she always was in his store; he could bite your head off for going anywhere without him, and usually at length.

He led them behind his tall, sturdy counter. Its sides were made of solid wood that had the patina of time and disregard, not craft. It was impossible to see most of the wood, it was covered by so many things. Papers, bits of cloth, needles, thread—she had never asked why he wanted those because his answers could be mocking and gruesome. It looked more as if it belonged in a bar than a store, but then again, most of the things in the store looked as if they belonged somewhere else; the only things they had in common were dust and cobwebs, and the occasional glint of something that might be gold, or steel, or captive light— a hint of magic.

Wedged between two hulking shelves that looked suspi-

ciously unstable was a very narrow door. Evanton took out
a key ring that Kaylin could have put her whole arm through
without trying very hard, chose one of three keys that
dangled forlornly from its thin, tarnished metal, and
unlocked the door. Like everything else in the store, it
creaked.

He opened it slowly—he opened everything that way—
and after a moment, nodded to himself and motioned for
them to follow. Kaylin started forward, and Severn, with
long years of practice, managed to slide between her and
Evanton so smoothly she didn't even step on the back of his
feet. And not for lack of trying.

They entered a hall that was, like everything else in the
building, narrow; they could walk single file, and if anyone
had tried to pull a sword here, it would have lodged in the
wall or the roof if they actually had to use it. Given Evanton,
this was possibly deliberate. It was hard to say where the
old man was concerned.

But at the end of the hall was another door, and judging
by the jangle of keys, it, too, was locked. "Here," he said
quietly, "is the heart of my store. Let me tell you again.
Touch nothing. Look at nothing for too long unless I
instruct you otherwise. Take nothing."

Kaylin bridled slightly, but Severn merely nodded. "How
difficult will that be, old man?"

"Maybe you are a Hawk after all," Evanton replied,
eyeing Severn with barely veiled curiosity. "And the
answer to that question is, I don't know. I have no
trouble." He paused and added, "But that was not always

the case. And I did not have myself as a guide, when I first came here."

"Who did you have?" Kaylin asked, tilting her head to one side.

He raised a white brow.

"Sorry, Evanton."

"Good girl. Oh, and Kaylin? I continue to allow you to visit here because of the great respect I have always felt for the Officers of the Halls of Law."

"But I haven't—" She stopped moving for a moment, and then brought her free hand up to her cheek to touch the skin across which lay a tattoo of a simple herb: Nightshade, by name. Deadly Nightshade, she thought to herself.

If it had *only* been a tattoo, it would never cause her trouble. It felt like skin to her, and the Hawks had become so used to it, she could almost forget it existed.

But this mark was—of course—magical, and it had been placed on her cheek by Lord Nightshade, a Barrani Lord who was outcaste to his people, and oh, wanted by every division in the Halls of Law for criminal activities beyond the river that divided the city itself.

Lord Nightshade had marked her, and the mark meant something to the Barrani. It meant something to the Dragons. To the other mortal races, it was generally less offensive than most tattoos. But clearly, it meant something to Evanton, purveyor of junk and the odd useful magic. He understood that it linked her, in ways that not even Kaylin fully understood, to Lord Nightshade himself.

But if Evanton's eyes were narrowed, they were not suspicious. "Here," he told her quietly, "there is some safety from the mark you bear. He will not find you, if he is looking." He pushed the door open so slowly, Kaylin could have sworn she could feel the hours pass. "Is he?"

"Is he what?"

"Looking."

She shrugged, uneasy. "He knows where to find me," she said at last.

"Not, perhaps, a good thing, in your case. But enough. You are clearly yourself."

"You can tell that how?"

"You could not have crossed my threshold if you were under his thrall."

She nodded. Believing him. Wanting to know *why* she couldn't have.

Severn spoke instead. "You sent a message to the Halls?"

"Ah. No, actually, I didn't. If you check your Records carefully, you will not find a single—"

Severn lifted his hand. "Where *did* you send the message?"

"Ah. That would be telling. And probably telling too much," the old man replied. "But people in power have an odd sense of what's important. I imagine one of them took the time to read my elegant missive."

"You expected this visit."

"Of course. Forgive the lack of hospitality, but I don't drink, and I can't stand tea."

And he held the door slightly ajar, motioning them in. Watching them both more carefully than he had ever watched Kaylin before. She wasn't certain how she knew this, because he looked the same—eyes and skin crinkled in lines around his lips, the narrow width of his face. He wasn't smiling, but he almost never did.

She meant to say something, but the words escaped her because from the width of the hall and the door she had expected the room to be tiny. And it was the size—and the height—of the Aerie in the Halls, where the winged Aerians who served the Hawklord could reach for, and almost touch, the sky.

Sunlight streamed down from above, as if through colored glass; the air moved Kaylin's hair across her cheeks, suggesting breeze and open space. As a fiefling, she had had no great love of open spaces, but daylight had always suggested safety. There was a hint of that safety here, and it surprised her—magic almost always made her skin crawl.

The wooden plank flooring, often covered with carpets that made the floors look both older and more rickety, rather than less, had given way entirely to…grass. Blue-green grass, thick and short, that was so perfect she was almost afraid to take a step on it without removing her boots. She couldn't see the far walls—she imagined this was because they were painted the color of sky—but she could see trees—tall trees—and the hint of water ahead, and to her left, the large curve of boulders seen between slender trunks.

A garden.

A magical garden.

"Yes," Evanton said, as the door clicked shut at her back. She turned slowly to face him and saw that he had changed. His clothing was different, for one, and he seemed to stand slightly taller; the stoop in his shoulders, the bend, the perpetual droop of his neck, had disappeared. He was not young, would never be young, but age had majesty here that it had never had before.

"Yes?"

"It is a magic, of a type, Kaylin Neya. If you stand here for long enough, and you listen carefully, you might hear the sound of your name on the wind." He paused, and then tendered her something shocking: A perfect, formal bow. "Lord Kaylin," he said quietly, "of the High Court."

"Don't you start, too," she began, but he waved her to silence.

"In this place, names have import, and there are rumors, girl."

"Never bet on a rumor."

His expression shifted and twisted, and for a moment she could see the man she had first met in this changed one. "Why not? You do." He lifted an arm; blue cloth clung to it in a drape that reminded her of Barrani High Court clothing. It was not so fine in line, and it hung a little long, and perhaps a little heavily, on his scrawny frame—but it suggested…gravity. Experience.

Maybe even nobility, and *no one* sent Kaylin to talk to the nobles. Or the people who—far worse—wanted to be nobles and hadn't quite made it yet, in their own minds.

"I bet small change," she began. Severn snorted.

"Small change," Severn told Evanton, unphased by the change in the man, "is all Kaylin ever *has*."

"So you bet everything you have, time and again? You really should choose different companions, girl. But," he added, staring at Severn again, "I don't disapprove of this one."

"You didn't disapprove of Teela or Tain, that I recall."

"It hardly matters, where the Barrani are concerned. And Teela is a slightly unusual case. I have known her for some time," he added, almost gently. "She was the first customer I had in this store, when I finally opened it."

"When you finally opened it?"

"Ah, yes. It took me some time to find my way back. From this place," he added, looking beyond Kaylin, his eyes slightly unfocused. She knew the look; he was remembering something. Something she was certain he wasn't about to share. "And she was waiting, with, I might add, her usual patience." Which would of course be none at all.

"How long had she waited?"

"Quite a while, from all accounts. It was well before she joined the Hawks," he added, "and she cut a formidable figure."

Thinking about the drug dealers on the banks of the Ablayne—the ones who had been unfortunate enough to sell Lethe—Kaylin said, "She's pretty damn formidable now."

"In a fashion. She was waiting for me, and she was not with Tain. She did have a greatsword, however, a fine piece of work. It predated the Empire," he added. "But I do not believe it was a named weapon."

"Don't believe? You mean you aren't certain?" Kaylin felt her jaw drop. Luckily, it was attached to her face, or it would have bounced off the grass.

"Not entirely certain, no. There was something of a glamour on it, and since it looked like a serviceable, if old-fashioned, sword, the glamour clearly wasn't there to make it look *more* impressive. But making it look less impressive, holding some power in reserve—that's Barrani all over."

She shook her head. "Teela doesn't even *use* a sword."

"If the sword she had with her that day were one of the named weapons, she wouldn't—she wouldn't insult the responsibility of ownership by using a lesser blade. What does she use, anyway?"

"Mostly hands or feet, but sometimes a great big stick."

He nodded.

Severn, who was the model of studied patience, finally spoke, scattering the pleasant gossip to the winds that Evanton had mentioned. "Why are you showing us this?"

"A very good question. I'm surprised Kaylin didn't ask it," he added, frowning at her, although he spoke to Severn. "She always asks too many questions—they try what little patience I've managed to preserve." But he said it without rancor. "This is not unlike the High Halls of the Barrani— and if I'm not mistaken, Corporal Handred, you are also entitled to be called Lord while you are in the High Halls."

Severn nodded.

"This place is, however, older, I think, than the Halls, and one of the few such ancient places within the city that are not governed by either Barrani or the Dragon Emperor himself.

"Although when I was called to answer for my stewardship of this place, I will say the Dragon Emperor was a tad…testy. I'd advise you to stay on his good side when you do meet him."

"You mean the side without the teeth, right?" Kaylin asked.

Evanton chuckled. "That side, yes, although the tail can be quite deadly."

She didn't ask him how he knew this. His words had caught up with her thoughts. "What do you mean when I meet him?"

His frown was momentary. "Never mind, girl. All in good—or bad—time. He is watching you, but even his reach is not so long that he can see you here. He is almost certainly aware that you *are* here, however."

"What do you mean?"

"He has my shop watched."

"Oh." She paused, and took a step forward into a room that was, in her eyes, almost devoid of any trace of human interference. But…it belonged to Evanton, and because it did, she could see odd things that lay on stone pedestals, on stone shelves, and in alcoves that lined the nearest walls. Things that held candles—candelabras?—that were lined up in perfect precision, unlit and therefore unblemished. There were books, boxes that looked as if they'd been left out in the rain—and the sun and the snow for good measure—and small, golden tablets that looked as if they had, conversely, barely been touched by eyes. Still, it was the candles that caught her attention.

"Are they ever lit?"

"Never," Evanton replied. "And if they are to be lit, let it be during someone else's watch."

She nodded and kept walking, and after a while, she said, "This is circular, this room?"

"A large circle, but yes." Evanton's eyes were gleaming and dark as he answered. His nod was more a nod of approval than Kaylin had ever seen from him. She took encouragement from it, and continued to watch the room with the eyes—the trained eyes—of a hawk.

Saw a small pond, saw a fire burning in a brazier; felt the wind's voice above her head and saw the leaves turn at its passing. Saw, in the distance, a rock garden in which no water trickled.

She said, "Elemental."

And Evanton nodded again.

"Severn?"

"I concur. But it is unusual."

"And the books, Evanton?"

"Good girl," he said softly. "Those, do not touch. You may approach them, but do not touch them."

"I doubt I'd be able to read them."

"It is not in the reading that they present the greatest threat, and Kaylin, if you spoke no words at all, if you were entirely deprived of language, these books would still speak to you."

"Magic," she said with disdain.

"Indeed, and older magic than the magic that is the current fashion. Fashion," he added, "may be frowned on by the old, but I believe that the trend is not a bad one."

She half closed her eyes. Listened to the voice of the wind as it rustled through slender branches; golden leaves, white leaves and a pale, pale bloodred, all turned as it passed. Heard, for a moment, a name that was not quite hers as she looked up, to feel its touch across her cheeks.

The mark of Nightshade began to tingle. It was not entirely comfortable. Without thinking, she lifted a hand to her face to touch the mark.

"The mark you bear affords you some protection. He must value you, Kaylin," Evanton said. He was closer than she realized; she should have heard his shuffling step, but she had heard only the wind. And felt, for a moment, the glimmering dream of flight.

His voice dispelled the wind's, sent it scattering, left her bound—as she would always be bound—to ground. And because he simply waited, she began to walk again.

To the pond, where small shelves and altars sat across moss beds. Books lay there, and again, candles, unlit, by the dozen. There were small boxes, and a mirror—the first she'd seen since she'd entered this room.

"The mirror—"

"Do *not* touch it."

"Wasn't going to," she said, although her hand stopped in midair. "But does it work?"

"Work?"

"Is it functional? If I wanted to send a message, could I?"

"Not," he replied, "to anyone you would care to speak to." It was an evasion. She accepted it. At the moment, the investigation—such as it was, since he hadn't actually *told them anything useful*—was not about mirrors or messages, but it was the first truly modern thing she'd encountered.

Yet even as she thought it, she looked at the mirror, and thought again. Its surface was tarnished and cloudy, and its frame, gold and silver, poorly tended. Unlike the rest of the small, jeweled boxes, the reliquaries—she recognized them for that now—this had been left alone.

"Do they all have mirrors?"

"All?"

"The elemental gardens. There should be four—the fire in the brazier, the water in this small pond, the rocks just beyond those silver trees. I can't see anything for air—"

"It is very, very hard to build a garden to air," he replied. "But it is here, and perhaps it is the freest of the elements because it can travel so readily. And the answer is no. None of them do."

"But this one—"

"Was brought here. It does not belong in this room."

"But you haven't moved it."

"No," he replied. "And until the Hawks deem it wise, I will not return it to its place. But do not touch it. The hand that held it last left some impression, but it will not, I think, be the equal of yours."

"You think of everything."

"I? Hardly. Had I, you would not be here now."

"Good point. Maybe." It was hard to leave the mirror, but she did, because the surface of the pond was everything the surface of the mirror was not: clean, smooth, reflective. The breeze that blew above did not touch it at all; she wondered if a pebble would ripple its surface.

"No," Evanton replied, as if he were reading her mind—

which she'd gotten used to in the last few weeks, but still didn't much care for. "It would not. The earth and the water barely meet here. The pond is not wide," he added, "but it runs very, very deep."

She nodded. "These footprints," she said, although she had barely grazed ground with her eyes, "aren't yours."

"No."

"You know whose they are?"

"I have some suspicion."

Severn knelt with care at Kaylin's side and examined the moss. He had seen what she had seen, of course. "There are at least two sets," he told them both. "The larger set belongs to a person of heavier build than the smaller. I would say human, and probably male, from the size."

Evanton's answer was lost.

Kaylin was gazing at the surface of the pond. Although the water was clear, there was a darkness in the heart of it that seemed endless. Deep, he had said, and she now believed it; you could throw a body down here and it would simply vanish. The idea of taking a swim had less than no appeal.

But the water's surface caught and held light, the light from the ceiling above, the one that Aerians would so love, it was that tall.

She could almost see them fly across it, reflected for a moment in passage, and felt again the yearning to fly and be free. To join them.

It was illusion, of course. There was no such thing as freedom. There was only—

Reflection. Movement.

Not hers, and not Severn's; Evanton stood far enough back that he cast no reflection.

"Kaylin?" Severn said, his voice close to her ear.

But Kaylin was gazing now into the eyes—the wide eyes—of a child's bruised face. A girl, her hair long and stringy in the way that unwashed children's hair could often be, her skin pale with winter, although winter was well away. She wore clothing that was too large for her, and threadbare, and undyed. She wore nothing at all on her feet, for Kaylin could see her toes, dirt in the nails.

She came back to the eyes.

The girl whispered a single word.

Kaylin.

CHAPTER 2

The first thing Kaylin had been taught when she'd been allowed to accompany groundhawks on her first investigation of a crime scene was *Do not touch anything or we will never bring you back.* This also meant, *Do not embarrass us by attempting to steal anything.* The Hawks were pretty matter-of-fact about her upbringing; they didn't actually care. The fiefs couldn't be actively policed, so it wasn't as if anything she'd done there was on record. If she had been canny enough to survive life on the streets of Nightshade, tough enough to emerge unscathed, and idealistic enough to want to uphold the Law rather than slide through its grip, so much the better.

It had been a missing-person investigation—which usually meant dead person whose body had yet to be found—and they'd walked the narrow streets that faced the fiefs without—quite—touching them. The Law still ruled in this old, boarded-up manor house, by a riverbank and a couple of narrow bridges.

She had been all of fourteen years old, and had spent six long months begging, badgering, and wheedling; when they said yes, she could follow them, she had nearly stopped breathing.

By that point, being a Hawk was the *only* thing she wanted, and she had held her fidget-prone hands by her sides, stiff as boards, while the Hawks—Teela and Tain for the most part, although Marcus had come along to supervise—had rambled about a series of large, run-down rooms for what felt like hours.

There wasn't much in the way of temptation on that particular day: nothing worth stealing.

Nothing she wanted to touch.

But this was so much harder. The girl was young. Younger than many of her orphans, the kitlings she visited, taught to read, and told stories—casually censored—of her adventures to. This girl was bruised; her eyes were wide with terror, her face gaunt with either cold or hunger. And she was real.

The water did not distort her; she did not sink into the depths, beckoning for Kaylin to follow to a watery, slow death. There was an aura about her, some faint hint of magic, but there would have to be.

Kaylin knelt with care by the side of this deep, deep pond, this scion of elemental magics. She did not touch the water's surface, but it was a struggle not to; not to reach out a hand, palm out, to the child whose dark eyes met hers.

As if he knew it—and he probably did—Severn was

behind her. He did not approach the water as closely as she herself had done, but instead put both of his hands on her shoulders and held tight.

"Corporal," she heard Evanton say quietly, "what do you see?"

"Water," Severn replied. "Very, very deep water."

"Interesting."

"You?"

"I see many things," Evanton replied. "Always. The water here is death." He paused and then added, "Almost everything is, to the unwary, in this place."

"Figures," Kaylin heard herself say, in a voice that was *almost* normal. "But whose death?"

"A good question, girl. As always."

"You usually tell me my questions are—"

"Hush."

But the girl didn't vanish until Evanton came to stand by Kaylin's side. "You're not one for obedience, blind or otherwise," he told her, with just a hint of frustration in a voice that was mostly approving. "But I believe I told you to look at nothing too closely."

"If you saw what I saw—"

"I may well, girl. But as I said, I see many things that the water chooses to reveal. There is always temptation, here, and it knows enough to see deeply."

"This *is not*—"

"Is it not? Here you sit, spellbound, horrified, gathering and hoarding your anger—which, I believe, is growing as the minutes pass. It isn't always things that tempt our basest desire—not all temptation is sensual or monetary in nature." He lifted his hands and gestured and the water rippled at the passage of a strong, strong gust.

All images were broken as it did, and the girl's face passed into memory—but it was burned there. Kaylin would not forget. Couldn't. Didn't, if she were honest, have any desire to do so.

"I know what you saw, Kaylin Neya. More of your life is in your face than you are aware of, in this place. And in the store," he added quietly.

"This is why you called me," she said, half a question in the flat statement.

"On the contrary, Kaylin, I requested no one. But this, I believe, has some bearing on the call the Hawks did receive. Even had I wanted to deal with the Law directly—and I believe that there are reasons for avoiding it—I would merely send the report or the request. The old, belligerent Leontine who runs the office would decide who actually responds."

"Marcus," she said automatically. "Sergeant Kassan."

"Very well, Sergeant Kassan, although it was clear by description to whom I referred." He paused, and then added, "Something was taken from this…room."

Her eyes widened slightly. "How the hell did someone get *into* this room?"

"A very good question, and believe that I have friends who are even now considering the problem."

"Friends?"

"At my age, they are few, and not all of them are mortal,

but," he added, and his face warped into a familiar, wizened expression, "even I have some."

"And they—"

"I have merely challenged them to break *into* the elementarium without causing anything to alert me to their presence."

"Good luck," she muttered.

"They will need more than luck," he said softly. "But I expect most of them will survive it."

She straightened slowly, her knees slightly cricked. It made her wonder how long she'd knelt there. The answer was too damn long; she was still tired from the previous night's birthing. But the elation of saving a cub's life passed into shadow, as it so often did.

"What was stolen?" she asked Evanton as she rose. Her voice fell into a regular Hawk's cadence—all bored business. And watchful.

"A small and unremarkable reliquary," he replied. "A red box, with gold bands. Both the leather and the gold are worn."

"What was in it?"

"I am not entirely certain," he replied, but it was in that I-have-some-ideas-and-I-don't-want-to-tell tone of voice. "The box is locked. It was locked when I first arrived, and the keys that were made to open it… It has no keyhole, Kaylin."

"So it can't be opened."

"Jumping to conclusions, I see."

She grimaced. "It has to be opened magically."

"Good girl," he replied softly.

"This isn't really Hawk work—"

"The Hawks don't investigate thefts?"

"Ye-es," she said, breaking the single syllable into two. "But not petty thefts as such, and not without a *better* description of the value of what's been stolen."

"People will die," he told her quietly, "while the reliquary is at large. It exerts its power," he added softly, "on those who see it and those who possess it. Only—" He stopped. His face got that closed-door look that made it plain he would say no more. Not yet.

"There were two people here," she said at last.

"Yes. Two. An unusually large woman, or a heavyset man, by the look of those treads, and an unusually small one, or a child, by the look of the second." He met her eyes.

And she knew who the child had been.

The shop seemed more mundane than it had ever seemed when Evanton escorted them back into it. His robes transformed as he crossed the threshold and the power of wisdom gave way to the power of age and gravity as his shoulders fell into their perpetual bend.

He was once again the ancient, withered shopkeeper and purveyor of odd junk and the occasional true magic. And this man, Kaylin had chattered at for most of her adolescence. If Severn was circumspect—a word she privately hated—she had no such compulsion.

"You think there are going to be murders associated with this theft."

He didn't even blink. "Indeed."

"Or possibly already have been. When exactly did you notice this disturbance?"

"Yesterday," he replied, his lips pursed as he sought his impossible-to-miss key ring.

"But you don't think it happened yesterday?"

"I can't be certain, no. As I said, I've sponsored a bit of a contest—"

She lifted a hand. "Don't give me contests I can't enter."

He lifted a brow. "Oddly enough, Private, I think you're one of the few who could. Possibly. You make a lot of noise, on the other hand, and it may—"

"Evanton, *please*, these are people's lives we're talking about."

"Yes. But if I am to be somewhat honest, they are not lives, I feel, you would be in a hurry to save."

"You're dead wrong," she said, meaning it.

"About at least one of them," he said softly. "But if I am not mistaken, she is not—yet—in danger. I feel some of the mystery of their entrance can only be answered by her."

"By a *child*?"

"You might wish to fill the corporal in on what you saw," Evanton told her.

"It's not necessary," Severn replied, before Kaylin could. "I have a good idea of what she saw."

"Oh?"

"She gets a particular look when she's dealing with children in distress." He paused and then said, voice devoid of all texture and all emotion, "Kaylin has always had a weakness for children. Even when she was, by all legal standards, a child herself.

"And that's not a look she gets when the child is happy or

looks well treated," he added softly. "Then, she's only wistful."

Evanton nodded as if everything Severn had said confirmed what he already knew. "Very well. You make a good team," he told them both. "He's much better for you than those two Barrani slouchers."

Kaylin sidestepped the question in the old man's words. Remembered the brief touch of Severn's palms on her cheeks. But that was personal. This was worse.

"What will the manner of death be?"

"That, I cannot tell you. It is very, *very* seldom that I invite visitors into the elementarium, and with cause. You felt compelled to touch nothing and take nothing, because that room had nothing to offer you."

"I felt compelled—"

"Yes, but not to *take,* Kaylin. Not to acquire. And I cannot yet tell you why the water chose to show you the girl. I can only tell you that what you saw was in some fashion true."

"She called me by name."

He spun so fast she almost tripped over him and sent them both flying—which in his case would probably have broken every bone in his frail body. She managed to catch herself on the wall.

"By name?" he asked, one brow melding with his receding hairline.

She nodded.

"Ah, girl," he said, with a shake of the head. He turned away again. "If I had found you first—"

"What does it mean?"

"I cannot say for certain," he replied. "But this much, I can guess—she touched the heart of the elemental water, and woke some of its slumbering intent. It wants you to find her, Kaylin."

"And that's a bad thing."

"It may well be," Evanton replied. "But if I told you—if I could honestly tell you—that it would mean the end of the Empire itself were you to pursue it, you'd pursue it anyway.

"Water is canny that way. It sees into the deeps that we hide." But he turned away as he spoke.

"Evanton—"

"Old man—"

He stopped as Severn and Kaylin's words collided, but did not look back. "If you're about to accuse me of knowing more than I've told you, stand in line and take a number," he said in a voice so dry a little spark would have set it on fire. "I'm a very busy man. Do come and visit again."

"Kaylin—"

Kaylin lifted a hand and swatted her name aside.

"You're going to crack the road if you don't stop walking like that."

"Severn, I don't have a sense of humor about—"

"Almost anything? Fair enough. I've been accused of that."

She stopped walking. Although his stride was easily the longer of the two, she'd been making him work to keep up. Not that it showed. Much.

Since her entrance into the ranks of the Barrani High Court, Kaylin had grown more aware of Severn; of where he was, how close he was, or how far. It was as if—as if something bound them, something gossamer like spider's web, but finer, and ultimately stronger. She had given him her name—if it was her name—and he had accepted it.

But he had never used it. When she shut him out, he accepted the distance.

It's not my name, he had told her quietly, *it's yours. If I understand Barrani names at all.*

I'm not Barrani.

You're not human. Not completely. But you're still Kaylin.

Could you? Could you use it?

He'd been quiet for a long time; she could still remember the texture of that silence, the way he'd stared at her face for a moment, and then turned away almost wearily. *What do you want me to say, Kaylin?*

She hadn't answered. She wasn't certain.

"We have to find her," she told him, her voice quieter now.

"I know. Any idea where to start?"

Missing Persons was a zoo. Almost literally. Although the offices that fronted the public square in the Halls were slightly better equipped and more severe than the interior offices in which Kaylin spent much—too damn much—of her day, they were in no way quieter.

For one, they were full of people who would never— with any luck—wear a uniform that granted them any kind of Imperial authority. For two, the people who milled about, either shouting at each other, pacing, crying or shouting at the officers who looked appropriately harried, were by no means all human; although here, as throughout most sectors of Elantra, humans outnumbered the others by quite a large margin. For three, many of the visitors were either four times Kaylin's age, or less than half of it. Kaylin recognized a smattering of at least four languages, and some of what was said was, in the words of Caitlin, "colorful."

Impatience was the order of the day.

Missing Persons was, in theory, the responsibility of the Hawks. Depending, of course, upon who exactly was missing. Some missing persons had left a small trail of death and destruction in their wake, and these investigations were often—begrudgingly—handed over to the Wolves, the smallest of the three forces who called the Halls of Law home.

The staffing of the office, however, was the purview of the Hawklord. Or his senior officers. None of whom, Kaylin thought with a grimace, were ever on the floors here.

She herself was seldom here, and of all duties the Hawks considered their own, this was her least favorite. She was not always the most patient of people—and people who were desperate enough to come to the Halls seeking word of their missing, and possibly dead, kin required patience at the very least.

She was also not quite graceful enough to forgive other people their impatience. But at least she was aware of hers.

"Well, well, well, if it isn't the vagabond."

And, if she were entirely truthful, there were other reasons for hating this place. Grinding her teeth into what she hoped would pass for a smile, she faced the worst of them squarely.

If it was true that the Barrani had a lock on arrogance, and the Dragons on inscrutability, it was also true that for petty malice, you really couldn't do better than finding a truly loathsome human. And to Kaylin's youthful disappointment, she hadn't actually had to look that *far* to find this one.

His name was Constant Mallory—and, give him this, if she'd had that as a name, and she'd been too stupid to *change* it, she might have developed a few personality ticks. He was, for all intents and purposes, the ruler of this small enclave. He answered to Marcus, and to the Hawklord, but his answers could be both disingenuous and fawning, and she thought he'd learned enough from the Barrani to dispense with truth entirely.

She was aware that he and Marcus had, as the office liked to call it, "history." She'd once asked why, and Teela had said, with some disdain, "You really *don't* pay attention, do you? How much of history is spent discussing happy children and fluffy bunnies?"

"It's true," Tain had half drawled. "If humans actually had a lifespan, things would have been a lot more interesting around here a few centuries ago. But that's the problem with mortals—they get a little power and it all comes tumbling down. It's a good thing you breed so quickly."

Teela and Tain had no problems at all with Mallory. They didn't *like* him, but then again, given the way they treated people they *did* like—and Kaylin had some experience with this—their lack of affection was a dubious negative. Like many humans, he treated the Barrani with respect and care. He had not always given Marcus the same respect.

Or rather, he'd given him exactly the same respect, but then again, Marcus took subtle office politics about as well as he took vegetarian menus.

Mallory had wanted the Leontine's job. Then again, so had Marcus. Marcus had come out on top. The miracle of the tussle, to Kaylin's mind, was that Mallory had come out alive. She gathered that not everyone had.

But getting people who'd been there to talk about it was more difficult than getting criminals to cough up useful information. And, as a harried Sergeant Kassan had finally said, "You're usually so proud of your ignorance. Learn to live with it, Kaylin." The implication being that living and living with it, on that particular day, were the same thing.

Mallory was tall. He was, by human standards, fit, and not even painful to look at: he was competent, quick-witted, and good with a sword. He handled his paperwork with care—a distinction that he did not fail to note on the rare occasions he was allowed to visit Caitlin's office.

But he was a self-important prick, and he was the only Hawk of note who had spoken against her induction. The latter, she was unlikely to forget. The former, she had come to expect from the world at large.

His greeting was not in any way friendly. Her smile was not in any way friendly. It was, as Marcus called it with some distaste, a human social custom. Probably because it didn't involve enough blood and fur.

But she had never come with Severn before.

And Severn became completely *still* beside her.

"Corporal Handred," Mallory said, greeting him as if that stillness were not a warning signal. "Our newest recruit."

Severn extended a hand, and Mallory took it firmly. "I see that they have you babysitting. It's unusual to see the private in any company that isn't Barrani. How are you finding the Hawks so far?"

"Interesting," Severn replied. At least he hadn't gone monosyllabic.

"Compared to the Wolves?"

Severn didn't even pause. "Yes. Longer hours. I confess that I've seen many reports from your office, but I've seldom had a chance to visit in person."

Mallory looked slightly at a loss, but he recovered quickly enough. "We do important work here," he began, straightening his shoulders somewhat. "It's here that most of the cases that require official attention are brought to the notice of the Law."

"I imagine you deal with a lot of reports. How do you separate the frauds from the actual crimes?"

Mallory looked genuinely surprised, and Kaylin fought an urge to kick someone—mostly because she couldn't decide whether or not she'd kick Severn or Mallory. Mallory took the lead, and Severn, walking by his side, continued to ask pleasant questions, his voice engulfed slowly by the office noise.

Leaving Kaylin on her own, with no Mallory vindictively standing over her shoulder. It was a trick not even Teela had ever tried.

* * *

There were two ways to get useful information about the missing persons being reported by the people who came to the Halls. The hard way—which was to take notes, to have the official artists employed by the Halls on hand, and to attempt to draw a picture of some sort that could be used as an identifier. This was both the least efficient and the most commonly used method of gaining some sort of visual information the Hawks could then use.

The second, and far more efficient, method involved the Tha'alani. And the reason it was little used was, in Kaylin's opinion, pretty damn obvious. She looked across the crowded office as if the people in it were shadows and smoke, and against the far wall, bordered on either side by finely crafted wooden dividers, and no door, sat a gray-haired man.

At least he looked like a man from the back. But he wore robes, rather than the official uniform of the Hawks; if he was finicky about detail, there *might* be a gold Hawk embroidered on the left breast of the gray cloth; if he wasn't, there would be nothing at all.

Kaylin preferred the nothing at all.

From the front, although he didn't turn, the illusion of humanity would vanish; the slender stalks that rose from his forehead would be visible in the hallmark paleness of his face. His eyes would probably be blue; hard to tell with the Tha'alani, but then again, she usually avoided meeting their eyes—it meant she was standing too damn close.

Those stalks were their weapons, their means of invasion;

they were prehensile, and they moved. They would attach themselves to the face of anyone—anything at all—in the Empire, and they would draw from that person's thoughts *everything*. Everything they were told to look for. Possibly more. All the hidden secrets, the private memories, the terrors and the joys would be laid bare for their inspection.

Officially, there were no Tha'alani in the ranks of the Hawks; they were, however, always on call should the law require their services. The only office that had a Tha'alani on staff was this one, and he was a grant from the Imperial Court. All of the Tha'alani who served the Law were seconded *by* the Dragon Emperor. A warning to anyone who might otherwise treat them like the invasive horrors they actually *were*.

It was probably the real reason she hated the Missing Persons office so much. Men like Mallory were so common in her life, she could only expend so much energy hating him. Most of the time.

To the left of the stall in which the Tha'alani sat, back facing her, was a long, slender mirror edged in gold that had seen better days. It was flecked and peeling. It was also out of sight of the public, tucked as it was against the other edge of the wall and the divider.

Records.

She squared her shoulders and moved toward the mirror on the wall. It was inactive and she could see Severn and Mallory bent over Mallory's impeccable desk, discussing something that no doubt would have bored her to tears. She probably owed Severn a drink or ten.

She walked toward the mirror, and forced herself to relax, to walk naturally. She tried to remember the one Tha'alani woman she had met that had not somehow terrified her. She was slender, and had reminded Kaylin inexplicably of warm sun in autumn. Now, however, was not the time to think of sunlight, or warmth. It made her job difficult. Instead, Kaylin tried to remember what Ybelline had said about the lives of the Tha'alani who *could* serve time among the "deaf," and by that, she had clearly meant humans. Kaylin's kind. No, wait, one of the Dragons had said that.

The Tha'alani woman, Ybelline, had corrected him gently for his unkindness, although Kaylin hadn't bothered to be kind first.

Ybelline had somehow made Kaylin feel comfortable and safe. Had taken memories from the sleeping child she and Severn had brought with them to the office—a child kidnapped by the undead, and almost sacrificed—sparing the child the waking experience of the Tha'alani mind-touch. Holding on to that memory, Kaylin did relax.

Until she was almost at the records mirror itself, and the Tha'alani rose.

He was older than any Tha'alani she had ever met, although he was by no means as aged as Evanton; his hair, which had looked gray, was gray, and his face was lined with age, with sun and wind. His eyes were slate-gray, not a friendly color, and his lips were thin and pale.

And the disturbing stalks on his forehead were weaving in and out among themselves, as if it were the only way he knew how to fidget. It came to Kaylin as she watched them warily that he was, in fact, fidgeting.

Had she ever noticed this before?

Did they all do this?

There was no Hawk on his robes, no official sign. She wondered if he was always in this office, or if he was only here on this particular shift. Wondered, with just a faint edge of hysteria to sharpen the humor, what he'd done to deserve it, if he was.

But he *bowed* to her, and by this, she knew two things: that he'd risen because she approached him, and only because of that, and that he'd been somehow waiting for *her*. It didn't make her comfortable. For perhaps the first time she noticed, as he rose, the deepening lines around his mouth, the slight thinning of his lips. As a thirteen-year-old girl, she had thought it a cruel expression, and that had left scars in her memory that had been slow to heal.

Now…she thought, as objectively as she could—and given she was Kaylin that was hard—that it might be a grimace of pain. And she felt, mingled with her own very visceral revulsion, a twinge of sympathy for a total stranger.

She tried very hard not to notice the way his stalks were swaying. But she *did* notice; they were swaying to and fro, but almost seemed to be shying away. From her. From, she realized, her revulsion.

She swallowed. Composed herself—as much as that was possible. "Private Kaylin Neya," she said, introducing herself. She did not offer him her hand, and he did not extend his own.

"I am called Draalzyn, by my people." The word was broken by an unexpected syllable. The Tha'alani had a language that Kaylin had never bothered to learn because as far as she could tell it contained no colorful—which is to say useful—words. It, in fact, seemed to be free of most words; when Tha'alani conversed, they conversed in silence, and only their hands and their stalks seemed to move. They also touched each other too much.

And she was projecting again. She could see that clearly by the subtle shift of his expression. She wanted to tell the bastard to keep away from her thoughts. It was her first reaction.

But a second reaction followed swiftly. She knew she was the proverbial open book; how often in her life had Severn just glanced at her face and known what it was that was bothering her? She'd never bothered to count. Probably couldn't count that high unless it involved a wager.

And the second thought, the Tha'alani almost seemed to sense, for his expression grew slightly less severe.

"Private," Draalzyn said quietly, "I hoped to see you at some point in time."

"I work inside."

He nodded. He knew where she worked; that much was clear to her. He seemed to have trouble speaking; he opened his mouth several times, as if searching for words. Or, as if he'd found them, and discarded them as useless.

She waited, eyeing the mirror, and catching a reflected glimpse of Severn as he ran interference. It wouldn't last.

At last the Tha'alani said, "Ybelline asked me to carry a message to you, if our paths should cross."

Ybelline. The one Tha'alani Kaylin had met that she had *almost* liked.

"Why me?" Unlike Draalzyn, Kaylin rarely bothered to stop the words that first came to mind from falling out of her mouth. But she remembered this honey-haired woman so clearly she felt almost—almost—protective of her. She had been so gentle with Catti, an orphan, as unwanted by the world at large as Kaylin had been at her age.

"She believed you could be of assistance to us," he replied quietly. "And the matter is of some urgency." He paused, and she realized that the pallor of his face was probably unnatural. He was *worried*. Or frightened. Or both.

"What's happened?"

"If you would come to her dwelling in the enclave—or if you would choose a meeting place that is not so crowded in the city itself, she will explain."

Kaylin nodded.

And the Tha'alani seemed to relax; his shoulders slumped a little in the folds of his robe, as if he had been expecting something else.

Fair enough. Had it been any other Tha'alani, any at all, Kaylin would have refused. Or worse.

"She is willing, of course, to promise that there will be no intrusion, and nothing will be taken from you without—"

Kaylin lifted a hand. "I know the drill," she said, "and you don't have to repeat it. I—trust her. And I don't have *time*," she added bitterly, looking again at the mirror's surface, and at Mallory.

"You wish to access records without interference?" he

asked. As if he had read her—no, she told herself forcefully. It was bloody obvious he had. You'd have to be blind *and* stupid not to recognize the fact.

"Yes."

"You are looking for?"

She stopped. Looked at him, truly looked at him, as if seeing him for the first time. The Tha'alani worked in this office for a *reason*. But—

The image of a bruised child's face rose up before her eyes, captured in water's depths. It was so strong, so clear, that she couldn't shake it. It was more concrete in that moment than the rest of the office.

The man waited.

She noted this, her Hawk's training in place. And she knew as well that all *real* images that went into records, any real information, would come, in the end, through him or his kin.

"You know what's in the records?"

"Not all of it," he began.

"The recent reports. You might know if someone came in looking for a missing girl."

"Of what age?" His eyes seemed to glaze over, as if he were a living embodiment of what the records contained, and he was accessing the data.

"Nine, maybe ten. Scraggly dark hair, dark eyes. Pale skin. Poor family, I think."

"How long would she be considered missing?"

"I...don't know. More than two days." Maybe, given her condition, many more.

He was still frowning.

And Kaylin clenched her jaw tightly, stepped forward toward him, and, lifting her hands, drew her hair from her forehead. She was shaking. But the girl's image was strong enough.

"You know this child?" he asked, understanding exactly what she offered.

"No. But I've seen her once."

"And you are willing—" But he stopped. He was, by law, required to give her a long speech full of unreassuring reassurances.

None of which she had time for. He did her the courtesy of not failing to read this clearly, and held her gaze for just that little bit longer than required. She didn't blink.

His forehead stalks began to elongate, to thin, as they moved toward her exposed skin.

"Don't touch the mark," she warned him.

"Ah," he replied. "No. I will not."

And they were feathery, those stalks, like the brush of fingertips against forehead. He did not touch her face with his hands, did nothing to hold her in place. In every way, this was unlike the first time she had submitted to the Tha'alani. But this was an act of choice.

And if he saw more than she wanted him to see, what of it? It made her squirm, the fear of exposure, and she balanced that fear—as she so often did—with the greater fear: the child's bruised face. The frustration, anger and, yes, pride and joy that she felt just being deemed worthy to bear the Hawk. The fear of failing what that meant, all that that entailed.

The Tha'alani stalks were pale and trembling, as if in a

breeze, but they lingered a long time against her skin, although she did not relive any memories but the memory of the water, its dark, dark depths, and the emergence of that strange child's face.

Then he withdrew, and he offered her a half-bow. He rose quickly, however, dispensing courtesy as required, and with sincerity, but no more. "I better understand Ybelline's odd request," he told her quietly. "And I do not know if what I tell you will give you comfort or grief, but no such child has been reported missing. There is no image of her in the records.

"But go, and speak with Ybelline, Private Neya. I fear that your partner is about to lose his composure." He bent to his desk, and wrote something carefully in bold, neat Barrani lettering. An address.

CHAPTER 3

"And you've never hit him?" Severn asked, as they left the crowded courtyard behind in the growing shadows of afternoon.

"No. He and Marcus have history. I couldn't find where Mallory'd buried the skeletons in his closet, so it didn't seem wise. Marcus, in case you hadn't noticed, has a bit of a temper."

Severn's dark brow rose slightly. "Wise? You *have* grown." He paused and added, "He probably doesn't have them in his closet—he probably has them neatly categorized by bone type in his filing cabinets."

Kaylin snickered. "You feel like a long walk?"

"Was that rhetorical?"

"No. Whatever that means. We can walk, or we can hail a cab."

"Given the pocket change you have for the next few days, we'll walk."

"Ha-ha."

"But I wouldn't mind knowing where we're going."

She frowned. "I know where I'm going."

"You know where you want to be," he replied.

"I know the city, Severn."

He shrugged. "I've been led to understand that you know every inch of every beat you've ever covered."

"And your point is?"

"Let's just say I take Sergeant Kassan's warnings seriously—and I have my doubts that you've covered this beat much."

"Why?"

"You're walking toward the moneyed part of town."

She shrugged. It was true. Marcus said that she could make dress uniform look grungy when it had just left the hands of the Quartermaster. You needed a certain bearing to police this section of town, and Kaylin had its opposite. Whatever that was.

Kaylin's unerring sense of non-direction added about an hour to their travel time. She cursed whomever had built the streets in gutteral Leontine, and the fifth time she did this, Severn let out a long sigh and held out his hand, palm up.

She shoved the address into it. "Don't even think of saying it."

He did her the grace of keeping laughter off his face, but his brows rose as he read the address. "You're going *there?*"

"Yes," she said tersely. Followed by, "How the hell do you know where it is?"

"I know Elantra, Kaylin. All of it that's in records. I know the historical shape of the streets, the newer sections, the oldest parts of the town. I'm familiar with the wharves, and the quarters given to the Caste Lords of each of the racial enclaves.

"I'm less familiar with the southern stretch," he added. He would be. That was where the Aerians lived. "The Wolves seldom run there."

Of course. He was a Wolf. A Wolf in Hawk's clothing. "Lead on," she said quietly. "And yes, I'm going voluntarily."

"Who lives here?"

"Ybelline."

"I know of only one Ybelline who works outside of the Tha'alani enclave in any official capacity." He gave her an odd look.

"Yes. It's the same Ybelline. We met her—"

"You met her," he said gently.

"—when the Dragons came to talk."

"You didn't seem to love her then."

"She's Tha'alani." Kaylin shrugged.

"Kaylin—why are you going? Your feelings about the Tha'alani have been widely quoted in the office memos whenever someone's bored."

She shrugged. "She asked to see me."

He stopped walking. "I'm serious, Kaylin."

Kaylin didn't. "I can tell." Severn's stride was long enough that he could damn well catch up. He did, and caught her arm; she was in good enough shape that she staggered a step before bringing her to a halt.

She thought about lying to him, because she didn't feel she owed him the truth. But when she opened her mouth, she said, "She didn't touch me. But—when I looked at her, when I saw what she did for Catti, I thought she *could*. That I would let her. That she would see everything about me that I despise and she wouldn't care. She would like me anyway."

"You trusted her."

Kaylin shrugged. She'd learned the gesture from Severn. "I always trust my instincts," she said at last. "And yes. Even though she—yes. I felt I could."

"Where are you going?"

Kaylin stopped. "I'm following you."

"Which is usually done from behind."

They had a small argument about Kaylin's insistence on logging the hours she spent walking, because, as Severn pointed out, at least forty-five minutes of those were her going in circles.

"It's not even clear that this visit pertains to any ongoing investigation in the department," Severn added, "and it may well turn out to be more personal in nature."

"Believe me," Kaylin snapped back, "if the Hawklord knew that I'd received even an informal invitation from any of the Tha'alani—"

"He'd be astute enough to send someone else."

"Very funny."

"I wasn't entirely joking."

She made a face. "If he knew—and if you're finished?—

he'd make it a top priority. We don't get much in the way of communication from the Tha'alani enclave."

"For obvious reasons."

"And there are at most a handful of cited cases in which the Tha'alani have sought the services of officers of Imperial Law in *any* context. He'd call it outreach," she added, with a twist of lips.

"That would be like diplomacy? He'd definitely send someone else."

"Like who? Marcus? Teela? Tain?"

"I was thinking of the Aerians. They're fairly levelheaded for people who don't like to keep their feet on the ground."

But as arguments went, it was verbal fencing, and it generated little rage. It also gave Kaylin something else to think about as she approached the gated enclave behind which the Tha'alani lived. They were not numerous for a mortal race, and they very seldom mingled with outsiders.

Kaylin had never been on the other side of those gates, and they had always held a particular terror for her, because beyond them was a whole race of people who could see— if they wanted to—her every thought, past and present. Who could, at a whim, make her relive every deed, every wrong, every humiliation.

It was kind of like the waking version of a familiar nightmare, in which she suddenly appeared in her office without a stitch of clothing on.

Severn seemed unconcerned, but he always did.

And she was competitive enough that she had to match that, schooling her expression as she approached the gate

itself. It was large enough to allow a full carriage or a wagon
easy egress, but it was—and would remain—closed, unless
there were reason to open it. No, the way in and out was
through the gatehouse itself.

Which she had also only seen from the outside.

Clint had brought her, when she was fifteen; he had complained about her weight for the entire trip because she'd
begged him to fly, and he had loudly and grudgingly
agreed—when she'd promised to leave his flight feathers
alone for at least two weeks.

From a distance—the safest one—the gates had still been
a shadow and a threat, and it was the only part of the city
she had refused to look at while he flew by. His words
carried—the lovely, deep timbre of his voice was something
she had never learned to ignore—but only his words, and
his words alone had painted the picture she now saw clearly.

She could still hear echoes of the words that the wind
hadn't snatched away, and the murmur of his Aerian cadences.

Severn took the lead, and she let him.

She had something to prove, but found, to her annoyance, that pride had its limits. Even annoyance couldn't
overcome them. Because the man—the single man—at the
gate was Tha'alani. And he wore not the familiar robes that
she had come to hate, but rather a surcoat in the same odd
gray over a chain hauberk whose arms glinted in the
sunlight, making clear that the Tha'alani were a lot more fas-
tidious in their armor care than the Officers of the Law—
or someone else did the cleaning.

"Severn," she said, stalling for time even as they approached the sole guard, "have you ever had to run down a Tha'alani?"

"Probably as often as you've had to investigate one," he replied. Answer enough.

"Do they never report their crimes?"

He shrugged. "Either that, or they never commit them."

He must have believed that about as much as she did. But if a crime did not affect a member of another racial enclave, it was the prerogative of the enclave—and its Castelord— to deal with the crime itself in the custom of their kind. And the racial enclaves were not required to submit any legal proceedings to the Halls of Law. Kaylin had thought it cheating when she'd first joined the Hawks, and had complained about these separate laws bitterly—until it was pointed out that were they not separate she would have to learn them all, and probably the languages they were written in.

Or growled in.

After that, she'd kept the complaints to herself.

The guard turned toward them as they approached, aligning first the stalks on his forehead, and then his face and body, as if the latter were afterthought. Severn appeared to take no notice of this, but Kaylin found it unsettling.

She could not see the color of his eyes, but realized after a moment that she *could* clearly see said eyes—that this guard, like the Leontines and the Barrani, wore no helm. Of course he didn't wear a helmet, she thought bitterly. It would cripple his most effective weapon. She shoved her hand into her pocket, and pulled out a crumpled piece of paper.

If it had taken her that damn long to notice something that damn obvious, she was letting her nerves get the better of her.

But Severn was ahead of her, and before she could even uncurl the wretched thing, he said to the guard, "We have come at the invitation of Ybelline Rabon'alani."

The guard's expression froze in place, and his stalks waved a moment in the air. He looked carefully at the hawk emblazoned on both of their surcoats, and then searched their faces.

After this silent inspection, he nodded, not to Severn, but to Kaylin, who stood in his shadow. "She will see you," he said, the words oddly inflected. "Someone will meet you on the other side of the guard house and show you the way to her home."

"Someone" was another guard, another man in mail. His hair was a pale shade of brown, but it was long, and he wore it in a braid over his left shoulder. His eyes were clear, not golden the way Dragons' eyes were, but still some shade that was paler than brown, darker than sunlight. He bowed, rising, and she thought him younger than the guard at the gate. His eyes were alive with unspoken curiosity, and his expression was actually an expression.

He stared at her, and she stared back.

"I'm Epharim," he finally said, his stalks weaving through stray strands of his hair. He waited, and then after a moment, he reddened and held out a hand.

Kaylin took it slowly, and shook it. If it was true you

could tell a lot about a person by shaking their hand, she wasn't sure what she could take out of this handshake. It was stiff, hesitant, almost entirely unnatural.

"Did I do that right?" he said, retrieving his hand, his gaze still far too intent.

"Do what?"

"Greet you."

"Yes, Epharim," Severn replied, stepping on Kaylin's foot before she could open her mouth. Well, before she could speak, at any rate. "I am Corporal Severn Handred, and this is Private Kaylin Neya. We serve the Emperor in the Halls of Law." He offered his hand in turn, and Epharim took it, repeating the gesture that was supposed to be a handshake.

He beamed. "And what does it mean?" Each word a little too distinct, as if speech itself were something new and unfamiliar. Or as if the language were. But he spoke the common tongue of Elantra, and if the cadences were off, they were, each and every syllable, completely recognizable.

Severn said, "We don't use names that have specific meanings." Clearly, Severn had been a master student in racial studies.

"You don't have a naming tongue?" Epharim's brows rose. And as they did, Kaylin noticed—with the training she had excelled in—that the passersby in the street all seemed to slow, that their stalks, from different heights, perched upon different shades of hair, seemed to turn toward them. Or toward Epharim.

"Are we causing a scene?" she asked in low tones.

Epharim looked confused. Well, more confused. "A scene? Like in a play?"

"No. A scene, as in everyone in the street for miles stops to stare at us as if we're insane."

He blinked. Looked at the people who were—yes— staring at them, and then looked back at Kaylin. "This…is a scene?"

Severn stepped on her other foot.

"People don't normally stop to stare like that."

Again his brows rippled, this time toward the bridge of his straight, perfect nose. "They don't?"

"No."

"Then how are they expected to observe?"

"Observe what?"

"You. Corporal Severn Handred."

"Severn will do," Severn said. "It is our custom."

"They're not supposed to," Kaylin replied, ignoring Severn. "They have other things to do, don't they?"

"They have things to do," Epharim agreed, still standing there, anchoring Kaylin in place while stragglers farther down also stopped walking and turned to look back. "But most of them have never seen one of your kind so close. They will remember," he added, as if this was supposed to be a comfort. She had the momentary urge to pull out her beat stick and approach them with a smile that was about as soft as steel, telling them to move along.

But there were children there, their stalks slender, and to her surprise, almost transparent, their eyes wide and openly curious. Too far away to see her own reflection in those eyes, she knew then what she would want reflected, and the impulse left her. She turned slowly back to Epharim, who was beaming at her with an expression she now recognized—a childlike wonder so out of place on the face of a grown man she had failed to see it at first.

She had never seen Tha'alani children before. Never seen their babies, or their elderly, their youths; she had never held one, never ushered one, bloodied and crying, into the world; she had never been called upon by the guild of midwives to save a mother who would otherwise die at what should have been the start of a new life.

Then again, she had never been asked to lick natal fluid off the hair of a Tha'alani newborn, so maybe she should be grateful. She wasn't, but that was the perverse nature of her universe. And as they stared at her, she stared at them, separated by yards of street and a gentle breeze. It was utterly silent.

One of the children—dark-haired, dark-eyed, pale-skinned, too young to be easily identified as either boy or girl—slid loose from his guardian's grasp and toddled toward her, his stalks weaving in the air so awkwardly she wondered if they could be combed out when they got knotted. It was an idle thought, and it held no fear.

As the child approached, she thought him a boy, and knew that she could easily be wrong, but she had to think him one or the other because *it* was not a pronoun she ever applied to children.

He was smiling, and he had teeth, and his cheeks began to flush as he teetered in the precarious almost-fall that was a young child's run. All of Kaylin's self-consciousness melted in the warmth of that smile, and she knelt slowly, bringing herself as close to the ground—and to his approaching height—as she could while still maintaining any dignity.

He wore a blue-and-red robe, gaudy, bright colors that had a sheen that caught light, and gold around one wrist. She held out her arms without thought, and he chortled with glee. Had he been Leontine, he would have had milk teeth, and she would have been a tad more careful while holding out uncovered hands.

But he was Tha'alani, and almost human, and the stalks that had terrified her were almost literally knotting themselves as they twisted. The terror they held for her, perched on the forehead of older men with grim, shuttered faces, was gone.

She thought he might slow his approach, but the momentum of his trajectory carried him forward, faster and faster, until he was leaning toward the ground; she caught him before the stones did. Swept him up, her hands under his arms, and held his face across from hers, laughing, because she *had* to laugh. He was laughing.

And as he reached for her, his slender arms dimpled with baby fat that had not yet disappeared with height and age, she let out a small squeal of delight that easily matched his, and she hugged him.

The stalks on his forehead untwined and touched her face, soft as feathers, but slighter and more insistent. They brushed her cheeks, her mouth, her nose, as if they were his fingers, and then rose toward her forehead and hovered there, waiting.

After a moment, they touched her forehead.

She should have been frightened, but it was *impossible* to be frightened in the face of his open curiosity, his imperious delight, the smug sense of certainty that loved children everywhere show. If she were a danger to him, he couldn't conceive of it, and she couldn't, either.

And if he were a danger to *her*, then she had grown so paranoid and so pathetic that… But she couldn't hold on to the thought. His stalks continued to bat against her forehead, and she realized that he was looking for *hers*.

"I don't have them," she told him gently, aware that she was confessing some inner fault. His smile faltered, and he looked at her face intently, his eyes wide. He hesitated a moment and then his stalks were moving again, this time more slowly; she could more feel than see them, because she was watching his expression. She thought he might be worried now, or afraid, because she was different, strange, unknown.

Instead, she felt a giddy delight and something else, the desire to be chased around in the open streets, the desire to laugh and to hide and be caught, over and over again. That and mild thirst. None of these were her feelings.

She glanced at Severn, who was watching her as intently as any of the Tha'alani in the tableau the street had become. She heard herself say, "He's—he's speaking to me…."

The Tha'alani had never spoken to her, not this way. They had pried, poked, pulled at memories; they had forced *her* to see what they were seeing. But they had never exposed themselves as this child had just so joyfully done.

Would it have made a difference?

She set the child down and he ran away, and stopped, and looked back, waiting for her to follow, to chase him.

She looked back at Epharim for guidance, but found nothing there that would stop her or warn her; he had no fear at all for the child, and clearly no sense of impatience at the delay in escorting her to see Ybelline.

"His parents—" she said, touching her unadorned forehead. "They won't mind?"

"Mind?"

But no parents magically appeared to scoop their wayward child back into the safety of their arms, to keep him from strangers such as Kaylin, and that was answer enough because the child was impatiently waiting to be *followed now*. She felt the words, rather than heard them. But she would have felt them from any child, of any race. She might have been a little more careful in the southern stretch, where wings were not yet strong enough to carry a child who chose to launch himself off the edge in mimicry of the adult Aerians, but here, a fall was just a fall.

She ran after him and his laughter filled the street, and it was joined by the laughter of literally dozens of other children as he ran past—other children, older and younger, and many of the adults. Like a multitude of voices sharing the same throat, the same joy, the same word.

She caught the child, knowing the game, and tickled him, lifting him and throwing him in the air, taking care to hold on to his armpits. And on the way down, she laughed, as well, and her laughter was asynchronous, out of step with the crowd.

But when she set the boy free and turned to face Severn and Epharim, she saw only joy in Epharim's expression. No resignation, no sense of lost time, no judgment and no fear.

And this was the part of the city that had so terrified her that she wouldn't even look down at it from the safety of the skies.

Epharim waited until she had joined them again and said softly, "You fear discovery. You fear your own thoughts." And he said it with pity. Kaylin was not the world's biggest pity fan. "Fear, we all know," he added. "And we all know rejection and pain. But none of us have ever suffered this fear of being revealed, this fear of being seen as we are." He was serene, and without judgment.

"The children will not sense this in you," he added softly. "They are not so powerful yet, and they are children. If they know other thoughts, they can't be bothered *listening* to the ones that don't concern them."

She nodded absently, wondering what it would be like to live an entire life in a world where every thought was known. Would it even be possible to lie? Would it ever occur to someone to try it? Would it be possible to love in secret, to desire the things you couldn't have?

Would it be possible to kill?

Epharim said, "We are human," but his tone was quiet. "And there are few of us who can enter your world and live with what we find there. Very few of you who could live in ours, and not be shocked or scandalized by what you would find here. We have very different ideas of what is natural, of what nature *means*.

"But the young are the young," he added softly. "And the child will remember you, now." He smiled and said, "I think he was shocked that you had no *ahporae*. Come. Ybelline is waiting."

"You know that from here?"

He nodded. "She is not far, and she is very, very sensitive."

"But she lives on the outside."

"She lives here. She travels at the behest of the Emperor. But Dragons are not mortal, and their thoughts are so vast and so strange they are more comfortable for us in many ways."

She wondered at a race that could find the presence of Dragons more comforting than the presence of humans.

"There is very little a Dragon fears," Epharim said.

And she didn't even resent the way he answered the things she hadn't said aloud. Perhaps her time with Nightshade had prepared her for this. Or perhaps the child had given her a small key.

"Fear?"

He nodded.

"It's the fear that's bad?"

"It is the fear that is most common. We frighten your kind."

She nodded, and with more force.

"Fear kills," he told her quietly. "It maims and it kills. It twists and it breaks. And among your kind, fear is part of the foundations upon which you build all thought." His face shuttered as he said this, and he looked at her with his pale eyes, his antennae drawn back and down across his hair. "It is why so few are chosen to go and be among your kind. It takes a special talent to dwell so long with your thoughts and not absorb them, becoming like you."

Kaylin couldn't even imagine a life without fear.

Ybelline's dwelling was not small. It was a manor, but all of its surfaces were rounded; even the corners of the building bent gradually, and looked to Kaylin's eye like a rectangle trying its best to imitate an oval, and not quite succeeding. It felt like stone to the touch, and she knew this because she did. But it was a brown that most stone didn't go without effort.

There were windows along the curve of the wall, but no balcony. Doors, the only flat surface she could see. Instead of steps, there was a ramp that sloped up gradually. Epharim lead them toward it.

"You don't have horses here?"

"There are horses where horses are needed," he replied. "But we find oxen more pliable."

"But they're food!"

He said nothing, but it was the kind of nothing that promoted stillness.

The doors slid open—literally disappearing into either wall—as he approached. "Ybelline will be in the back," he told her. "She's expecting you." He paused, and then added, "We understand your fear, Kaylin Neya. It is not entirely groundless. But if I have said we live without fear, I have not been entirely truthful. We fear your kind."

She started to say something, managed to think the

better of it before the words left her mouth, and said instead, "So do I."

"Help us, if you can."

Before she could ask him more, he turned and left them. Kaylin looked at Severn. Severn was quiet and remote. "What do you think is going on?" she asked softly.

"Nothing good." He began to walk and Kaylin fell into step beside him. "You did well, out there."

"Hmm?"

"With the child."

"The— Oh." She opened her mouth and he lifted a hand.

"Don't tell me you didn't do that on purpose."

"But—"

"Because it doesn't matter. Be yourself here. It's enough."

"I'm always myself," she said, half-ruefully, thinking about Marcus and the Hawks.

"I know. I've watched you, remember?" He shook his head. "I couldn't have done that."

"He was a child."

"I know. But—they were willing to touch you."

"No one touched—"

"Your thoughts, at that moment. They all did."

She hesitated; a momentary revulsion gripped her.

"They're afraid of us with more reason than we fear them," he told her quietly. "Study the Tha'alani. Those who walk among the deaf will come back injured, or insane— by their standards—if they go too often. They absorb our fear and our terrible isolation.

"We're a race of insane people, to the Tha'alani. Think

about it, Kaylin—a home where there can be no misunder-standing. Where all anger is known and faced instantly, and all fear is addressed and calmed. Where all love is known, and all desire is accepted."

"Oh?" Kaylin said, after a moment. "Then why am I here today?"

Severn said quietly, "Bet you dinner that it has some-thing to do with the deaf."

"Meaning us."

"Meaning our kind, yes."

She thought about it for two seconds. It was a sucker bet, and she didn't make those on the losing end. "No deal."

His smile was brief and dark. It suited his face so perfectly, with all its nuance, that she realized he was right: it was not a smile she could even imagine on Epharim's face.

Ybelline was waiting for them in a garden that was both sedate and seemed, at first, very simple. She sat at a table in the open air, and there were empty chairs around it—two empty chairs. Kaylin bowed briskly; Severn's bow was extended. But genuine. He obviously knew Ybelline, and Ybelline's graceful nod implied that she remembered him. They'd met before. Maybe they'd even worked together. Seven years, Severn had lived a life that Kaylin knew nothing about.

Did you see what I can't see? she thought with a pang. *Do you know what he won't tell me?*

As if in answer, Ybelline turned to Kaylin. But her antennae were flat against the honeyed gold of her hair, and her eyes were dark, a color that sunlight didn't seem to penetrate. Kaylin had seen that color before in Tha'alani, but she wasn't certain what it meant.

"Please," Ybelline said, her voice rich and deep, but still slightly odd. "Be seated."

They both obeyed her easy request as if it weren't a thinly veiled command—and Ybelline was so gracious, it might not have been. She offered them tea, and like the color of her hair it was warm and honeyed. Severn drank without pause, although Kaylin knew he didn't particularly like sweet in beverages. Kaylin, on the other hand, thought they should be desserts.

"What you did, Kaylin Neya, was good."

Kaylin was confused.

"Ah, I meant with the son of Raseina. The boy. Epharim told me about it." She did not smile as she spoke, but her tone conveyed gratitude. Which was odd. "You are fond of children," she added, "and now, the collective knows this."

Collective?

"The Tha'alaan," Ybelline said, raising one brow. She looked at Severn, who was wincing. But she didn't miss a beat, and her brow fell. "Your introduction to my kin was not a kind one. Perhaps not harsher than you deserved, but still, harrowing."

Kaylin nodded at both statements.

"I have been gathering my own thoughts among my kin," Ybelline continued, "and I would have conveyed what I felt in you the first time we met—but this was better. The child touched you—he is strong—and what he felt, the Tha'alaan felt. Your people believe in lies," she added, "because they cannot *hear* truth.

"But there is no lie in that affection, although you fear us."

"He's a child—" Kaylin began.

"He is, but he will not always be a child, and many of your kind would fear him for what he might see, or how they might affect him with their fear and their secrets, the things they cannot help but hide. Hiding didn't occur to you when he ran toward you."

"It was a test?"

"No. Not a planned test, but perhaps the gods are kind."

Kaylin had her doubts, and was aware that keeping them to herself around this woman was impossible. Then again, she generally didn't keep that particular thought to herself, so no big loss.

But Severn said, before she could continue down that path, "Why was this fortunate, Ybelline? Why would it have been necessary to make such a statement to the Tha'alaan?"

Kaylin looked at Severn with surprise and a complete certainty that his question was actually one she *should* have been thinking.

"Yes," Severn said, not bothering to spare her because, well, Ybelline would probably hear it anyway, "it was. But where children are concerned, you seem to forget simple things like thinking."

Funny man. She thought about hitting him. Briefly.

Ybelline's stalks rose and fell, as if thought itself were too heavy. She was silent for a long while, staring at Kaylin, and at Severn. Then she rose, leaving the table behind, and turned her back on them. Even among humans, this would not have been considered a good sign.

"You are very guarded," Ybelline said to Severn. "And I choose to trust you without touching your inner thoughts."

"And Kaylin isn't."

"No," Ybelline said softly. "And I think she may have more that she feels needs to be hidden."

Severn said nothing.

Kaylin froze for just a second. But Ybelline's voice was so gentle, so free from censure, that the moment passed, and Kaylin let it go. She wanted to trust this woman. She had wanted to trust her the first time she'd laid eyes on her. Kaylin didn't remember her mother very well—but something about Ybelline reminded her of that past. Never mind that the past was in the poverty of the fief of Nightshade.

Ybelline lifted her arms, wrapped them around herself. Kaylin could see her fingers trembling in the still air, the warm sun. "We need you to help us," she said quietly.

With anything came to mind, but didn't leave Kaylin's lips. Of course, the fact that this didn't matter occurred to her only after she'd successfully bit back the words; they were *so* loud.

"One of our children is missing."

CHAPTER 4

Missing.

The word was heavy. It opened between them like a chasm created by the breaking of earth in the aftermath of magic. Kaylin did not look at Severn, but she was aware that he was watching her. Not staring, not exactly, but aware of her reaction. She schooled her expression—a phrase she hated—with care, entirely for his benefit.

"You haven't reported her as missing." Not a question.

"No," Ybelline said, and she almost shuddered. Did, although it was subtle, a ripple that passed through her and left her changed.

"You don't believe that she just wandered out of the quarter on her own." Flat words.

"No," Ybelline replied.

Which made sense. The young child Kaylin had so un-selfconsciously lifted had had the attention of everyone in the street simply because he wanted it, and the adults were happy to indulge the simple desire of someone who was certain he was loved. Any child, Kaylin thought, would have that certainty, among the Tha'alani. She felt a pang as she thought of the orphans in the Foundling Halls, Marrin's kits. They had never been certain of that.

Kaylin stepped back, but not physically. She was a Hawk, and reminded herself that that was what she had chosen to be. And a Hawk asked questions, sought answers, sifted through facts. No matter how much they dreaded them.

"What happened?" she asked, not bothering to hide that dread.

Ybelline did not close her eyes as she turned back to them, and her eyes were dark. The color, Kaylin thought, of either sorrow or horror. She still wasn't sure.

"She was not at her home," Ybelline began. "Understand that we have a…looser sense of home…than your kin. We are aware of where our children are, and we watch them, as a community. We listen for them. We hear their pain or their fear, and any one of us—*any*—will come to their rescue if rescue is required.

"Mayalee is a wanderer," she added. "A young explorer. And she is fond of night, and stars, and navigation. She is bold—" The words stopped for a moment. "She is afraid of very little. Not even heights or falling.

"And none of our children—in the Tha'alaan—are afraid of strangers. We have no word for it," she added, "that does not mean outsider. And no outsiders come here."

"You think one did."

"One must have," Ybelline said bitterly. But something was not right, something about the words hinted at evasion. Kaylin looked at Severn to see if he had noticed, but she read nothing on his face, nothing in his expression. He was, as Ybelline had said, careful.

Kaylin was not. "You're not certain it was an outsider," she said at last.

Ybelline raised a golden brow.

"Epharim said—he mentioned—that we define insane, for your kin. My kin," she added, "and I won't argue the definition. He might be right. I've often thought—"

"Kaylin, topic," Severn said curtly.

"Right. If insanity can be defined, it means there are, among your kin, those who *are* insane."

"The deaf," Ybelline said, and there was pity in her voice. "Those that are born deaf. Those that become deaf through injury."

Kaylin nodded.

"It is like losing the ability to speak," Ybelline added, "and to hear. And to touch. And to walk. It is all of those things, at once. It is the loss of kin. Many do not survive it."

"And those that do?"

"They are our kin," she replied, "and we care for them as we can. They have no place in your world. They are of the Tha'alaan even if they can no longer perceive it."

Kaylin nodded. "What happened?" she asked again, but this time her voice was gentle.

"Mayalee is five years old, by your reckoning. She is still

in all ways a child, by ours. She is aware of the Tha'alaan, and the Tha'alaan is aware of her.

"She was out, near the roof gardens of the center. It was late, and the moons were full—it was just after your Festival. She likes the Festival," she added softly, "and although we forbid it to our kin, some of the magefire that lights the sky can be seen clearly from the terrace.

"So she went there, to watch.

"After a time, she climbed down, and she headed toward the guardhouse wards. She is such a clever child," Ybelline added, and the affection was swamped with regret and fear—and a certain sense of failure.

Profound failure.

"She was not afraid, simply determined. Her aunt—I think you would use that word—headed out to find her. But before they reached her she met someone.

"A man," she added. "He was not in the Tha'alaan, but Mayalee was not afraid of him. Not immediately."

"And she went with him?"

"She went with him. Her uncles came, then, and her mother," Ybelline added. "I was on call to the Emperor at the time, or I would have heard her."

"How far away can you hear your kin?"

"I? A great distance. But it depends entirely upon the individual. Some of us can reach far, and some can touch only the heart of the Tha'alaan.

"She was afraid, when she left our quarter. She did not want to leave. She told us this much—but not more. We could not clearly see the man she saw," she added. "And this—"

"Magic?"

"We fear magic," Ybelline replied. "But it is worse—she began to tell us something and then—she screamed." Ybelline closed her eyes. "She screamed. It was the last thing we heard of her—that scream. She is no longer in reach of the Tha'alaan."

"She was taken that quickly?"

"That is our hope," Ybelline said, but there was little hope in the words.

Kaylin was confused. Severn rose. "You think she was crippled," he said quietly.

"We fear it," Ybelline replied. "We fear that they damaged her somehow, to break the contact. Those who are powerful can sense each other—but even the weak can touch the Tha'alaan at all times."

"But they could have just knocked her out, couldn't they?"

"No. Not conventionally." It was Severn who replied. "The Tha'alani would be aware of her, even were she sleeping."

"But how—" Kaylin bit back the question. "Her stalks. Her antennae."

Ybelline nodded, and this time, her face showed open fear.

They were silent for a time. Even for Kaylin, who had dreaded the Tha'alani for almost half her life, the sense of horror was genuine. It was as if she had been told someone had blinded a child to stop the child from identifying where she was being held captive.

"Why have you not approached the Halls of Law, Ybelline?" Severn again. Kaylin let him take over the questioning because he was so calm, his voice so soft, facts somehow seemed less threatening.

"We are not certain that it is a matter for the Common Law," Ybelline replied carefully.

"You cannot think one of your own—" He stopped. "One of the deaf."

"It is possible," Ybelline replied. "One is missing."

"How long?"

"We cannot be certain—but he was not to be found after Mayalee disappeared. She would not fear him," Ybelline added. "She might pity him, but she would not fear him."

"I'm sorry," Severn told her. "I wasn't clear. How long has he been deaf?"

"Almost all of his life."

"And he has lived here?"

She was silent for a time. "When he reached the age of maturity, and the madness was upon him, the Tha'alaan itself could not reach him, as it reaches those who are not—deaf. He...injured himself. And he left the Tha'alaan, searching for his own kind, as he called you."

"He injured himself."

"He cut off what he referred to as useless appendages," she said carefully. "And bound his head with warrior markings, so that the wounds might go undetected. I think he truly felt that among your kin, he would find peace and acceptance."

"He wasn't accepted here." Kaylin's words were flat.

"He was, Kaylin," Ybelline replied, just a hint of anger in

the words. "And he was loved. We would no more turn our backs upon our own children than you would turn your backs upon one born blind or silent.

"But he felt the separation keenly at that time, and nothing we could say or do would dissuade him. We are not jailers," she added bitterly. "And in the end, it was decided that he might, indeed, find truth among your kind."

"But if he was living here—"

"Our world and your world are different," Ybelline replied. "And fear is so much a part of yours. He would be considered—would have been—childlike and naive by your kin. By you," she added. "He was not the same when he finally returned to us. He was silent, and he smiled little. He was injured," she added, "but we did not ask him by what, or how. He did not desire us to know.

"He was ashamed, I think," she added softly, "and that is almost foreign to us. He recovered here. He spent time with his friends and his kin."

"How long was he gone?"

"Six months."

Six months, Kaylin thought. Six months could be such a long time. You could learn so much in those months. Or so little, she thought ruefully, remembering her months on idle behind a school desk in the Halls of Law.

"Yes," Ybelline said, looking at Kaylin's face carefully. "He learned, we think, to lie. To smile when he was unhappy. To be silent when he yearned to scream. More," she added. "But it hurt us, and we did not press him." She looked away. "Were you of my kin," she whispered, "you would know how much of a failure that was—we, who know everything, did not attempt to learn, to seek *his* truth."

"But if he didn't want you prying—"

"You think like a human."

"Hello. My name is Kaylin. The last time I looked—"

Severn stepped on her foot beneath the table. Hard.

"You seek privacy because you fear discovery," Ybelline told her. "And in the end? We *let him be like you.* We did not want to touch his fear, and draw it into the Tha'alaan. He chose to be isolated, and we let him."

Kaylin understood by the tone of Ybelline's words just how guilty she felt—but she couldn't see *why.* So she did what she could as a Hawk, instead; she had nothing to offer the woman otherwise. "Where was he last seen?"

"His mother saw him," she said quietly, "and those of his friends he chose to keep company with."

"Was he behaving differently?"

"How were they to know? He is like your Severn in his ability to hide from us."

"Can we speak with these friends?"

She hesitated. "They are younger than I," she said at last. "Your age, perhaps slightly older."

"So?"

Ybelline turned to Severn.

Severn nodded. "We are not here, I think, in official capacity. I doubt the Hawks would allow Kaylin into the Tha'alaan as a representative in any case. Her dislike and her fear are well known."

Ybelline said, "It is a deep fear, but it is a narrow one. There are things she fears more, and in the end, things she loves more. I am willing to trust her. Are you?"

Severn nodded. "With my life," he said, an odd smile on his lips. "She's not noted for being all that careful with her own, however." He rose and approached Ybelline, his back toward Kaylin. "Show me," he said quietly. "Show me who his friends are, and where we might find them."

Kaylin rose, as well, moving slightly, so she could see them in profile. Could watch Ybelline lift her face, could see the fluttery movement of her dreaded antennae as they brushed the surface of Severn's forehead in a light caress.

Kaylin shuddered, but Severn merely closed his eyes and nodded. There were whole days where she didn't understand him. And there were days like this—where even the thought of understanding him seemed impossible.

"All right, you win."

"We didn't have a bet here."

"What exactly is the Tha'alaan?"

"It's their community," he said slowly. "Their...living history. No, it's more than that—it's like a thought they all share, whenever they choose to touch it. The Tha'alani individually have exceptional memories of their personal experiences, and they share these. They share what they've felt. They can almost relive it, and in doing that, the community relives it. The Tha'alaan is like a collection of all their experience, past and present, living and dead, all their hopes, and all their fears."

"I thought they didn't have any."

He raised a brow. "Anything alive knows fear. Ybelline is terrified now, and she is under some strain. She keeps much from the Tha'alaan and that is costly. Were she not trained for service to the outside—were she not schooled in handling the deaf, as we're called—she would not be able to master her thoughts in this fashion.

"Not all the Tha'alani can. Some have aptitude, and those are trained and tested. Those powerful enough, they surrender for a time to the Emperor's service."

"Or to anyone who can pay?"

"No, Kaylin. There are perhaps one or two in the history of their kind who have *chosen* to work for the deaf, but they are the exception that proves the rule. Most of the Tha'alani would live forever in their own world, seeking no contact with any outsiders, were it not for the Emperor's dictate."

"They don't want to do—what they do."

"No."

"But they do it."

"Yes. Those who can. They rotate service—the length of time they can work outside of the Tha'alaan differs from person to person." He paused. "Ybelline is very strong. Strong enough to be gentle," he added quietly. "She doesn't pity us, and she doesn't fear us. She half understands."

"She can…keep her experience of our world to herself."

"Exactly."

"So it doesn't pollute the hive mind."

He frowned. "They're not insects, Kaylin. But yes, there are experiences that they would *never* otherwise have, and

only those who can live with the isolation of individual experience can serve. It is very, very hard for the Tha'alani."

They had no escort as they emerged from the large,
rounded dwelling. Epharim was gone, and no one in armor
stood ready to take his place. Kaylin was nonplussed. "She
chose to let us walk here," Severn told her.

"She didn't seem to worry about you."

"No."

"Why?"

"We've met before," he replied carefully. Where *carefully*
meant completely neutrally in that don't-ask-me-questions
way. "I am not, perhaps, the ideal person from whom to
draw information, but neither was I afraid of her, or her kin.
They can't create memories," he added. "They can't erase
them. And what happened, happened."

"I'm not proud of a lot of my 'what happeneds,'" Kaylin
said in a quiet voice. "If I wanted people to know, I'd tell
them."

"That is a luxury," he told her as he continued to walk.
"And a daydream. Learn to care less about what other people
think."

"I don't want my life paraded through the office like yesterday's gossip."

"It already is yesterday's gossip."

"You know what I mean."

"Yes. I do. I don't agree with you, but I do know what you
mean. We don't have privacy, Kaylin. We have the illusion
of privacy. Nothing more, nothing less."

"And we have no secrets?"

He shrugged.

"I don't want my children to know—to know about things that I've done." She thought of the Foundling Halls, and the children she visited there. Shuddered to think of how much it would hurt them to know what she was capable of.

"That, I understand. Children are very absolute in their judgment. Do you truly think she would tell them?"

"Not her."

"And the others?"

Kaylin cursed in Leontine. "Not them. But the people they inform—"

"Would you change your past?"

"Parts of it. In a heartbeat."

He shrugged again.

"You wouldn't?"

"I can't. I don't waste time thinking about changing what can't be changed."

"And you're never afraid that someone will judge you? That they won't misunderstand you or misconstrue you as you are now?"

"People judge me all the time. Be careful of that," he added, pointing at a trellis that grew near the roadside. Vines were wrapped around it, and they rustled in the nonexistent breeze.

"But they don't have the right—"

"They have the right to form their own opinions. I have the right to disagree with them in a fashion that doesn't break the Imperial Laws."

"But—"

"I'm not afraid of the judgment of strangers," he told her quietly. "I live with my own judgment. That's enough. And I judge others, and live by those judgments, as well."

"I don't—" *want to be despised or hated.* She couldn't quite frame the words with her lips, they sounded so pathetic as a thought.

But Severn had her name; she felt it tug between them, its foreign syllables not so much a sound as a texture. *Ellariayn.*

He stopped walking and caught her face in his hands, pulling it up. She met his eyes. "Then stop despising and hating yourself, Kaylin. We're not what we were. We're not what we will be. Everyone changes. Everyone *can* change. Let it go.

"If you are always afraid to be known, you will never understand anyone else. If you never understand anyone else, you'll never be a good Hawk. You'll see what others see, or what they want you to see. You won't see what's *there.*"

She pulled herself free. Said, thickly, "Let's go find these friends."

Because he was Severn, he let her wander around in circles before she realized that she had no idea where those friends were. Because she was Kaylin, it took another fifteen minutes before she asked him where they were going. He didn't laugh. Exactly. And she didn't hit him, exactly.

But she watched the streets unfold as she walked, half-lost, in this section of the huge city of her birth that she'd never willingly visited before today. Saw the neatly tended houses, the profusion of *green* that seemed to be a small jungle around the rounded domes. If there was order to it, it wasn't the kind of order that the human nobility favored; each garden—if that was the right word—was its own small wilderness.

Every so often she could see one of the Tha'alani, dressed in a summer smock that seemed so normal it looked out of place, kneeling on the ground, entwined by vines and flowers. They were working, watering, tending; they didn't even look up as she and Severn passed.

The children often did, and one or two of them waved, jumping up and down to catch her attention. She had the impression of chatter and noise, but they were almost silent, and their little antennae waved in time with their energetic, stubby hands. They were curious, she thought, but they weren't in any way afraid. And they were happy.

She waved back. Severn didn't. But he walked more slowly, and as he did, the nature of the streets changed, widening as they walked. The greenery grew sparser—if things that grew could be sparse in this place—and the buildings grew larger, although they never lost their rounded curves. Street lamps, guttered by sun, stretched upward along the roadside; even the Tha'alani couldn't see in the dark, it seemed.

"Where are we going? The market?"

He nodded slowly. "The market is there," he said.

She recognized evasion when she heard it. But she was now curious herself; markets were markets, but the streets here were not so crowded as the streets surrounding any of the city markets on her beat.

There were children here, as well, but here there were fences. They were short, often colored by clean paint, and obviously meant as decoration and not protection; the children were almost as tall as the fences, and could be seen poking arms through them and touching leaves or petals. Adults came and went, and it was hard to attach any particular child to any of the adults who walked or milled around the street in silence.

And that was the thing that was strangest to her: It was eerily silent, here. Once or twice the children cried out in glee or annoyance, and the adults would murmur something just out of audible range—but there was no shouting, no background voices, nothing that wasn't the movement of feet against the cobbled ground.

For the first time, Kaylin understood why she was referred to as deaf by the Tha'alani; she felt it, here. The deafness, the odd isolation her need for the spoken word produced.

"Where's the market?" she asked Severn, to break the silence, to hear the sound of words.

"Beyond the lattice," he replied, and pointed.

Fountains blossomed like flowers with water for petals and leaves of intricately carved stones. The slender spires of water that reached for the sky seemed almost magical to Kaylin as she stared at them. Small children were playing at their edges, and squealing as the water fell down again. No language was needed to understand the urgency of their pointing little hands, or perhaps all languages encompassed it.

"You've been here before, haven't you?"

"Yes," Severn replied, using that voice again.

"Who were you hunting?"

"Someone who understood the Tha'alani geography, but not the Tha'alani themselves," he replied. "It didn't take long to find him."

She knew better than to ask what had happened to the man once they'd found him. Severn had probably already said too much.

Kaylin approached the fountains that were spread out on the points of an invisible grid. She dodged a running child, and avoided a spray of misaimed water or two. The fountains here clearly did not hold the invisible Do Not Touch signs that the fountains in the rest of the city did.

In fact, nothing seemed to.

Do not touch also did not extend to *do not wade,* and several of the children who were too old to be called little and to little to be thought of as anything else were thoroughly soaked—or entirely naked—in the low rise of the water. They made the noise that the rest of the streets seemed to lack, and Kaylin gravitated toward them, promising to never again curse the sound of voices. Even when she was hungover.

But she stopped short because it wasn't only children who were making themselves at home in the water. Severn bumped into her back at her abrupt halt.

Entwined, legs tangled, half sitting, half covered in the shallow water, were two Tha'alani who were obviously, but quietly, making love.

* * *

But the children played *around* them, sometimes over them, in their mad scramble to catch falling water; one or two of them had stopped to stare for a moment, and were still staring, but not the way Kaylin was. If her jaw hadn't been attached to her face it would be bouncing across the slick stones. She managed to control the urge to grab one of the children who was watching and haul him to safety.

Barely.

But there *were* other adults here, and they seemed entirely unconcerned. They barely seemed to *notice,* and this was almost as shocking as watching the couple themselves, skin water-perfect as they moved. Their eyes were closed, and their stalks intertwined; they were blissfully unaware of the world around them.

Kaylin teetered on the edge of action for a moment, and then began to walk forward toward them, half-embarrassed and half-outraged. Severn caught her upper arm.

"Don't," he said very quietly into her ear. "It's considered rude."

"Stopping them from—from—there are *children* here, Severn!"

"Stopping them from expressing their love and desire. Yes. It's considered intrusive here."

"But—but—" she spluttered as if she were the one who was half drowning. "The children—"

"The children are aware of them," he said. "And as you can see, they are not concerned. They haven't yet learned not to attempt to disturb, but that's expected of children."

He paused, and then said, "No, Kaylin, they have no shame." But the tone of the words conveyed no contempt and no horror, no shock, no judgment.

Certainly no embarrassment.

"They want what they want. They are aware of it in the Tha'alaan from the moment they touch it. They love as they love, and it is considered as natural as breathing, or eating, or sleeping. They make love without fear of exposure because in some ways there is no privacy. The thought and the impulse is extreme, and it is felt regardless of where they are.

"But it isn't condemned," he told her. "Not by them."

"But—"

"This is the other reason why the deaf are seldom allowed entry into the enclave. No race, not even the Barrani, can understand the total lack of possessiveness that this entails."

"It doesn't—doesn't bother you?"

"No. But I couldn't live with it, either. They are not lovers in the way we would use the word. They have no marriage, no fidelity, no sense of ownership or commitment. They feel no jealousy," he added, "or if they do, it is minor. It does not drive them to acts of rage or despair.

"They have no privacy because they don't need it."

Kaylin shook her head, almost compelled to watch, and uncomfortable in the extreme with the compulsion. A world with no privacy? It would be like hell. But worse. She could never escape—

Escape what?

"Do they never get angry?"

"Oh, they can."

"Do they never dislike each other?"

"Possibly," he said. "I've never seen it, but I can't imagine it never happens. They are not all of the same mind."

"But they can't hide it?"

"No. They don't try." He drew a sharp breath, and she knew that despite his composure he was not unaffected. "But so many disagreements between people occur because they simply don't understand each other. Or they cannot see a viewpoint that isn't their own.

"The Tha'alani never suffer from that. They understand each other perfectly. Or as perfectly as I think it's possible to understand another person. They don't get trapped by words. They don't interpret them differently. They can't lie to each other. And even if they could, they have no reason to. A lie is a thing we tell to hide something—and they cannot hide from each other.

"Love, hatred, fear, insecurity—all of these things have been felt before, and will be felt again, and all of them are part of the Tha'alaan. Long before pain festers or breaks someone, it is felt, addressed, uprooted.

"At least that is my understanding."

Kaylin looked at Severn, at his expression. After a moment she said, "You really like these people, don't you?"

"Yes," he said softly. "They're almost entirely innocent, Kaylin. But I couldn't live among them."

"Why?"

"Because I'm not. Because even understanding them, I could not live as they live. I know why you fear them. But between the two of us, you could live more easily in the

Tha'alaan than I, in the end. What I want isn't part of their world." He turned and met her gaze, and his lips turned up in an edged half smile. "I don't like to share."

She almost took a step back. "We should go," she said, her voice low.

His smile broadened, but it lost the edge, changing the lines of his face. "Unfortunately," he said, "we can't."

"Don't tell me—" She couldn't even finish the sentence.

"These are the two we want to speak with."

It was several long, embarrassing minutes later. Maybe even half an hour. Kaylin hid it—if it was possible—by engaging the children who were tugging at her legs with their wet little hands. She joined them in their fountains, assiduously avoiding line of sight with the couple; she couldn't actually watch them without feeling as if she'd accidentally walked into someone's bedroom. Or worse.

And explaining *why* she felt this way was not high on her list of priorities. Explaining why their nudity was embarrassing, explaining why public lovemaking was unacceptable behavior in the rest of the city—the words came and went, and she knew they would make no sense to these people.

They made so little sense to Kaylin.

But eventually Severn demanded her attention. He didn't speak. It was as if the Tha'alaan had seeped into his expression. He tugged at her name, at the shape of it, and she felt him suddenly, was aware of the way he was watching her, was even aware that he had been watching her the entire time she had been playing with small, gleeful strangers.

She hoped the two lovers had gotten dressed. She didn't fancy her chances of normal questioning if they didn't; they were young, and they were sun-bronzed and almost perfect. They were so wrapped up in each other—both literally and figuratively—that she wanted to go away and come back some other day.

But a child was missing.

And missing as well was a Tha'alani who was both deaf, and who had spent six months living in Kaylin's world. She felt a pang of something like pity for him, for someone who had grown up among people who were guileless and sympathetic to everything. The world outside must have come as a shock to him. Or worse.

Had he kidnapped the child?

Was the child in some way the child she had seen in the depths of the water in the back of a shop that was far too small to contain what it did, in fact, contain? She didn't think so; there had been no evidence of antennae, no evidence of the scabbing and bleeding that would no doubt be the result of their removal. And the child in the water was older.

Severn was standing by the couple when she at last emerged from the water, disengaging very small fingers from her waterlogged pants. It was warm enough that she had chosen to forgo leather for comfort, and she was damn glad of it. It didn't wear well in water.

They had, indeed, donned clothing, and if they were still wet, their hair plastered to skin and neck, their antennae weaving as if they were drunk, they wore loose robes that must have taken yards of material to make. Not dark colors, in this sun, but pale blues and greens.

"Kaylin," Severn said, speaking Elantran. "This is Nevaron, and this is Onnay." He pointed first at the male, and then at the female. "The man that we seek is Grethan, and they have been friends for a long time."

His words sounded out of place, so few other voices could be heard. But she nodded, attempting to regain her composure. It was easier than she had expected; they were calm and happy and completely free from either guilt or fear. They had not been discovered; no parent would be festering in fury.

They just…were.

And they were, to Kaylin's eye, almost beautiful because of it, which she hadn't expected. They were perhaps a year or two younger than her. It was hard to tell. They might easily have been a couple of years older.

But they would never know her life, and instead of resenting them, she felt strangely peaceful. Embarrassment faded, and she let it go, showing it out the figurative door as quickly and cleanly as possible.

"Ybelline sent us here," Severn said quietly, "so that we might ask you a few questions about Grethan."

Their stalks moved toward each other, touching slightly; they did not exchange a glance. Then again, they probably didn't have to. The touch would give them room to say anything they wanted.

"We haven't seen Grethan for two or three days," the young woman said. Her words were oddly accented—and

Kaylin realized, listening to them, that it wasn't so much the accent as the enunciation; they pronounced each syllable slowly and carefully, as if speech were both new and foreign. Which, of course, it would be.

"When you last saw him, was he unhappy?"

"Grethan is always unhappy," Onnay said quietly. "We can touch him," she added, "and we can feel what he feels, and he allows this—but he cannot do likewise for us. We can speak to him when we touch him, but it is...invasive." She dared a glance at Kaylin.

Kaylin nodded quietly.

"He did not allow us to touch him," Nevaron said, after a pause. "Not in the last day or two. There were very few whom he would allow even that contact before then, and we accept this. It has happened before," he added. "And it will no doubt happen again."

"He is not in the Tha'alani quarter."

Onnay's brows rose. "What do you mean?" she said, each syllable still perfect, still slow.

"He is not at his home. He is not in the market. He is not where we believe he works."

As they hadn't *actually* done any of the legwork to ascertain this, Kaylin guessed that Ybelline had communicated this information to Severn when she had almost caressed his forehead with her antennae.

"We believe," Kaylin said, speaking almost as slowly as they did, as if they were children, "that he has left the quarter and found a home outside of it."

"With the deaf?"

"With, as you say, the deaf."

Onnay shook her head forcefully. "That's not possible," she said at last.

"Why?"

"He lived there some time."

"We are aware of this."

"And he came back—" She shook her head. "He lived a nightmare there. Here, he could wake and be at peace. He was happy to be home," she said. "And we were happy to see him return.

"He shared some of his life on the outside with us." She could not suppress her shudder, and didn't even bother to try. "And it hurt us," she whispered. "We did not ask him to share all. I do not think—"

Nevaron shook his head. "It was not easy for him to share, and it was not easy for us. Onnay did not touch him, that day. I did." He lifted his chin slightly. "I am of the Tha'alanari."

"You will find work on the outside," Severn said quietly. It was not a question.

"Even so."

Severn nodded. "And you kept much of this from the Tha'alaan?"

"They would be—what is the word?—darkened by it."

Severn nodded again. "In the memories that you touched," he said softly, "were there no happy ones?"

"None that I would call happy, if I understand the Elantran word correctly."

"And he met no one, found no one, that he might consider a friend?"

"Friend," Onnay said, and looked at Nevaron.

"It is an Elantran word," he replied, carefully and politely. "Ybelline sent them," he added. "It means people who care."

"Then we are *all* his friends."

Nevaron's antennae danced away from Onnay's for a moment and her brows lifted. She smacked his chest. Kaylin laughed. "My apologies," Nevaron said gravely, "but Onnay doesn't pay much attention to racial differences."

"Well, it isn't as if I will go Outside." Onnay frowned.

Kaylin laughed again. "Oh, Onnay," she said, at the girl's quizzical look, "no one ever really knows *what* they'll be doing until they're in the middle of it."

"And the Tha'alaan contains very little about Outsiders," she continued, obviously still annoyed.

"True," Severn said, before Nevaron could dig himself into a deeper ditch. "But if he has left the quarter, he must have had some destination in mind."

Nevaron hesitated for a moment longer, and then said, "I can show you where." And Severn, as if he did this every bloody day, bowed his head and bent his face down so that it was within reach of Nevaron's antennae.

He stiffened suddenly, but did not withdraw, and Kaylin could see, in the clear lines of Nevaron's expression, some shock. "You know this place?" he asked, his voice low.

Severn's brief chuckle was so dark, Kaylin knew instantly what the answer would be.

"Yes," he said quietly. He turned to Kaylin, and his expression gave her no hope at all.

"Nightshade," she said softly.

"The fief, yes," Severn replied. And then, after a moment, added, "And the fieflord, Kaylin."

CHAPTER 5

Kaylin was silent on the walk home. She didn't even try to lead; she followed Severn as if she were his shadow, a part of his movement, impossible to separate from it.

"Kaylin?"

She shook her head. "I'll go," she said quietly.

"Alone?"

"I think it— I think so."

"I despise the fieflord," Severn said in a flat and neutral tone, "but his taste has never run toward the mutilation of children. Not her age." He paused, and then added, as if it were dragged from him and he was unwilling to let it go, "I do not think, even if it did, that he would pursue it while you lived. There are some things that you do not forget."

"Did Nevaron give you all of Grethan's memory?" She felt almost dirty asking. Like a gossip, but worse. And she hated herself for it; she was doing what she herself feared might be done to her. Hypocrisy and Kaylin were not close friends.

"No," Severn replied. "It was not his to give. He is Tha'alanari. He understands why barriers must be placed, and where."

She nodded. The answer was both a frustration and a comfort. "Just an image?"

"More than an image, but not a whole story," he replied. "The image of Mayalee is not the same as the description of the girl you saw in Evanton's…shop. I do not think they are the same child," he added, "although neither have been reported as missing. As neither have been officially reported," he added quietly, "I'm not sure we'll be allowed to officially investigate, either."

She nodded absently. "Subsection of the human rights code v.8 states clearly that—"

"Those who are incapable of stating a case are still protected by the dictates of law."

"It was meant to make provisions for—"

"Abused children, or those sold to brothels by their parents, often for transport to the fiefs."

"You're good," she said with a half smile.

"As are you, which is probably more surprising given your general academic history." His smile was fleeting, but genuine. "But the first case almost certainly involves magic."

"And the second?"

"It involves Nightshade," Severn said quietly. "What do you think?"

"Magic." She said the two syllables with the emphasis she usually reserved for Leontine cursing. "Gods, I hate magic."

"Don't start, Kaylin."

"All right. I won't."

"And speaking of magic—"

"Yes, damn it, I know."

"You're late."

"Did I not just say I know that?"

"Have you ever been on time for one of your lessons?"

"Once. I think it almost gave Sanabalis a heart attack. If," she added darkly, "Dragon lords have hearts."

"I believe they have four."

"Probably because they ate three." She started to run because Severn had begun to jog.

"I have a few questions to ask the sergeant," Severn said. "I'll meet you after you've finished."

Lord Sanabalis of the Dragon court had that aura of aged wisdom that had not yet declined into dotage. She found him both comforting and frightening—but then again, she'd *seen* a Dragon in its serpent form, so that was understandable.

He was also, in his own way, kind. The day she had been on time, he had been late. In fact he had taken to arriving about half an hour to an hour later than their scheduled appointment, probably to put Marcus at ease. It was not something she thought other Dragons would do; even Tiamaris, technically still seconded to the Hawks, would not have condescended to show that much consideration for the merely mortal.

Especially not when it was Marcus.

Today, Sanabalis was waiting for her in the West room, in the chair he habitually occupied. It was the largest chair in the office, and it was made of something so hard you could probably have carved swords out of it and they would still have maintained a killing edge.

Dragons were not exactly light.

She bowed when she entered the room, her hair askew. She had, as usual, flown through the office at a run, and paused only to let Caitlin fuss a bit.

But she sagged slightly when she saw her nemesis sitting on the table: a pale candle with an unlit wick. Grimacing, she took her seat opposite Sanabalis.

"Good of you to come," he said. This was code for *I've been waiting half an hour.* She had thought she would only be half an hour late, and revised that estimate up by about thirty minutes.

"I was delayed," she said carefully, "by a request from Ybelline of the—"

He lifted a hand. "It is not my concern."

He waved toward the candle, and Kaylin said, without thinking, "Instead of trying to get me to understand the shape of fire, can you teach me the shape of water?"

His utter silence was almost profound, and his eyes had shifted from calm, placid gold to something that was tinged slightly orange. Red was the color of death in Dragon eyes.

Orange just meant they might pull an arm off for fun.

"It is very interesting that you should ask that, Kaylin. You will of course amuse an old man by telling him *why.*"

Kicking herself was not much fun, but she did it anyway. "It's—"

His eyes shifted shades. His inner lids began to fall. Certainly made his eyes a more vibrant color. "Why water, Kaylin? Why now?"

Because she was either brave or stupid, she said, "Why do you care so much?" She didn't tilt back in her chair; she couldn't affect that much nonchalance in the face of a concerned—she liked that word—Dragon lord. But she did try.

It wasn't the answer he was expecting. She could tell by the way he blinked; the last few weeks had given her that much. "Water is pervasive," he said at last, and his eyes had shaded back to gold, but it was a bright and fiery gold, unlike the normal calm of Dragon eyes. Too keen, and too shiny.

"All of the elements—and that is a crude word, Kaylin, and it conveys almost nothing of their essence—have faces. They are death, if you discern that shape, but they are life, if you discern others."

She thought of the shape of fire. Looked at the candle. It wasn't life or death she had been struggling with. It was just lighting a damn wick. "Fire burns," she said at last.

"Yes."

"And without it, we die in the cold, if we're unlucky enough to live there."

"Yes."

"There's more?"

"Yes."

"You're not going to explain it, are you?"

"No. But I am not unpleased, Kaylin."

"Why is that, exactly?" She didn't often say something right to her teachers, and she thought it might be useful if she ever wanted it to happen a second time.

"Water," he said. "Tell me what you think."

She knew she was chewing on her lower lip. "Well," she said at last, "you can drown in it."

"Yes."

"And the storms at sea—"

"Yes."

"But if you don't drink it, you die."

"Very good."

"And so do the plants, in a draught."

"Indeed."

"And there's more." But this wasn't a question. *Water is deep.* "Water is deep," she said, musing aloud.

"Yes. Those are the words of the Keeper."

"The who?"

"You met with him today," Sanabalis added softly.

"Oh. You mean *Evanton?*"

His brow rose at the tone of her voice.

"Well, he's just an old—" And fell again as her voice trailed off, remembering him in his elemental garden.

"He was one of my students," Sanabalis said quietly, "but he does not visit, and cannot." He looked at her carefully. "He showed you his responsibility."

She nodded slowly.

"And you saw something in the water there."

She nodded again. "A girl," she said quietly. "Bruised face.

Dark hair. Wide eyes. She called me by name," she added softly.

"Did you recognize her?" His gaze was keen now, sharp enough to cut. Had she been a liar, she would have fallen silent, afraid to test that edge. But she was Kaylin.

"No. But I—I need to find her, Sanabalis."

"Yes," he told her softly. Where in this case *soft* was like the rumble of an earthquake giving its only warning.

"You know about this."

"I don't, Kaylin. Or I did not. But water—it is the element of the living. It is the element to which we are most strongly tied, or to which you and your kind are. It is the element that speaks most strongly to the Oracles."

Kaylin failed entirely to keep from grimacing.

"You disdain the Oracles?"

"They speak in riddles when they speak at all, and afterward, they tell you that whatever gibberish they said was of course true."

"It is only afterward that the contexts of the words have their full meaning," he replied patiently.

She stopped. "You've been talking to the Oracles?"

"Yes."

"Why?"

"The Emperor desired it," he replied, carefully and slowly. "And in truth, they came to him, and they were ill at ease."

"How ill?"

"Perhaps a week ago, perhaps a little more, they were woken from their sleep by a dream."

"All of them?"

"All of them. Even those who are mere apprentices and have not yet earned the right to live in the temple and its grounds."

"It wasn't a good dream."

"It wasn't a dream at all."

"A—what do they call them?"

"Vision." His momentary impatience was clear.

"Of what?"

"Water," he told her.

"Water."

"Yes. The waters are deep," he added, speaking almost exactly in the tone and style of Evanton. "And things sleep within those depths that have not been seen by even the living Dragons, save perhaps two."

She froze. "Something is waking."

"In their dreams, yes."

"What?"

"They're Oracles, Kaylin," he replied.

"So you don't know."

"No. They're certain it's not a good thing for the city. Which has a port. The Sages have been poring over the words and symbols," he added, with just a flicker of his brow.

"And they get what anyone sane gets, which is confused."

He actually offered a slight smile. "It is not yet clear to them, no."

"Something big is going to happen."

"Big enough to wake the Oracles—all of them—no matter where they lay sleeping."

She was silent for a moment, candle forgotten. "And did they have any sense of timing?"

"Time is not as concrete for people who see into possible futures," he told her quietly.

"That would be no."

"That would indeed be no—but there is urgency. And I cannot think that it is coincidence that you came to me today to ask me about the element of water." He paused. "The Keeper summoned you."

"Well, no—" She stopped. "Maybe."

"Then the child is someone connected to the water, I think."

Kaylin nodded. "I have no idea where to start," she added. "But…Ybelline also invited me to visit her…at her home in the Tha'alani quarter."

Dragon brows rose. "And you accepted?"

"It wasn't official," Kaylin replied. "And…yes. Because I was in Missing Persons…" She trailed off. "Dragons don't believe in coincidence, do they?"

"Not in this city," Sanabalis replied. "They do, however, believe in lessons." He stared at the candle.

"If the world were ending—"

"You'd still have work to do."

The contempt in which candles were held by Kaylin could not safely be put into words in front of a Dragon lord—but it was still a close thing. Sanabalis, however, did not lecture her. He was quiet during their lesson, and his lower lids flickered often as he studied her face. At length he stood.

"Perhaps," he said, as if grudging the word, "you require a slightly different approach, given your remarkable lack of success. Very well, Kaylin. The day after tomorrow, we will look at the shape of water. Be prepared," he added softly. "There are many reasons why water is not the first element we approach. And why, in some cases, it is better not approached at all."

He rose and left, and she sat in the West Room, staring at the plain surface of a nearly invulnerable table, seeing her future. Which would be in Nightshade, where so much of her past had unfolded.

It was well past midday when Kaylin made her way across the Ablayne, idly watching its banks for trouble. Almost hopefully watching the banks for trouble. It was a safe trouble—in as much as people trying to kill you or beat you to a messy pulp could be called *safe*—compared to the trouble she faced in Nightshade.

And fate, as always, thumbed its nose at Kaylin. The bank was mockingly empty. Too close to night. Even at the edges of the fiefs, the howls of Ferals crossed the water and they could be seen as packs of roving shadows in a distance that never seemed quite safe enough.

The feeling of dislocation as she stepped off the bridge on the wrong side of the river—by the city standards—had never been so sharp; even the air seemed different as she took it into her lungs and held it a moment. The air was night cool, but humid; the moons were high. The sky had retained the clarity of the early day, and the wind that came from the port was so faint it was barely worth calling it breeze.

Everything was different. Everything was the same. It was not yet night, and the Ferals were not a danger, but people were already creeping inside and barricading the doors where they could.

Kaylin felt the faint tingle of the mark on her cheek not as pain, but as warmth, as she walked the streets. She wore her uniform; she hadn't thought to change, and had she, wouldn't have bothered. This was the only armor she had, and the only armor she wanted.

She wasn't paying a social call.

The streets seemed smaller as she walked them. Narrower, but less confining. And why wouldn't they? She didn't live here anymore. She never had to live here again. The poverty, the hunger, the desperate thieving—they were behind her. But so was all of her past, and she felt herself standing on it as if it were a pile of badly teetering crates. She *hated* this place.

But in some ways, here, she could stretch her arms, could breathe, could feel at home. She didn't have to mind her manners, she didn't have to know the laws; the only thing she needed to know was when to get off the streets, and who to avoid when the streets were in theory safe. The only Barrani she had to speak was the guttural Barrani of the fief itself.

She shook herself, and even smiled, although it was rueful. No home, here. Not marked as she was. And if the sun set any faster, no safety, either. She hated to hurry, but it was second nature when the sky was turning shades of pink and purple and the moons were beginning to make themselves felt.

* * *

The castle guards were waiting for her.

She knew that Lord Nightshade was likewise waiting. She could almost hear—or feel—the syllables of his name in the pleasant cool of the night air. Secret name. Hidden name. In theory, all Barrani had them, and in practice, they didn't share them with anyone who could speak about it later. Not that Kaylin could—she'd tried, in private, to speak the name aloud. It wasn't possible. Every variation sounded wrong to her ears. It was almost like someone trying to describe something she had seen to someone born blind, except that both of those people were her.

Even as it got darker, she slowed her stride. The castle itself looked faintly luminescent in her vision. She had never seen it look that way before.

But she walked toward it now, thinking—trying to think—of missing children, and of a deaf Tha'alani boy who had thought to find understanding in the world outside the Tha'alaan. Grethan. What understanding had he come by that had led him to Nightshade?

What could he offer, in the end, that could buy his escape? And what did he have to do with a missing Tha'alani child who could no longer be felt in the Tha'alaan?

And Nightshade answered, *Come inside, Kaylin, and you will have your answers.*

Entering the castle was never, ever going to be a pleasant experience. It was like a slap in the face, but with fists. It disoriented, blinded, and added a sickening lurch—like a fall, but somehow worse—for good measure, before she stumbled into the vestibule that served as an entrance. She wished that a door—a normal, functional, door—could take the place of the illusionary portcullis that was actually a magical portal. Partly because it wouldn't be magic, and partly because it wouldn't make her want to throw up so badly.

She swore she was going to find the bloody back door, because something this size *had* to have one. It wasn't a thought that had ever occurred to her before, because she had grown up in the Castle's shadow, with the certain knowledge that entering the castle was courting death. Well, more accurately, running past courtship straight into a very, very short marriage.

He met her at the door, and he offered her a deep bow. His expression, as always, gave away about as much as a felonious banker. He was wearing dark blue, simple enough to catch the flickering light of far too many stones that glittered in the ceiling above.

"Have you your Lord's permission to attend me?" He asked softly.

She frowned. "I'm here as part of an ongoing investigation. I don't talk to the Hawklord every time I have to ask a question—oh. You mean the Lord of the High Court."

"There is no other."

"For me, there is." She paused. "There is only one."

"And yet you are a Lord of the High Court, Kaylin Neya."

"The Lord of the High Court understands who and what I am." *More or less. Well, maybe less.* "I'm a Hawk. I'm here."

"You bear the mark of an outcaste."

"I bear your mark, yes." She shrugged. "It doesn't interfere with my duties."

"To the Hawks? No. But you will have duties to the High Court at one time or another. Play with care, Kaylin. You have never liked fire."

She almost laughed. Didn't. "You know why I'm here."

"No, actually, I don't." He held out an arm, and she realized after a moment that he meant for her to follow, or to precede him in the direction he was pointing. "But some conversations take time," he added, "and possibly privacy if they are of a delicate nature."

"They don't send me out on 'delicate' cases," she said firmly, wanting to stand her ground. Following anyway.

"In our youth," he said quietly, "we were concerned about perfection." He had taken his seat across from Kaylin in a room she had never seen. Not that she had seen much of the Castle itself. The walls were pale, eggshell-blue, and the ground was a sheen of light over wood; a window, like the sundered half of a huge circle, let in moonbeams, hints of starlight. Before him, low and slightly concave in the center, as if to suggest an ebon palm, was a table that gleamed with a sheen of light over dark, dark brown. Water flowers swirled to a breeze-called eddy in a low, flat bowl that was simple white ceramic with no adornment she could see. Such austerity seemed at odds with the Castle and its usual decorations, but she liked the simplicity.

"It is worth far more than flakes of gold," he said coolly, but with the hint of a smile. "And the flowers that live for mere days in the waters it holds, far more valuable still. But you did not come to criticize my decor, nor to marvel at the flowers that I chose to grace this room."

"No. You know where I went today."

"Indeed. You are a part of my...clan," he added softly, "and therefore it is my business to know."

She didn't ask him why or how because it didn't matter.

"I admit some surprise that you chose to visit the Tha'alani quarter—your dislike of their natural gift is well known. But you are a Hawk, and if that is where you must circle, you circle." His eyes were dark as he studied her face, as if reading, in each expression, each turn of lip or flicker of eye, the whole of a story that she herself conveyed but couldn't understand. "Did you find what you sought?"

She shook her head.

"And is it connected in some way with the Keeper?"

"The Keeper?"

"You call him... What is he called by your kind? Ah. Evanton. A querulous old man of indeterminate age who will occasionally condescend to perform magic, if it strikes his fancy."

"We call them enchantments," she said stiffly. "And no. At least, it doesn't appear to be connected."

"Ah."

Something, she thought. He knew something.

"We spoke with Ybelline Rabon'alani."

"She is seconded to the Emperor, is she not?"

Kaylin nodded. This much, she did expect him to know. The Barrani seemed well informed about the affairs of the

Emperor, whereas Kaylin—well, curiosity was well and good, but living was better.

"One of her people is missing from the enclave." She paused and then said softly, "No, two. Two are missing."

"Unusual. They are?"

"A five-year-old child, a girl named Mayalee. And a young man, maybe twenty, called Grethan."

She waited for a shift in his face, some subtle hint that the name was one he recognized. He met her gaze without once altering his expression, but…he did recognize the name; she felt it, rather than seeing it. Lifted her hand to her cheek almost awkwardly, as if to hide the mark there. As if to hide herself.

He failed to acknowledge the feeble attempt.

"It's not the first time he's left the enclave," she said, after the pause had grown *awkward,* at least for her. He never seemed to be aware of what the word *awkward* meant, and she resented it, as she often resented the perfection of the Barrani. The only time they were bearable was when they were drinking. Or when they were saving her life.

Even then, it was a close call.

"Continue."

"He was born deaf." She chose the word with care. "By the standards of the Tha'alani, he was born deaf. He can hear, of course, and speak—but the way they speak to each other—that, he can't do."

"And he left the enclave once because he felt isolated from his kind, and he wished to find those who would understand him."

She nodded slowly.

"But he found, instead, a world of people who were accustomed to *being* deaf; who had no idea of what they were missing, of what they had lost by their essential deformity. He discovered lying," he added, "and a level of violence and abuse that he had never dreamed of in the confines of the enclave."

She nodded again, but slowly, acknowledging the middle of a story that wasn't pleasant, but seemed almost inevitable.

He rose. "Will you partake of refreshments if they are offered?"

She started to say no, realized that she was hungry, and nodded instead, still thinking about what he had said. About what Severn had seen when he had willingly allowed himself to be touched by the tendrils that adorned Tha'alani brows.

"How did you find him?" she asked as he rose and turned away from her, walking toward the door they had entered. He opened it and when it shut and he turned back to her again, he was carrying a simple tray as if he were a servant.

She had expected a servant to come.

But he seemed to suffer no lack of dignity by pouring wine into clear goblets, nor any from offering her bread and fruit. She waited while he carefully set things upon her tray, arranging them carelessly so that they looked like a small artistic statement.

Which eating, of course, would destroy.

"I have ties," he replied at length, when she did not choose to further fill the silence, "in the city across the bridge. I know many of your kind there, most of whom you would dislike, if you did not kill them outright." He shrugged. "They are of use to me from time to time, and I will admit that I have killed a small number of them myself."

"Murder," she said, but it was almost rote.

"Indeed. But no investigation was launched, nor was one called for." He watched her eat, and then, after a pause, he ate, himself, the perfect host.

"Grethan?"

"You are impatient, Kaylin, but your age is almost excuse enough. I said, when we sought this room, that in our youth we were concerned, always, with perfection. We strove for it in all things—in all arts, whether of peace or of war. In our music, in our poetry, in our plays, in the style of our dress. We forged great weapons," he added softly, looking past her shoulder, "the art of which is not entirely lost to us now. In those years, our struggles with the Dragons were great, and many a forest was destroyed in the wars waged. But even that—even that was a kind of perfection."

She nodded; nothing he had said surprised her.

"But perfection," he said, lifting the glass he carried so that he could meet her eyes over the rim, and leaving it there, as if it were a lowered veil, "is tiring, in the end, because in the end, the perfect, the flawless—it is all *alike*. It is achieved, and it is static.

"And some of our kind looked instead to other things. To the flaws and the imperfections to be found in the natural world. In the Consort's garden," he added, "there is some hint of that wilderness, of life wending its way, making its choices."

She hadn't noticed it, but she'd been kind of bleeding and falling over with exhaustion at the time.

"You are a Hawk, child. Half-dead, you notice everything."

"Everything of import."

He shrugged, lifted the glass to his lips, drank. "Learn to define *import* by the people you study, and not by your own narrow life. It is significant, there."

She bit her lip. Mostly to stop herself from snapping. "Grethan?"

"I am coming to Grethan. I am not, for my kin, young. My youth is long past me, and the time when I idled in that mysterious drive for perfection is lost. I, like the Consort, look now for the unique, for the things that life has made imperfect, each in its own way."

"For the crippled?"

He frowned. The expression should have frozen his wine. It certainly froze Kaylin in place.

"I am not Grethan. I will never be Grethan. What he sensed in his crippled communication with the Tha'alaan, the Barrani have never had, nor will they ever achieve it. The Tha'alaan in all its alien glory is something that would be achieved only by our destruction, if by that at all. We are *ruled*," he said. "We value power. The Tha'alaan does not seem to even understand it.

"But Grethan came to understand it in his brief time among your kin. Power, and the lack of power that comes with it. Pain. Lying. He learned each of these things in turn, and each of these things scarred him, twisting him.

"When he was offered to me," he added softly, "he was Tha'alani in form only. The exotic appeals to many men— and few women—of all races. Very, very few of the Tha'alani are…accessible to those who live outside of the enclave. And those that are, are seconded to the Dragon Emperor, and very closely guarded.

"And when he was brought for my inspection, I saw many things in him, Kaylin, that intrigued me. I saw the stumps, scarred because of their clumsy mutilation, that were all that remained of the most obvious physical difference between his race and your own. I saw the scars, as well, that do not show, and I chose to offer him a way out of his situation."

"What situation?" she asked sharply, more sharply than she had intended.

"Come, Kaylin, don't be naive."

The wine tasted as if it had already soured; the food in her mouth, like ash. She set things down, her arrangement a small chaos compared to his own plate. This, she did notice.

"It happens to many naive people, often girls who have run away from their strict parents, often boys. They come to Elantra with dreams and hopes—and very little in the way of money or employment. Some are lucky, but most find themselves indebted to men who extract a very high return for their initial investment.

"Grethan was incapable of lying directly. He was very easily led into a state that would be considered very illegal by your Hawks or your Swords. What he discovered of the races outside the enclave was unpleasant indeed."

"And of the Barrani?"

Nightshade offered her a rare smile. "Very little at all, Kaylin. I offered him a way out of the debt he had incurred in his foolishness, and although he was at that time wise enough to be suspicious, my offer—whatever it might entail—seemed far better than what he could look forward to for the rest of his short life.

"He accepted my invitation," he added, "and he came to live in Nightshade for a space of a few months. He has seen more of the Castle than you."

"You—you—"

He laughed, then. "No, Kaylin. I did not touch him. That was not my interest in him, although I believe it took him a month to believe that was not the nature of any trap I might set. I merely watched him. Spoke with him. Allowed him to speak to other inhabitants of this place. It is my belief that the Castle would accept him should he choose to enter it again, but it is probably not his belief."

"What did you do to him?"

"Very little, I assure you. We spoke about his people. We spoke about yours." He paused. "But he spoke, as well, to some of my associates who are less obvious in the way they avoid the dictates of law."

"What do you mean?"

"Powerful men," he replied. She knew it was all he would offer. "Not all of the Barrani avoid me, as you have seen, although I am Outcaste. There are some, still, who will barter with me, and when they come here, they come as guest, not as their Lord's agent."

Some fleeting thought wondered what those interests were, but it couldn't grip strongly enough to hold on. There was really only one person she was interested in hearing about. "Why did you expose him to these people?"

"He asked it, as a favor."

"But—but why?"

"The Tha'alani are not mages," he replied. "They do not appear to be born with the talent, and if they are, they do not come forward to have it trained. If they did, they would be under Imperial control, Imperial dictate. They would live among the deaf."

"And Grethan—"

"Seemed obsessed with the magical."

She closed her eyes. "He wanted to *fix* what was wrong with him."

"He did indeed."

"And you let him believe—"

"No, Kaylin. He chose to believe. I was not unkind—that, he had already experienced. Nor was I kind, for he had walked away from kindness, which informed the whole of his life until he found your people. I told him the truth—that there was no cure to be found that I knew of."

"And he didn't believe you."

"He had no desire to believe me, and for many of your kind, belief and desire are one and the same."

"When did he leave you?"

"That would be the first intelligent question you have asked."

"I could have asked why."

"That, too, would be intelligent." He paused. Rose. Walked over to where she sat, her brow furrowed as she tried to imagine what she would do were she Grethan. She could understand some of his life; some of it, she had lived. It made her squirm.

And the touch of Nightshade's hand on her chin made her freeze in place. "It is my belief," he told her softly, "that one of the men to whom he spoke offered him the cure that he desired. I do not know what was said. The meeting itself, the first meeting here, was innocuous. But Grethan was not confined to the Castle. I did not require it, and I was curious to see what he would do with freedom, if he had any sense of it at all remaining.

"But he did meet again with one of my colleagues."

"And then he returned to the enclave."

"Yes."

"Who did he meet with?"

Nightshade shook his head. "That," he said, as his hand left her chin, "was not at all subtle."

"I don't need—"

"But you do, Kaylin. You need to make the person who has the information feel that it is either in their interest, or amusing enough, to give it to you. A gift requires no payment, and no barter."

"Look, the child—the missing child—was last seen talking to Grethan. I think they disappeared at the same time. I think he took her with him when he left."

"And that," Nightshade continued, as if she had not spoken, "was equally unwise. You are now claiming *need* for the information, and need implies desperation. When someone is desperate, they will often pay far more than mere information is worth."

"Nightshade—"

He bent suddenly and brushed her lips with his own, the taste of wine sweet on his breath.

"The Barrani are not a scrupulous people," he said as he stepped back. His eyes were cold. "But we understand our prey.

"Very well, *Erenne*. You wish information from me, and if I am not mistaken, that information will be costly, for I will undoubtedly lose that contact within the city."

"And…from me?"

"From you I will ask for information in return."

CHAPTER 6

She tensed.

"You went to visit Evanton."

She nodded. "And I lost contact with you there."

"Do you understand why?"

"Not completely."

He raised a brow and met her gaze, unblinking. Cat's eyes—but a large cat, capable of destroying much before it could be brought down. If it could. "Do you understand Evanton's role, in this city?"

"Not really."

"I see."

"Do you?"

He surprised her with a rare smile. "No, not entirely. But I understand that he has, at his command, the elemental powers of a bygone age, and he has chosen—he will *always* choose—to keep them leashed. There is no power that could move him to use what he holds, and no threat that could be dire enough that he would do so. Were the entire of Elantra to be destroyed, I believe his shop would still stand, where it has stood in place since before the creation of the Empire."

"He can't be *that* old."

"No. He is not the first Keeper. He will not be last. And he is aged." He studied her face for a moment. "What did you see, Kaylin? What did he dare to show you?"

"His garden," she replied tersely. "And yes. Fire. Water. Earth. Air. You could almost hear voices."

"He showed you these things even though you bear my mark."

"He didn't seem concerned about it. He said you wouldn't be able to even enter the store."

"Ah."

"But…Teela could."

"He has less to fear from Teela. She is a rebel, and known for it among our circles."

"He's not exactly—"

"He is known to us. He is treated with deference."

"Why? If you know he won't *use* the power—"

"He is Keeper for a reason. There are those among our learned who believe that were the elements to be un-leashed, they would destroy the world. Or remake it. Tedious debates, which you will no doubt forget or I would lay them out before you, have occurred about this for centuries."

Centuries. Kaylin almost shuddered.

"What did you see, Kaylin? It concerned you. Where did you go in his garden, and what did you choose to listen to?"

"He told me to listen to nothing."

"He is wise. You, however, are not. You were agitated when you left his abode. Tell me this much, and I will tell you what you need to know."

"I—" She hesitated. There would always be this hesitation around Lord Nightshade. His presence was larger to her than the long, tall shadow the Castle had been for over half her life. "I looked to the water," she said at last.

"To the water."

"There was a small pool. Pools that size aren't usually very deep."

He laughed. The laughter was genuine, but not entirely free from condescension. And not free, when it ended, from concern. "So," he said softly.

"So what?"

"Tell me, Kaylin, before I ask further what you found in that water, why you went to Evanton at all."

"I was sent there by my sergeant," she replied.

"Pardon?"

"He received information that required some investigation, and he sent groundhawks to investigate. Why do you look so surprised? It's what I do for a living."

"But it is odd that it was you that he chose to send."

"Not really. I like Evanton. Evanton likes me. Well, he bites my head off less than other people when *I* ask him questions he considers stupid."

"What questions would those be?"

"Any questions at all."

"Since Evanton is easily offended, Sergeant Kassan thought there was little risk in sending you to handle the investigation. Very well. Pardon my intrusion and continue with your story."

"I— The water was deep."

"Deeper by far than you can imagine, Kaylin."

"I couldn't see the bottom."

"That *is* what I just said."

"But I could see the surface clearly. The water there is very still, even though the breeze is strong. And yes, I'm not an idiot. I understand that the air and the water do not mix in that place.

"I saw—I thought it was my reflection, at first."

"And he did not stop you from approaching the water?"

"No—there were footprints in the moss bed that led to the edge of that pool. I followed them there."

At this, Lord Nightshade stilled, as if he had received his first real surprise of the day.

"Not Evanton's."

"No. We wouldn't have been called for otherwise."

"How many?"

"This is official business—" she began.

"And the information you require of me is for official business, as well. That is the way of the Law, to ask for the aid of those who understand its underside. You bribe people," he added. "And each of us, in our fashion, is susceptible to bribery."

The problem was that it *wasn't* official. But she'd be

damned if she now admitted this. "All right, but the people we often ask for information are trying their best to stay out of the Hawks' eye. You—"

"Yes. I rule here, Law or no."

"But if you—"

"You are my *Erenne*," he told her softly. "And you will give new meaning to that word, in time. New meaning, and old."

She forgot what she had been about to say; the tone of his voice was almost intimate, and it traveled the length of her spine, making her stiffen, causing her hands to draw in toward her lap, in easy reach of her daggers.

Not that they would do much good.

"What you do, however, is private, now. No information will be given, Kaylin, to anyone. What you know and what I know are no longer separate, and I will not weaken my house."

She nodded, her mouth dry. She took a gulp of liquid to wet her lips and wine burned its way down her throat, causing her to cough. A lot. All in all, it hadn't been her most dignified day.

"I saw the face—the bruised face—of a girl who was maybe ten. Possibly twelve. It was hard to tell. She wasn't standing in a lot of light."

"And you remember her face clearly?"

"Completely clearly."

"What did she say?"

She started to play that game, to ask him, *Who said she said anything?* But she couldn't play games here, not with this man. "My name," she whispered. "I think she was asking for help."

"Where was she?"

"I couldn't see. Believe that I tried."

"How long did you have?"

"Long enough for a Hawk."

He nodded. "It is interesting that you went to the water, or that the visitors that Evanton did not himself lead into the garden also went there."

"Why? Sanabalis—Lord Sanabalis—asked me about my interest in water, as well."

"Because there are portents," he told her. "As Lord Sanabalis must have told you. In the Oraculum. And elsewhere."

"End of the world portents."

"Something close."

"I have to find that girl."

"That is my belief, yes."

"I mean—"

"I understand what you meant. But she is not the only missing child you must find. I cannot say for certain that Grethan took the child. It is not an act that I would have considered within his capabilities. But I can tell you where Grethan went before he returned to the enclave."

"Was it across the bridge?" she asked.

"Yes, Kaylin. It was not within the fiefs. Very few of the wise here—and they exist, but hidden—would risk the journey from one fief to the lord of another."

"Give me a name," she said briskly. "Um, and a race."

"He is human," Lord Nightshade replied carefully. "And he is a member of the Arcanum."

Kaylin wilted visibly, although the Castle itself did not seem to be affected by the heat of the sun and the humidity that the ocean cast across the city.

"I will write it down for you," he added.

"Why?"

"Because he is careful, and because speaking his name can act as a summons."

"To you?"

"Indeed."

I loathe magic.

Then you loathe yourself, Kaylin.

Something Severn had also said. She took the paper he offered, wondering where it had come from.

"I will see you soon," he told her quietly.

"I don't—"

"You will be back." It wasn't an order, and it wasn't a request. It was a simple statement of fact.

And she couldn't deny it.

She didn't hurry out, but she didn't linger; he escorted her to the portal that was, as far as she could tell, her only exit. She had once seen him jump through a mirror, but the Castle was his.

When she reached the portal, she hesitated, and only partly because she disliked throwing up on principle. "Did he come back to you?"

Lord Nightshade raised a perfect brow. His smile was cool, but genuine. "Yes, Kaylin. Briefly."

"When?"

"Recently." More than that, he would not say; she knew it. Wanted to press, anyway, and would have had he not been standing so close.

"Why?"

"Because the deaf—the mortal deaf—have a desire to *be* understood, and I understood him. I still do." He paused and then said, "He does not desire love, for that, we are not capable of giving, and he understands this, now. But he desires a place that is his. He wants to belong."

"To what?"

"To the dream of the Tha'alaan, Kaylin. And that was a poor question. You could answer it yourself."

"I wanted to see what you would say."

He raised a brow again, but this time, his lips turned down in a slight grimace, and she found herself changing the subject.

"Did he ask for your help?"

Lord Nightshade said nothing.

"Did he bring the child with him?"

"No."

"And if he had—"

"There are some things, Kaylin, that should never be put into words. I have killed children in my time, and I have seen them killed. But…you will find him, I think. Whether or not you will find him in time remains to be seen."

She paused for ten minutes outside of the castle walls, mostly because she wanted her stomach to stop heaving. The portal's method of swallowing her and spitting her out—in either direction—was fast becoming something she planned on fixing. Where fixing involved large hammers and a small army of people intent on destruction.

It was night, of course, and the moons were high; the air was still humid, and the humidity clung to the heat of the earlier day. Leaving at night was not the wisest of choices, but staying—staying seemed less wise. *Had* seemed less wise.

It had been a long day. A tiring day.

And the image that returned to her at its end made her blush slightly. Two bodies rolling in a fountain, surrounded by splashing children and nonchalant parents. And was that so bad? She had always dreaded a world without privacy. Had always hidden small weaknesses and small imperfections of which she was ashamed.

But it had never occurred to her that a world without privacy might just accept those flaws in the same way she accepted rain; might not only overlook them, but embrace them. And in that world, why would love be hidden when nothing else could be? If nothing could be hidden, there could be no lies, and no need for lying.

It was a world that should have been alien to Nightshade, and perhaps it still was; perhaps that was why the boy had interested him at all. Or perhaps they were both outcasts—still alive, but unable to connect with their own people.

She drew her dagger as she headed down the wide path from the castle and into the nighttime fief. Listened carefully for the familiar and unwelcome howl of hunting Ferals, and thought better of her desire for home.

And a shadow moved in the moonlight, a single shadow. She shouldn't have recognized it in the darkness, but she did. Something about the way Severn moved would always be familiar.

"How long have you been waiting here?" she asked as she approached him.

He answered with his characteristic shrug. "Long enough."

"It's not safe—"

"It's always been safer in packs," he replied. "It's always been safer not to be alone."

She looked at him for a moment. "Aren't we, though?"

"Alone?"

She nodded.

"Sometimes, yes," he replied softly, understanding the whole of her question. "We aren't the Tha'alani. We'll never have that perfect understanding, either of ourselves or of each other."

"I think I want it."

"You wouldn't, if it were offered to you now."

"Why?"

"Because there are things you—and I—have done, Kaylin, that the Tha'alaan could not accept. *We've* learned to, or we've tried. What they see in the deaf *is* there. But this is the only way we can live, because we're not Tha'alani."

But I can speak to you.

He startled, and then turned to face her.

And you can call my name.

"Yes."

She wanted to say more. But she held it back, because in the end, there were some things she didn't even know how to put into words, and without the words to contain them, she wasn't even sure she understood them herself.

"Did you get what you came for?"

She nodded. Reached into her shirt and withdrew the folded paper. "A name."

"May I?"

"I doubt you'll be able to read it in this light." But she handed it to him anyway.

"Probably not. But we'll go where there is light."

"And not where we can sleep?"

"You won't," he replied. He was, of course, right. She was tired, but not so tired that she could leave this until tomorrow.

Because time was an issue. Nightshade had said so.

Marcus, to their great surprise, was still at the office. He was absently retracing old furrows his claws had put in the hardwood surface of his antique desk. Well, that was what the merchant carpenter had called this particular desk—*antique* sounded a lot better than *cast-off* or *used*. To some people. To Kaylin, given the desk, it was one and the same, and she'd been perfectly willing to insult the smug little man in order to get the price down. Which was why, of course, Marcus had taken her. Marcus seemed to need new desks a lot, and the Quartermaster didn't dock *his* pay.

Among the Leontines, the women were usually the ones

who bartered. Men were either above that sort of petty squabble—which Kaylin doubted—or prone to take offense and kill the squabbler. Which was, as everyone in the office knew, technically illegal, if tempting.

The sergeant looked up when they entered, although given Leontine hearing, he'd heard them a good ways off. "You're back," he said, and gestured to the two chairs that just happened to be placed facing him, in front of the intimidating piles of paper that *always* adorned his desk.

Kaylin slumped into one chair; Severn took a seat more fluidly and gracefully. He did, however, hand Marcus the piece of paper he had taken from Kaylin's shaking hands.

"What's this?"

"The name of a man who has connections with the fieflords," Severn replied.

"And it came from?"

Severn shrugged.

Kaylin said quietly, "Lord Nightshade."

"You were sent to visit Evanton this afternoon. Whatever it was you found missing there, it must have involved a misplaced...person."

Apparently news of their visit to Missing Persons had, as it often did, traveled.

"While technically I would appreciate a report, practically, I won't actually *read* it unless it involves a kidnapping or a murder. And Evanton doesn't have children."

Kaylin hesitated and Marcus growled, but without much fang in it. Clearly, it *had* been a long day at the office. "It must have something to do with children, Kaylin—you never head to Missing Persons unless it does. You whine about records access otherwise. Pretend I'm not stupid. It's a career-advancing move.

"You returned and managed to weasel your way around the idiot in charge of records—" *idiot* was about as kind a term as Marcus ever dredged up for the man "—and came up with nothing.

"However, there is currently in that division a Tha'alani who is seconded to the Imperial service. I believe you were seen speaking with him, Kaylin. More than that— someone said that you allowed him to actually touch your face."

"We all have to grow up sometime," she said, adding a growl to the words that she hoped made them sound like Marcus. He recognized her mockery, but said, "You sound like a drowning kitling."

She gave up, although gods knew he'd said worse things about her attempts to use Leontine. Swearing, of course, came naturally—but it was hard to get that wrong in any tongue.

"I took the liberty—at some personal expense—of re-viewing your inquiries into Records," he added. "The fact that you're here strongly implies that you didn't find what you were looking for."

"Nothing's ever that easy in this damn place," she muttered. Damn, she was tired.

"Kaylin, where did you go afterward? Straight to Night-shade?"

"No."

Marcus nodded, as if he already knew the answer and was

hoping to catch her out in a lie. Given his mood, Kaylin didn't want to become a desk substitute for those claws, and as far as lies went, she was only *slightly* better than Marcus at telling them.

"And where did your investigation take you?"

"Actually," she said quietly, "it wasn't part of the investigation. It was a—I was—we were paying a social call."

Bushy Leontine brows rose a fraction, although if you weren't familiar with the furrows of that furry, huge face, you might not have noticed. "Social call. During work hours."

The bastard was going to dock her pay.

And she was going to let him. There were entire days where being awake was overrated. And then there were days that were worse.

"And the visit to Nightshade?"

"It was…part of my investigation." Not, technically, untrue. She hadn't said it was official.

"Ah. And why?"

"Evanton, as you're well aware, is a purveyor of fine—"

"Junk, and the occasional genuine enchantment, yes."

"This involves a genuine enchantment. Something in his care has gone missing."

He growled. "And what would that be?"

"A box. A reliquary, I think. He's had it so long he doesn't know what's *in* it, but he was worried anyway."

Leontines didn't really appreciate magic much more than Kaylin did, were in fact the only race she knew well enough to know hated it more.

"We discovered that more than one child is possibly

missing," she said with care, "and that their disappearance, or the way the information was conveyed, ties in with magic."

"With elemental magic, hmm?"

She flinched. Thought for a moment. "Sanabalis—"

"Lord Sanabalis."

"*Lord* Sanabalis came to see you."

"Yes. He found your lesson somewhat unusual, given his own duties at this time."

"But I—"

"You asked him an entirely coincidental question about the nature of water. Unfortunately, Dragons don't actually *believe* in coincidence."

"They don't?" she asked, momentarily sidetracked.

Marcus wasn't having any of it.

"Not at all."

"Does this mean I'm off the hook for lessons while he—"

"Almost exactly the opposite, you lucky girl."

"Yes, sir."

"Good." He barked a command that only Caitlin could actually reproduce, and the lights flared up, giving the office a ghostly look, to add to the almost haunting silence left in the wake of absent gossips. Speaking of which… "Severn?"

"Yes?"

"Did Jadine actually dump Lorenzo, or did she—"

The loud bark sent the question ducking for cover.

"You are going to be the death of me," Marcus growled. "After I kill you."

"Justifiable homicide," Severn said with a smile.

She gave them both a sour look.

Marcus then turned his attention to the paper Severn had so quietly handed him. He unfolded it, looked at the name, and winced.

"You recognize it?" Kaylin asked.

"What have I told you about asking the obvious?"

"Don't. It wastes air."

"Good."

"But do you—"

"Don't breathe, Kaylin."

"The name?" Severn asked quietly. "It was dark, and I could not easily read what was written. Lord Nightshade has a fine hand."

"Donalan Idis."

Severn became completely still. His expression didn't change; he did not reach for his daggers or the chain he wore at his waist. His eyes, however, did not leave Leontine eyes; his gaze did not falter.

"How by two moons did you come to be mixed up in this?"

"You sent us to—"

"Fine. Blame a tired, old sergeant."

"Yes, sir."

"Less cheerfully, and a lot less smugly."

"Yes, Marcus."

"Good. You may, if you wish, enlighten Kaylin, Corporal. But if Idis is involved—" He paused. "Nightshade has a fine hand?"

"The name, of course, was provided by Nightshade, sir."

"I…see. And what does he want in return? His kind don't last long if they're seen to cooperate with the Halls of Law."

"I imagine that he could cooperate with the Emperor himself should he so choose, and none could unseat him."

"I see. What information did he request of us in return for this, Kaylin?"

She shook her head. "Not much."

"Fine. I want a full report of yesterday's—"

"Today, sir?"

"Not unless you're an oracle." He flicked a claw toward the wall. "It's *very late*."

Which was, of course, why the mirrors were covered.

"Your wives are going to feed you to their litters one day, sir." It was a Leontine phrase.

Marcus laughed. If Leontine laughter could be rueful, this was. "My wives have each other and they say the household runs more smoothly when I'm not in it. Now get out."

"Sir."

"Report. *Full* report. In the morning. On my desk."

As if he'd notice it. Kaylin nodded briskly anyway.

"By way of Caitlin," he added when she had almost cleared the office.

Her curse and his subsequent laugh were the only two sounds she could hear.

"Donalan Idis was a member of the Arcanum."

"In good standing?"

"I don't know. It's not a phrase the Arcanum actually uses, to my knowledge."

They were wending their slow way down a nighttime street that did not have the fear of Ferals to mark it. It was almost unworldly to Kaylin, and she felt out of place in it, as if she were walking in dream. Childhood dream, dream of safety, Severn by her side.

"How do you know him?"

"The Wolves know all of the members of the Arcanum," he replied, his tone remote. "As well as all names of the Imperial Order of Mages, and their apprentices."

"And this one?"

"He is slightly more familiar to the Wolves," Severn replied, "for his early work with the Inquisitorial Services."

"The what?"

"Torturers."

She would have blanched. Didn't. "But they don't use—"

"This was before the Tha'alani…offered to work within the Imperial Service. I believe that some were drafted into Emperor's service prior to the compact made by the Tha'alani and the Dragon Emperor, but it was a dismal failure."

"How many years ago was this, Severn?"

"Well before your time or mine," he replied. "But I would guess maybe thirty."

"So he's old."

"He's human, and he is not young. But *old* is probably not the right word."

"Why?"

"Because, Kaylin, he is still alive."

She thought about what he had said for a few minutes. "Do you think he had a hand in the attempt to draft the Tha'alani?"

Severn was silent for a full minute. "If I were to guess, yes. I can attempt to confirm it tomorrow."

"Through the Wolves."

"Not officially. But yes."

The departments in the Hall—all three—had different duties, and of course, each one felt theirs was the most important, so there was a bit more than just friendly rivalry, especially after Festival season, during which the Wolves had what the harried Swords and Hawks called "their bloody vacation."

The Swords kept the peace, if there was much peace to be kept—and they were probably at their busiest during the Festival season. The Hawks were left to pick up the pieces when peace did *not* ensue: they investigated murders, thefts, missing persons and other breaches of the law. It wasn't uncommon for the Swords and the Hawks to work together when the city was in chaos, and Festival described that more or less neatly.

But the Wolves…were a special investigative branch of the law; they kept to themselves. They were called in when everything else had failed—where everything else meant things like arresting a suspect or a known criminal. Especially if the attempted arrest had involved injury or death.

Severn had been a Wolf.

"Severn?"

"What?"

"Can you find something else out for me?"

"Possibly. What?"

"How did they choose the Tha'alani they attempted to draft?"

"My guess? The ones that weren't ash. The Emperor doesn't take kindly to any refusal of a direct command."

"But they—"

"It was a disaster, yes. But it drove the Tha'alani to come up with a compromise. And that compromise has worked for decades."

"What happened to them? The ones that were pressed into service?"

"Kaylin—"

"No—you seem to know a lot about the Tha'alani. What happened to the ones who—failed?"

"They went home," he said tersely. "And they put the fear of the deaf into the Tha'alani in a way that nothing else could have." His lips tightened and closed. If there was more to say—and she could tell there was much, much more—it wasn't going to come from Severn. Not tonight.

He walked in silence to the front door of her apartment, but he did not offer—or ask—to stay. "Tomorrow," he told her. "Tomorrow, I'll tell you what I can about Donalan Idis. But, Kaylin—"

"Don't expect the news to be good."

He nodded.

CHAPTER 7

Morning happened, like a waiting disaster.

Except, of course, you could predict it. Kaylin dragged herself out of the sagging middle of an old mattress, glared expectantly at the mirror—which, miracle of miracles, remained silent and reflective—and started sorting through the pile of laundry she mentally classified as "clean."

The midwives hadn't called her in, and this was good; she was still recovering from the last delivery, and the taste of birth fluids and almost nonexistent hair lingered in her mouth. Still, Leontines were among the most devoted and grateful of peoples, and the child, named in some ways after her, was a sign of goodwill between the pridlea and Kaylin that only kin-murder would break. Word would travel—had probably already traveled—between the various pridlea that constituted the complicated Leontine pack system. She would be marked as more than just a friend to the cubs' family. Given that she was already unofficially considered Marcus's kit, she could be relatively certain of safety among the Leontines.

Friends in high places were supposed to be something to strive for, but Kaylin found that friends in the quiet and un-expected places were often the ones who really helped in ways that counted.

And among those friends, complicated and scarred, was Severn, whom Kaylin tripped over when she opened the door.

"What are you doing?" she said as she righted herself on the banister—which creaked under her weight, damn it all.

"Listening to you snore."

"I don't snore."

"You scared the mice, Kaylin."

"Ha-ha." She gave him the "later in the drill circle" look the Hawks were so familiar with—as if he were a Hawk, had always been a Hawk. Funny how odd that expression felt when your face froze there as your thoughts caught up to it.

"You've got the key," she said, turning away.

"Yes. I kept it after the fight in Nightshade. You were un-conscious for most of the week." He paused, and then added, "I don't really need a key."

"I don't want to know." She pushed the door open and held it for him, looking into her room with the newly self-conscious gaze of someone who has an unexpected visitor.

He knew an invitation when he saw it, stood, and entered quietly. He also closed the door at their backs, and after examining the chair that was sometimes referred to as an open-plan closet, he walked across to her bed and jumped up to the ledge of the window, perching there.

"I brought food," he added, handing her a canvas sack. He glanced at the mirror.

"Don't," she told him, before he could move.

"Don't?"

"Don't mute it, or whatever it is you think you were about to do."

"For security reasons, Kaylin—"

"The orphan hall and the midwives," she replied.

He gave in with a shrug. Against those, there wasn't a damn argument he could offer that would move her, and he knew it.

"I was a Wolf," he said, as Kaylin reached into the bag he had handed her. She broke the loaf of bread she found there, and also broke a chunk of cheese from the long wedge that was likewise in the bag.

She nodded, her mouth full.

"I was a Wolf for three years before the Wolflord called me to the Shadows."

Her mouth was full but it had stopped moving. She lifted a hand, her eyes wide.

He waited, with a look so impassive it made stone seem like cheesecloth. "Believe that I choose my words with care, Kaylin. But to understand what I'm going to tell you, you have to understand a bit more."

"This is Wolf business," she said, when she could manage to chew and swallow again. "It's not Hawk business."

"Most of the Hawks' business is actually not your business, but it doesn't stop you from nosing around."

"Yeah, well, nothing I find out about the Hawks is going to buy me a shallow unmarked grave."

"Nothing I tell you will end that way, either."

She was silent; the words were spoken softly. Clearly.

"Severn—"

"Three years a Wolf. Four years a Shadow Wolf. There is a reason that I understand the Tha'alani so well. The current Wolflord is not himself a man who could walk in the Shadows—as he put it."

"Probably needed to keep his hands clean."

"That is uncalled for, Kaylin." Sharp words. Severn clearly respected the man.

"Sorry."

"Lord Merlin is wise," Severn added.

"Merlin? Isn't that a—"

"Bird, yes. The irony is often remarked on by newer recruits. His family is, however, an old family, and his father— who is still alive—retains a seat in the council of the Caste-lord.

"As for keeping his hands clean—ask Lord Grammayre one day what happened eighty years ago, give or take a few."

"What happened?"

"I'm not Lord Grammayre."

She continued to eat, wondering where he was leading her. Not really wondering whether or not she would follow. He was Severn, and some part of her was still a fiefling in his care, whether she liked it or not.

"Live in the Shadows for long enough, and all you see is danger, death, insanity. Evil, if you want to use that word."

"You don't?"

"It's too simple."

"Fair enough. I like things to be simple."

"I know." He folded his arms across his chest. If she had done that, she'd have tipped off the window edge. "You lose the ability to judge men. You look only for the things that will make them a danger. And at some point, all living things can be a danger, either now or in the future. To rule the Shadow Wolves, you *must* be able to see more clearly than they can see."

"But he—"

"And you must choose with care who you consign to the Shadows."

"Because you don't want—"

"Because you will ask those men and women to do things that are only legal *because* you've asked it. And they must do those things only upon your command. You must trust them to do what is perceived to be a necessity, because you won't be there to guide them.

"You must trust them never to do so otherwise." He paused. "And people who *can* do what is asked, for the right reasons—if they exist at all—are not as easy to find as one would hope."

"He chose you because—"

It was Severn's turn to lift a hand. "My past influenced his decision," he said rigidly. "And he offered me the promotion."

Promotion wasn't the word Kaylin would have used, but

she didn't say anything; she knew she shouldn't want to hear what he said—but she desperately wanted to hear it.

"I accepted," he said softly, "because among the memories offered me by the Tha'alani—"

"Offered you?"

"Yes." Terse word. "They did the same for you, yesterday."

"But—"

"Leave it, Kaylin. I understood the need. I submitted willingly."

She nodded slowly.

"The Imperial Inquisition has existed in one form or another for many years. It was a much less pleasant arm of the Imperial Guards for most of those years, and I won't bore you with the details while you still have an appetite. But until the Tha'alani made their peace and their compact with the Emperor, it was crude and somewhat ineffective.

"Among those who helped the Inquisition to retrieve necessary information from those who did not wish to part with it were members of the Imperial Order of Mages, and also members of the Arcanum. Oracles have some play in this, but they are not considered reliable."

She rolled her eyes.

He didn't respond. He almost seemed a statue, sitting there as if motion would betray him.

"You're not going to eat?"

"I ate."

"Why are you telling me all of this?"

"Patience is useful sometimes. Learn it."

She ate a bit more, willing to play his waiting game.

"As a Shadow Wolf, you have access to information that you might need. Donalan was part of the Inquisition that existed *at the time* of the unrest between the Tha'alani and the Emperor, and experiments—and that is a kind word for what was done—were performed on the Tha'alani, to see if their talents could be magically duplicated. If they could be, the Tha'alani would be rendered superfluous.

"They could not be, but the experiments that eventually ascertained this were overseen by Donalan Idis.

"He was almost obsessed by it. This is not uncommon for those who make magic their study. He felt—and in this he was entirely correct—that the innate ability of the Tha'alani would make the task of the Inquisition much simpler.

"But the damage done to the members of the Tha'alaan was enough to convince the Tha'alani to cooperate with the Emperor. The relations between the Dragons and the Tha'alani has been…poor. But they will not thwart the will of the Dragon Emperor again, and they have begun to choose with some care the people who will serve the Emperor in the world of the deaf."

She nodded again.

"Those people are called the Tha'alanari. For the Tha'alani," he added softly, "*those* people live in the Shadows, Kaylin. They must be able to separate themselves from the Tha'alaan. They must be able to keep secrets, something that is anathema to their kind. They are chosen, like the Shadow Wolves, with care.

"Ybelline is the woman in charge of that choosing," he added quietly. "And there could be none better. What she has seen, and what she has been forced to extract, has not deadened her or scarred her. Her natural empathy has taken from the world of the deaf an understanding of what *our* lives must be like. Our unrealistic expectations of either good or evil, our judgmental nature, our desperate need for privacy and secrecy, our sense of shame—all of these things she can see as caused by our lack of the Tha'alaan. She can imagine what she might be, had her life been our life, can imagine what *we are*. It is why she can be gentle," he added.

"You catch more flies with honey than with vinegar."

"You catch more flies with shit," Severn said, smiling sharply.

"Yeah, I never understood that one, either."

He laughed. "You never fail to amuse, Kaylin."

"Thanks." She paused and set her bread down. "Donalan Idis had no such empathy."

"None whatsoever. What he needed and wanted was a tool he could use to accomplish his duties."

Kaylin raised a brow, her expression the definition of skeptical.

"This was, as I have mentioned, before my time—but not by much."

"And Donalan Idis?"

"When an understanding was reached between the Tha'alani and the Imperial Court, and the various compacts were devised and signed, the studies were, of course disbanded. Reparations of some sort—unspecified reparations—were offered the Tha'alani for the harm done their kin."

"They disobeyed the Emperor and he offered *reparations?*"

"There is a reason that he is both Dragon and Emperor, Kaylin. He is not Ybelline. I doubt that any Dragon is capable of her kindness. But he understood that what had been done had harmed not a handful of men and women, but the whole of a race, for as long as that race survives. And he also understood that to fail to acknowledge the damage done to children not yet born, and to their children, and so on, would be an open statement of ignorance. He *is* deaf. But he could understand what was explained to him."

"So it was finished, with that."

"Yes."

"And it wasn't."

"No."

She was silent, food forgotten for a time. When she spoke again, she was a Hawk. "Did the Tha'alani who were captured resist?"

His silence was longer than hers, deeper, and more disquieting.

"You don't want to answer me," she said softly, "because you already know they give me hives."

"They were mad with pain and isolation," he replied, obviously choosing his words with care.

"That's a yes. Tell me what happened."

"They drove several people insane."

"And Idis was one of them?"

"He's of the Arcanum."

"So he was already insane."

"Pretty much. But paranoid. Whatever insanity moves him, he was probably driven by it long before he met the Tha'alani for the first time."

"How, Severn?"

"They shredded their tormentor's memories," he said neutrally. "They pulled out the earliest, and the most ugly, because—if I were to guess—they were looking for the commonality of fear and brutality."

"They'd find it, there."

"Oh, they did. It's clearly documented. The Tha'alani were, for some time, considered a threat. It was not until Ybelline's predecessor bespoke the Emperor that the Imperial Court was reassured, and the full nature of the Tha'alani was made clear."

She thought about this for another long moment. "There would have to be proof of her claim."

Severn nodded. "Proof enough to satisfy an immortal Dragon."

"The Emperor did not expose himself to their touch?"

"No."

"But—"

"Yes. Among the Court, there would have had to be one Dragon lord who was willing to take that risk—and given how several of the Inquisitors had fared, it *was* a great risk. Although there are many among the mortal who are trusted by the Emperor, there are none who could be trusted to make judgment of an entire race and its intent. The Dragons are, in their own way, at least as arrogant as the Barrani, but they also hoard their secrets."

"Sanabalis." It wasn't a question.

Severn gave her a look of mild approval—the type of look that one or two of her teachers had favored her with when she had struggled with the schooling the Hawks insisted on putting her through. Or putting the teachers through.

"And Donalan Idis?"

"Many of the Inquisitors were retired in one way or another," Severn replied with care. "Donalan Idis, of course, relinquished all claim to his experiments, and the documentation survives only in the Royal Archives."

"If he's involved in this—"

"Yes."

"He never stopped."

"No."

"Severn?"

"Yes?"

"Did the Wolves hunt him?"

He didn't answer. And Kaylin didn't ask him again.

When she entered Evanton's store, he looked up from his perpetual hunch. He appeared to be beading a piece of cloth with a very fine needle, and his eye—the left eye—was covered in something that looked like a tube. Kaylin had used one before, once or twice, when sifting through shreds—literally shreds—that might be evidence. It had seemed magical to her then.

"Private Neya," he said as she closed the door behind her. "Please come in. I'm a tad on the busy side, and my store is less tidy than it should be."

It was always less tidy than it should be. Kaylin kept that thought behind her lips, instead of just blurting it out the way she usually would.

She managed to find a stool, moving the books on top of it to a corner of the desk where they teetered precariously for a moment. She didn't even bother to examine them; she'd tried once or twice on previous visits and had found the language—or the writing—completely impervious to fumbling attacks by her meager understanding. It was almost as if Evanton's store was designed to make her feel stupid.

She said, as she perched, finding room for her elbows as she watched the old man work, "I don't understand why you called us in."

"Don't you?"

"No. Generally, I like to appear to be smart. I don't admit being stupid when there's any hope I'm not."

He actually cracked a smile at that, the lines of his face shifting, but never really smoothing out.

"Good girl," he said genially. "If you never make mistakes—"

"It means I've never tried anything. I know, I know." She hesitated. "You implied—you said—that someone was going to die because of something that had been stolen from your—your garden."

He nodded, frowning at his handiwork. With a gesture of his gnarled fingers, light shone on it, and the beads glittered brightly, like caught rainbows. They were actually pretty, in a way.

"You might recall that I also told you to listen to nothing."

She shrugged. "What's done is done."

"Yes."

"The water—"

"Yes?"

"Well…the Oracles—"

"Oh, Oracles." He said it in such a dismissive tone of voice, Kaylin almost laughed. It was the tone she usually used.

"You can't trust Oracles for anything. They're smug and *mystical,* and they're only certain of their predictions after the fact."

"That's what I said. I would have been demoted, too, if there had been a lower rank. I think they considered inventing one."

"You probably said it while they were standing in front of you."

True enough.

"But even so…they seem to have spooked the Imperial Court."

He nodded, as if this was not news to him.

"There seems to be some indication that—"

"That all of the Oracles, and their apprentices—whatever they call them these days—were troubled by similar dreams."

She nodded.

"They've reason to be afraid."

It wasn't what she'd hoped for.

"But that's not why you came."

"Part of it."

"Not all of it. I'm a busy man, Private. Don't waste my time."

She nodded firmly and said, "Have you ever met a Tha'alani boy named Grethan?"

He continued to work in the oddly magical light that he'd called forth without a word. "Yes."

"How?"

"I'm afraid I don't remember."

"Liar."

He raised a brow, but without looking at her. Squinted a bit more at the glittering beadwork before removing the glass from his eye. "All right, I remember, and it's none of your business."

She shrugged. Severn's shrug. "It wasn't Grethan who came here, that night."

"No, Kaylin, it was not."

"Was it Donalan Idis?"

This, finally, caused him to stop his work and place it to the side. She now had more of his attention than she actually wanted; he was still an intimidating man, even given the aged stoop.

"An odd question, that. Why do you ask, and why that particular name?"

"You know him?"

"I know of him, yes. He's a member of the Arcanum. I can, with some ease, recite the names of most members of the Arcanum, past and present. It is a surprisingly long list. The shorter list—much, much shorter—would be the names of those who are welcome to cross my threshold, and that name would not be among them. At the moment," he added, "the short list would also coincide with the historical list."

"Oh?"

"They're all dead."

She nodded. Dead Arcanists were more to a Hawk's liking than living ones any day.

"But you have linked two names—Grethan and Idis—and I am curious. Why? The boy—" His expression shifted into something that look suspiciously like pity. But words didn't follow it. Then again, Evanton probably knew they didn't have to.

"Grethan is missing from his home in the Tha'alani enclave," she replied, her voice thickening. "And so is one of their children."

He seemed to get older as she watched his shoulders stoop at some invisible new weight.

"It is possible," he said at last. "Was the missing child you speak of connected in some way to Grethan?"

"I...think so." Remembering Ybelline's face, darkened by worry and a fear that drove Kaylin even now. But *also* remembering that Ybelline did not consider this a matter for Common Law.

"And the water?"

She shook her head. "What I saw there doesn't appear to be part of it."

"Yet."

She didn't really like the tone of the word.

"If it is Idis, Kaylin, be cautious. He is not a man who can be crossed with impunity. The wolves were sent to hunt him, and they failed."

She didn't ask him how he knew. "What does he want, Evanton?"

"Oh, probably power."

Fair enough. "Why do people who want power always threaten thousands of lives?"

"That is a better question. Possibly because power is something that calls out to be used." He paused and then said, "Hurry, child. Whatever it is that the Hawks do, do well, and do it quickly."

"Why?"

"Because you still have time, but not much of it."

"If the Imperial Court and the Oracles—"

"What concerns them, in the end, does not concern you in the same way. What you can do, you must do." He smiled, and if it was weary, it was genuine. "What you did in the High Court," he told her, "and what you do every time the Foundling Hall summons you, every time the midwives call—you think of them as small things."

"No, I damn well don't. It's just—"

"But large things are built on small, and sometimes, broken by them in unexpected ways. No, I don't know *what* your task is. I therefore have no idea how it is to be accomplished, and even had I, I would not tell you."

"Evanton—"

"You *must* learn. Lord Sanabalis is teaching you, if I am not mistaken."

She thought of candle wicks and grimaced. "He's trying." A thought occurred to her. "As a mage, did you—"

But he lifted a hand. "If it was only magic," he said, as if he were talking about selling vegetables, "it would be less important. Not everything he will teach you is about your own power, not directly.

"And he is canny, for a Dragon. He understands mortals better than any Dragon I have ever met."

He handed her the patch that he had been working on. It was a beaded representation of the Hawk in flight. "For you," he told her quietly.

"You knew I was coming?"

"I guessed. Put it on. Leave it on."

"But it—"

"It's still a Hawk."

She nodded. Cringed. "I can't really sew well—"

"It doesn't need to be sewn on—it will adhere to whatever you place it on. I'd suggest your uniform."

She nodded again, failing to notice the bite of his condescension. "Thank you," she said, surprising herself as she opened her hand and stared at his handiwork.

"I hope you will, girl. Why are you staring at it? It doesn't bite."

"It…doesn't hurt my hand."

"Hurt it?"

"It doesn't feel like…magic."

"Maybe it's not," he said with a shrug. "Maybe it's just a folk charm from bygone days."

"But you—"

"I'm a busy man, Private Neya."

You never really wanted to disobey that wizened little man. Or to mock him. Or, and she looked again at his handiwork, to be in his debt.

"Are you still standing there?"

"No, sir."

"Good."

The front door seemed promising, and she took it. On rare occasions, she could take a hint.

"Neya," Marcus growled as she entered the office. Loud growl, but then it would have to be—the office was packed.

"Sir?"

"Where the hell do you think you're going?"

"To check the betting—" She paused. "Nowhere, sir."

"Good. Sharks lost," he added as she about-faced and came to his desk's side. The heartless bastard didn't even look up. "Sit down."

"Sir. Am I late for something?"

"Yes."

She tried to think back on her admittedly chaotic schedule and came up blank. Sadly, she did this frequently when she did, in fact, have some meeting or other to attend. "Sir?"

"Don't even." He looked up from his paperwork then, and his eyes were bleary and pale orange. It was an odd combination. He was tired—and angry. But not furious. Not yet. Having seen him furious once or twice, Kaylin knew better than to push.

"Lord Sanabalis is waiting for you," he told her.

"But I—"

"I don't believe this involves a lesson. If it does, he's doing it for free."

"What else does he— Wait, what do you mean for free?"

"It means that we're not paying for this one."

"What— *We're* paying for these lessons?"

"Yes. And consider yourself lucky that they aren't coming out of your salary." He paused and added, "Because your salary wouldn't cover them."

She was momentarily silent. In that gaping, embarrassing sort of way.

"West Room, Private. He's been waiting for almost an hour."

"But I was out on the beat—"

"Yes. That's why you're not in trouble."

"Yes, Marcus." She turned away from the desk, only to be dragged back by his growl.

"Sir?"

"Why," he said, "just tell me *why*, does every damn case you become involved in deal with children in one way or another?"

"I don't know," she said, and this time her expression was shorn of anything but worry. "Maybe because—"

"It was rhetorical, Kaylin," he told her. But he stood, his eyes still that pale copper, his brows still bristling if you knew enough to recognize it. "I asked Kalaya."

The leader of his pridelea, his oldest wife. "What did she say?"

"Because humans desert their children, by dying. It's bad to have only two parents."

"That's not their fault—"

"And because you care, Kaylin, and you're marked by magics we don't and can't understand. She thinks if you cared less—"

"I'd be less involved?"

"They'd die more. She also asks me to tell you—nicely—that she would like you to be careful. Possibly because she doesn't have to deal with you daily."

It took her a moment to realize just how highly his wife had praised her. She wasn't all that great at accepting compliments—they were almost a type of charity. But she managed a nod, and he offered the same in return, letting the words pass by.

Lord Sanabalis was waiting for her the way he always did: with characteristic patience. Which is to say, he was playing with something in his hands and idly glancing toward the door every minute or so. As if, she thought sourly, he hadn't actually heard it being opened.

She took her customary seat across from him, and even thought about going to get a stupid candle. But if she'd been any good at going through the motions—any motions—she wouldn't still be a private. "Iron Jaw said you wanted to see me."

"I do."

"Why exactly?" She paused and then said, "And how much do you charge for these lessons, anyway?"

"Oh, money," he said, with the vague wave of a hand. "I'm not personally in charge of fees. That is a duty left to the Imperial Order."

"Which doesn't mean you don't know."

"Of course not. It merely means you may discuss it with a bureaucrat."

He bent toward the floor and opened a case by his feet. It was a worn, black case, with tarnished metalwork and a faded engraving. It was also flat and wide.

He pulled a long piece of paper out of it, and then set the case aside on the flat of a spotless table. "I merely wished to ask you a simple question," he told her quietly.

She nodded, more curious than annoyed.

Until he laid out the paper, and she saw that it was a drawing, sketched in pencil and shaded with something that had either smudged or bled.

"Do you recognize this girl, Kaylin?"

Staring at her, with wide, almost bruised-looking eyes, was the face of the girl the water had shown her in Evanton's elemental garden.

"I will take that as a yes."

"You've seen her?"

"Not exactly, no." He gestured at the paper. "She has been seen, in a manner of speaking."

"What do you mean?"

"The Oracles."

"The *Oracles* drew this?"

"This? Gods, no. This was drawn by a young Tha'alani, a rather sheltered but very sensitive boy. He is not in service," he added, "not yet, and if I had any say, he would *never* be in our service. But he was able to untangle some of the dreams that lay upon the Oracles themselves, and the imagery was shattered enough that the dreams were just that to the boy—dreams. Or nightmares. Both exist in the Tha'alaan, and both have a quality that removes them from reality. I deemed it safe to request aid, for that reason. Ybelline suggested the boy. He is gifted in his chosen art. The Oracles, with one or two notable exceptions, are not.

"There are other drawings," he added softly.

"The boy did the others, as well?" She could not take her eyes off the contours of the girl's face.

"No. Would you care to see them anyway?"

"I don't know if it would help or not."

Sanabalis had not yet resumed his seat, and it became clear a few moments later that he would not. "I would like you to accompany me, Kaylin."

"But I have—"

"I have asked permission, of course," he added.

"Of course."

"Corporal Handred is not required, but if you wish his presence, he may also be seconded. I leave that up to you."

"You'll be with me, won't you?"

"Indeed."

"Then what could go wrong?"

Lord Sanabalis visibly grimaced. "You clearly do not believe in angry gods," he told her, as he carefully slid the drawing back into its case and handed the case to her. "Be careful with that, it's quite old."

"Yes, Lord Sanabalis."

"Good girl. My carriage is waiting."

"Your carriage?"

"The *other* drawings were done by a boy who lives with the Oracles."

"He's an Oracle?"

"Of a type, yes."

"Why didn't you just bring those?"

"He draws what he sees," Sanabalis replied, "and Oracles see everything. You cannot direct them without great effort, and some cannot be directed at all."

"The Tha'alani boy?"

"Touched the Oracle boy, yes. This is what was safe to call forth."

His carriage was an Imperial carriage, with fine painting, fine gold leaf, fine emblems, and wheels that probably weighed more each than the horses did, in Kaylin's estimation.

She clambered up after Lord Sanabalis, still carting his unwieldy case.

"Set that on the floor," he told her. "It won't be harmed there." Or more harmed, his tone implied, than it had been by her handling of it. He pulled the curtains back as the carriage began to move; the ride was smooth, but here, the roads were well made.

She looked at the unlidded eyes of her companion for a long moment, and then drew a breath.

"Yes?"

"I was wondering if I could ask a small question."

"Smaller than that one?"

"Well, maybe a bit larger."

His smile was weary. "I half expected to be interrogated for our entire journey. For someone who disliked learning, you're very curious."

"What did happen with the Shadow Wolves eighty years ago?"

"Why do you ask?"

"Ummm, curiosity."

"You aren't a Wolf, Kaylin. You are *certainly* not Shadow material. Believe that if you were, you would have been dead long ago."

"Thank you. I think."

"I meant it as a compliment. Of a sort. And a warning, as well."

"It's history…"

"Yes. It is. And I deem it not harmful to answer your question, although you should have known far better than to ask it, for your corporal's sake."

She was silent, then. Mouth first, thought later. Severn had always said that about her, and he was right.

"There was some difficulty with the Wolflord of the time," Sanabalis finally said. "He had made some powerful friends among the less pleasant members of society, and his estimation of both his worth and his ability to skirt the Imperial Laws had grown beyond the reality of his situation.

"He felt himself to be careful enough and powerful enough to avoid those laws, and in the end, he posed a risk to the Court that could not be easily overlooked. Some word reached him of a possible replacement, and he had that man killed almost before the words themselves had been uttered. In all, it was not a good time for the Wolves. Their leader was privy to much information that the Wolves *must* have.

"There were a few more deaths, and a great deal of ugliness, before things were sorted out."

"Sorted out how?"

"The Imperial edict against the Dragons assuming their form within the bounds of Elantra was broken by the only person who could freely break that law and be certain of his survival."

Kaylin looked at the impassive face of the Dragon lord; he was watching her instead of the passing streets.

When he failed to see whatever it was he was looking for in her gaze, he said, "The Emperor flew. It rained fire, Kaylin."

CHAPTER 8

"Take everything you've learned about Oracles," Lord Sanabalis told Kaylin, as the carriage drew to a stop, "and throw it out the window. That one," he added, with a slight glare that didn't really change the color of his eyes. "The Oracles are often a little...scattered. Some of them are also easily offended. Or easily frightened. We believe that they have some understanding of what they've glimpsed, but an inability to communicate it—and shaking them until their teeth rattle does not produce the desired effect."

"What do you mean?"

"The most gifted of their number almost never speak with outsiders. The *least* gifted are usually the most functional, but they are ambivalent about their position, and ambivalence in humans is something to be wary of."

"Oh, and it's not in Dragons?"

"We are seldom ambivalent, and yes, it is." He paused and

added, "We naturally believe ourselves superior. Our ambivalence does not make us foolish, but cautious."

He paused for another moment, and then said, "One or two
of the people you may meet today will not even speak at all.
They seldom introduce them when I am present, however."

"Oh?"

"I frighten them."

She looked at him. "Well, you *are* a Dragon."

"Yes. And while most of history—mortal history—has
forgotten what that means, they can still taste it in the air I
disturb simply by breathing. It is an interesting truth of the
Oracles. They are all human, your kind, Kaylin, and to
those who already know what it is they've seen, their prattle
actually does make sense.

"Mortals, however, have learned to love the dark, to love
ignorance."

"That's a little harsh," she said, substituting her first
reaction with a swiftness that would have impressed Severn,
had he been there.

"Is it? You are mortal. By definition, Kaylin, you will all
die, no matter what you do. There is no precaution you can
take that will save eternity for you. Death is the road you
walk, from the moment you first breathe. It surrounds the
fabric of your living. You are always saying goodbye.

"My kind, and the Barrani, have oft overlooked the im-
portance of life *to* the mortals because it is so very brief, and
because so little is lost—in our eyes. A handful of years. If
I chose to sleep, I might have missed the whole of your
life—and it seems long to you, even though you are young.

"But there is an urgency about mortality that creates wonder, that heightens both joy and fear. To my eyes, you live an eternity in a short span."

She shrugged, thinking about death. The deaths that had scarred her because they had happened long before she could understand them; the deaths that scarred her because she couldn't prevent them.

"It is my belief that you love life more because you have so little of it. You live in a moment that eludes us in anything but acts of war. Because in war, we face death, the loss of eternity. Our greatest moments, our greatest acts of nobility, our profoundest acts of cowardice have always occurred in war."

"Why are there no Oracles from the other races?"

"I have thought about this," he said, his voice rumbling as he paused in the act of opening the door, the hinges creaking ominously beneath his weight. The fact that the carriage hadn't quite *stopped* didn't seem to bother him. "The Tha'alaan holds moments of birth and moments of death while the race lives to remember it. They know death, and they may fear it, but it does not drive them. In some sense, they are never forgotten. They are *remembered*.

"The Leontines have so much in common with beasts it's a small wonder they can speak at all. And I would thank you *never* to repeat that, as it is considered—"

"An offensive racial position to take, sir."

"The *sir* is not necessary, Kaylin. Technically, the *Lord* is, but I will not hide behind formality. Neither is your extreme sarcasm. I understand that you are fond of your Sergeant and I wish him no ill. But they have many bestial instincts, and even their tribal system is fraught with the—let me call it the *earthy*. I do not believe they fear death in the way that humans do."

"And the Aerians?"

"The Aerians have, in the past, had their Seers," he told her quietly. "But those Seers have never been granted to the Oracles. Whether they are exalted or shunned, I do not know. They are few. In ways, they are most like your own kind, even though your kind is denied the gift of flight. But they are more tribal than your kind, because they are less numerous. They cede very little to others."

She was silent for a moment. "In the Foundling Hall," she said at last, as the carriage wheels sprung up at the sudden loss of his weight, "there are only human children, as well."

He held the door open for her. "It would almost be best," he told her gently, well aware of the fact that in different circumstances, one of those foundlings might well have been her, "if you thought of the Oracle Hall as a similar place to the Foundling Hall."

"They have no Marrin," she told him.

"No," he replied, his gold eyes lidded, the arm he offered a reminder of her brief time at Barrani Court, and also a command. "And I think it a loss, for those here. What I have never fully understood is why the Foundling Halls *have* Marrin."

"It never occurred to me to wonder," she answered, because it was true—up until this moment, it hadn't. "She started the Hall. It's *hers*. She's made the orphans her life, and she'd give her life to protect them. She sees that they're safe, fed, clothed, and as well-educated as they let themselves be."

"And she had no pridelea of her own, no cubs, no mate, on which to spend this endless devotion?"

"I—I don't know."

"You are surrounded," he told her, "by works of art, by acts of magic, and by things that are unique or unusual— you are one such. But in a way, so is your Marrin. You do not question why she has made the choice she made. She does not question why you are gifted with a talent for healing that beggars all healers the Imperial Service has discovered over the years.

"But I digress. You have that effect on me, child."

She bristled very, very slightly.

"It would be best if you thought of the Oracle Hall as a place similar to the Foundling Hall, and yes—" he added, lifting a hand to forestall the words that were about to fall out of her mouth, "you will see why for yourself."

The why was not answered when they were met at the gatehouse by men who wore more metal than Imperial Officers of the Law. They also wore swords, but as they were technically *not* in a public place, they were slighting no laws that Kaylin could easily recall. They did not wear surcoats, and the metal caught sunlight like sharp, pointed spears of light, it was *that* polished. She pitied the apprentices whose hands had done *that* work.

Her instinctive fear of armored men had long since given

way—it would have to, as she often *was* one—but in its place, she harbored a mild resentment. They could hide in safety behind what they wore.

And they now challenged her as she neared the guard-house. On the other hand, they didn't lack a certain bravery—they also stopped Sanabalis, and it would have to be obvious, even to the most ignorant, that he was a Dragon. "Halt and state your business," one articulated tin can said.

"I am Lord Sanabalis, in service to the Emperor, and I have been invited to attend Master Sabrai after the contemplations this afternoon."

The shining tin can turned and spoke to another tin can behind him, and the second man hunkered off, making a lot of noise as he walked. Sanabalis didn't seem put out by this. Then again, formalities never seemed to bother Dragons when they weren't actually in a hurry, and he seldom seemed to be in a hurry. As if he could read her mind—and gods knew everyone else seemed to be able to today—he said, "When you have all eternity, the word *hurry* is relative."

"And the guards, being mortal, have less of it, and their version of *sluggish* doesn't approach your version of *fast?*"

"Something very like that." He looked past the man—the Dragon lord was tall, although he usually hid it by slouching, and added, "The gardens here are surprisingly tranquil, and if we are given the opportunity, you should visit them."

"I'm not much of a gardener."

"Pity."

"You are?"

"Not as such. That was always more of a Barrani pastime."

"It still is," she told him, thinking of the High Court. "But I wouldn't use the word *tranquil* to describe their gardens."

"*Tranquil*, like *hurry*, is a relative term."

The second man returned, and, lifting his visor, spoke a few words to the first man.

"The Master will see you," the guard said, and, signaling the others, stepped aside. "He will also allow you to bring your guest." If there was criticism in the words, it was slight and hidden by formality.

"That is kind of him," Lord Sanabalis said. "I have been busy of late, and asking the requisite permission slipped my mind."

"Lord Sanablis," the guard replied, bowing in a way that all that damn plate should have made impossible.

With a regal nod of the head, Lord Sanabalis preceded Kaylin through the gatehouse doors.

The gardens weren't much in evidence as they walked the path from the gatehouse to the Halls. Well, maybe they were, but they didn't seem all that impressive to Kaylin. They might have, had she come here at thirteen or fourteen, when she had been new to the Ospreys, and many of the Hawks who failed to remember how sharp the memory of a young and homeless girl could be had often called her their mascot.

But she'd seen enough since then to think *Grass, grass, more grass. Pretty nice grass, for grass, though.*

"It burns very easily," Sanabalis said quietly. "And it is ap-

parently quite soft to the touch. People would be upset if
one were to take a true breath, here."

"People," she told him archly, "would be upset *anywhere*."

"True enough. And please do not even think of quoting
the Law at me, Kaylin."

"It's one of the few things I *can* quote."

"And I hear it makes a very good lullabye."

"Only hear?"

"Dragons don't sleep much."

She nodded.

"And the Emperor, never. He watches what he's built."

She nodded again. "Do you like him?"

"Like him?"

"The Emperor."

"The Emperor is above things as simple as 'like' or 'hate.'
And I will say that this is possibly the first time I've been
asked that question. Why did you?"

She shrugged. "I don't know."

"Have a care what you ask," he said quietly. "Mortals are
allowed more leeway for folly, but in truth, not much." His
eyes were a pale gold, but they were lidded; he walked with
a slight stoop to his shoulders, which robbed him of height
and made him seem, well, ancient. Clever, that. Pointless,
but clever.

"You will understand what I mean when you meet
him," he added.

"*When?* Not *if?*"

"The Hawks have done what they can to keep you from
the Imperial Court, but I can see the day coming when they

will no longer have that choice." His expression was completely neutral; his face seemed like a mask. But when the lines shifted, he smiled. "But most certainly that is not today. Today we have nothing more terrifying than the Oracles. Have a question prepared for them, Kaylin."

"What kind of a question?"

"Something harmless."

"Why?"

"Because it is customary to come to the Oracles *with* questions. It focuses their thoughts, and leaves them less leeway to babble."

"And that's going to be a problem?"

"You'll see."

Dragons were enormously arrogant, and known for it. They seemed to be in a close race with the Barrani, but as there were more Barrani around, most people gave the nod to the Barrani. Kaylin wasn't so certain. Dragons were definitely quieter about it, though. She'd give them that.

But maybe more smug.

They were met at the front doors—the wide, tall doors with ascending peaks that looked ridiculously ornate to Kaylin—by armed…matrons. Which is to say, women who looked like human versions of Marrin, the Leontine who guarded the Foundling Halls. The armor admittedly helped; Marrin, being composed of bristling fur, obvious fangs, and claws that left indents in hardwood, didn't really need it.

They were a bit less friendly than Marrin was with strangers, but then again, Marrin depended on the generosity of strangers, and had to rein her protective instincts in whenever someone crossed the threshold.

But their eyes—hard to tell the color, really—were like Marrin's eyes when she gave someone as much of a once-over as she was allowed by polite multiracial society. They grimaced at Sanabalis, but most of their suspicion centered on her; clearly, they had met the elder Dragon before.

Kaylin, however, was wearing the Hawk, and while she personally hated being sneered at, she could swallow that. Mostly. Sneering at her while she was in *uniform,* on the other hand, was a whole different story. She straightened up, and assumed as formal a position as she ever did.

Sanabalis stepped on her foot.

This was not the reaction she had been expecting—she hadn't expected him to react at all. But Dragon feet were bloody *heavy,* and if he spared her some of the weight, it wasn't much. Still, she was pretty sure nothing was broken.

"Kaylin," he said, speaking to the twin matrons, and not to his student, "has never been here before. Believe that I sincerely regret the disruption of your routine, and the routine of the Oracles, but the Oracles themselves are in a state of near-panic at this time, and if there is some solution to be found to their *current* panic, it is most likely to be found by this young woman, as improbable as that may seem. She has come to view Everly's artistic endeavors."

"He's been in a state all morning," one of the women told Sanabalis grimly. "And you never know what will set him off. You *know* he reacts a bit strangely to the sight of you," she added.

"He generally dislikes most of the nobility."

"I'm as far from nobility as they get," Kaylin told them both, edging her feet out of Sanabalis's easy range.

"Dear," the second woman said, relenting slightly, "if you've never been here before, things are a bit unusual. Everly doesn't speak," she added. "He draws. Sometimes he draws maniacally. He has drawn some *extremely* unflattering portraits of his visitors before, and it has caused us some difficulty."

Kaylin nodded. "I don't really expect him to speak."

"He does. But with his hands. With pictures." She paused and then added, "He's a good boy. We're all very fond of him." She spoke the last two sentences in the soft voice of death threats everywhere.

"You're certain about this, Lord Sanabalis?"

"Unfortunately, Sigrenne, I am. And I cannot guarantee that it will not be upsetting for him."

The two women exchanged a glance, and then the woman he had named Sigrenne sighed. "Very well. Do *not* speak to the people you see in the halls," she told Kaylin sternly. "The Oracles often wander when they are in vision or dream states, and only people who've been properly trained know how to handle them without causing them alarm. There are people here who will see that they do not walk off balconies or stairways.

"Do *not* touch them at all. Even the Oracles to whom you are introduced in the rooms where visitors are normally sequestered are not to be touched unless they request it."

She paused to see if Kaylin understood, and Kaylin nodded, wondering just what kind of Hall she'd entered.

"Do not make loud noises. If you feel the need to shout or scream, hold it in, or you will be escorted off the premises and denied any chance at further entry."

"Got it. Anything else?" She attempted to keep the sarcasm from totally overwhelming her voice.

She might as well not have bothered; the sarcasm that was already there was pretty thick and they seemed to have missed it entirely.

"Usually the list of rules is sent to the supplicant in advance of their visit," Sigrenne said, frowning over Kaylin's head at Sanabalis. "And we have not allowed supplicants to enter the Hall for a week."

"Lord Sanabalis being a special case, I take it."

"All direct servants of the Emperor being excepted, of course." She gave Sanabalis a decidedly odd look, and then added, "But they've been good about who they send. Lord Sanabalis upsets many of the Oracles, but fascinates many more."

Sanabalis nodded amiably in her direction. "We have no desire to upset the Oracles," he said quietly. "It suits neither of our purposes."

"Well, try to remember that," Sigrenne said curtly. "Let's get this over with. It'll be lunch soon."

The first thing Kaylin noticed about the occupants of the Hall—and it was possibly an odd thing to notice first, given her occupation—were the colors they wore. Their clothing was garishly mismatched, something that Kaylin generally avoided by wearing blacks or undyed cloth. If the matrons guarded their charges with recognizable ferocity, they certainly didn't dress them.

Here and there were deep shades of purple, brilliant shades of red, a cacophony of blues and greens and turquoise, a hint of yellow-gold. Whole robes looked like quilts, and Kaylin had to do a double-take the first time just to make certain that the one that caught her eye had sleeves, and was not, in fact, pulled off a poor bed.

Some of the robes looked like a small child's idea of magic—dark blue, with golden stars, golden swirls, and vivid, red eyes. Well, the eyes were maybe not so small child, but the rest was. Although the person wearing the robes was definitely long past the age at which *child* could be remotely applied to him, there was something about the way he looked around, picked up objects—like, say, the lamp, which made one of the two Matrons cringe slightly, although she said nothing—and looked at them with curiosity and open wonder that made him seem young.

"Christen is new here," Sigrenne said, by way of comment. "He was not treated entirely well in his former home, and he is perhaps a bit unusual by even our standards. He speaks," she added, "and has not yet adapted to our rules."

Kaylin nodded. Her eyes wandered around the room, taking in the clothing—one man was wearing a very real crown, and sported a beard in a style that was better suited for stiff portraiture than life—and the silence of the occupants. She had thought that Oracles were like the so-called nomadics who wandered in during the summers and sold fortunes by the pound. Of gold. She thought that they were possibly pretentious liars. That they indulged in mystery and the mysterious—seeing so very few people—for reasons of commerce, of manipulation.

She had even met one or two in the Halls of Law—but they were *nothing* like this.

What Sanabalis had told her to do before they'd left the carriage, she did now: she threw out all of those conceptions. She understood in that one sweeping, slow glance why so few were allowed here. It would be very, very hard to take anything these people said seriously. If they spoke at all. It would be hard not to treat them as deranged, drunken idiots. Or just idiots.

And…she understood the reaction of the Matrons to new people, because on occasion, as if furtively, these steel-haired women did throw an alarmed or affectionate glance at the strangely attired men, women and children who roamed freely in the wide spaces, or who plastered themselves against the walls of the long hall, or who draped themselves limply over the stair rails, kicking their feet slowly and steadily behind them. These ferocious women clearly had no desire to see their charges exposed to ridicule or condescension.

This was supposed to be a house for very odd people, who might have a glimpse into the future. Kaylin wasn't certain she believed this, but given how odd the people were, she was certain *they* did. And intent mattered, both for the law and for Kaylin.

Sanabalis did not speak, and their passage through the hall drew no attention until they were almost at the far door. But when they were about ten feet from its safety, a small child darted out—in a green-yellow dress with large purple patches—and latched onto Kaylin's leg.

Her hair was sort of braided, although strands of fine gold had worked free; her eyes were a wide gray-blue that should have looked cold in the pale white of her face. Her lips were small, and they were moving; Kaylin thought she might be all of six years old, although she could be younger or older by a year or two.

The order not to speak flew out the window, and out of Kaylin's mind, as the child turned her face up to Kaylin's and pulled on her knee—a universal request for the larger person to get down to the child's level. Kaylin knelt at once. The child reached out and touched the mark on her face—the nightshade, pale blue against decidedly less pale skin.

And then she said, "You're a book."

Kaylin nodded, as if this made sense.

"There is writing all over you," the girl added in a soft, matter-of-fact tone. And it was true, although none of that writing was actually exposed. It lay beneath shirt and pants and collar and hair, hidden. But not to the child.

The child could see.

So…

"What does it say?" Kaylin asked quietly, breaking one of the rules she had been told to follow at risk of permanent ejection.

"Well," the girl replied, "I'm not sure. I don't want you to leave yet, though. I want to read the whole story."

"I don't think it's finished yet."

"Oh?"

"It's just a guess."

Serious-eyed, serious-voiced, the child said, "But it's yours, so you should know. The words are fighting, though," she added. "Maybe when they finish, there'll be an ending."

Before she could stop her mouth—a habit that had never taken hold except in formal interrogations—Kaylin said to the girl, "Will I survive it, do you think?" And the steel-eyed doll of a child looked at her for a long time as she considered not her face, but her arms, her legs, as if looking at clothing. But then she moved around Kaylin's back, and Kaylin sat utterly still, as if such inspection were natural. Kaylin knew what she was looking at. The writing that had appeared last.

The silence went on for a moment, and then the child said, in a voice that was high and fluting, a girl's precocious voice, "We all die."

"Marai," Sigrenne said quietly, "you will alarm our guest." She had bent slightly in her gleaming metal, and the child looked not the least intimidated.

"Oh, she's seen *lots and lots* of death," Marai replied confidently. "And I don't scare her at all. I can make a scary face," she added, with less confidence. "But that only works on Mika."

"Have you eaten lunch?"

"Lunch?" Marai replied, as if Sigrenne had just asked her if she knew what the moons were made of. "Is it lunch-time?"

"It is past lunchtime."

"Well then, I must have eaten."

"And what did you eat?"

"Noodles and cheese and the funny salty rolled meat."

"No dear, that's in two days."

"Or last week."

Sigrenne smiled. "Go and find something to eat, Marai. Remember what Master Seltzen said. You must remember to live in the now sometime."

Marai nodded somberly, and with a regretful glance at Kaylin, she backed away.

Kaylin rose and was met by the stony glare of slightly orange Dragon eyes. The eyes were lidded. "Sigrenne," he began, but Sigrenne had turned to Kaylin with a thin-lipped frown already forming across her weathered face.

"I believe I made the rules clear," she said coolly.

Kaylin nodded, sparing the child a backward glance, as fascinated by her as the child had been by the writing that she *could not* have seen by any normal means. "But she's a child," she said, with a bit of a guilty inflection. "And she was speaking to me."

"Yes. And because *she* is a child, she will not be in too much trouble for *also* breaking the rules."

"They have rules?"

"Yes. They are not to speak to strangers."

"Oh. The usual rules."

"The usual rules, yes. And," Sigrenne added, relenting, "they follow rules as well as most children that age do."

"I'm sorry—I'm not used to ignoring children."

"Oh?"

"Private Neya," Sanabalis said, stepping in and speaking in a smooth, almost officious tone, "does much of her volunteer work with two worthy organizations. The guild of midwives, and the Foundling Hall. She has spent many of her adult years around children who feel isolated, and I ask, as a favor, that you overlook her gross infraction."

"The Foundling Hall?" Sigrenne said, raising a brow and looking at Kaylin for the first time as if she were another woman, and not a possible criminal. "You know Marrin, then?"

Kaylin's brows rose higher. "You know Marrin?"

"Aye, I've spoken with her a time or ten," Sigrenne said with a wry smile.

"I know her, yes. Her fangs are still sharp and her claws still draw blood."

Sigrenne frowned, and Kaylin reddened slightly. "It's a translation of a Leontine saying, but it basically means she's not in her dotage yet."

"That old lion will never be in her dotage. She can be an infuriatingly territorial—"

"She is Leontine."

"Aye, she is that."

"And the children she takes in are in some ways her pridelea, the kin she has chosen. I don't know why she doesn't have a pridelea of her own, and I've never asked."

"I have," Sigrenne said, wincing. "Don't."

"But—but how do you know her?"

Sigrenne's face grew serious again. "You met Marai?"

Kaylin nodded.

"And you didn't recognize her?"

"No."

"Ah. She wasn't at the Foundling Hall for more than a day or two. Marrin has a sixth sense, I swear. I mean, an almost Oracular sense. The child was dumped on the grounds, and brought to Marrin by the groundskeeper— what is his name again?"

"Albert."

"Ah, yes. Albert. She'd been left there. Many, many of the Oracles are abandoned by their parents. Some are killed," she added, and here a flash of fury colored her cheeks for a moment.

"But—but why?"

"The less affected the Oracles are by their gift—and in early childhood, they are not quite as lost as they can later become—the more often they ask inappropriate questions about things like their parents' infidelities. In public places. They know things they shouldn't know and see things they shouldn't see, and very often they are viewed as witch children and a great evil.

"They are feared," Sigrenne added, "without understanding."

"Some of those that survive are found by Marrin, and she will call us. She's not terribly good about releasing the children, and believe that she's paid us a visit or ten just to make sure that her children aren't suffering."

Kaylin laughed at that, and the unnamed woman also

chuckled. It made her seem younger than her armor or her bearing. "So some of Marrin's kittens are here."

"Not so many, but yes, some of them are here. Some are much older than Marai, but Marrin found them and kept them safe. One boy was badly burned," Sigrenne added, "when Marrin found him. Apparently his uncle came back to try to finish the job. There wasn't a lot left of the uncle, from what I heard."

"From who?"

"I have friends in the Halls of Law," she replied coolly.

"So do I," Kaylin said with the hint of a grin. "And at the moment, suicide isn't illegal."

"It wasn't exactly suicide—" And then Sigrenne also laughed. "I see you *do* know Marrin."

"She has my mirror," Kaylin replied. "And she's not afraid to use it."

"Very well, if you've worked for the old beast, we'll overlook this. Marrin is quite protective and ignoring one of her kits in that particular way would probably cost you a hand."

"Well, finger."

"Infection happens."

Kaylin found herself liking this older woman. "And these," she said softly, "are your kitlings."

"Yes."

The Hawk found herself completely relaxing. Because this was now a place she understood. "I won't harm them," she said. "Or I'll do my best not to alarm them."

"Aye, you will. But *try* a bit harder, girl. They sometimes want company, and some of them don't know how to ask for it very well."

Kaylin nodded.

"And if they scream and run at the sight of you, don't take it personally, and try not to jump or scream in response."

"Got it. Personally, several of my coworkers already have that reaction to me, and I've found it's best not to encourage them."

They managed to get out of the long, open space without further incident, and Sanabalis's eyes had already returned to the calm gold of Dragon ease. He even gave Kaylin a slight nod of approval at her handling of the affair, which she accepted even though she knew it was undeserved.

They were led to rooms that seemed both sumptuous and plain; they were obviously designed in a way to impress visitors of rank and leisure, but they were not so ornate or gaudy that they made Kaylin uncomfortable.

"Wait here," Sigrenne told them both. "And make yourself comfortable. It is not always easy to disturb the Oracles, but the Master of the Hall is expecting you, and he is much less wayward."

"He deals with visitors?"

"We call them supplicants—or he does. And yes, every single person who wishes to pose a question to the Oracles must first speak to the Master. He usually throws out about a hundred requests a month as trivial and foolish wastes of both time and money."

Kaylin's brows rose.

And fell as she noted the subtle shift in the folds of the Dragon lord's robes, which indicated that he might be prepared to step on her foot again, and finish the job by breaking it. But the expression on her face had nothing to do with her normal contempt.

"He—he lets nobles talk to the—the children?" For as she said it, it came to her that they *were* in their way like lost children, even the oldest among then, in their brilliant, scattered and mismatched regalia.

Sigrenne's face cracked a genuine smile, then. "You *are* Marrin's," she said, voice gruff with approval. "And you understand why we're protective. Not all of the Oracles are…as lost…as the ones you just saw. You've met Oracles before, in your line of work, surely?"

Kaylin nodded.

"You're here to see some of them," Sigrenne added. "But the Master first."

"I'll be good." She looked at Lord Sanabalis and added, "I'll try to be good."

CHAPTER 9

The words *The Master* always had a certain tinge of authority to them that set Kaylin's teeth on edge in *any* institution. Respect, she could grant—but some stubborn part of her felt it had to be earned. It wasn't something she could just toss around lightly, like dirty laundry at the end of a long, messy day.

And the man who eventually entered the room, followed by servants who carried simple, but obviously silver, trays, suited the words. The contrast between his attire and the attire of the inmates of this strange interior world could not have been more pronounced; had he been in a throng of pretentious nobility it would have been impossible to pick him out. He was impeccable. His hair was salt-and-pepper black, and he sported a pointed, well-groomed beard; his eyes were a dark brown, and nested under a thick welt of brow that broke only slightly when it crossed the bridge of his nose.

He was a tall man, and his subtle stance made it clear to Kaylin that he was accustomed to taking advantage of his height when it suited him. At the moment, it didn't suit him, and he stood almost at ease, examining her. He spared Sanabalis the shortest of glances, a certain sign that he was familiar with the Dragon lord. And yet…she had been told that he was an Oracle.

And that those with the weakest power were often the ones who could most easily interact with the outside world by its own rules. She could well believe it now.

"Lord Sanabalis," he said at last.

"Master Sabrai," the Dragon replied, inclining his head, "this is Private Kaylin Neya, of the Imperial Hawks."

"The investigative branch?"

"Indeed."

"And what do the Halls of Law require of the Oracles on this fine day?" He asked the question of Sanabalis, but he directed the brunt of his scrutiny toward Kaylin, the newcomer. There was, however, no disdain in his gaze. It contained a certain amount of weariness and, yes, hostility—but none of the contempt that she had come to expect of people who dressed the way he did.

She took a breath and turned it around. "It's not exactly what the Halls require, but what the Oracle Hall needs."

He was silent in his brittle regard.

"Sanabalis—" She paused as the dragon cleared his throat loudly, and started again. "*Lord* Sanabalis brought me a sketch—a color sketch that's really quite good—indirectly attributed to one of the children here. For some reason, he thought I might recognize the girl in the picture."

"And you did?"

She nodded. "I've seen the girl once before."

Master Sabrai froze in place. Kaylin had heard the expression a hundred times, but only a handful were truly descriptive. "In life?"

"No."

"In—not in dream?" His brows rose, changing the distant and well-kept expression of his face. The eyes that had looked so dark seemed paler as they rounded, like windows, like a glimpse of vulnerability and uncertainty. Nor did he struggle to contain it, as many a noble might have done, and she realized that he *was* an Oracle.

Wondered what it cost him to be so different from the others who lived here, and wondered what he did when he wasn't forced into this role.

"No, not in dream, either."

He relaxed slightly, and the weary look on his face became, for Kaylin, the look of a man who wasn't anxious to sleep much, and needed to.

"How, then, did you see her?"

"On the surface reflection of a pool of very, very deep water."

"W-water?"

She nodded, watching him carefully now; she had ceased to be a worry in one way, and had brought home all worry in another.

"Lord," Master Sabrai said to Sanabalis.

"Yes, Master Sabrai."

"The other drawings?"

"It was to get your permission to speak with the artist that we came. That and to see the rest of his impressive work."

"She knows the rules?"

"She has been fully apprised of the rules, yes."

"Good. You have my permission. I would like to attend, as well."

"Of course."

Kaylin could smell the room before she could see it. It wasn't an unpleasant smell—but it *was* a dusty, strong smell, and an unfamiliar one. They had been escorted through a different set of doors than the one they had entered, which she hadn't expected.

"Don't we usually speak to the Oracles in your office?"

"Yes, that would be the usual method. But Everly is somewhat unusual, and he does not speak at all." He hesitated for a moment, and then added, "He is not generally exposed to the public. On the few occasions that we have felt his presence germaine, it did not turn out...well. And the full effect of his expression of talent cannot be had in my office."

As he wasn't looking at her, Kaylin didn't bother to nod.

"You will see, among his collection, some portraits you may or may not recognize. It's not exactly his specialty, but—he tends to anchor things *to* people."

"That's unusual?" Kaylin asked. Mostly because she

couldn't see how a future that didn't concern living people was much of a concern at all.

"Try chatting with a tidal wave," Master Sabrai replied.

"Good point." She paused for a moment as his back hurried off. "Was that just a random example?" And moved her foot just in time to avoid Sanabalis's. For someone who affected age, he could move *fast*.

"Lord Sanabalis has been here before, obviously." Master Sabrai stopped at a closed door that looked sort of like any other closed door in the narrow hall. "Some of the Oracles…don't like Lord Sanabalis."

"It's the Dragon thing, right?"

"Something like that," Master Sabrai replied, and pushed the door open.

Into the fury that was the jaws of a dragon. Kaylin's knees had bent and her hand had dropped to her dagger hilt before she realized that *this* Dragon was actually…a huge painting.

"Impressive, isn't it?" Master Sabrai said over her shoulder. "It's the one that most fascinates Everly. He never quite finishes it. He adds to it here and there."

Kaylin turned slowly to look, not at Sabrai, but Sanabalis.

"I think it a good likeness of the days of my youth," he said, without so much as cracking a smile.

"If that's what the Oracles all see when they see you, I'm surprised they let you in *at all*."

"Not all of the Oracles will see Lord Sanabalis that way," Master Sabrai said quietly, as he motioned toward the room itself. "But enough of them do."

"And you?"

"I see him as he presents himself."

"Ah." Kaylin tilted her head to one side for a moment. "And me?"

"You bear an unusual mark," he said.

Which, Kaylin decided, proved the point about sane and powerful—the more sane, the less powerful. She thought briefly that this might apply to everyone, thought of the marks on her arms, her legs, her back, and decided she distinctly disliked the direction her thoughts were taking her.

So instead of thinking, she chose observation. Kaylin looked around a much larger room than she'd expected, and realized that the painting of Sanabalis had to be *huge*.

"It's life-size," Master Sabrai said, because he could probably hear her jaw hit the floor. "It was rather difficult to get the canvas for it, and unfortunately, it was also rather necessary."

"Oh?"

"He's an Oracle," Master Sabrai added, as if it were an explanation. It wasn't, really.

"Is that why it's not framed?"

"Oh, most of his work isn't. The work on display is otherwise framed, yes, but Everly doesn't care about frames. They do, however, often impress the few dignitaries who request permission to view his gallery."

And that was the word for this room.

Wall-to-wall paintings stretched out toward the devouring jaws of a Dragon in fury, and above those paintings, light shone from layered windows in the ceiling. The light didn't directly touch the paintings themselves; someone had designed this room with at least that much care.

She started to walk toward the right wall, and stopped there. A bed was tucked into the corner, beneath an impressive set of cupboards, and a desk was pressed against the wall that held the door. A chair was tucked into it, but the layer of dust across its back made clear how often that desk was used.

"Where is the Oracle?" she asked Master Sabrai.

"He is there," Master Sabrai said, and lifted a robed arm.

Tucked kitty-corner from the bed was a very tall easel, which held a canvas.

"At work," he added, lowering his voice. The two words held concern.

"It's not good for him to work?"

"It is. But not…like this."

"No?"

"He doesn't eat unless he's fed. He doesn't sleep unless he's drugged. While many of the other Oracles confront their nightmares, he confronts his—but he doesn't require sleep to do so."

"He does need sleep," she began, and then bit her tongue. Sometimes it flapped way too much.

"He won't be aware of your presence," Master Sabrai told her.

Kaylin nodded. "Does it disturb him if we watch him at work?"

"Not usually."

"And if it does?"

"You'll know."

She wasn't sure she liked the tone in which the words were delivered. She also wasn't sure she liked the Dragon on the far wall, but she had to approach it to see the boy because it was directly at his back. What kind of child could paint something so obviously deadly, so beautifully savage, and remain unperturbed by the reality of it?

An Oracle, idiot.

She approached the canvas as if it were a manor wall, and she were climbing over it instead of going through the guardhouse, the way visitors who were welcome usually did.

She wasn't wearing too much in the way of armor, so she didn't make a lot of noise. But as she was at last within touching distance of the back of the stretched cloth, she could hear the boy's breath, could hear the small clunk of a palette being settled on what looked, to her eye, like the flat of a bar stool. She couldn't see the boy yet, but could see the hand that had set it down.

Master Sabrai was behind her, and Lord Sanabalis had chosen to approach at a vastly more leisurely pace than Kaylin, so neither of them were close enough to stop the small noise that came out of her mouth when she finally rounded the edge of the easel and came face-to-face with what the boy was painting.

It was *her.* It was Kaylin Neya.

The boy's brush hand stopped for a moment; the fine, fine hairs of his brush hovered steadily above the canvas, almost in midstroke. His eyes were a milky blue, and he turned them toward her, staring as if lids were decoration and blinking was a fashion statement. One that he was above making.

She almost introduced herself, remembering the manners that her mother had tried to teach her in a different place a lifetime ago. But her eyes were drawn to the painting and held there, and anything she thought she might say about herself seemed suddenly superfluous.

What, after all, could you say to a boy who was painting the marks that lay hidden beneath your uniform? What could you say to a boy who had removed the uniform, exchanging it for a backless, armless gown, so that the symbols that adorned her skin were, in their entirety, laid bare?

She was half turned away from him, in the painting, so that three quarters of her back could be seen; her hair, which she always wore up when she worked, was in fact pulled high above her neck and pinned there by something he had not yet added. If it were true to life, it would be a stick of some sort. Certainly nothing ornate.

But this *wasn't* true to life; Kaylin had never worn a dress like this one; she didn't even *own* something that came close. It was simple, at first glance—but first glance was something that she gave it only because the marks were so accurate and so prominent they dwarfed everything else about the portrait.

"He's been working on this one for almost a week," Master Sabrai told her.

"Interesting, isn't it, Private Neya?"

The old bastard could have warned her, she thought, but the annoyance was halfhearted enough that she couldn't even put it into words—and annoyed was something she was *good* at. The brush started to move again.

"He works in oil?" she asked Master Sabrai.

"He works in whatever he can get his hands on, and

many of his most…useful…works have been done in pencils and watercolors," the Master replied. "But if oils are here, he tends to use them. The paintings are much clearer, and much cleaner, when he does. They also take much longer," he added quietly. "This *is* you, isn't it?"

"You can't tell?"

He took one look at Kaylin's street uniform, and then looked at the painting. His raised eyebrow said the rest, and she had to agree with him. If she didn't know herself, she probably wouldn't have made the connection so easily.

"But Sanabalis, you said—"

"I said the image of the girl was taken from his memory with his permission," the Dragon lord replied.

"But you implied—"

"Kaylin. Be a Hawk."

But the Hawk was not in the picture; not yet. Just Kaylin herself, and the dress, and the markings. Without a word, she unbuttoned one bloused sleeve and shoved it up past her elbow. It fell, and she cursed in Aerian—it being somewhat quieter and less likely to be known than Elantran—before she *rolled* it up so it would damn well stay put.

Stroke for stroke, dot for dot, line for line, the marks were the same. She had known they would be, but…she had had to check.

"Why?" the Dragon lord asked, and she realized that she was half muttering to herself. She was flustered.

"You can see," Master Sabrai told her softly, "why many find Everly disconcerting. Even when the portrait is flattering—which, to be honest, it seldom is."

Kaylin nodded. It was as if someone had not only walked over her grave, but had come back to do a little song and dance, and to paint graffiti on the headstone.

"Are these—these portraits—are they accurate?"

"How do you mean?"

"I mean— Well…you know when Oracles tell you things, they don't make any sense?"

Lord Sanabalis trod on her foot.

She hastily added, instead of the *ouch* that was appropriate, "I mean, until you know more of the context." It was lame, but clearly Master Sabrai was accustomed to worse.

"Yes," he said drily. "I am well aware of what most people think of Oracular information."

"I don't—I don't even own a dress like that one. It's… It's not even *decent*."

"Kaylin—"

"No, I mean really—I wouldn't even sleep in something like that!"

"Understood," Master Sabrai replied, "although you must understand in turn that current fashion and the Oracle Halls are not well acquainted. And to answer your question, Kaylin, the portraits themselves are indicative of some future state, but like the verbal prophecies, they are not always about the present, not always about the future. They are possibilities, but not certainties."

"But is it significant?"

The boy was painting almost furiously now. It was a small wonder that his hands weren't shaking, he was moving so quickly. It gave Kaylin hives. It also gave her an excuse to actually look at the *rest* of his face; the eyes had been…hard to look at. His hair was a kind of matted brown, and it was long enough to be pulled back from his face in much the same way hers was—although she thought she saw a paintbrush shoved in the knot that hung slightly to the right of center. His skin as almost translucent; the sunlight that came in from above might add color to the gallery, but it revealed none in Everly.

He wore something that made sackcloth look good, except for the splatters and smears. She thought the color had once been a natural shade of ivory, but now it was a riot, and she imagined that no one—not even the most compulsive of cleaners—could restore it to its original state.

His legs were crossed beneath him. His shoulders, however, were straight. His lips were almost the color of his skin, and his eyes were ringed with dark circles.

"This is what you wanted me to see?" she whispered to Sanabalis.

"No. But I thought you should."

She nodded.

"How did you know to look—"

"For the girl?"

She nodded again. She did not mention the Tha'alani boy who had done the watercolor that she had instantly recognized.

"I didn't," he replied quietly. "But *all* of the Oracles, even those who are not yet living upon the grounds, or those who are accomplished enough at dealing with the present to now live beyond them, had nightmares, Kaylin.

"And you thought—"

"Yes. Since they woke, since it began, since *before* it began, Everly has been painting your portrait."

"And the others?"

"Those who have some drawing skill—and who are not obsessed with it in the way that Everly is—have drawn bodies," he said quietly. "Or buildings. Many of the buildings would be ones you recognize. I believe you cover much of the city on your rounds."

"Bodies."

"Yes. Usually facedown in water. Sometimes trapped too far beneath the surface of it to float."

"You said many of the buildings?"

"The ones that are mostly standing." He had joined her now, and his foot was almost pressed against hers.

"That tidal wave you mentioned—"

"Yes," Master Sabrai said wearily. "It was not a chance comment." The Master's hand covered his eyes for a moment. He started to speak, and the seven syllables that left his mouth were not in a language that Kaylin knew. Not, she would have said, one that she had ever heard before, and given how many she *had* heard in Elantra, it was surprising.

But he stopped himself, and she realized that he had not intended to speak at all. His very Elantran cursing, on the other hand, she had no trouble with.

Lord Sanabalis lifted a hand. "Shall I send for Sigrenne, Master Sabrai?" He spoke slowly and carefully.

"No. No, I'm—fine."

"We will not detain you further."

"You will," he said firmly, "stay for as long as you deem necessary."

"If you—"

"I *said I was fine*."

"As you wish."

Kaylin watched them both. She had a question or two about what he had started to say, but she *liked* walking, and she hazarded a guess that she wouldn't be if she asked. But she looked at the painting again, her left sleeve rolled up. "I haven't changed," she said. "Or the marks haven't."

"No."

"The dress—"

"It is not a current fashion, no. But I think it significant in some way."

"Why?"

"Look away from the markings, Kaylin. Look at the rest of the painting."

"It's not finished yet."

"No."

She frowned. "It's—there's someone else there."

In pencil, in faint outline, blocked out, waiting for color and brush to give it life.

"Yes. At least one person. Possibly more."

"You think the dress is ceremonial somehow?"

"I think it probable, yes."

She swallowed and looked at the dress. It was white, not ivory, but it was edged in gold, and the gold itself was bright and almost metallic. There were words embroidered there, words that seemed in shape and form very similar to the ones that marked her skin. They were smaller, and less detailed, and they did not glow in the way the marks did. Because in Everly's painting, the marks *were* glowing faintly.

Her hands were outstretched, or at least her arms were; he had not yet painted the hands, and what they held, he therefore kept to himself. But the dress seemed formal for all its simplicity.

"When do you think he'll finish?" she asked Master Sabrai.

"Soon, if the gods are kind."

"And if they aren't?"

"Soon."

Sanabalis did not step on her foot. "I think—I think I need to see the finished painting."

"Yes. So Lord Sanabalis has said."

"But—"

"But you are not entirely comfortable watching him work?"

It embarrassed her. But it was true—she wasn't. She had thought to pity him, and she was now ashamed of the impulse; he wasn't so much a child as a conduit, and Kaylin was not Tha'alani; there were things about herself that she didn't want anyone else to see.

And she couldn't control what he *did* see.

"Can we talk to him?"

"You can try," Master Sabrai said. "But he is not always easily distracted."

She held her breath for a moment, wanting to ask both Sabrai and Sanabalis to leave. Knowing that it would be the wrong thing to ask. Then she said to Everly, "My name is Kaylin Neya."

He didn't appear to notice. His hands continued their manic dance, stopping only to touch palette, to pull some color out of a mixture of two or three, as if by magic, and to transfer that to canvas.

Okay. That was a dead end.

She thought about grabbing his brush, and decided against it because she wasn't certain that Master Sabrai wouldn't break her fingers. She thought about it for a moment longer, and then looked at the palette itself. Looked at the canvas, at the area that had been blocked out in some fashion, but still lay shrouded in the near-white of paintless surface. Frowning, she said to Master Sabrai, "Does he often work in pencils?"

"Almost never, although as I have said, he does use them."

"Where would they be?"

"Behind him, in the box on the floor. He keeps everything in it that might be of use. We take out the food before insects or mice find it," he added helpfully.

Kaylin moved around Everly, and opened the long, rectangular case. Then she found what she was looking for—a slender stick of gray charcoal. She rose, went to stand beside Everly, and watched him work.

Then she lifted the charcoal and began to draw on the canvas.

She heard the sharp intake of breath from both Sabrai and Sanabalis, but she ignored it. She expected Everly to say something, to *do* something.

But what he did do was not what she'd expected. He set

his brush down on his palette, but instead of reacting in outrage, he got down from his stool, and reached for the same box Kaylin had opened. He drew out a long piece of charcoal and came back to his stool, where he clambered up on the seat.

It was the only thing that reminded her that this very disturbing child was, in fact, a child.

But he turned before he touched the canvas, and he looked at her, and his eyes—she almost froze in place. Did freeze. They were the color of water.

He touched Kaylin firmly, grabbing the hand that held the charcoal, and pushing it toward the canvas. She dutifully followed his lead, and began to add something to the work itself.

She didn't touch the image of herself—couldn't, really; this close, it would have been like carving your initials in the wooden arms of a throne—say, the Imperial Throne, with the Dragon Emperor *in* it. Instead, she touched the area in the background that hadn't been touched yet, beginning to draw, awkwardly and self-consciously, extra bodies. Not many. The boy's hand pushed hers away, but not in anger; he wanted space to add to the work himself, to join her awkward, jerky lines with lines that were smooth and graceful.

But she had been attempting to draw someone Severn's height, and Everly was drawing something else. Not quite someone, yet, but she thought it would be. And since it wasn't her, she was fascinated by it.

"Private Neya," Lord Sanabalis said, in a cool tone of voice.

At the sound of *his* voice, Everly looked up. He didn't, however, look terrified. He just…looked.

"I believe that what you are doing would be forbidden by the Oracles if it had ever *occurred* to them that someone would *try*."

"Oh."

Master Sabrai's voice joined in, but she was too busy watching Everly's handiwork to look up.

"It does not disturb Everly," the Master of the Oracle Hall said in a hushed voice. "Indeed, he seemed to welcome the input. I would not have thought it possible," he conceded, to the chill of Sanabalis's voice, "but perhaps because she *is* the subject, she has…some say."

"Some say in the future?"

"We don't control what we see, as you well know. Nor do we control what is done with what *we* see. But…"

Kaylin lifted a hand.

"Private Neya?"

"It's her," she said quietly. "He's drawing her."

"Her?"

"The girl I saw in the water."

"So. She is part of his vision."

Kaylin nodded.

"But you are a larger part."

"I have to find her. And I think I must because she's here."

"Where is here?"

But Kaylin had no answer to that—there was no scenery yet. Still, it gave her hope, in spite of the dress.

CHAPTER 10

Sanabalis was quiet on the ride back to the Halls of Law. It wasn't unusual for him to be quiet, but his quiet was usually a wall in the face of Kaylin's tirades. Now, it was something more contemplative.

She contented herself with silence, as well, thinking about the shock of Everly's eyes, the certainty of his movements, the sense that he was simply a tool in the hands of...of his vision. Lame, Kaylin.

When they were well past the finer grounds of manors that lay behind sturdy fences and even sturdier guards, Lord Sanabalis looked at her. His eyes were not quite gold, but not yet orange, and they were lidded. He wasn't angry, then, but he was probably concerned.

"Well, Private," the Dragon lord said, "what do you think of the Oracles?"

She shrugged almost helplessly. "I don't think it matters."

"A good reply. It doesn't, to them. All of our skepticism, all of our beliefs—they mean nothing to the Oracles. They see what they see."

"I didn't ask a question, though."

"Hmm?"

"You said I should have a question prepared. I didn't. And I didn't ask."

"I rather think you did. But I would not have thought of asking in that particular fashion."

"Do you think—"

"The picture is literal? No."

"But the Dragon—"

"Yes." His inner membranes dropped. It made his eyes seem less vulnerable, oddly enough. "He sees what I *am*."

"Not what you will be?"

"Perhaps he sees that, as well. The Dragons live in the present, and if the present stretches out in all directions, it does not change this fact."

"We didn't ask them about water—"

"No."

"Or about—"

"No."

"Are we going back?"

"Yes."

"And am I going to carry all of this conversation?"

At that, he smiled. "That would make this day little different from any of the others. But no, Kaylin, I merely muse on what was already there."

"You'd seen it."

"I had. I wished to see your reaction." He paused and added, "The marks on your arms?"

"Matched the painting exactly. I couldn't check the ones on my back."

"Good. I note that you did not wear the bracer, in that painting."

She looked down. Looked out the window. Saw the Halls of Law as the carriage drove past them.

When she looked up at Sanabalis, one of his silver brows was lifted. "We are not yet done with our day's lessons," he told her quietly.

"I hope you're not charging the department for your time."

"I told you—my time has value to bookkeepers. It is with them that you must take up all complaints that you have in this regard."

"Fine."

"I believe it will cause the department some paper-work, however."

Her eyes narrowed. Had Sanabalis not been a Dragon, she would have kicked his shin. As it was, she grimaced and said, "You win."

"I was not aware that we were involved in some sort of contest," was his distant reply. "And winning? The games we play now measure such things in the number of lives we will lose before this is done. I am given to understand that betting was a way of life in the fiefs."

"We didn't bet on lives."

"No?"

"Well, not often."

Sanabalis shrugged. It was an elegant motion, but it was also a heavy one. "We have studied the Oracles text," he said at last.

"You mean the Imperial Order of Mages?"

"Do I?"

If hearts really could sink, Kaylin's was busily rearranging her internal organs. "You mean the Dragon Court."

He said nothing. Loudly.

"And the paintings?"

"Everly is the only Oracle who is currently completely visual in his prophecies. He is also, at the moment, implacable in his determination to finish your portrait. He works at a speed that is tiring to watch. But even at that speed, it is not fast enough. I had desired to see the location in which you were standing, although with Everly it is impossible to predict the existence *of* location. So far, it is nonexistent. I do not think, given the various records, that he has missed a *single* mark.

"Well, not the exposed ones, at any rate."

"It would not greatly surprise me if he had already painted the ones the dress hides," Sanabalis replied, glancing briefly out the window.

"Why do you think there might be no location?"

"There seldom is, in his paintings."

"Then how are they useful?"

"Spoken like a Hawk," he replied, but without the usual approval to take the edge out of the words. "Everly is concerned only with the people he can see. Where they are does not interest him. His entire world is that gallery, and I do not think he is even consciously aware that other worlds exist beyond it. Even the dining hall causes him confusion.

"But there is much about a person that one can tell by simple things—clothing, weapons, age."

"But—"

"Yes?"

"The clothing—I don't own anything like it."

"It could be symbolic. Fashions, like climates, change over the passage of time. But it will be significant in some aspect, even if it is not, to your mind, accurate."

"You've seen clothing like that."

He said nothing, glancing again out the window before turning his gaze upon her.

"Where are we going, by the way?"

"You asked me to teach you the nature of water," Sanabalis told her gravely. "And I have decided to accede to that request."

If ever there was an example of "be careful what you wish for," this was it. Kaylin spent some time wishing that someone *else* had been stupid enough to ask.

And then she forgot that part, because the carriage had come to a halt in front of gates that she recognized, even if she had only seen them from a very safe distance. Imperial gates.

The guards appeared at the window of the carriage, and one look at Sanabalis made them disappear more quickly. The gates themselves, at this time of day, were open, although they weren't exactly open to the public. Kaylin had flown over the vast estates that the Dragon Emperor laid claim to in the heart of the city, but even in flight, Clint had soared higher, complaining the whole time about her weight. Aerians served the Emperor as guards, and they patrolled the skies above the palace. They did not seek to stop Clint, but he did not approach their territory, marked invisibly across a stretch of what seemed, at her age at the time, to be freedom.

Liveried men waited for the carriage in the courtyard, and liveried men opened the door in which Sanabalis was framed. He stepped out and spoke a few words, and the same men appeared on the other side of the carriage, silently opening the door and equally silently offering Kaylin a hand. They had placed a small step just beneath the door itself, which Kaylin nearly fell over; she was used to just jumping out.

If they were bothered by the fact that they were forced to carry more of her weight than courtesy demanded, they were utterly silent about it; a smile would have cracked their faces. Or a frown. Or any expression at all, really.

Sanabalis was waiting for her. He offered her an arm, just as Severn had done in the High Halls of the Barrani court. There, Kaylin had worn a dress fit for a queen. Well, fit for a really, really rich person with more money than common sense. Here? She wore her daily uniform, and was acutely aware of how much she needed new clothing. The leather legs were actually patched.

But the men who had stopped her from falling flat on her face now took the reins and lead the carriage away to wherever it was that carriages went, and Sanabalis did not seem to be aware of just *how* underdressed she was.

"Does Marcus know I'm here?" she asked in a very quiet voice.

"Marcus? Ah, Sergeant Kassan. No, I do not believe he does. Nor does the Hawklord. With luck, there will be no reason to remedy their ignorance."

"Are you joking?"

"I? Dragons are seldom accused of humor."

"Have you paid attention to what my luck is actually like?"

"I have heard rumors that you faced a dragon, Kaylin, and won. I consider, given your race, that you are blessed with luck."

"Someone lucky—"

"*When* you need it."

"Which I will if I don't shut up?"

"Possibly. I advise you to make as little fuss as possible while you are in these halls."

"Ahead of you," she said, her voice dropping to a whisper.

"We are not going to Court," he added, "but to the Royal Archives. There is also a gallery. Four galleries, to be precise. And three different libraries. At the moment, the difficulties under consideration do not involve the Imperial Order of Mages, and given that you've offended a third of the most important men who comprise it, I consider you…lucky."

Lucky, she thought glumly. The *servants* were better dressed than she was. She felt like something the cat dragged in, except for the being-half-a-corpse-and-bleeding part. Hopefully that wouldn't follow.

But silence was a burden for Kaylin, and while she promised herself that it was one she would carry, she shed it in a small shriek when she rounded the huge, gaping corner of the huge, palatial hall.

"Tiamaris!"

Dragons never looked surprised. Kaylin was certain that there was a rule book somewhere that had that as the number-one law of dragonkind. Given that Dragons were immortal, it was probably etched in stone, but still.

Tiamaris, seconded to the Hawks for a short period of time, and still in theory on the duty roster although he wasn't sent out on patrol, raised one dark brow at her. Then he nodded gravely. "Kaylin."

"What are you doing here?"

"He lives here," Sanabalis replied drily.

"Yes, but—"

"Lord Sanabalis, is this entirely wise?"

It was Sanabalis's turn to raise a brow, although his was distinctly silver. "It is entirely unwise," he replied. "What have I taught you about asking a question to which the answer is obvious?"

"Much," Tiamaris replied. "But even more about the nature of what is obvious and what is merely contextually difficult."

"Very good. Well done. Yes, you may accompany us." He lifted Kaylin's hand and offered it to Tiamaris, who stared at it for a moment too long before holding out the bend of his elbow. Kaylin laughed.

The entire hall had damned impressive acoustics.

"You weren't just waiting for us?"

"No."

"You're sure?"

"As certain as I can be."

"But—this is a *huge* place. How did you—"

"Kaylin," Lord Sanabalis said, in a deep and suspiciously rumbling tone of voice, "please, a little respectful silence is in order."

Before she could open her mouth to reply, Sanabalis added in perfect Elantran, "Shut up."

Which more or less caused her jaws to snap together in shock. She dared a glance at Tiamaris, and to her chagrin, he was smiling. "It seems," he said, "that I still have much to learn from you, Lord Sanabalis."

"Do not make me repeat myself," was the curt reply, although it was offered in his habitual Barrani. It caused Tiamaris to chuckle, and this much mirth Kaylin had never seen him show. Then again, the last time she'd seen Tiamaris, they'd been investigating the gruesome deaths of children in the city, so there hadn't been a lot to laugh about.

"Why are you here?" Kaylin whispered.

"Private Neya, it may have escaped your attention, but I am *not* deaf."

"Never mind."

The halls could have been an Aerie. There were no winged Aerians flying above them as they walked, but they could easily have stretched their flight feathers here. It would have been welcome. The lack of any noise but footsteps—and Dragons don't have light feet—was beginning to make Kaylin nervous.

Nervous gave way to something else when Sanabalis at last stopped. He stopped because there were doors that were half the hall's height in the way. And the doors bore a mark that was at the level of a grown man's reach.

Door-wards. Kaylin hated them.

Sanabalis reached out and placed his palm against the mark. The doors didn't open—that would be too much to hope for. Tiamaris let go of Kaylin's arm and also walked to the door, where he placed his palm against the same mark. And of course, the damn doors stayed closed.

"Private Neya? In your own time."

Which meant *touch the bloody door now so we can get going*. Dragons might speak in Barrani, but tone of voice was universal.

She walked up to the door, gritted her teeth, and planted her palm against the ward as if she hoped it would go through it.

Blue light enveloped her, snapping at the air. The strands of her hair that *never* stayed up flew out to the sides as if trying to escape her skull.

She started to shout something, bit her lip, and waited; her arm was numb.

But the door-wards had taken whatever it was they were looking for, and the doors began to swing slowly inward.

"That," said Tiamaris in a low voice, "was impressive."

She would have cursed in Leontine, but she liked her tongue where it was.

"I imagine that anyone of note in the palace now knows you're here," he added.

* * *

If they—the nebulous *they* that always made Kaylin slightly nervous—were aware of her presence, they didn't choose to do anything about it. No alarms sounded; no guards surged through the open doors to greet her. Instead, she was hit with *silence*. It didn't so much descend as stomp. Where the halls had been cold and shining marble, the floors here were carpeted for as far as the eye could see. That much, Kaylin expected, and she didn't find it strange. The fact that the carpets slid up the walls, on the other hand—where walls could be seen—she found a bit unusual.

In between the bits of visible wall were shelves that stretched from floor to ceiling, bisected neatly in the middle by a narrow catwalk that followed their precise contours. There were ladders, which were sensible, given the height of the shelves, and smaller ones rested on the catwalk above the main floor, leaning up against the space between shelves. There were more books than Kaylin had dreamed existed.

She stood, her jaw temporarily unhinged, as she stared. Even the quiet click of the doors at her back didn't easily draw her attention. Sanabalis had said there was more than one library, but he hadn't said they were all in one place.

"Private," Lord Sanabalis said tersely, "you may have all day to stand there and gawk. I, however, am a busy man. A *very* busy man."

"If it would please you, Lord Sanabalis, I can escort Kaylin from here."

"It would not please me to see the two most difficult

students in the history of the Imperial Order left to run rampant in this august wing," Lord Sanabalis replied curtly.

Tiamaris shrugged. "So the rumors are true," he said to Kaylin.

"Which ones?"

"That you are his pupil."

"More or less."

"Knowing you, Kaylin, you probably did something to deserve it."

She stepped on his foot. He kept walking. His hold on her arm tightened so that she didn't go flying across the carpets. "You already knew."

"Of course. Had the Imperial Order chosen to listen to me, you would not have been given the opportunity to offend so many of its constituency."

"They were arrogant, know-it-all, judgmental—"

Tiamaris raised a brow. "Your conversation is almost certainly being captured in Imperial Records," he told her. "You might consider what you say with care."

"They were inflexible."

"A much better choice of words." He spoke Elantran, as he had done when he walked the streets as a Hawk. "You might *also* consider speaking in Barrani while you are here. It's harder to make the same verbal mistakes in that tongue."

She shrugged. "Why? Given who's likely to be listening, it won't make a difference."

He conceded the point.

"Why did he bring me here?"

"I can only guess," Tiamaris replied gravely. "And as you

will know soon enough, I will keep that guess to myself. But your progress has been followed in the Court. You went to visit the Keeper?"

"You mean Evanton?"

"Indeed."

"I visit him all the time, Tiamaris."

"And when you returned, you asked Lord Sanabalis about the nature of water. That can hardly be a coincidence."

She shrugged, a Hawk's shrug. "It wasn't. Well, I mean— no, it wasn't."

"What did you see?"

"Tiamaris," Lord Sanabalis said, the syllables colliding in a snap of sound that implied large jaws and brimstone.

"My apologies, Lord Sanabalis." Tiamaris turned back to Kaylin. "The Dragons have never seen what must be watched," he told her.

"Curiosity is for the mortal," was Sanabalis's cool reply. "And, Kaylin?"

"Yes?" She stopped herself from adding *sir*.

"Evanton may have been unwise enough not to warn you against speaking of what you saw. It is, however, ex- ceedingly unwise."

She hesitated for a moment and then turned to Tiamaris. They had progressed farther into the library, and it showed no sign of ending. On the other hand, it was a fairly straight route to the exit, if the doors opened at all.

"Something was stolen from—from his care."

She walked *into* Sanabalis, which was a lot like walking into a lumpy stone wall. The Dragon lord turned to look down at her, and he *was* looking down; all of the assumed slouch of age had deserted his spine.

"Why did you not inform me of this sooner?" Sanabalis snapped.

"Well, it's in the report—"

"You haven't filed a report!"

"Well, that is—I think Severn…" The words trailed off. "Marcus probably wouldn't *read* the damn thing, anyway. He's still buried under Festival writs and notifications."

"I assure you, Private Neya, that you are wrong. In this case, you are utterly wrong."

"I was worried about the girl—"

"The girl is *one child*, Kaylin. If by some miracle we escape this with one death—with a hundred—we will be counted the recipient of undeserved miracles by historians a millennia hence."

"Tiamaris, what's going on?"

"I am not, myself, certain," he replied carefully. "But I have been given the reports generated by days spent in the company of Oracles, and I would have to say—"

"Nothing," Sanabalis said coolly.

"I can't investigate *nothing*," she said, with a lot more heat.

"This is not a matter for the Hawks, the Swords, or the Wolves," Sanabalis replied curtly.

"It is if—"

"There has been no missing persons report, am I correct?"

"Well, yes, but—"

"And there has been no writ issued for any theft?"

"We're having a bit of difficulty classifying the item, and

without classification, we don't have a specific law to apply to—" Her voice trailed off; his eyes were orange, with just a hint of red at their center.

But she hadn't finished, although she really, really wanted to be. "Donalan Idis," she said quietly. Just that.

Tiamaris frowned. "Where did you hear that name?"

"Legal history."

"Liar." Elantran was, Kaylin realized, not always a blessing.

"Donalan Idis *is* under the purview of the Halls of Law. A writ was issued for his retrieval, and he was never found. No countermanding writ was ever issued."

"The writ was issued to the Wolves, I believe."

"Who are part of the Halls of Law, and who serve it as the Hawks do."

"What *exactly* does Donalan Idis have to do with the matter at hand? Think carefully, Kaylin. I am almost at the end of my patience."

"I don't know," she replied, moving as if she were surrounded by leaping tongues of flame.

"She is telling the truth," Tiamaris said, his voice soft, the cadences of it wrong.

Sanabalis replied in a language that Kaylin didn't actually know. But it was loud, each syllable a roar in miniature.

"Stand behind me," Tiamaris told her quietly.

She *moved.*

Tiamaris replied to his former master, and his voice was also lost to the sound of thunder, the roar of Dragons. She had seen Tiamaris assume his Dragon form only once, and had no desire to ever see it again.

* * *

But a third voice entered their conversation—if it could be called that—a third roar, louder in all ways than theirs.

For a moment, Kaylin thought she was dead—she thought the Emperor himself must have heard the shouting and come from Court to see what it was about.

But the Emperor had not come. Either that, or the Emperor was a compact man with a crown of hair that failed to cover his skull. He had whisper-thin whiskers that trailed from a mustache that was paler than Sanabalis's beard.

And he commanded instant, and utter, silence.

He looked… He looked a little like Evanton, except three times his size. His skin was wreathed in lines, and those lines were decidedly not smile lines. His eyes were glowing orange, and unlidded.

He turned and looked at Kaylin the way Kaylin looked at mice. But when he spoke again, he spoke in formal Barrani. "The library is not a place for idle conversation. People come here to work in silence, and you are disturbing their studies."

She instantly bobbed her head up and down. "I expect no better from you," he added, without bothering to mask his disdain.

Kaylin didn't even bridle.

"If you gentlemen wish to debate, you will find a different venue for your words. Do I make myself clear?"

"Yes, Arkon," Tiamaris said, bending so that his head was almost in reach of his knees.

"Good." He turned and strode off. Stopped, his robed back

toward them, and added, "I am aware that Lord Sanabalis is under a great deal of stress, so I will overlook this incident."

"Thank you, Arkon."

Sanabalis himself was utterly silent.

A second set of doors came as a relief to Kaylin, even with a door-ward in plain sight. This ward tingled the way normal ones did, and she touched it first, without prompting. There were definitely some things that were worse than magic.

But the doors opened into a rounded room, a squat hall with narrow windows and wide doors between them. Six sets in all, including the one that they had just exited.

Sanabalis surprised her; he bowed to her. "My apologies, Kaylin. The Arkon is of course correct."

"Who *was* he? I thought there were only a few Lords and—"

"He is not a Lord. He is the Arkon. These rooms, the libraries and the galleries, are his hoard. He is not young," Sanabalis added.

"I saw that."

"And he is not kind. If you needed a reason to disturb *nothing* without permission, you have now been given it."

She nodded. Hesitated. "I really did forget about the theft," she said quietly.

"Of course you did. The girl would drive almost anything sensible out of your very thick, mortal skull." He frowned. "If we understand the Oracles correctly, however, we have two weeks left."

"Two weeks left until what?"

"You misunderstand me. We have two weeks left, period. In two weeks there will be no Elantra. And it is highly likely that the loss of Elantra involves a great deal of water moving from one spot—the ocean that happens to front our port— to another. The fact that Everly began to draw you is either a sign of hope or a sign of doom," he added. "It has been much discussed. I did not consider it worth mentioning until the discussions were resolved. Until you asked me about the nature of water.

"And we are coming to the gallery. I would not leave you in a library here if my hoard depended upon it."

Gallery was a word, like any other word.

Clearly Dragon translation, even into Barrani, left a lot to be desired. Kaylin had thought Everly's room huge, and it was. But this? This was larger than the library. And it housed not canvas, but things older—leather hides, chunks of sheared rock, carved statues that were short a limb or three.

"You have labored under the burden of ignorance, and we have allowed it," Sanabalis told her. He sounded like himself. Like her teacher. The Dragon was gone from his voice. Tiamaris was likewise quiet, but his eyes were a shade too amber.

"We have allowed it because we ourselves are without explanations. The marks you bear," he added, "would be recognized by the Arkon, and perhaps by one or two others. In the history of our kind, others have borne those marks," he said. "No, I am not being entirely accurate. Not the marks you *now* bear. They have changed, with time, and the magic of the outcaste. But the marks as they first appeared.

"You went to the High Court of the Barrani. You were privileged to witness the vulnerability of their *Leoswuld*. You were privileged to bear witness to the birth of a new High Lord. And you were stupid enough to venture into areas that you should never have seen at all.

"It is something that no Dragon would have done, had one been invited to attend. You speak little of what you witnessed, which is commendably wise on your part, if surprising. And you bear the burden of the High Court, whether you acknowledge it or not.

"But rumor has wings, as they say. You touched the source of their lives, Kaylin, and it marked you. It is a subtle mark. Tiamaris?"

"I...sense no change in her."

"A very subtle mark," Sanabalis said drily. "You will never bear witness to a similar ceremony among the Dragons. But Kaylin, what the Barrani possess, we also possess. What gives them life, gives us life.

"None of us are certain how the mortals arrived on our world. We are almost certain about the timing, although we may be off by as much as a century."

"What do you mean, arrived?"

"I believe that I used the correct word."

"Um."

"Yes? It is safe to speak here. It is not, however, safe to touch *anything*."

"I thought you were hatched?"

Tiamaris and Sanabalis exchanged a glance.

"To be fair," Tiamaris said to Sanabalis, "none of the racial classes she failed concerned themselves with reproduction. I don't believe it's considered relevant to police work."

"Having had her as a student for what feels like a long time, I'm disinclined to be fair."

"So that's a no, no eggs?"

"That's a no, no answer," Tiamaris replied. "And, Kaylin, neither Sanabalis nor I have forgotten the theft you spoke of. What, exactly, was taken?"

"A box. A reliquary, I think."

The silent exchange of glances was beginning to get on her nerves.

"He said it couldn't be opened by any key. But he also said—well, implied—that it *could* be opened by magic. He didn't say what was in it. I don't even know if he's seen the inside of the box." She paused, and then added, "I'm not really supposed to say this, but there seem to be reliquaries associated with each of the...elements. The one that was stolen—"

"Yes, we could deduce that."

"And this is bad because whatever threatens the city has something to do with water."

"Good. We'll make an excellent student of you yet. But it was not for that reason that I brought you to the galleries."

"Okay. One more question?"

"One." It sounded a lot like *none*.

"You and Tiamaris—you were kind of roaring at each

other back there. Should I be ducking behind that statue for a bit?"

Tiamaris laughed. "We were having a discussion, Kaylin. I assure you, if there's ever cause to duck behind that statue over there, as you so quaintly put it, you'll know. You won't make it *in time,* but you'll know."

But Kaylin was now approaching "that statue over there." It was, as were all the pieces in this gallery, close to one of the walls; there was a plaque in front of it that said something she couldn't actually read. It was one of the few statues that had not suffered the amputations over time that so many of the others had, although it had been worn in places so that it was almost smooth.

Standing on a pedestal that was definitely not part of its original construction, it towered above her, but had it been flush against the floor, it would only have loomed. It was missing its left ear, and the strands of stylized hair now fell like a pocked blanket down its shoulders—and possibly past them, since she couldn't really see its back. But the right ear marked the statue as Barrani. Tall and slender, it was almost impossible to tell whether the original had been male or female, and it didn't seem, to Kaylin's admittedly untutored eye, to be something made *by* Barrani. It was too lifesize for that.

And all of this was inconsequential; the Hawk saw it, catalogued it, and let it go. Because the Barrani's arms were exposed, and the robes were cut so low they didn't *have* a back.

Because they didn't, because she could see the Barrani's arms clearly, she knew why Sanabalis had brought her.

They were marked with curved symbols and dots, familiar lines. They had been carved there, rather than painted or tattooed, or time would have worn them away. Almost unconsciously, she lifted one of her arms—the arm that was unfettered by heavy, pretty gold.

"Yes," he said softly. "They are—or were—the same as the marks you first received."

CHAPTER 11

"Tiamaris—"

"I told you that were you to show your arm to someone who could read it, you would probably not remain attached to it," he said quietly. "There are those among our number who can read some of what is written, but they find it disquieting."

"Why?"

"Because of this statue," he replied softly. "The Barrani Lord who bore those marks was a legend long before Sanabalis was born. I do not know if the Barrani themselves remember him."

"They probably don't—*they* don't have the statue."

"It was not created for the Barrani," was his quiet reply.

"Then for whom?"

"We are not entirely certain. Nor, before you ask, are we certain *by* whom."

"Where was it found?"

"I do not believe the ruins that it was taken from even exist anymore. It is old, Kaylin."

She nodded.

"But…" He hesitated.

Sanabalis took over. "It is not the only idol of its kind that we are aware of. It is merely the one that was best preserved in the fall."

"The fall?"

"There were wars," Sanabalis told her gravely, "which changed the shape of the world. They are in the past, and it is the desire of the Dragon Emperor—and many others who labor in silence in Elantra—that they remain in the past.

"But, Kaylin, mortals have existed for a long time in the world, and you are the first one—the only one to our knowledge—who has been graced by such marks. Had you been Dragon or Barrani, one of two things is likely to have occurred. The first, you would be dead. But I have a suspicion that your death would merely mean that another child would bear those marks in your stead.

"The second, however, is more certain."

"And that?"

"The Dragon outcaste whom we do not name would never have attempted his magics to take control of the words themselves. To change their shape through arts that are generally considered sympathetic magic—"

She snorted.

"The words would have a weight, and yes, a significant power, were they inscribed upon one of the firstborn. We *are*, in some sense, a word. These words have power," he added softly. "You have used them from the moment they first appeared, to heal the injured. You use them in that fashion now. Had you used them differently, I do not think you would have fared so well against your enemies.

"The names that give us life are the language of the Old Ones. And these marks are part of that language. They are both more and less complex. In and of themselves, they cannot create life, or waken it.

"But they add to the name that *did* waken life."

"They're like names—" She stopped.

If he noticed, he didn't say as much. "But on a mortal? We are not even sure what it means. There are theories about the Old Ones, but mortality eludes them. Theories are always confounded by your kind."

"What did this Barrani do?" She asked it looking up at the time-worn contours of his face; there was little in the way of expression left, and she could not discern what he might have been like.

"He won wars, Kaylin."

"That's all?"

"He won wars that changed the shape of the world, time and again. It is not a small thing."

"I can't—"

"We're not at war." But his eyes were amber. "And I pray—well, you would if you had religious convictions— for the sake of your kind, that we never are."

"But, Sanabalis, something doesn't make sense."

"Much lacks sense or logic. What in particular do you mean?"

"How did Ma— How did the outcaste *know?* How could he somehow strip the undead of their names?"

"A name, like a life, can be surrendered," was the quiet reply. "But your first question has troubled the Court since the deaths began when you were a child. We were not certain, Kaylin, and yes, before you ask, the Oracles were consulted heavily at that time.

"But the time passed, and no new power awakened to challenge the Dragon Emperor. We thought that whoever was responsible for the deaths was trying to somehow mimic history, but on mortal children. That way, if the experiment proved successful, or rather, too successful, the damage might be more easily undone."

"Undone?"

"It would be easier to kill you."

"Got it."

"And then you arrived in the Hawklord's tower, some time after the deaths had stopped. You, a child—do not make that face, Kaylin—and a mortal, bearing marks out of legend."

"That's why Tiamaris wanted me dead?"

"It is why most of the Court wanted you dead," he replied, as if he were talking about a common sea squall. "But the information came to light slowly—in your terms— and by that time, the Hawklord and his subordinates were attached to you. Why, I can only ponder."

"But if the Emperor—"

"You are *mortal,* Kaylin. You were watched closely, and some information about your skills as a healer came to light. The Hawklord argued your case, and the lone Leontine to serve the Emperor directly growled it. Some heated words were exchanged between the members of the Court and the Officers of the Law.

"It is my belief that were the Emperor to order your death, the Hawklord would have complied. But not your sergeant, which would have been something of a loss to the Hawks. Lord An'teela also presented herself in Court to argue on your behalf. She argued not as a Hawk, but as a representative of the High Caste Barrani Court."

"But she couldn't do that—"

"Very well. I am addled and my memory is clearly wrong."

"I mean she couldn't *legally* do that."

"I highly doubt that she had permission to do so. I highly doubt that the Castelord was *aware* of her petition."

"And it was made in his name," Kaylin said very quietly.

"Yes. And I must say that she was quite clever in her presentation, which is more than can be said of Sergeant Kassan. She did her best to belittle you, and in so doing, to belittle those who were afraid of a human child."

"And you argued?"

"I? No. I merely watched. Tiamaris was most vehement."

"Lord Sanabalis," Tiamaris said coolly, "that is unnecessary. You know well—"

"I knew well," Sanabalis said mildly, "that all arguments on either side of the debate had been aired, some with subtlety, and some without. And I knew also that in the end, the Emperor's word—and not one of ours—would decide the matter. He was impassive," Sanabalis added. "Even for a Dragon, he was inscrutable. I myself was uncertain which way things would go.

"But in the end, the Hawklord brought memory crystals to the Court, and each of us were allowed to view what they contained. They were trivial, really—I believe one of them involved your misunderstanding of the word *bookmaker*— but they were of you.

"He summoned the Tha'alani, and the Hawklord submitted to an examination. Lord An'teela professed herself willing to do the same—but that proved unnecessary. And the mind of a Barrani would not be a pleasant place for any Tha'alani, even the strongest, to visit.

"I did think that you would be seconded to Court, which would, in the light of your general attitude toward formality, have been most unfortunate. But the Emperor chose to leave you with your beloved Hawks. And so you have remained.

"But I better understand him now, I think. What was not clear to any of us, even the most aged, has become clearer as you have grown. There is a reason for your existence at this time, and in this place.

"The Dragon Emperor *is* Emperor for a reason. He sees deeply, and he looks a long way off. If the libraries and galleries are the Arkon's hoard, the Empire is the Emperor's."

"What's yours?"

"Kaylin!" Tiamaris sounded *shocked*. He looked quickly at Sanabalis and said, "She failed racial interactions, Lord. She is not—"

But the older Dragon lifted a hand. "I will not, of course, answer the question," he said quietly, "but I understand that she meant no offense by it."

In Elantran, Tiamaris said, "Never, *ever* ask another dragon that question."

"And never," Sanabalis added, "ask *this* Dragon that question a second time."

She nodded and turned back to the statue for a last lingering glance. "What killed him?" she asked softly.

"No one knows. If you are wondering what *could* kill him, Kaylin, the answer is the same. Not one of us knows. Perhaps when the time had come and the Lord had served the purpose written in those ancient words, the words—and their power—faded.

"Now, come. There is more."

"But I don't understand," Kaylin whispered to Tiamaris as they followed Sanabalis down the long gallery. "He *told* me what the Arkon's hoard was, and what the Emperor's is. If it's okay to know that, why is it such a big crime to ask?"

"Both the Arkon and the Emperor have made clear what they hoard," Tiamaris replied in a very low voice. "It is a matter of public record. But big or small, all Dragons have those things which they prize and value above all else. It is their weakness," he added, "and often, their strength."

"I thought it was just gold and jewels and stuff."

"And perhaps you thought that because those stories were told by humans, who value gold so highly," was the curt reply. But after a moment, he added, "And in some cases, it was that simple. A long time ago, perhaps. But think, Kaylin—how many Dragons do you know?"

She could count them on the fingers of one hand. Well, two hands if you included the Emperor, but "know" in this case wasn't exact. She held up one hand. Sanabalis hadn't interrupted them yet, and she didn't want to press her luck.

"There were more. There *are* more, and perhaps in other empires, they also rule. Or sleep the long sleep," he added quietly. "So many of our kin chose to take the long sleep rather than surrender to the rule of another."

"Sleep as in dead?"

"No. Dragons seldom use euphemisms where fire and brimstone will do."

The irony—and condescension—was not lost on Kaylin. "There is *no damn way* this was covered in any classes about racial bloody integration."

"True enough. Only those dragons who were unusual enough or young enough could willingly accept the Emperor's claims to these lands and those within it. To be forbidden both flight and hunt was no part of their desire, and to control those urges, no part of their constitution. You saw me," he added softly, "when I assumed my true form."

"This isn't true?"

"It is a form that is…less primal."

She nodded. "I saw. I knew why."

"And you understand that I knowingly courted my own death by making that choice."

"Yes."

"Were the Emperor himself not…flexible…we would not

now be speaking. But I made the choice because I have duties to the Dragon Court, and in the end, the Emperor saw the necessity of that choice, and accepted it."

"Or you'd be dead."

"Indeed."

"But the Law—"

"There *is no Law* but the Emperor's, Kaylin. Should he desire it himself, he could fly through Elantra and burn down the cursed mendicant's guild—"

"Merchants?"

"Yes, I believe that is its official title. He could devour whole whomever he felt might satiate hunger. He could do *anything* he desired. No Law would be broken, because he *is* the Law."

"But he made *our* Laws," Kaylin said, her voice rising. "And he tasked us with their keeping. Do you think we would just stand by?"

"No. I think you would—to a man—perish."

"And you?"

"Kaylin," Lord Sanabalis said. "We are almost in the oldest of the libraries. As we approach it, I wish you to consider the wisdom of the question you just asked."

"He's still a Hawk," she said, some of the heat leeching out of the words.

"Indeed. And the Hawks are sworn to serve the Emperor's Law as it is written and handed down. I do not question your loyalties. I do not even doubt them. Were the Emperor to break the Laws you have sworn to uphold with your life, you would be honor bound to stand against him. He understands this," the older Dragon added, as they at last reached a very small, very modest-looking door.

"And it was much discussed at the time of its inception. But mortal laws are for mortals, with their fleeting power, their brief span of years. Those Laws were of his creation, Kaylin, and the vows taken and made by those who serve them were *also* of his creation. For *you,* child, there can be no other answer.

"But Tiamaris was seconded to the Hawks *as* a Dragon lord. There is only *one* answer that he can offer you. Only one, ever. Do not ask him to dissemble. We *are* Dragons. We who made the choice to remain and watch are those who chose to accept the rule of the Emperor. We are part of *his* hoard, Kaylin. We are part of the Empire. Do you not understand why there are so few of us?"

And she did. Suddenly, she did.

Her silence trailed on for minutes as the weight of the words took root.

"I was not required to take the Hawk's oaths of induction," Tiamaris told her, almost gently. "And in truth, I thought them foolish and inconsequential. But..." He turned to face her fully, and raised one hand to his neck, to a fine, fine chain that surrounded it. Beneath the weight and color of Imperial robes, she hadn't seen it clearly.

He pulled it up, and it came easily, until she could see what dangled, like a pendant, at its end. A silver hawk.

"I was proud—I am proud—to bear the Hawk," he told her gravely. "And in its service, I was allowed to *wake,* Kaylin, to taste air and flesh and the dust of ages. To *breathe.*

"And were the time to come again, when the question of your fate balanced on the fine edge of our Lord's whim, I would not now offend the sergeant so gravely with my arguments."

"Tiamaris was young, when the Emperor rose," Sanabalis said quietly. "Too young for the long sleep. Not too young to die. But he is here, and he is as you see him. Of the Court, he argued most vehemently for your death, but of the Court, he is most at home in this strange and cluttered environment you call a city.

"You will be pleased to see there are no door-wards here," he added.

She had hardly noticed.

He opened the door by taking a key out of his voluminous robes and inserting it into the lock. It was a very strangely shaped key, to Kaylin's eye, but there was nothing inherently magical about it.

"This," he told her, "is the oldest of the libraries, and in it are scrolls and tablets that could not be bound into a form that can be easily organized. It was not tried more than once," he added. "And the man who tried had the foresight to imprint what he read in a memory crystal, which is also now a part of the library."

"I won't be able to read any of this," she said. There wasn't even a question in it.

"Actually, there may be some phrases or words that you would recognize. High Barrani has changed very little over the ages. But then again, the form of writing it *has* changed, so maybe you are correct.

"I feel I must offer a word or two of warning before we enter, however."

She nodded. "Will the Arkon be there?"

"No. He knows that you are escorted by two Dragons."

"Good."

"Touch nothing, Kaylin. If you feel the urge to do so, tell us instantly, and we will prevent it."

"O-kay…"

"There is a reason for the lack of a door-ward. It may or may not become clear as we enter."

"Is this some sort of test?"

"Indeed. Everything that doesn't kill you is."

He pushed the door open into darkness.

"Mind you," he added, "surviving doesn't always mean you passed."

He could be such a comfort.

The first thing she heard as the door swung shut was a mild curse.

"You didn't bring a lamp?"

"There are lamps here."

"I notice they're not lit," she said, struggling to keep the heavier sarcasm out of the words, and succeeding as well as she usually did.

"No. Would you care to light them?"

"Light them? I can't even *see* them!"

"Oh, very well." Sanabalis was suddenly illuminated by the glow of an oil lamp.

"You didn't use magic?"

"No."

"Then how did you—"

"I breathed on it," he replied.

"What—you can breathe *fire* in this shape?"

"Of course. The tricky part is breathing only enough to light the wick."

"I couldn't," Tiamaris told her.

"If you cared to practice, it would come easily."

Kaylin had the feeling that the Dragon definition of *easily* encompassed more than her life's worth of years.

Tiamaris's fireless snort was as much of an answer as he cared to give.

She watched the old dragon as he traversed the room— which looked oddly like a cave to her eyes. He kept his back toward her, but every time he passed an unlit lamp, it woke in his wake, little tongue of flame leaping at dead air. And it *was* dead air. There was no movement of breeze in this place, and nothing to suggest that breeze had ever touched it. Certainly no breeze had disturbed the dust and the numerous cobwebs that clung to it.

"People don't come here much, do they?"

"What gave you that idea?" Dragons, clearly, could be just as sarcastic as any other race. "Don't feel it necessary to make idle chitchat, Kaylin. I enjoy the rare moments of silence I'm granted."

As her eyes became accustomed to the light, which was gloomy and orange, she stopped walking. "Sanabalis—"

"Yes?"

"Tell me that that isn't a body in the corner."

"I can tell you that isn't a corner, if it's of any help," he replied. "And technically, *body* is perhaps too fleshy a word."

Technically true. It was a skeleton, ribs curving up toward the light as it lay supine across floor. "Why is it here?"

"If you mean, how long has it been here, the answer is a good number of years. If you mean why is it considered part of the library, you could try moving it. You could, however, only try *once*."

"You told me not to touch anything."

"Good girl."

"Would the Arkon kill me?"

"I doubt he would have the chance, although the inclination would probably exist."

But the skeleton seemed to be wearing a helm of some sort, one that revealed empty sockets. Its long arms were bare, but its wrists were girded in—in something that looked suspiciously like golden bracers. Around what remained of its neck—which really wasn't much—an amulet caught light, returning it in a flash of blue and gold. If the blue was sapphire, it was a round dome of sapphire, the size of an egg, surrounded on all sides by gold and smaller gems.

Kaylin inched toward the skeleton, and Tiamaris picked up a lamp that stood on a dust-covered pillar. The dust came with it, like a graceless cloud.

"Lord Sanabalis," Tiamaris said softly.

The figure of the robed, elder Dragon stopped moving. He turned slowly to face his former student, as his current student knelt carefully before the skeleton, keeping her hands above her lap as she undid her shirt's buttons at the wrist, and pulled them up to reveal the bracer that she thought of as her own personal cage.

"This came from here," she said, a hint of question in the statement.

"Yes," was the quiet reply.

"What kind of a library signs out artifacts?"

"This one, obviously."

She looked at her wrist and inhaled dust sharply. "The gems—"

But Sanabalis had come back, and Tiamaris was standing above her. They could both see that the gems that studded the bracer—the gems that had to be pressed in sequence in order to open it—were flashing in quick bursts of light, with no hands to touch them or invoke them.

She watched the sequence with wide eyes. "It's not—it's not—"

"No. It is not the pattern to open the bracer." His pale brow rose slightly. "Why did you think to look?"

She shook her head.

And cried out in shock as her arm lifted of its own accord.

Tiamaris caught her arm at the elbow, taking great care not to touch the bracer itself. She thought he would break her arm, because her arm kept *moving*, and dragging the weight of a grown Dragon with it as it went. Kaylin was struggling to help Tiamaris in any way she could, but she wasn't his match in either size or strength, and what he couldn't do, she had no hope of achieving.

"What are you trying to touch?" Sanabalis asked sharply.

"Nothing!"

But she knew that her wrist was moving in a straight line toward the body itself, toward the pendant that still glowed a shock of blue, incandescence trapped in crystal. "The pendant—"

"What pendant?" he asked, his voice even more sharp than it had been. The day had just gone from bad to worse, something she would have bet her own money against being possible.

"The *glowing blue pendant around his neck.*"

"Tiamaris?"

"I do not see it, either, Lord."

"Pick her up and take her out of the room, now."

"She seems to have gained a lot of weight in the past few minutes," was his reply, although it was strained. He was trying to lift her, one hand on her arm, and the other around her slender waist. And it wasn't working. "Any aid you would care to offer would be appreciated," he added.

Sanabalis cursed softly—softly enough that Kaylin, with her special affinity for swearing, couldn't catch the words. He set his lamp down somewhere, and he came to her other side, catching the arm that wasn't moving and attempting to pull her back.

"Tell me what you see," the Dragon said in her ear, as he grunted with pointless effort.

"He's wearing a gold necklace. It has a large pendant that's weighing it down. Big rock. Looks like a sapphire, except no facets. It's circled in gold, and there are gems in the gold—"

"Kaylin!"

"Flashing gems," she said, and cursed in Leontine. "You can see the bracer?"

"Yes. Of course."

"I think it's flashing in time with the stones on the pendant—two diamonds, two rubies, two sapphires."

His curse this time was distinctly louder, and she still couldn't understand it. Tiamaris, however, could. "She was not to know," he said, breathing heavily between syllables. "There is not one of us, save perhaps the Emperor himself, who understands the workings of the artifact she wears."

"Yes, and it's *that* Emperor who is going to be asking the questions if we don't get her out of here."

Inch by agonizing inch—which was a pretty accurate description because it felt as if her tendons were going to give—she drew closer to the pendant. Close enough to touch it, although her hand was curled in a fist, denying till the last what seemed inevitable. Sanabalis's weight and strength, combined with Tiamaris's, had slowed her enough that she could now clearly see what she hadn't seen before: there was a mark at the center of the smooth, round crystal, and it was the mark itself that radiated blue in such profound brilliance.

She said, "It's a word."

"What?"

"There's a word at the heart of the pendant."

"What word?"

"I can't read any of the ones on me," she snapped. "But it's the same language."

Indeed, a voice said. And not a voice she recognized.

"Sanabalis?"

"Do not touch it—"

"I don't think it matters anymore."

The empty sockets beneath the helm began to glow, and the color was orange, the exact orange that heralded the slow build of Dragon rage.

The skeleton rose.

And this, this evidence of life where none existed, was plainly obviously to both of the Dragons who were clinging to Kaylin. "I don't suppose either of you knew who he was—"

"No," was Sanabalis's grim reply. "But I've no doubt we'll soon know more than any Dragon before us save perhaps the Emperor or the Arkon."

Daughter.

He rose, and as he rose, the glow from his eyes spread out across his bone structure, covering it, masking it in light, if flesh could be light. She could see through it, but only the Hawk in her noticed.

Why have you come?

"Can—can either of you hear him?"

"No."

"He's talking to me—" The bracer at her wrist clicked, opened, and fell. Kaylin and two dragons suddenly toppled backward in an awkward splay of limbs. They scrabbled to their feet just as awkwardly, Kaylin's hand hitting the sheath of her dagger as she steadied herself.

Sanabalis *roared.*

And so, too, did the stranger.

"Sanabalis, *don't*—"

But he had heard the roar, where the words had been silent to him, and he stilled. It was not a relaxed stillness.

She said, "Oh my God, he's a Dragon...."

Tiamaris whispered something that Kaylin couldn't understand, and Sanablis lifted a hand to stem the words.

But the dead man—Dragon—had heard them anyway. Because he could.

"Yes," he said, his voice dry as dust, but somehow heavy and deep and resonant at the same time. "And I died as you see me."

Tiamaris closed his eyes and looked away. Sanabalis, older, did not, but he bowed his head, and Kaylin thought it was merely to avert his gaze for a moment. Nor was she wrong.

"We did not know," he said when he again lifted his head. "Forgive us. We did not know."

Kaylin looked at the three of them, the two who were undeniably living, the one who was not. "It's bad to die...as a man?" she whispered at last.

"It is why so many chose the long sleep," Sanabalis replied, "who might otherwise have chosen to serve. This is the death we fear," he added. "Trapped, in every way, in our frailty and vulnerability, denied our hoard and the roar of the wind."

Dead is dead, she started to say. Thought better of it, for once, before the words left her mouth. After all, dead men didn't speak, and this one was. He was *speaking.* And glowing.

"I earned my death," the dead Dragon said, speaking,

she knew, in Dragon, although she could understand him. "I failed."

"But you—you're here now."

"Yes. I am trapped here, now."

"And you want to be free?"

He laughed. It was a roar; her body shook with the sound, as if she were crystal and his cry the resonant note that would shatter her. She lifted her hands to her ears without thinking. It made no difference.

"That would be a yes," Tiamaris said in quiet Elantran.

"Kaylin, I do not mean to alarm you," Sanabalis added in slightly strangled Barrani, "but your arms are glowing."

She took them from her ears and saw that he was partly right: the symbols were glowing, pale blue and misted orange, a blend that should have hurt to look at, but didn't. It wasn't, in the end, much different than the colors that marked the dead Dragon. "That part where there's supposed to be no magic in this room—I just broke that rule, didn't I?"

He nodded. "I was foolish," he added in a soft voice.

The roar had died into a heavy silence.

"What is freedom to the dead?" Her voice. She was surprised to hear it because everything about it sounded wrong. She was not as surprised, however, as Tiamaris; Sanabalis was impassive.

"You come late," he told her quietly. "I waited, and you did not come, and my watch failed."

The fact that she wasn't alive at the time seemed irrelevant. "I could not hear you," she said at last. "I could not hear your call."

"Not bound as you were, no. I will not ask you how you came to be so bound. I have freed you from the binding with what little strength I could gather."

Again, the fact that she could easily—if not completely *legally*—free herself, seemed to belong to a different story. She bowed instead, as if in thanks.

"But my failure was not complete if my kin still live," he said slowly. "And perhaps it was for this moment that I waited. Come, Chosen. Take the burden I can no longer bear, as is your right and duty." His head lifted, his tarnished helm glinting oddly, his eyes—for she could see them clearly now—unlidded luminescence.

"Kaylin—" Lord Sanabalis said, making of her name a warning.

But Sanabalis for a moment was no more part of this story than the words Kaylin had managed not to utter. She shrugged herself free of his restraining hand. "Trust me," she told him, looking only at the ghost.

"To do what?"

"Oh fine, ask the hard question."

But the Dragon, dead, was not deaf. "Child," he said to Sanabalis, "do not seek to interfere. My hoard is scattered, my wings are broken. Will you face me?"

"Not all of your hoard is scattered," Kaylin told him, stepping forward slowly, her arms tingling, her spine aching. Words all over her body were coming to life; she could feel them as they were written, and written again, over and over.

His smile was sharp. "Duty became my hoard, Chosen. And it is not a hoard that the dragons understand. I failed—"

"*No*. You did not fail." For she could see, now, that the pendant was the same color as the runes on her inner arms, and she understood what it meant. For just a moment, she understood. "Look. You still bear it, burden and hope. And we have need of it now."

"I cannot invoke it."

"No," she said, her voice softer. "But *I* can. I will take it," she added, "and your story, in this place, will finally come to a close—and the Dragons will remember, forever, that what you guarded with your life, you guarded, as well, with your death."

"And you will tell me the end of my story, Chosen?"

"I will write it," she whispered, and her throat was raw by the time she had finished speaking. Dragon was not, apparently, a language meant for mortal vocal cords.

He seemed to shrink in on himself, the light fading from his bones until only those bones were erect, illuminated by the glow of eyes and the glow of pendant. "Then tell me, Chosen. I am too weak to continue."

"No," she said again, but more quickly. She reached out and caught his dusty, bony fingers, and held them fast. Light raced down her arms like a flash of lightning from a thunderous sky.

"Take it," he said, as the light enveloped him. "Take it now."

"I cannot take it. It can only be given." This wasn't even a guess; she *felt* it, and knew that she had probably never spoken truer words in her life.

"And will you guard it with your life? Will you care for it, as I have done? Will you bind yourself to its purpose and seek no other treasure to replace it?"

But she shook her head, understanding what he asked as if, for a moment, she *were* a Dragon. "I have taken my hoard," she said. "And it is as you see it. And I will not cheapen your efforts by lying. But I promise you this—I will find someone who will guard it with the whole of his life, seeking no gain and no power. He will not touch it, he will not wear it, and he will use it for no lesser purpose than you yourself sought."

For she could read what lay at the heart of the crystal she had thought was simply a sapphire.

"My hands, Chosen," he told her, and she realized that she was still gripping them tightly. She released them, slowly, and saw that light still bound them together, when nothing else did. Understood that words were his power, here—and that she was the parchment upon which they had been written.

A thought came to her, unbidden. What did *these* words do to the word that gave life to the immortals?

But she did not ask it. Instead, she waited, while he lifted what could not in theory be lifted: hands stripped of all muscle, all tendons, all flesh. "I hear it," he told her softly. "It is waking, now, and it is dangerous. Use this, if you can. Prevent what I could not."

She couldn't hear a thing that wasn't his voice, but wisely said nothing. She felt, not pity, but something like awe and sorrow, as he lifted the chain.

Dread would come later.

He took it from his neck, but it caught on the edge of his helm. Kaylin did not hesitate; she reached out and pulled the helm from his skull. It was heavy and cold and dead in her hands, and she would have tossed it aside in disgust had Tiamaris not removed it.

With nothing to impede its progress, the chain traveled over the Dragon's head, and his eyes flashed a pure, pale gold. Still, she waited, and as the chain approached her own head, she bent forward slightly to receive it.

Everything else would come later, she knew. All cost, all anger, all regret. But for now, she began to speak, and if the speaking was painful and wrong in every way, it was also *right*.

"Teyaragon, eldest of his line, gave over the gathering and the hunt, and retreated from the skies and their freedom when he was but eight hundred years old in the reckoning of his kind." Her legs and her arms were burning, and she could *hear* the words on her skin, because they were so like the ones she was speaking for a moment, they might have been the same thing.

"A duty was placed upon his kind and he chose to bear it alone, and he faced the heart of Water, bearing only its name, and when the Water was awake, he fought its coming, and he perished in the fight.

"But he fought for long enough, and with all of his power—which was great, even reckoned among his kin— that his people had time to take to the skies, where they could without deserting their hoard. And the Water, in the end, found nothing to sustain it, and it died, upon the land, as Teyaragon himself had died.

"But he kept his oath and he fulfilled his duty, even in

death, trapped and lessened by the form he had been forced to take to bear *this* sigil. And in time, when his ancient enemy began to stir, he came from the edge of death to greet the Chosen, come at last at his call."

The light in his eyes was fading, but it was still pure gold. Kaylin wanted to look away. She couldn't bear to see empty sockets there. She felt the weight of the pendant as he dropped it, at last, around her neck.

But she hadn't finished yet.

"And without his burden, having fulfilled all duty beyond even the expectation of those who placed the geas upon him, he was free at last to return to his rightful form." And she gestured, and her hands flew up, palms out, and the words surged *through* her. She heard the snap of thin wood as her hair streamed free, and strands of it stood on end, as if she were a lightning rod.

"The winds which had waited for millennia gathered, even in the darkness of his tomb, and they whispered his name, and he heard it."

Light flared around him; light that was bright, but pale now, not blue and not orange but not quite blinding white. Where the light he had somehow summoned in death had been amber and man shaped, the light that took him now was larger in every possible way. It spread through the darkness like fire, consuming it. Wings of light passed through the walls and tongues of white flame left his jaw as his face elongated.

And there *was* a wind in the closed chambers; heavy, brittle pieces of parchment fluttered by, swirling up toward the ceiling and the far walls.

"And the winds carried him aloft, to the open skies."

The light began to climb; the wings were flapping. She could *feel* the gale, and stood in the center of it, unharmed. Unmoved.

He roared in triumph and in joy, and the whole palace must have shaken with the sound of it; had it been no more than a whisper, she thought they must feel it anyway, because of what it contained.

"Go," she whispered. "I give you back your name, and your death, and your freedom."

And rising from her—from within her—was a single bright sigil too complicated to memorize, too significant to ever forget.

But she knew there was one less mark on her body.

Darkness descended.

Even the pendant, which had glowed so brightly when she had first laid eyes on it, was now a part of the dark, dusty room. Well, the dark room, at any rate; the dust had kind of scattered like a routed army. With the light went all of her energy, all sense of certainty, all power.

She dropped to her knees, and by some kindness of fate managed to put her hands in front of her face before her face hit the ground.

CHAPTER 12

When she woke, she rolled out of bed.

She hadn't intended to—but in her flat, the wall would have stopped her. Which meant, she thought, as she lifted herself off the floor, she wasn't at home. She couldn't be; the floor was softer than her bed, and it was a deep, rich blue. Carpet. She pushed herself off the ground.

"I was beginning to wonder if you would ever wake," a familiar voice said.

"I wish I hadn't." But she teetered to her feet, and sat heavily on the side of the bed she'd accidentally deserted.

Tiamaris was standing some distance away, his hands behind his back. The room came into focus around him, but then again, he had always had a habit of filling a room. Even when it was crowded and full of other people. He had changed his clothing. It matched the carpet, which was a bit hard on the eyes.

"I'm still at the palace."

"Observant as always."

She made a face.

"I took the liberty of sending word to Sergeant Kassan. Or rather, of having word sent."

"What? What word?"

"You have been sleeping for almost a day," he replied. "And while being late is something the Hawks expect, I believe he knew where you were going."

"What did he say?"

"Something about your pay."

She groaned.

"Lord Sanabalis apologizes for his absence," he added, "and I was given permission to attend you. A physician was brought—an Imperial Physician—to examine you. We told him you were drunk," he added.

"And he didn't ask about the lack of anything alcoholic?"

"He's not paid to ask questions, Kaylin. Merely to answer them."

"What did you ask him?"

"If you were going to survive. He said yes."

It was hard to tell, with Dragons, whether or not they were joking.

"The room—"

"Stay still. Lord Sanabalis took the responsibility for explaining the disturbance to the Arkon. I believe they are still conversing. And before you ask, yes, there is some difficulty. The Arkon would probably prefer that you take the place of the skeleton which no longer exists."

"No longer—"

"I believe a very fine layer of bone ash is mixed with the settling dust."

"What—what happened?"

The Dragon raised a dark brow. "You don't remember?"

"I remember what *I* saw. But I want to know what you saw."

"A fair question. Let us just say that we saw the skeleton rise to its feet. We heard it speak, and we know what it said. What you said was…harder for us to understand."

"I did speak."

"You spoke," he said, "with the voice of history."

She wished, as a stabbing pain made her clutch her temples, that he could be straightforward. What the hell was the voice of *history*, anyway?

"And we saw you remove his helm, Kaylin. I took it. He lifted his hands and removed something from his neck, and this, he placed around yours. But you accepted his burden," he added. "You accepted the responsibility of his burden."

"I had to."

"No."

"I *did*." It had all seemed so *clear* at the time, too. It had made so much *sense*. Which should have made her either more suspicious, more cautious, or both. "I didn't promise him I would guard it," she added. "I told him I would find someone who would."

"Guard what?"

"The pendant."

"Is that what you saw?"

"I'm wearing it—" She reached up and put a hand to her throat. "Oh." There was, of course, nothing there. "You never saw it?"

"No." He lifted a hand before she could speak again. "We believe that he gave you something. We believe that you could see it. Neither of us, however, could. What did you take from him?"

"A word," she said softly.

He nodded as if this made sense.

"I had to take it," she said in a lower voice. Talking loudly made her head throb—maybe being hungover wasn't so very different. "If I didn't take it, he couldn't leave. He was bound to it," she added.

"Yes, that much we understood. And you freed him, and for that, Kaylin, you have the Emperor's gratitude."

"You heard him, then?"

"Every Dragon in the city must have. It did cause some minor difficulty," he added with a slight grimace. "Because the voice we heard could not be uttered by a Dragon who was not in his true form. The Emperor is aware of us, of course, and aware to a lesser extent of those Dragons who exist at the outreaches of the Empire. He was satisfied that none of us broke his edict. This took some time, but you were not necessary to the discussion and Lord Sanabalis felt you would appreciate being absent from it."

Nodding made her head hurt, but it was automatic.

"I, however, requested a leave of absence. I am to return you to the Hawks, where the Hawklord is waiting for your personal report of events."

She winced.

"And for the duration of the next two weeks, I am once again seconded to the Hawks." He nodded slightly, and removed a small crystal from his pocket. It was smoky quartz with a heart of sky. "Information that may prove necessary," he told her softly, "has been extracted from the Imperial Archives and will be added to the Records of the Halls of Law."

"What information?"

"You asked about Donalan Idis, if you recall."

She didn't, but took his word for it; he was hardly likely to make it up. "And that?"

"What we have of his studies and his duties here. It is not as much as we would like. But, Kaylin—you did not explain why you asked the question, or where you came by the name. And like most of the Dragons, I don't believe in coincidence."

"It's... It's complicated."

"With you, it could hardly be anything else."

"And it's not technically official," she added, wretched now because she could clearly see the look on Ybelline's face. "And it might have nothing to do with the—the current investigation."

"Which investigation would that be?"

"Um, the one where we all die in two weeks?"

"Ah, that one," he said drily. "We have one missing artifact, and according to Sanabalis, one missing child whose absence has not been reported to the Halls of Law."

"Two," she said, giving up.

"Two?"

"Two missing children. Donalan Idis may or may not be connected with the second missing child." She hesitated.

"And the second missing child has likewise been unreported."

"Yes."

"But you know of the child—boy or girl?—how?"

"Girl. I know because someone asked me to look into it." And she'd spent a day sleeping. She stood. Managed not to fall over.

"Food was left for you. I suggest you eat it."

She could honestly say she had never really seen Tiamaris look shocked before. Given what they had been through together, this said something about his demeanor. But as she told him, haltingly, of her visit to the Tha'alani quarter, his brows disappeared into his hairline.

"She asked for *you?*"

"You don't have to look like that. It's not as if—"

"*Kaylin,* your views on the Tha'alani are very, very clear. You didn't happen to mention this to anyone sane in the Office?"

"No. It was a personal visit."

Tiamaris shook his head. "You went alone?"

"I went with Severn."

"Good. Forgive my interruption. You went at the request of Ybelline, and she informed you that one of the Tha'alani children had gone missing?"

"During the Festival, toward the end."

"And Donalan Idis came up?"

"Not…precisely."

"Which means not at all."

She thought he could have at least had the grace to make a question of it. "She didn't mention him, no." Her hesitation was more marked. "I don't know if they're connected. The two missing children, I mean."

"Ah. Among the Hawks, you have a custom. It's called *betting*. I am willing to bet that they are."

"What odds?"

"Pardon?"

She rolled her eyes. "Never mind. I wouldn't take that bet. Did Sanabalis tell you about the Oracles?"

"You refer to Everly?"

She nodded.

"He mentioned it. He also mentioned that you…directed the picture somehow."

"I was trying to figure out how to *talk* to him."

"While he was in the middle of his vision?"

She shrugged. "It seemed like a good idea at the time."

"I'd also be willing to bet that those are the last thoughts of any number of people. Dead people," he added.

"I caught that part." She finished eating what was, she had to admit, a really good sandwich. "We'd better get going. I can't afford to lose much more in the way of pay."

The streets were pretty much the same streets, and the sun was low enough that she wouldn't pass out from the heat, but walking was still tiring. On the other hand, she wasn't bruised or bleeding, which counted for something as

278 CAST IN SECRET

far as long, unpleasant walks were concerned. Tiamaris, by presence alone, kept people at bay; even if you didn't know a Dragon on sight, you knew trouble when you saw it.

He said very little, and although she wanted to ask him a hundred questions, she was silent, as well, thinking about missing children, about a deaf Tha'alani boy, and about Oracles.

Thinking about anything, in fact, that was not Sergeant Kassan. But when Tiamaris escorted her to the open doors of the Halls of Law, Clint and Tanner were on duty. Clint's wings rose slightly as he saw her.

"Kaylin!"

"I know. I'm late."

"That, too." He smiled. "We were beginning to get worried."

"Betting worried?"

"We weren't allowed to place bets."

"What?"

"Corporal Handred did not think betting was appropriate."

"And anyone listened?"

Clint winced. "Look, Kaylin, you should probably know—" He stopped and looked at her companion. "Lord Tiamaris."

Tiamaris inclined his head. "It was thought best that I return to active duty for the time being," he said. "And part of that duty was escorting Kaylin to the Hawks."

Clint lifted his halberd to allow them both to pass. "Hurry," he whispered. Kaylin's fingers brushed his flight feathers, and for once, he didn't seem to notice.

* * *

To call the office *a bit tense* was to call a razor *a bit sharp*.
Marcus wasn't even sitting at his desk; he was *prowling* the
room, and as Kaylin entered it, she could hear the thrum of
his growl. But he was watching her as she rounded the corner.

"Kaylin." He stopped pacing. In general, this was a good
thing. In specific, she wasn't so certain. His glance strayed
to Tiamaris and remained fixed there.

Tiamaris, however, offered the sergeant a very proper
bow. "Sergeant Kassan," he said quietly.

Said sergeant glared at the Dragon for a little longer than
was comfortable—for Kaylin, at any rate, as Tiamaris didn't
seem to notice—before he again looked at Kaylin.

She walked up to him, stopped in front of him, and bared
her throat. But he wasn't angry at her; he didn't touch it.
"There's been a disturbance," he told her gravely. "The
Hawklord wishes to speak with you. He's been waiting."

"I'm sorry—I was tied up—"

"At the Imperial Palace. Yes. I heard."

"We all heard, dear," Caitlin said, rising from a small
mound of paper. "You're looking a bit peaked."

"It's nothing."

"Hmm."

"I ate," she added defensively. She looked around the
crowded office, and added, "Where's Severn?"

"Corporal Handred is with Teela and Tain," Caitlin said,
looking pointedly at the back of Marcus's head. Kaylin edged
away from Marcus and into the radius of Caitlin's voice. "He
wasn't happy to leave, dear."

"Why?"

"There was some concern about the length of your absence, given where you'd gone."

"Oh." She turned to Marcus and said, "I went to visit the Oracles, and after that, we went to the library. There wasn't much danger. It's not as if the books could jump up and swallow me."

"And the roaring *Dragon* had nothing to do with you?"

"The…roaring Dragon…" She turned to Tiamaris and gave him a very black glare.

"I said any Dragon could understand it," he said mildly. "I do not recall saying that anyone else was rendered deaf."

"He was a happy Dragon," she said, wincing, as she turned back to the Leontine who could make her life a living hell. "And he wasn't exactly in a position to do anyone any harm."

Tiamaris covered his eyes with his hands, rubbing either side of his temple with his thumb and forefinger. "The Hawklord wishes to see us?"

"He made no mention of you," Marcus snapped. But then, as if finally certain that by some unforeseen miracle Kaylin still had as many limbs as she'd left with, added, "But he'll want to see you once he knows you're here."

"Where are Teela and Tain?"

"Investigating a double murder," old Iron Jaw snapped. Seeing the look that instantly transformed her face, he softened his voice. "No, no children. A man and a woman."

"Where?"

"Go see the Hawklord, Kaylin."

"But—"

"*Now.*"

Tiamaris, knowing how much she loved door-wards, preceded her up the winding circle of climbing steps. He stopped briefly at each landing to nod at the guards posted there before continuing, something that Kaylin usually failed to do. Then again, she was *usually* late, in trouble, and in enough of a hurry that polite and *unemployed* seemed synonymous.

But he kept his pace measured, and when they approached the door, he lifted his hand and placed it firmly against the ward. She felt the prickle of magic that would unlock it, but that was all. It wasn't her hand that glowed a faint blue as the door-wards took the information they needed and processed it, dumping some of it into records and the rest, gods only knew where.

The doors swung inward, rolling slowly and silently to the sides as the rounded dome of the tower shed light in abundance across the floor—and the lone man who now occupied the Tower. His wings were folded at his back, and they were almost all she could see of him; he was studying an image in the mirror before him, and it clearly wasn't his own.

"Lord Tiamaris." He turned, gesturing, and the image in the mirror dissolved. "Kaylin."

"Lord Grammayre," Tiamaris replied, tendering a deep bow. Kaylin followed suit.

"Lord Sanabalis has been keeping you occupied," the man who commanded the Hawks said quietly. She wasn't sure whom he spoke to.

"He has," Tiamaris replied, clearly not as uncertain as Kaylin.

"I trust you did nothing to endanger the Hawks while you were in his keeping."

"No. Yes. I mean, I didn't get us in trouble." Kaylin knew whom he was referring to with that.

"Good. I believe we have enough trouble as is." He was standing in the circle etched in stone on the floor. "While you were gone, two bodies were discovered near the merchants' quarter. Not the foreign merchants'," he added, knowing how exact her sense of geography was. "I would have sent you to investigate, but as you were otherwise occupied, sent Corporal Handred in your stead."

"Has word come back?"

"Not precisely, but yes, I have received a preliminary report. They felt it was urgent."

"Why?"

"The two—a middle-aged couple who owned a number of the buildings in the area—were found drowned."

"They were drowned in the merchants' quarter?"

"Apparently without the aid of water."

She was silent for a long moment.

"There was no sign of a struggle—or rather, there were signs of flailing, as one might expect, but no bruising that could not be attributed to their own movements."

"No bath—"

"There was a bath, but it was empty."

"Recently emptied?"

"Not according to the Corporal. The bodies do not appear to have been moved. They were not near the bath when they were discovered."

"Who discovered them?"

"Their daughter. She was expecting them for lunch, and when they failed to join her, she went looking for them." He paused. "There will be more information shortly."

She nodded.

Tiamaris stepped forward. "I have some information for your classified records," he said quietly. "I do not know if it is pertinent to the investigation at hand, but it may well become so." He handed the Hawklord the crystal he had shown Kaylin in the Palace.

The Hawklord accepted it without comment. "Kaylin," he said softly. "How much have you been told?"

"I don't know," she replied. "I know what the Oracles fear. I know we have two weeks, if the Oracles can be trusted."

"Then you know enough. You visited Evanton in Elani Street."

She nodded again.

"We require you to visit him again. Ask the questions you deem wise. Fail to ask the questions that are ill-advised. Do you understand the import of this?"

"Off record."

"Good." His wings shifted; she heard the feathers brush against each other and looked up as he spread them. "I

myself have a meeting to attend. I will not ask what trans-
pired at the Palace until after the meeting.

"But, Kaylin, the words of the Oracles are *not* meant for
public consumption. Is that clear?"

The words *no one listens to them, anyway* hovered
briefly—and rashly—on her lips. She nodded instead. She'd
seen what panic could do to a crowd, and she really didn't
want to see what it would do to a whole city.

"Red is waiting for the bodies. He'll examine them when
they arrive. The daughter was reluctant to part with the
remains."

Kaylin nodded again. It happened a lot—although why
people thought the dead cared one way or the other, she'd
never understood.

The dome of the Tower began to collapse to the sides as
it opened. She watched the Hawklord take flight, envying
him the freedom of the skies. Only when he was gone did
she whisper a single word.

Water.

Elani Street had still not quite recovered from the
excesses of Festival spending; although it was not yet
evening, the streets were practically empty. Good for
policing, bad for business. Severn had still not returned to
the office by the time she'd come down from the Tower, and
Tiamaris was sent as her partner.

"He won't let you in," she said quietly.

"He will let me into his store," was the equally quiet reply.

"You're a Dragon."

"Yes. But I am also, for the foreseeable future, a Hawk. He will not dishonor the uniform."

"You're barely *wearing* a uniform." His robes, however, did bear the Hawk, and it was not a small piece of embroidery, either.

"I am willing to make a small wager."

Kaylin laughed. "I'm not."

"Oh?"

"I wouldn't bet my own money against a Dragon."

"That's odd."

"What?"

"It seems a wise course of action—but you still, according to your office, seldom have any money of your own."

"How much are you getting paid?"

"To work as a Hawk?"

She nodded.

"It is considered part of my service to the Court," he replied.

"Which means 'nothing.'"

He raised a brow.

"Well, add a small number to that, and you have what I'm getting paid. Meaning, it's not my fault I'm broke."

He smiled, and his eyes were golden, like the sun without the burning intensity. She walked in his shadow, tired but calmer somehow for his presence. Which, given he was a Dragon, said something; she'd puzzle out exactly what it said, and about whom, later.

Evanton's door opened before she could ring the bell. Her hand was halfway to the pull and she froze at the sound of its little chimes. Evanton, still wizened and bent, frowned at Tiamaris for a moment longer than necessary, but he did open the door and get out of the way.

"I guess you heard," she said quietly.

"I heard." He shut the door firmly behind them, and then reached up and drew the curtains shut. "You need some sleep by the look of you."

"I had a day of it."

His look redefined the word *skeptical*. "I have water boiling."

"For what?"

"Tea."

"Oh. I ate." Evanton was not much of a tea lover; he made tea for guests. Sometimes.

"Eat more."

He looked, to Kaylin, older and wearier. "There were two deaths in the merchants' quarter today."

"Drowning deaths."

She nodded.

"Without the benefit of water."

And nodded again.

He closed his eyes and his shoulders slouched downward, as if he were surrendering to gravity. Or age. "Evanton?"

"I had so hoped it wouldn't come to this."

"But you thought it might?"

He nodded.

"You could have said something."

"I did. I said there were no murders yet."

"Why would two middle-aged merchants be worthy targets for a murder? And why, if they were, would someone be stupid enough to kill them in a way that practically screams magic?"

"All very good questions. Answers, however, would be better." He waved her forward, and then stopped. "Lord Tiamaris," he said gravely, "I am offering you the hospitality of my home *because* you wear the Hawk and I happen to respect it. I would have bet against the Emperor creating laws which in theory he can't break, but I thought it was well done.

"However, I invoke the right of hoard law here, before you take another step into my store. You may choose to abide by it or leave. If you feel that you cannot make that choice, leave now."

"What's hoard law, exactly?" Kaylin asked, as the ancient shopkeeper and the Dragon stared at each other.

Tiamaris replied in Dragon. Kaylin thought her ears would pop and she cupped them protectively with both of her hands. But although the voice *was* a roar, there was no change at all in his expression. Or rather, there was—but if anything, he looked more respectful.

"You know I can't understand that," she said, when she thought she might actually be able to hear the sound of her own voice again.

"I wasn't speaking to you," Tiamaris replied.

Evanton seemed satisfied with whatever the answer was. He beckoned them into the back of the shop, where his kitchen lay hidden behind a small door. There were no large doors in this place.

The kettle started to whistle. Evanton made a straight line

toward it. Or as straight a line as could be made; the kitchen wasn't anyone's definition of tidy. He swept a stack of books off one chair and set them on the table, where they perched like an accident waiting to happen.

Evanton brought the kettle to the table, and around another stack of books, cups appeared. "That is the second time I've heard a Dragon speak in two days," he said conversationally. "It's not at all common these days."

"No," Tiamaris said agreeably. The look he gave Kaylin was less agreeable, but Evanton missed nothing that happened in this place.

"I see you've been keeping busy, Kaylin."

She cleared her throat. The cups—she'd learned this the hard way—were too hot too pick up, and they were without the usual handle that made hot things safe to touch. Evanton liked them. Kaylin liked her fingers more. She waited while the liquid cooled.

And daring a glance at Tiamaris, she said, "I think I have something that belongs to you."

"If you had it, girl, there wouldn't be two dead people in the merchants' quarter."

"Oh—not that. Something else."

"I gave you the crest. Which I see you're wearing."

"Not that, either."

"Well?"

"Um."

He waited with something like patience. For Evanton. "Kaylin, now is not the time to play games."

She wasn't sure how to tell him that she was wearing something she couldn't touch and couldn't actually see.

"Keeper," Tiamaris said when the silence had grown a little too stretched.

Evanton raised a white brow. But he didn't correct Tiamaris.

"The first Dragon you heard yesterday—what did it say?"

"It didn't say much. The closest I could come in Elantran is *freedom,* but it lacks the gratitude and joy that I heard. I could, if you'd like, repeat it."

"No!" Kaylin said as forcefully as she could.

Evanton took a sip of tea; obviously Tiamaris was considered a *real* guest. Tiamaris picked up one of the delicate cups and held it by its rim and its base. Of course, Tiamaris could probably stick his hand in a fire and not notice that it was hot. Kaylin stared mournfully at her own neglected cup.

"He wasn't actually alive," she said. "The Dragon, I mean."

"Ah. By which you mean he was actually dead?"

"Long dead."

"And you found him."

"In the library."

Evanton's brows rose. "They let *you* into the Imperial Libraries? And you *walked out alive?*"

"I didn't take anything—" Which wasn't technically true.

"My dear, I wouldn't have vouched for your safety there in any case. The librarian is one of the few living creatures who could probably read what's written on you."

"Well, yes, but—" She stopped. "W-what do you mean?"

He actually grimaced. "Kaylin, you come from the fiefs. I expect you to be *good* at lying."

She would have bridled, but it was Evanton.

"I know what you are, girl. I always knew it."

"Could you explain it to me?"

"Not easily, no, and you probably wouldn't understand half of it. I'm too old to have the patience to try. But I know that you bear the marks. This *is* my home," he added. "And very little comes into my home that I cannot see clearly."

"You always knew?"

"I always knew."

"And you let me into—"

He lifted a hand.

"Sorry."

"Good girl. I trust your intent, Kaylin. And I have ways of protecting myself against hazardous accidents. This is probably one of very few places in which you could be safe."

"From what?"

"Yourself. But I interrupted you. Please continue." Steam rose between them like a tattered curtain. "A dead Dragon?"

"Oh. Yes. Very dead. For some reason, they kept the skeleton—"

"In the library."

She nodded.

"He was very loud for a dead creature."

"You're telling me. I—"

"Kaylin." Tiamaris frowned.

"Oh. Right. He—" She hesitated again. "He was trapped

in the library. But not by the—the librarian. He'd—damn it, it was all so *clear* yesterday."

"Magic often works that way," Evanton replied. "I won't ask for details or explanations that you're not capable of giving me. Have a biscuit," he added. "Before the mice get them. And tell me what you think happened. I'm sure Lord Tiamaris will correct any infelicities."

"Well—he was trapped by something he was guarding. But it was more than just guarding. It was his—his—hoard, I think. But it wasn't so much gold or treasure—"

"She has a human understanding of Dragons," Tiamaris said, with just a hint of frustration.

"Well, she is human. Mostly. What was it, Kaylin?"

"It was a pendant. No—it was more than a pendant. It was a *word*."

The cup of tea froze halfway to the old man's mouth. "A…word."

She nodded. "He was entrusted with its keeping. No, not even with its keeping—he was to guard it and to use it when the need arose, because it *could* be used by someone strong enough. He was powerful, in life, and I think he was young for a Dragon when he accepted the responsibility.

"But the responsibility didn't end with his death."

Evanton closed his eyes and set the cup down heavily. "He is gone now."

She nodded. "He thought I was—I was someone else."

"And you lied to him."

"No!" She swallowed. She had sort of lied to him—but

it hadn't *felt* like a lie. Not when she'd been speaking. Not when she'd been there. "He saw—I guess he saw whatever it is that you saw when you first saw me. I— He—" She shook her head. "He thought I was someone else." Lame, lame, lame. "He said he had called for me, and I failed to arrive in time. And I wanted to *be* someone else, for him. So I…apologized. For being so late. I'm good at that," she added with a trace of bitter humor.

"If he saw what you think I saw, he saw truly," Evanton said almost gently.

"He wanted me to take it. And I did—but I told him I would find someone else who could do what he did. Who could guard it with his life—or more than that. Who could use it when it needed to be used. And only when it needed to be used." The last part, she realized, was important. She stopped talking for a moment and absently picked up her cup. The spill as she set it down—quickly—was almost invisible. "He had power," she said softly, "but he wasn't chosen for his power. He was chosen because he had no desire to *use* it."

Tiamaris shook his head. "He had the desire, Kaylin."

"How would you know?"

"He was a Dragon. And by your own words, a young Dragon. What he had, as well, was the ability *not* to use the power."

"And he used it late."

"Perhaps. Perhaps he could not trust himself with its use until it *was* too late."

And, ashen now, Evanton said, "I know what you saw. He gave it to you?"

She nodded. "I think I'm supposed to give it to you."

"Would that it were so," Evanton replied. "But I am not its keeper."

"Can you see it?"

"No more than you can, now."

"But I think it belongs in your…garden."

"Garden?"

"Garden."

"It has been missing for a very long time. But if it belongs in my garden, as we shall call it, so, too, does its bearer. And that person is not me, Kaylin. I'm sorry."

"Then who?"

"That, I cannot tell you. But I think you have very little time in which to find the answer."

"But it—" She stopped. "He said he could hear…it. His enemy. The thing, I think, that killed him in the end."

Evanton nodded. "And if you bear his burden, girl, and you listen very, very carefully, you will hear it, as well. I do not, however, suggest that you try."

"Why not?"

"Because you are currently sane."

"And listening would—" She stopped. "The Oracles."

"Yes. They do not know what they hear, but they hear truly. They are not, by anyone's definition, sane. And they cannot prevent themselves from hearing the voice. Think about being an Oracle."

"No, thanks."

"Then do not listen."

She nodded. "Do you know what killed the couple?"

"Water."

She started in on sarcasm and stopped before she opened her mouth. "Tiamaris—remind me to ask what kind of water they drowned in."

The Dragon nodded.

"Very good," Evanton said.

"Could a mage have done it?"

"Done what?"

"Well—drowned them. Put water in their lungs."

"Only the old-fashioned way."

"Tiamaris—"

"The Keeper is correct, Kaylin. Of the mages that currently practice in the Imperial Service, there is not one who has the power or control to do what was done there. With fire, yes, but fire is the easiest element to master. Earth, in its time, is simple, as well, although devastating. But air and water? No."

"The Arcanists?"

"That is less clear to me. If, however, you are obliquely referring to Donalan Idis, then the answer would once have been no."

"Would once have been?"

"He was gifted, and powerful. He is no longer a part of the Arcanum, and we therefore have no idea what he has been doing. Or learning."

"What is the difference between an Arcanist and a mage, anyway?"

"A mage serves the Emperor."

"Oh." Pause. "That's it?"

"The Arcanum existed before the Empire. Had the

Emperor wished to raze it to the ground, he could have done so—but there was a small risk that the Empire would have joined it in the ashes. The Emperor chose to be pragmatic."

"Too bad."

"Indeed, the Arcanum is not well loved by the Officers of the Law. But it is—again in theory—subject to the Law, and the truce that has existed since the founding prevents the Arcanists from breaking said Law."

"They are their own Law," Evanton added with a small frown.

"What does that mean?"

"It means they wish to remain free from the constraints that the Imperial Mages labor under, and they kill any of their own who might be justifiable cause for the loss of that independence. There might possibly be one or two who could do what was done—but at a significant expenditure of power."

"You don't think it was them."

"You've already pointed out why it would be foolish."

"Then how—" She stopped. "The reliquary."

"Yes."

"You think they've opened it."

"No. Not yet. But I think they—whoever they are—are close to being able to open it."

"What's inside it, Evanton?" she asked.

"I told you, truthfully, that I have never seen the inside." She nodded.

"If I had, I, and this entire City, would most likely be dead."

CHAPTER 13

Tea took a long time to cool. Kaylin stared at Evanton. "The entire City."

"Yes."

"And you leave it *lying around?*"

Something suspiciously like a Dragon's foot stepped on hers. "Forgive her impertinence, Keeper."

"Always."

"Well—does it have a mark or a note that says *open this and kill everyone???*"

"No. And if it did, some enterprising idiot of a mage would spend his entire adult life trying to open it anyway. Trust me," Evanton added darkly.

She looked at Tiamaris, who seemed to be completely unsurprised by anything that had been said so far. "Why the hell would anyone *want* to open it?"

"Because it's powerful, and people who are certain of

their own power cannot conceive of a power they cannot control." Evanton replied.

"Very, very few people are aware of what it contains," Tiamaris said, as if Evanton had not spoken.

"No one could steal something like that by accident."

"I would have said no one could steal it at all," the Dragon lord replied gravely. "And anyone who could—" He paused. "Keeper?"

Evanton bowed his head. "The fault, as you are careful not to suggest, is mine."

Tiamaris began to speak, but Evanton swatted the words away. "I will not invite you into my garden," he told the Dragon lord.

"Nor would I expect it, Keeper. But you took Kaylin, and her companion, to see what the Dragons and the Barrani have never seen. I admit that we were curious. You understand something of the nature of Kaylin's...unique talents. I would have guessed that she, like the Dragons, would be excluded, and for similar reasons."

Evanton shrugged. "I have only instinct to go by. When I see a Dragon—on the rare occasions one has chosen to visit—it is seldom comforting. The Barrani, one trusts only when one is dead."

"And Kaylin?"

"Is Kaylin. She is as you see her. She says too much, too easily, she has a temper, and she has an overwhelming weakness for the very young and the very old. She jumps to conclusions, and frequently it is not unlike jumping off a cliff when one thinks it is a hillside. She is also a Hawk, and whether or not she grew up as a thief in the fiefs, she believes in the laws she swore to uphold. The desire for power is part of her nature only in daydreams, and she is fast becoming aware that those idle dreams are far removed from reality. I do not fear her."

"And you invited her into your…garden because you do not fear her?"

Evanton's face was about as friendly as stone—a great slab of it, falling forward to crush someone. But if it lacked any friendliness, he didn't order Tiamaris to leave. "I invited her, as you put it, because I am now too old to do what must be done—if I could ever have done it."

"Wait—what are you talking about? What must be done?"

He stared at the surface of his tea, as if he could read something in his own reflection. "You must find the reliquary," he said at last.

But Kaylin was still troubling over the words he and Tiamaris had exchanged. "You let me in. But you didn't let them in."

"No."

"Which means they had to let themselves in."

"Obviously."

"How?"

He was silent again, and it went on for a while. At last he said, "I am old, Kaylin. I was not old when I took possession of this store. I was also not the first person to come to the man who owned it. I was merely the last. He could find no better at the time."

"What happened to the others?"

Evanton said nothing. Loudly.

"So…whoever did come here…*could* come here."

"Yes."

"And that's significant."

"Of course."

She was thinking ahead of herself, and trying not to stumble over the thoughts. "Whoever it was, they didn't come alone. And…whoever came with them didn't mean for them to stay."

He nodded.

"Would they know, Evanton?"

"Before they came? No, Kaylin. I highly doubt that. They must have suspected, but the knowledge could only be gained for certain when they were in the…garden. But once they were here? Yes. I think they would know."

She looked up at him, her eyes narrowing. "The girl."

"The girl?"

"In the water. The girl who spoke my name."

Evanton nodded quietly. "She could touch anything here, I think, with safety."

"And she took the reliquary."

"That is my belief."

"But—"

"Find her, and you will find it."

"And what else will I find?"

"I don't know, Kaylin. I would go myself, but at *this* time, I cannot leave."

"Evanton, do you think she killed that couple?"

His face was pale. "She has no guide, no tutor," he said at last. "And she may not have the power required. *I do not know*. But it is possible, Kaylin."

"If she killed them—"

"Yes."

Kaylin said, rising, "We should go."

Evanton nodded, not pointing out that she hadn't touched her tea. Well, hadn't drunk any of it.

"But I don't understand. How, in this entire city, could someone find the one person who could come here at all? How would he *know* what to take? How would he even—"

"These are all good questions," Evanton replied. "Their answers are beyond me. Let me say this—there is likely to be more than one person in the Empire to whom these doors would not be locked. He would only have to find *one*."

"But he'd have to know *what* he was looking for!"

"Indeed."

"And only the Barrani and the Dragons seem to even have a clue what you've got hidden here. Hells, I've *seen* it, and I still don't."

"That," Tiamaris said drily, "would be the *other* reason it would be safe to allow you entry here."

She didn't kick him, but it took effort. He rose, and Evanton rose, as well, bent by age and worry. He led them to the door of his shuttered store and unlocked it—although she hadn't remembered him locking the door when they'd come in.

"When you find the girl," Evanton said quietly, "and if she still lives—and, Kaylin, I think there is a very high chance that she does not—you will find the guardian you seek for what you carry."

"And if she's dead?"

"You will carry it for some time yet." He paused, and then added, "I am old, Kaylin. It was an act a hundred years ago. It is not an act now. I hear the voices that the Oracles hear. I fear for the loss of the city.

"And I fear, as well, that my time is passing. That what has stood here for millennia will not stand at the end of two weeks. There is a power here that you cannot conceive of, and I ask only that you think of that power in the wrong hands."

If, she thought bitterly, I can't conceive of it, how the hells can I imagine it in the wrong hands? But Evanton was as smart, in this case, as he thought he was—because she could, and she didn't much like what she came up with.

"How many more drownings," she whispered, half to herself.

Tiamaris stepped firmly and heavily on her foot, and then all but dragged her out of the shop.

"It is a small wonder to me," he told her, as he walked briskly away from the small Elani Street shop, "that you've been allowed to enter that place more than once."

"Why?"

"You do *not* understand the burden of the Keeper."

She rolled her eyes. "No. I don't. I understand the burden of the Hawks, and that's enough for me. Besides, it's not like he's explained—"

"He shouldn't need to explain. I cannot believe—" He slowed down, shortening his stride. His steps were still thunderously heavy, though. "He is respected, Kaylin, by the Dragon Court. He is not entirely trusted—he stands outside of our Laws, and our ability to enforce those Laws. When the earth devoured the cities that stood before this one was begun, his garden remained. Do you understand?"

"No. But I understand that the Barrani and the Dragons understand it." She paused for a long moment. "Do you want to explain?"

"No. But I will say this, since you've seen it—the Dragon you rescued from death, the Dragon you freed—it was his fate to guard *less* than the Keeper now guards."

"He failed."

"Yes." Tiamaris now mimed a leisurely pace, which Kaylin could easily match.

"And Evanton is failing."

He stopped walking and closed his eyes. "Yes," he said softly. "The Keeper is failing. It is his failure that caused the death of the couple in the merchants' quarter. It is his failure that may see the deaths of every living being in the city, and if, indeed, he has failed completely, not even his shop will in the end withstand what is to come."

"But *what the hell is to come?*"

"I do not know myself. Water, certainly. We must find this child of whom you both spoke, and I must speak with the Dragon Court."

"In that order?"

He hesitated. "It is far worse than we feared," he told

her at last. "And it is also exactly what we feared. No, I do not need to report immediately."

Severn was waiting when they returned. He was waiting in that kind of grim silence that keeps everyone else at a safe distance. Sadly, Kaylin had never mastered the art of grim silence. Grim words, yes. But not silence. Where she went, the office trailed.

She went directly to Severn.

Severn looked up without surprise at Tiamaris, and nodded his greeting. He also handed Kaylin her bracer. It had kept the habit of returning to Severn, no matter where she let it drop. She held out her wrist like a penitent child, and he snapped it securely shut around said wrist.

"You heard," he said.

She nodded. "We went to talk to Evanton."

"And he had useful information?"

"Not exactly."

Severn, knowing her better than anyone, waited.

"The reliquary that was stolen," she said at last, putting a few extra syllables into the ones that she was hesitantly speaking.

"Yes?"

"He thinks—no, he's certain—that it's behind the deaths. What did Red say?"

"Death was caused by drowning in both cases. Bruising was self-inflicted."

"Did he say what kind of water?"

"Yes. Sea water."

"Tiamaris doesn't think it's possible that a mage caused those deaths."

"I concur. Possibly an Arcanist, but the Arcanum is not being particularly helpful."

"Is it ever?"

"No." He stared at her for a moment, then he shrugged his shoulders in one elegant motion and covered his face with his hands. When he lowered them, he looked exhausted, but the grim anger was—for the moment—leashed. She frowned. She had just noticed that he was wearing black. All black. Not even a Hawk adorned his shirt.

"What's with the mourning?"

He raised a brow at Tiamaris, who had, until this moment, said nothing.

Tiamaris shrugged. "Have you had a chance to access the records?"

Severn nodded quietly. "The information was not complete, but there was information in the records that I hadn't seen before."

Kaylin frowned for a moment. She hated coming in on conversations in the middle, but really hated it when she'd actually been there at the start, and still couldn't follow it. "Donalan Idis?" She hazarded a guess.

Severn nodded.

She looked at his clothing again. "You've spoken to the Wolflord." It wasn't a question.

"Yes."

"You're a Hawk—"

"I am a Hawk, yes. But the Halls of Law *are* the Halls, Kaylin, and we are in theory working toward the same goals."

"Not the Shadows."

Severn said very little.

"Severn, do you understand what Evanton does?"

It was Severn's turn to look slightly confused. "I understand," he said after a moment, "what he feels he is doing, yes."

"But did you know before you saw it?"

"No. But I've done some reading since then."

"What? Where?"

"The library."

She snorted. "Which library?"

"The Imperial Library."

"You found out about it from *books*?"

"I spoke for some time with the Arkon," he said quietly.

Even Tiamaris looked surprised. The surprise, however, faded. "You hunt Donalan Idis."

Severn nodded. "The Wolves don't like to fail," he replied softly. "And Donalan Idis is one of three men we've failed to apprehend. He was considered dangerous when the writ was signed," he added quietly. "Kaylin?"

She frowned. "I want to know."

"You have to know. Come." He left the desk he was standing in front of—it wasn't his—and led her to the West Room. Tiamaris followed.

"Teela will join us shortly," Severn told them both, as he placed his hand on the door-ward and waited for the door to open.

It did. The West Room, with its single table and its heavy chairs, waited in carpeted silence. They entered, and each took a seat.

Teela arrived five minutes later, and when she did, Kaylin winced. She was wearing, not the uniform of the Hawks, but rather the very expensive and exquisite gowns of the Barrani High Court; her hair was pinned about a thousand different ways above her very long nape. She looked taller than she usually did, and seemed infinitely more delicate.

And more dangerous.

She also looked a bit irritated, and when she sat, she uttered a very un-Barrani-like curse.

"We believe," Severn told Kaylin quietly, as Teela rearranged the folds of her skirt, "that the two drowning victims were killed in the building they oversaw."

"They were killed at home."

"Not their own, no. But they had rooms within the complex."

"You think they died in the rooms that the killer occupied?"

"Let us assume that there was a killer that can occupy normal rooms. If we can safely make that assumption, then yes, that is indeed what we assume."

"But why?"

"It's possible or even probable that they entered into the rooms in question—for reasons that are not clear—when the occupants were in the middle of something they did not wish made public. What that was, we can only guess."

Kaylin frowned. "Do we *need* to speak High Barrani for a reason?"

And Teela laughed out loud. "No," she said in Elantran. "It's habit forming, and it's a much easier language to say almost nothing useful in."

Severn grimaced.

"Who was living in those rooms?"

"That would be the odd thing. According to the financial records which the daughters of the deceased gave us, no one."

"According to the other tenants?"

"Ah. According to the other tenants, a widower and his daughter."

Kaylin leaned forward. "When were they last seen?"

Severn hesitated. "People weren't very clear on that. They were certain that an elderly man and his daughter lived there, but no one could say for certain when they were last seen."

"Did they have any visitors?"

"Not frequently, but yes, although one of the neighbors thought the visitors were relatives."

"How long were they living there?"

"Again, the neighbors are slightly unclear. If we average out their guesses, about six months."

"None of the neighbors visited?"

"Not often. The daughter was shy. She was also, apparently, mute."

"*Mute?* As in, couldn't speak at all?"

Severn nodded. "They're all shocked by the deaths," he added quietly. "The couple wasn't terribly friendly, but they were good landlords."

"The occupants would have had to leave in a hurry," Kaylin said. "How easy would it be to find another set of rooms?"

"Since they didn't appear to be paying for the rooms they were in?"

"Good point. What did the mages say?" She *hated* to have to ask that question.

"They're still combing the rooms and arguing a lot," Teela chimed in.

"They're mages." Kaylin hesitated and then said, "Did you call in the Tha'alani?" She hated that question even more.

"No."

"Why?"

"Because the description of the man in question was the same no matter who we spoke to. I do not believe he went to the trouble of disguising his appearance—that of a frail, somewhat downcast middle-aged man. I believe that the man used magic to avoid paying rent, which means he had very little money. No mage in hiding would use magic if it were unnecessary. No one knew what he did for a living, if he did anything. But he is not the only widower in Elantra, and he is certainly not the only one with a child or two."

"He's probably the only one with two corpses in his living room."

Severn nodded and looked to Teela.

Teela made the type of face she generally made when someone served her bad ale. "First," she said, in Elantran, "the Lord of the High Court sends his greetings to Lord Kaylin Neya and her *kyuthe*, Lord Severn Handred."

Kaylin looked irritated.

"Don't give me that look," Teela snapped back. "You

didn't have to stand there for an hour while he offered the damn greeting."

This made Kaylin laugh. When her laughter subsided, she said, "I'll buy you a drink. I'll buy you an hour's worth of drinks."

"With what money?"

"Probably mine," Severn said drily.

"Second, the Lord of the High Court expressed both his concern at the current investigation—and no, before you ask, I didn't mention it first—and also his willingness to help you in whatever way he can.

"Unfortunately, whatever way he can doesn't extend to giving a direct order to Lord Evarrim."

"Evarrim?"

"He's an Arcanist, you might recall."

"I try not to think about him at all."

"Well, try less hard for the moment. He's an Arcanist, and he worked with Donalan Idis, in as much as a Barrani Caste lord is willing to work with one of the merely mortal."

Kaylin was silent for a moment. "When you said the Lord of the High Court expressed his concern—"

"He, like the Emperor, has been consulted by and has in turn been consulting with, the Oracles."

"And he takes it as seriously as the Emperor does."

"More, I think." She was silent for a while, looking at her perfect gloves, her slender hands—things that were designed to accentuate the ways in which she was not a fumbling human. But Teela was, among the Barrani Hawks, the one most likely to swear and get drunk. Second only to

Tain in betting, she spoke Elantran as if it were her mother tongue. Kaylin didn't like the Court version of the Teela she'd known since she was thirteen.

She particularly didn't like the way this Teela raised her chin slightly, as if mulling over words Kaylin was suddenly certain wouldn't bring her any joy.

"The Lord of the High Court has an unusual request," she said at last, and Kaylin wilted.

Severn was leaning back in his chair, affecting ease. But his expression was on the rigid side. "What request?"

"It's for Kaylin," she said at last. "And it is strictly a personal request. It has no weight in the High Court, and your refusal of it would likewise have no weight. Nor could it be counted against you."

"Not legally."

"No. But I don't think it would count against you anyway. The Lord of the West March still considers you *kyuthe,* and he is known to be unwisely fond of you. He was present when the High Lord made his request, which, as I mentioned, does not have the weight of the Caste behind it."

"Why?"

Severn cursed in Leontine. He seldom did that—most of his swearing had been learned with the Wolves. But sooner or later, Marcus got to everybody. "Nightshade," he said curtly, when the swearing had died down.

Teela nodded slowly. "As Nightshade is outcaste, the Lord of the High Court cannot directly acknowledge his existence. This made the request a long and tedious affair," she added, with just a hint of smugness.

Kaylin looked at Severn. Nightshade had given them the name. Donalan Idis. The man himself, they had not yet found.

"This is another game," Severn said bleakly. "Nightshade's game."

"He gave us—"

"He gave us information, yes. But did he give us all the information he had?"

"I highly doubt it," Tiamaris said quietly.

"You have met the outcaste on a number of occasions," Teela said, more as a question than a statement.

"Our studies in the fiefs led us across his path. He did not seek to hinder us, and in one or two cases, may actually have been of aid."

"What game does he play?"

"I am not a Barrani lord. I do not know."

Teela nodded as if this made sense. From the standpoint of Barrani arrogance, it did.

"But he gave us the name. Donalan Idis."

"Yes. But the name was not involved in *this* case," Kaylin began—and then reddened. Severn raised a brow, but didn't even try to save her from her own big mouth.

"Which case did the name concern?" Teela asked, with perfectly feigned nonchalance.

"Severn, help me here."

But Severn was silent.

You like the damn Tha'alani, she thought, with bitter anger. *I don't.* But she could still see the fear and the exhaustion in the lines of Ybelline's beautiful face. It was not something she wanted to add to. Not in this way.

Not when a child—and the sanity of a race—was at stake.

"Do you think the widower was Donalan Idis?" she asked, by way of avoiding her own gaffe.

"I think it possible," Severn replied. "Because the two are dead in this unexplained fashion, and because an Arcanist would be capable of such killing. But...he has been careful, for all this time. I don't think it was his power which killed the couple."

"No sigil."

"None. There was *no sign* at all that magic had been done by any of the means our mages can trace. And we have one who can detect the signature of the mage on cases that are more than two decades old, if you can point him at the traces."

"It shouldn't be possible, though—no signature at all? No trail?"

"Kaylin," Teela said, very, very gently, "you *are* going to have to answer the question."

She looked at Tiamaris, and at Severn. "We should talk with Ybelline," she said at last, defeated.

"Ybelline? Ybelline Rabon'alani?"

Kaylin nodded.

"When—and why—were you talking with Ybelline? She is the Castelord of the Tha'alani."

"I don't think that word means that much to the Tha'alani," Kaylin replied weakly. "And I went to see her because she asked me to come."

"You *hate* the Tha'alani! Was the Hawklord out of his mind?"

"She didn't send the request through the Hawklord. She

didn't send the request through the Halls. It was strictly a personal visit."

"So personal that you didn't think to inform the Hawklord before you went?" Teela was practically gaping. Normally, this would be a small personal triumph, but Kaylin's sense of triumph was pretty much ash.

"I didn't think it was any of his business."

Teela's eyes swept upward, as if the Barrani believed in heaven and she were actually imploring one deity or another for patience. "What did she want?"

"She wanted my help," Kaylin said, her voice dropping until it was almost inaudible. "There was some difficulty in the quarter."

"If she asked for your help—"

"It's a caste case," Kaylin added firmly.

Teela stopped talking for a moment. She didn't look less grim when she started again. "You have no business in Tha'alani caste cases. They have their own investigators for that."

"Their investigators—such as they are, and they are in *no way* a body of law enforcement—do not leave the quarter, Teela," Severn replied.

"You'd better tell me," Teela told her, fixing Kaylin with that blue-eyed stare that spoke of imminent Barrani temper. The bad kind. Severn, apparently, had not spoken.

So he tried again.

"It is not Ybelline's wish that this be publicly known, and if it is brought up, it will upset the balance between the Tha'alani and the Law." Severn sounded like a schoolmaster, albeit a young and attractive one. "She will claim it as a matter for the Caste, and any chance we have of aiding her—any chance we have of building a bridge between the Tha'alaan and the outsiders—will be lost."

"Fine. Tell me off the damn record."

"There's no way to keep it off the records," Kaylin said bitterly, "if Donalan Idis is somehow involved in both cases."

Silence, then. Teela, however, was not much one for silence that didn't suit her. "Try."

Kaylin glanced once at Tiamaris. His gaze was golden, although his lids were raised. "The Dragon Court fully understands its crimes against the Tha'alani," he said quietly, "and the Emperor will also understand. Where it is possible, the Tha'alani will remain outside of the scope of this investigation. Even if Donalan Idis is, in the end, found in residence there. I will take what responsibility needs be taken for your disclosure."

"You can't," she said bitterly. Knowing that they were all right. The Hawk was heavy, but she wore it anyway.

"A Tha'alani child is missing from the enclave," she told Teela.

Teela was silent. The silence did not last. "I understand why she sent for you."

"I don't. She didn't touch me. And the Tha'alani who did certainly didn't get anything—" She closed her eyes. "Never mind."

"She touched Catti, Kaylin. She touched Catti's memories. Catti is from the Foundling Halls, and as you had just saved her life, I can't imagine that her thoughts weren't full of you."

Kaylin shrugged. "We're not talking about me. We're talking about a missing Tha'alani girl. She was last seen— in the Tha'alaan—in the company of a Tha'alani male who was born deaf. Deaf by the standards of the Tha'alani. He can be touched the way any thinking being can, and he can be read if he so chooses. The others can read what he remembers. But he can't actually touch the Tha'alaan himself.

"He ran away," she added. "When he was a teenager. He came *here* to find people who would understand him." Even saying the words cut her. "And he went back, and he wouldn't share his experiences here. But…he had one friend, or someone he felt was a friend, in the city outside of the Enclave."

"Who?"

"Lord Nightshade."

If Teela had been holding anything in her hands, it would have snapped in two. As it was, she looked around the empty, pristine room for something she could break.

"And he also met once with Donalan Idis while he was gone the first time. At least once. Donalan Idis had some interest in the boy."

"Nightshade?"

"I don't know, Teela. He lived with Nightshade for some time before he returned to the Tha'alani. He *isn't* with the Tha'alani anymore, and neither is the child. But it's worse."

"It always is."

"The child was in contact with the Tha'alaan, and the contact was broken suddenly, and with great pain to the child. If she were sleeping, she would still be in reach, or would have been. I don't know what the range is—I didn't really ask."

"You suspect—"

"That she may be injured or crippled, yes."

Teela was silent. "We can be glad of one thing," she said heavily. "It was one of their own, and not one of ours, that did this."

"I—I can't be certain of that. Grethan, the deaf boy—he *knows* what it means, never to be able to touch the Tha'alaan. I—I don't believe he could knowingly cripple a small child—"

"You don't know that for certain."

"I know that I wouldn't—"

"Kaylin, a small child could rob you and stab you in the thigh and you would make excuses. You're completely blind when it comes to things like this. Some people resent the ease that others have, and they could *easily* do harm.

"Where did he meet Donalan Idis?"

"In Castle Nightshade, the first time. I don't…I don't think Nightshade approved of the meeting. I don't think it happened again *in* the Castle."

"What was Donalan Idis doing in the Castle?"

"I didn't ask. If I had, I doubt I would have gotten a useful answer."

"Well, *ask*, Kaylin."

"What could they hope to get from a Tha'alani child? My only guess would be access to other people's memories—but if they crippled her—" and she *hated* to even use the word "—then that's not what they wanted. And what else is there?"

"It would depend," Severn said, slicing into the conversation with the tone of his voice, "on whether or not Donalan Idis was as unsuccessful in his early attempts to appropriate Tha'alani abilities as he claimed."

"What do you mean? If he had had success—" But the cool words that Severn had spoken suddenly became glaringly clear. "He didn't finish," she said dully. "He was deprived of subjects."

Severn nodded.

"And if he were almost finished, if he thought there was a way—"

"Yes."

"Oh God."

CHAPTER 14

"Severn—you accessed the records Tiamaris brought—"

"Yes. On the surface, there is very little there that the Wolves don't have in their archives."

"Why do the Wolves—oh, never mind. The writ of hunting."

Severn nodded. "Most of the information is not new to me. It is…more clear. The Tha'alani drove men mad in their own pain and fear."

"Was that all they did?"

"The cases are here," Severn said quietly. "But in the light of new information, old secrets might become clearer. I will say that Donalan Idis was not well loved by those in the Emperor's service. He was arrogant and frequently imperious.

"But given the disposition of the men who serve in that particular section of the Imperial Service, I would say their disdain for him had very little to do with the destruction of the Tha'alani lives given to his care."

"Let me access them."

Tiamaris now lifted a hand and placed it gently on Kaylin's shoulder. "I think Severn has spent the time necessary to acquaint himself with the information."

"But he—"

"No," Severn said quietly. "Kaylin should see them."

"We have need of her elsewhere."

"Yes. But she should see them, and time is something that we are short on, no matter what we do." Severn's expression was so carefully neutral, Kaylin *knew* she wouldn't like what she saw.

"What do you expect her to see, Corporal?" Tiamaris's eyes had shaded, in an instant, to orange. Kaylin had seldom seen such a total change in a Dragon's mood before. And Severn, well aware of what that color meant, met the Dragon's stare with an intensity all his own. His eyes didn't *have* to change color.

"Tiamaris," Kaylin said quietly, "I *want* to see the records. I need to know what I'm dealing with."

"Kaylin," Tiamaris replied, eyes still orange, "some children *want* to jump off the docks in the port."

Which more or less decided that.

They went from the West Room into a room down the hall. It had a much more prominent mirror, and the records access was clearer. Teela tagged along, still kitted out in full Court gear. Her eyes were a shade of green that was almost blue, but Kaylin couldn't tell who, of the three of them, was irritating the Barrani Hawk at the moment.

"Records," Severn said, lifting his palm and touching the mirror. "Corporal Handred, accessing Imperial Research Data entered today."

The mirror shivered in its frame. It took a few seconds longer than it normally did, and it normally didn't require a palm print. If this was information delivered to the Halls, it was clearly not meant to be perused by any eager student. Not that Kaylin had ever *been* one, but still.

"Imperial Security Studies, classified. Tha'alani. Group one."

There appeared, in the mirror, larger than life, a solitary man. His hair was black, with pale streaks, and his face was so severe a smile would have cracked it in so many places it would have left bone exposed. His eyes were dark, but his skin was pale, and his hands were long and fine. He *reeked* of money.

"Donalan Idis," Severn said, although it wasn't really necessary. The man in the mirror, frozen in time, was not a young man, but neither was he old. He was not ugly, but there was in his cold hauteur nothing attractive to Kaylin. She disliked him on sight.

The color of his robes, the red of the Arcanum, would have had that effect in any case. He was speaking, though. Grudging every word, Kaylin said, "Volume."

And the mirror replied, "Classified."

Severn said, "Volume." To Kaylin's chagrin, Donalan Idis now had a voice. It was a dreary voice, better suited to a bureaucrat, in Kaylin's opinion, than an Arcanist. On the other hand, she lived in dread of bureaucrats, having been trained by Marcus, so maybe this wasn't too surprising.

Donalan Idis was not, in fact, standing in front of a mirror for the entire time he was visible. "Did he know he was being recorded?"

"I consider it highly likely that he knew," Tiamaris replied, saving Severn the effort. "But as he wished to conduct the experiments on behalf of the Security Services, he had little say in the matter."

"Could he have tampered with the mirrors?"

"Of course. He could not, however, have continued his studies. Such tampering would not fail to be noted."

Group One, as Severn had called them, were three Tha'alani—two males, and one female. All adult. They were not entirely conscious, and they were also not at liberty. At all. They were bound, arms to their sides, legs strapped, to long, curved tables. They were bruised and pale.

But their stalks were weaving in the air, thrashing in a way that the rest of their bodies could not.

"The rooms were magically sealed," Tiamaris said quietly. "They could not reach the Tha'alaan. This was not, unfortunately, a precaution that was taken immediately, to the bitter regret of the Court, and the Tha'alani themselves."

"Donalan Idis believed that their gift was magical in nature. As such, he felt that it could be mimicked if it were clearly understood."

"There's nothing magical about those stalks," Kaylin said flatly.

"I did not say that everyone agreed with him. But given the refusal of the Tha'alani to cooperate with the Emperor at the time, and given our lack of understanding of the Tha'alaan, it was considered a possibility worth exploring."

"He's not touching them."

"No. He is, however—" and Tiamaris raised his voice so it could be heard over Idis's loud and angry shout "—instructing those people who were volunteered for this experiment."

Kaylin watched as Idis did the hand-waving that seemed to please Arcanists everywhere. It was, of course, accompanied by light, by a certain sense of power. Because she was watching it at a remove, she couldn't feel it, which was about the only thing she was grateful for. The light that emanated from him concentrated in his hands, and these hands he placed above the quivering Tha'alani stalks.

"Why," she asked, as she flinched and looked away from the expression upon the captive male's face, "did it take the Dragon Emperor so long to *decide* that the Tha'alani would somehow be useful?"

"A good question," Tiamaris replied, in his most neutral tone of voice.

"And a good question, as I was often told, deserves an answer."

"You were often told this by people who were failing you."

She shrugged. She had hated the Tha'alani. She really had. But watching them thrash, or worse, suddenly freeze in place, made her feel worse. All she really wanted was that they be locked away in their own part of the City where they couldn't put their hands on all her dirty secrets, all the parts of her past that were hidden *for a reason*. Unfortunately, it had never occurred to her prying little mind that that was all *they* had wanted, too. "What is he trying to do?"

"Study the physical and chemical reactions that occur in their stalks when they are presented with external thoughts or memories. Which," Tiamaris added, "you would know if you listened more carefully."

"That's not what he said."

"It's what he hasn't finished saying. He is in the process of saying it."

It made her twitchy. The watching. Her hands were clenching and unclenching as she did. And because this had *already happened* and there wasn't a damn thing she could do about it—even supposing that she would risk her career and quite probably her life for one of the Tha'alani—she clung to the question she had asked. "Why did it not occur to him before?"

"Perhaps it did. Or perhaps the abilities of the Tha'alani were not as manifestly clear as they became."

"More of the latter," Severn said quietly. He was standing quite still, his hands behind his back, his expression now unreadable. "The Tha'alani have some difficulty with either Dragons or Barrani. It's only the thoughts or memories of other mortals that come clearly and easily to their touch."

"They can't read the thoughts of Barrani?"

"They can," Teela said coolly.

"But not more than once?"

"No."

"And if they couldn't penetrate Dragon thoughts or Barrani thoughts, they weren't considered worth exploiting?"

"Kaylin," Tiamaris said coolly, "although this may seem odd to you, given what you are observing, the sole purpose of this venture was to save pain—and lives. I guarantee that the previous methods of interrogation—which methods are sometimes still resorted to in rare cases—would never meet with your approval."

She watched in the mirror, and in the end, she had to have the volume turned down completely. The Tha'alani were not mute; they could scream. And plead. And beg. They could whimper and when they did, half of their sentences were so fractured they reminded Kaylin of the Oracles. Of the Oracles without protectors, such as the two large and forbidding women who watched their doors had been.

The men who were exposing memories along those slender stalks did *not* fare better. But they weren't bound, and if there was a sword at their back, it wasn't obvious. Throughout it all, Idis took notes, and watched from an impatient, cold distance. Every so often he would perform some small magic, which he did not trifle to explain, and he would either nod or frown. Of the men who had been forced to endure the terrified touch of the Tha'alani, his only comment was, "Clearly we'll need more volunteers."

She really took a distinct disliking to him.

"You let this happen?" she said when the mirror froze at the end of what seemed a day of horror.

Tiamaris gave her a very irritated look. "It's the Interrogator's office," he said coldly. "What do you think happens there?"

She'd never really bothered to think about it. She knew that people who were suspected of grave crimes were often exposed to the Tha'alani, and that the Tha'alani ferreted out the information required. For all of her life on the right side of the river, this had been her common knowledge. Hells, she'd been *subject* to it.

"Who suggested this?" she asked Tiamaris.

"I cannot honestly recall."

"It wasn't a Dragon."

"Probably not."

"Please tell me it wasn't Idis or the Arcanum."

Severn said, "It was Idis."

Tiamaris raised a brow. "That is information that I did not possess."

He shrugged. He wasn't particularly pleased with what he was watching; his face didn't betray it, but his body did. He was ready to fight. And possibly ready to injure or kill. She could see it in the tension of his neck, the way he held his jaw, the way he was careful and deliberate in all his movements.

"What happened to the Tha'alani in these records?"

"They were returned to the care of the Tha'alani," Tiamaris replied. "I do not know what happened to them after they left Imperial hands. They were in custody for some length of time, however."

"And the test subjects?"

"Pardon?"

"The volunteers?"

He frowned. "Reports were taken. They were not free men," he added quietly. "Some were condemned men."

"All?"

"What he's trying to say," Teela drawled, "is that they were mortal. It wasn't significant one way or the other."

As Kaylin had had a lifetime to get used to this arrogance, she bit back further words and turned to the other person in the room who, by race, was also considered insignificant. Severn met her gaze. "Do you know what happened to them?"

"Not yet," he replied. "The Wolves had some transcripts and other recorded images of Idis, but this is the first time I've seen this material." He paused and added, "It's therefore the first time that I've had any chance to catch their names."

"He spoke to some of them."

"Yes."

"No—I don't need to hear it." She turned to Tiamaris again. "How many of the people who allowed the contact with the Tha'alani were left in the care of Idis?"

"They were all, in some measure, in his care."

"And you kept the interviews on record?"

"The interviews that were pertinent are now in your records and can also be accessed."

"Severn?"

He nodded grimly. "You won't like it any better."

But another thought had occurred to Kaylin—and she was certain it had occurred to Severn, as well. She turned very sharply on her heel and perched her hands lightly on her hips. "You said that the Tha'alani were cut off from the Tha'alaan during the course of the experiments."

The Dragon lord nodded.

"But you didn't know about the Tha'alaan until the experiments were underway?"

"We were…eventually informed."

"When did that occur?"

"During the studies of Group Three."

Kaylin had seen enough with Group One. A bureaucrat's name for people who had lived, and possibly died, in great pain.

"And Donalan Idis touched *none* of these?"

"None at all. He understood what they were capable of, and as an Arcanist, it can be expected that he highly prized the contents of his mind."

"You've got names," she said to Severn.

He nodded. "All of them, or all of the names spoken. For the most part, the men who were test cases did not remember their own names afterward."

Kaylin said, "Find them."

Severn said, "The Wolves are already working on it." He glanced at Teela, and then back to Kaylin. "You have other work," he told her softly.

She did. And she wasn't sure which she dreaded more: visiting Lord Nightshade again, or returning to Ybelline. But both had to be done.

* * *

It was to Ybelline that she chose to go first.

Ybelline, with her honey hair and her perfect skin and her mother's worry. For she was very like a mother, Kaylin thought, and the Tha'alaan itself, the memories of all her children, past and present.

Kaylin wore the Hawk, and she wore it, for this one day, with less pride than usual. If she hated the Tha'alani—if she *had* hated them—she was now burdened with guilt for what had been done to them, and it was hard to shoulder guilt with pride.

She had failed to mention to Marcus where she was going. She had failed to mention it, in fact, to anyone; Severn knew, and certainly Teela and Tiamaris were smart enough to guess. But it was all unofficial at the moment, and given how easy it was to offend people *without* an honest day's effort, that was best for the Hawks.

The guards waiting at the gatehouse were the same polite and distant Tha'alani, in the same armor. But she felt no fear of them now, and when she approached one, and told him her business, she also felt no qualms when his face slid into blank neutrality and his stalks quivered above his hair. *We wanted to steal this from you,* she thought. *And you paid.*

But what she said was, "I'm here to speak with Ybelline, if she's not too busy."

He was silent for a moment, in that strange blankness of expression she often saw on Tha'alani faces, and then his eyes focused and he looked at her. "She will see you, Kaylin Neya. Do you know the way?"

"I've been here before."

Half an hour later, she was certain she could *feel* Severn's exasperated laughter. But honestly, the last time she'd been here, she'd spent her time paying attention to other things— the children, the people who had stopped to stare as one large, single-minded crowd, the young man who had been their guide, and, if she were truthful, her own fear. She'd kind of followed Severn, and remembering *the route* was causing some difficulty.

Today, there were other children, so it wasn't a dead loss; she was stopped—or stopped walking—half a dozen times, just for the pleasure and indulgence of watching them laugh, or gape at her obvious disfigurement.

She was not a person who loved to be touched, but pudgy, harmless fingers were in an entirely different country, and she could return the favor, lifting a total stranger and tucking him, for a moment, into the curve of her arms. This was not the childhood of her youth, but she didn't *want* children to suffer that childhood, and it was oddly comforting—if she tried very hard not to think about the one missing girl—that this quarter existed.

Finding Ybelline did not, in the end, prove a problem. Ybelline, leaving the oddly oblong rounded dome that served as a house, found *her*. And, given that she was knee deep in children at the time, and that they were touching the emblem of the Hawk just as often as they touched her stalkless forehead, it seemed somehow right to look up and see Ybelline standing, quietly, a safe distance away.

Kaylin threw the children up into the air, caught them, each in turn, and then shoved them gently toward the waiting crowd of watchful—and amused—adults who would, with luck, keep them from running back too quickly.

"Sorry," she said, although the regret was more courtesy than real. She straightened out her tunic and tried to look more official.

"Never apologize for bringing a moment of joy into their lives," Ybelline replied gravely, her eyes smiling in a way her lips didn't. "Their joy—and their sorrow—is so immediate and so clean, the Tha'alani often draw on it in times of trouble. It brings us peace. Even their fears do, because they are so easy to calm.

"But come to my home, Kaylin. It is a better place to discuss anything of import."

Kaylin nodded, and, grateful for a guide, followed Ybelline. This time she made a careful note of how the streets turned, and in which direction; they weren't laid out in a grid at all. If streets could meander, these ones did; you could probably spend all day walking across the damn street.

But the house was familiar, with its odd door, its odd curves, its trailing greenery. Ybelline did not pause to unlock the door, but Kaylin would have been surprised had it been locked. Locked things were hidden things, and very, very few of the Tha'alani could hide in any meaningful way. She knew that now.

Also knew that Ybelline was one of those few.

She entered the house behind Ybelline, and they went to the sitting area that opened into a garden. Ybelline offered Kaylin a chair, and Kaylin took it with some gratitude. It was composed of woven strands of something that gave slightly as weight sunk into it.

Then she sat there, groping for words.

The ones she finally used were, "Donalan Idis."

Ybelline, seated across from her, actually flinched. "He is known to us," she said wearily. Her skin was pale in the light of day, pale and slightly gray. This is what *ashen* meant.

"No," Kaylin said quietly, "it's not an idle question. I'm sorry."

"It wasn't a question," Ybelline said, speaking more firmly. "But I know the name. We all know it," she added. "It came to us in the nightmare years."

"Severn explained some of the history of the Tha'alani and the Imperial Court to me. I was young, when it happened."

"I do not believe you were born," was the soft reply.

"*Very* young."

This drew the slightest of smiles from the older woman. But her words were not happy words. "Why do you come asking of Donalan Idis?"

"He was never found," Kaylin said quietly. "But...I do know that he found Grethan when Grethan left the quarter." She hesitated for a moment, and then said, "I'm sorry, but circumstances forced me to mention that one of the Tha'alani children had gone missing."

Ybelline nodded, looking unsurprised. "Had I not

decided to trust you, Kaylin Neya, I would never have asked for your help. But this…this is worse than fear."

"We're looking for him now." She hesitated again, and then said, "The Tha'alaan remembers what Donalan Idis did?"

"It remembers what he *is*," was the low, low reply. "What he did—yes. That, too, is remembered."

"But how? He didn't—according to our information—touch the Tha'alaan in any way."

Ybelline raised a golden brow. "Your researches are incorrect," she said at last. "He did not intentionally touch it. But he was responsible for the selection of his subjects, and on one occasion, one of our most powerful members had cause to touch him. I think he hoped to explain the Tha'alaan to Idis—I think he thought that the *explanation* would stay his hand."

"He tried to explain the Tha'alaan by *showing it to him?*"

Ybelline nodded. "There is no other way," she said softly.

Kaylin said, quietly, "The Tha'alaan contains the racial memories of the Tha'alani."

"Yes."

"How specific are those memories?"

Ybelline said, after a quiet that filled the room with melancholy, "I heard the Dragon's cry."

"And you understood it?"

"Yes."

"One of these days you're going to have to explain to me what brought the Tha'alani to this city."

"One of these days," Ybelline agreed.

"Do you understand Barrani, as well?"

"Yes. All of us can, if we try. The children are not as conversant with the memories. They're like…those black birds that like shiny objects. Magpies. But they will be changed by the Tha'alaan in time, just as the Tha'alaan will be changed, in small ways, by their lives."

"How easy is it to navigate these memories?"

"They are not like your Imperial Records," Ybelline replied. "They are not moved with a simple command, not at first. The young are aware of the Tha'alaan, they can speak to it, they can be comforted through it—but like everything else in their world, there is constant change. As they grow, as their capacity for thought grows and changes, they take to the Tha'alaan more naturally. The Tha'alaan watches them," she added. "I think that is the wrong word. It does more than watch, but—I think that is the best translation I can come up with. The Tha'alaan is aware of our children. Aware, in some ways, that our children need time to develop some sense of themselves as other, or separate. It approaches infants very differently than it would approach an adult. Differently," she added softly, "but in some ways, each first encounter is the same."

What do you mean? hovered on Kaylin's lips, but didn't leave; Ybelline was still struggling with words, and Kaylin had enough patience to be silent.

"Children assume that what they see and know is *all* that is seen and known. When they are young," Ybelline added. "At some point, they become aware that what *they* see and know is, in fact, different from what others see and know. It is at this age that they begin their struggle to encompass our past.

"What they first reach for, in the vast depths of history

and memory, are those memories and thoughts that are most like their own. What they first look for are those actions and experiences that they themselves understand firsthand. Does this make sense to you?"

Kaylin nodded.

"What the Tha'alaan might offer them, when they first touch these memories, are the experiences of those who were *also* present when the memory first touched becomes part of their awareness. In this way, the child learns that there are many ways of seeing the same event, and no one of those is wrong."

"And children like Grethan?"

"We spoke to him, individually," Ybelline said quietly. "And those of us who were strong enough could invoke the Tha'alaan for him. I do not know if this was a kindness, but it is what we have always done for the deaf."

"And not everyone can do this?"

"No."

"But if you can all reach the Tha'alaan—if it touches all of you—"

"To reach it, Kaylin, is almost to live in a different place. Your kind speaks of the weight of history, as if it were some-thing to be borne. Imagine that you are living it—can you speak of it coherently at the same time? Can you speak of it in a meaningful way to someone who can only see or hear you?

"At best, most of my kin can speak of it after. They can share their own experience. But the sharing of that experi-ence is not the experience itself, and even then—it is not the whole of the Tha'alaan. The Tha'alaan responds to what it finds. It is not merely records, be they as detailed as you would like."

"It…responds to what it finds."

Ybelline nodded.

"But—in the case of Idis—it could only be seen or touched through an intermediary."

Again, there was silence. Ybelline finally nodded.

"Ybelline—what did he see?"

Ybelline's eyes were wide and round as she turned to Kaylin. She did not touch Kaylin, but Kaylin thought that she didn't really need to. Ybelline had touched enough human minds in her time to understand people. Even deaf or insane ones.

Finally, Ybelline moved. And closed her eyes. "That is not the question you must ask," she said quietly.

"I think I need an answer."

Ybelline shook her head. "Not to that question, Kaylin."

As if this were some sort of test. Kaylin had failed many tests in her time. But those tests hadn't mattered. She said quietly, "What did the Tha'alaan see?"

"Power," was the single word she whispered.

"What did the Tha'alaan offer?"

"Power."

They sat opposite each other in silence. Ybelline was subdued, and seemed, to Kaylin's eye, smaller and somehow more fragile. Conversation of the type that Kaylin was used to—where people used actual words that made noise—was, it seemed to Kaylin, left to her.

She picked it up slowly and reluctantly, as if it were somehow harmful. "There are no Tha'alani mages," she said quietly. "No Tha'alani Arcanists. No Oracles."

Ybelline nodded.

"I always thought it was because they were Tha'alani. That's not true, is it?"

Ybelline shook her head.

"So in the past there were mages?"

She nodded again.

"And their memories are part of the Tha'alaan."

"Yes."

"Do they speak often to your people?"

"No."

"And your people don't somehow find them?"

"Some do," Ybelline replied quietly. "And we watch them with care."

"Why?"

Words slowly returned to the Tha'alani woman. "Because it was long ago, Kaylin. The world then was not what it is now." She paused for a moment, and then said, softly, "And because those who touch *those* memories are touching the oldest part of the Tha'alaan."

"It didn't always exist?"

"No. Our early history is lost to us, except for that which survives in the Tha'alaan. The world was harsher, then. And so, too, were my ancient kinsmen." She said, after some moments had passed, "When the Emperor chose to imprison members of the Tha'alani, when he chose to give them to Donalan Idis, the Tha'alaan was aware of it.

"And it...responded. Like a parent," Ybelline said, "whose child is threatened. Memories that had almost passed from view rose up, at the call to battle. Things that had never troubled our lives—any of our lives—suddenly broke into our dreams, and our waking visions. We call them the Nightmare years."

"But it didn't last years—"

"Kaylin, it *did*. You are the sum of your experiences, for good or ill. We are the same. There are some experiences that we were not meant to have, even in the Tha'alaan. And every waking Tha'alani who lived at that time experienced those things. Whole lives," she whispered, "calling out for vengeance and battle. People who had never so much as raised a hand against another—people like me—now remember murdering those who stood against us. And we remember those deaths without pity, because we *had none*. We remember what it was like to commune with the elements, to break the earth at our whim, to summon fire, water and air. We *remember* the words that we spoke when towers toppled. We remember the size of the armies that waited upon our word.

"And we remember watching those armies form.

"To calm the Tha'alani at that time was not a simple task. But to do otherwise was to court our destruction as a people. Whatever we may have been, we did not war against Dragons."

And Kaylin, guided by only instinct, said, "but you could."

Bitterly, Ybelline nodded. She covered her face with her

hands, and those hands were shaking. "In the quarter, there was anger unlike any anger that I have felt, before or after. And it was *because* of Donalan Idis. Because of Imperial ignorance. But those of us who were older, and who could extricate themselves from the Tha'alaan, *did*. And we could see with our own eyes, and feel only our own thoughts, and we met, and we discussed what might be done to preserve our people *as we are now,* and end the torment of those who had been taken from us.

"If at one point in our existence we wanted or needed power, that time has passed."

"And Donalan Idis saw it."

"Yes, Kaylin."

"But he *has* power. And he would know that your people don't. Why would he want—" She grimaced. Stopped speaking for a minute to let the nagging thought she couldn't quite catch grow stronger. "There's something I don't understand."

"There is probably much that you don't understand," Ybelline said, but without any edge of condescension, without any pity. "I scarce understand it myself."

"Wait. When you said you could remember summoning—"

"Yes," Ybelline said starkly. Her back straightened, and her shoulders, and she lifted her chin slightly. Her eyes were still honeyed, but they were bright now, the pupils so small they seemed to have been swallowed by color.

She lifted her hands, palm up, as if in supplication, and she spoke a single word.

Fire appeared in the air above those hands, a fire that was shaped like an Aerian.

Kaylin spoke a few words of her own, and not quietly.

But what Ybelline did next stopped even that: the stalks on her forehead stretched out, and out again—and from the fire, small tendrils of ruby and orange and gold stretched out to meet them.

CHAPTER 15

Remember the essence of fire. Remember the name of fire. Remember the shape of fire.

Hours—days—spent staring at the pristine wick of an unlit candle while a frustrated Dragon glared at her had not prepared Kaylin for this. Hells, throwing a *fireball* in the caverns beneath the hall of the High Lord hadn't. She had risen to her feet, and her hand was on her dagger, when the fire turned to face her.

And the fire was raging. She could see the way the heat distorted the air around its perfect shape. It was taller than either Kaylin or Ybelline—although that wasn't hard—and infinitely more majestic. It carried a sword of flame, whose heart was blue, and no shield. It was almost a man, although heat blurred its features, the cast of its nonexistent bones.

But not the color of its eyes.

They were Ybelline's eyes.

"So," the fire said, and it spoke with her voice, "you understand."

Kaylin did. "You could speak with the elements," she said flatly. "In a way that none of *us* could."

"Yes," Ybelline said quietly. "There are perhaps twenty-five of the Tha'alani who could do what I am now doing—but not one of them has."

"And you can…keep this secret."

"It is because I can that I am willing to risk this at all," Ybelline replied.

"And he saw this."

"Yes."

"And he wanted it. Not the Tha'alaan. He must have known that that was beyond him. But *this*—the ability to *be* the fire…" She shook her head. "Can you put it away now?"

"Yes. But it is more difficult than calling it forth. I am not the fire," Ybelline said, her voice slightly louder. "And the fire is not me. But it is living, Kaylin. In its fashion. It thinks, but not in a way that you or I think."

Twenty-five. For just a moment, Kaylin could imagine what a city at war would look like after twenty-five such mages had joined the battle. "Tha'alani are supposed to find Barrani and Dragons difficult to read."

"They are *very* difficult to read."

"But fire's easier?"

"Yes."

"Why exactly?"

"I don't know." She folded her hands, slowly, together, and as she did, the fire dwindled. But the heat remained in the air, distorting it. "Possibly because there is only *now*, with fire."

Something about the way she said the last two words made Kaylin's day worse. "And with the other elements?"

"Earth is slower," Ybelline replied. "Air is very, very hard to touch this way, and therefore much harder to control. Water, we do not—did not—call."

"Why?"

Ybelline said nothing. And looked very much as if she would go on saying nothing.

"Ybelline—have you heard the Oracles?"

The Tha'alani woman shook her head and spoke slowly, as if speaking were difficult. "We were summoned to speak with one of the Oracles. A boy who paints. The Dragon Court has been concerned with the Oracles. I have…had my own concerns."

"They're the same concerns," Kaylin said urgently. "And I need to know about water. We have, according to the Oracles, two weeks of city left." But something bothered her. Something Tiamaris had said…

Ybelline was watching her face now, reading the expressions that passed across it in rapid succession. Marcus had always said that Kaylin was loud, even in thought.

"Ybelline," Kaylin said slowly, "the child—Mayalee. You said she was abruptly cut off from the Tha'alaan?"

Ybelline nodded. Something in her face had grown sharper; perhaps the color of her eyes. It was hard to say exactly what it was. Maybe, Kaylin thought, it was the shape of fire, slow to fade. Her eyes had been *burning*.

"Had she not been, you would be able to find her?"

Again a nod.

"Donalan Idis had some method of cutting the Tha'alani off. From the Tha'alaan. One of the Dragons mentioned it," she added. "The Tha'alani themselves didn't—"

"Very, very few *can*, Kaylin. Had they the choice, they would have—but it is when we are most distressed that we reach for its comfort. Even if they could normally pull themselves away, what they suffered at the hands of the Imperial Service was *not* normal. Not even among your kind."

"I don't understand something," Kaylin finally said. "How did Idis manage what the Tha'alani themselves couldn't?"

Ybelline shrugged. "Magic."

The way she said the word would have made Kaylin smile on any other day. It appeared they had a few things in common. But any other day wasn't part of the two weeks they had left. "Donalan Idis was never allowed to finish his experiments. Did he take the child in order to do so?"

This time, the Tha'alani woman flinched. "That is now my fear," was her quiet reply.

And Kaylin thought, That was always your fear.

"Do you understand why we cannot speak of this?"

"Yes."

"And why, in the end, we chose to serve the Emperor, no matter how much he had damaged us?"

"Yes. No. I don't know. I don't think I could have done it."

"I think you could have, Kaylin. Because the consequences to the young would have been very, very high, had we done otherwise. All of us, as we can, protect our young."

Kaylin wanted to argue the point, but didn't. As a child in the fiefs, her experience spoke against the blank claim.

"You had power like that—you *have* power like that—and you hide it. Forbid it." She shook her head.

"Using the power would not have saved us," was the quiet reply. "Even had we won, even had we managed to survive, it would not have saved *what we are now*. You hide your own power. You are not as good at hiding it because were you to deny it entirely you would fail at the duties you've undertaken."

Kaylin's frown was sharp. "How do you know?"

"You are much spoken about, at Court," was the evasive reply.

Twenty-five. The city would be ash and ruins; the Dragon lords were also quite capable of summoning fire.

"Don't they want to use it?" Kaylin said at last.

"The others? No."

"But—"

"Were you to touch the Tha'alaan, Kaylin, you would understand why."

"I…"

"You don't want to."

She did, sort of. She wanted to see for herself what Donalan Idis had seen, however briefly. She wanted to know exactly what he knew, because if she did, she had some hope of understanding him, some hope of stopping him.

"I want to see the Tha'alaan," she said quietly, "but I don't want it to see *me*. And I don't know of any way to stop it."

"No. But in this case, I think you would find something you could understand in a way that most of my people can't."

"Why?"

"Because by our definition, the man whose experiences *gave* me fire was insane."

"What do you mean?" She paused for just a moment, and then said, "Like the deaf?"

"Yes, Kaylin. Like your kind."

"But—he *had* the Tha'alaan to guide him. How could he be…"

Ybelline again said nothing. "I cannot tell you more about water," she said, "because we do not summon water. And more than the fire, I will not risk. It is *felt*," she added, "when it comes."

"But you said you could keep it from the Tha'alaan."

"I can. But your mages sense magic, when it is done. If my kin are *not* mages, it is choice that compels them. They would know. And they would come to me," she added, with just the hint of a wry smile.

"I think Donalan Idis wants to summon water. And given the Oracles' visions, I think he may well succeed."

"Stop him."

"We're trying. We can't *find* him. But…" She looked at Ybelline. "We did find the people we think were his last landlords."

"Where?"

"Near the merchant quarter. They were dead," she added, and then, "drowned."

Ybelline was silent, absorbing this information. "I assume that they weren't drowned in one of your baths?"

"No."

"And you think the Tha'alani would understand how they were killed?"

"I didn't think you would," Kaylin said. "Until I came here today. I thought it was something only Idis would understand."

The hesitation that she would have said didn't exist was picked up by Ybelline. "You have your secrets," she told Kaylin.

"I have my job," Kaylin replied, punting. "The day I received your invitation, I had just returned from an investigation that involves another missing child. A girl. She's older than Mayalee," she added. "And I think, stranger."

"You've met her?"

"No. But I've seen her. She knew my name."

Ybelline said nothing for a long time. And then she said, "It is time for you to leave, Kaylin. There are now matters I must discuss with my kin."

Kaylin nodded. Something made no sense to her. But until she could figure out *what the damn thing was,* she wasn't going to be asking questions that would give her anything like a useful answer.

Ybelline saw Kaylin to the gates. She did not speak as they walked, but every so often her face would lose all expression, and her eyes... Her eyes were like crystal, absent any wine to give it color. The color would return, slowly, but in any case, Ybelline did not stop walking.

When they reached the gatehouse, Kaylin stopped. "Donalan Idis had a way of cutting the Tha'alani off."

Ybelline nodded slowly.

"Maybe that's what he did with Mayalee. We think—if she's with him—that she's still alive." She wanted to offer more, but there wasn't anything more she *could* offer. Yet.

Squaring her shoulders, she left the quarter, which seemed so much smaller and so much less threatening than it once had—when she'd had the bird's eye view, and the safety of distance. Funny, how things changed.

The sun was setting by the time she reached the Ablayne, and the familiar bridge that crossed it. The banks were deserted, and the streets on the wrong side of the bridge had already started to empty. Which only made sense. The Ferals were waiting, somewhere, for night to fall. When it did, they'd own the streets of the fief. No fieflord had ever attempted to stop them.

She toyed with the idea of removing her uniform, but she didn't really have the luxury of time. Castle Nightshade wasn't exactly at the edge of the fief, and she wasn't in a carriage; she could walk there at a good clip before things got dangerous. But not if she stopped to change. Not if she dawdled on the bridge, as she so often did. It was a barrier, that bridge. And this river.

Funny, how often she and Severn had come to the Ablayne, had stood on the wrong side of its banks, had stared with longing at the freedom that lay on the other side—all without crossing the bridge itself. No guardhouse protected the bridge; no guards patrolled it. They could just as easily have walked across it, to see for themselves how the free lived.

But they had stayed in the fief. Had told themselves stories about what lay across the bridge. Dreams, she thought, as she crossed it, heading toward her past. The reality? Freedom took work.

And if Nightshade had his cages, the Emperor had his Interrogators.

No, she thought. *It's not the same.* She imagined the Foundling Halls, the Halls of Law, the market—none of these things existed in Nightshade.

In Nightshade the only law *was* the fieflord.

But in Elantra, the only law was the Emperor. It hadn't saved the Tha'alani. And if the Oracles were any judge, it wouldn't save Elantra, either.

And what will?

Kaylin began to walk quickly. Sunset, liberal with pink and purple, began to turn buildings into silhouettes. Two missing children. Two.

But…there had only been one child in the merchant's quarter. A girl. If Donalan Idis was somehow involved with the other child, wouldn't there have been another? Or was one of them already dead?

She hated the thought, and she couldn't dislodge it, so she walked faster, until she was almost trotting. The silhouettes, the skyline here, were easy to follow because Castle Nightshade was so distinct. It wasn't as tall as the Imperial Castle, edict or no—but it was the tallest building in the fief.

It was also guarded, this close to night. Two guards, armored, no surcoat in sight. She walked up the length of the path to greet them, and paused some ten feet away.

One of the guards bowed low. She recognized him, even though the scant light robbed his features of sharp definition. "Lord Andellen," she said as he rose.

"Lord Kaylin," he replied gravely. She hadn't the heart to tell him to call her anything else. To Andellen, the title had a meaning beyond "let's make Kaylin uncomfortable."

"Have you been to the High Court lately?" she asked him softly.

"No, Lord."

"But you can."

"I can, yes. But it would not be wise at the moment. The Lord of the High Court is much occupied of late." There was a question in the words.

"I haven't been," she replied, as if he'd asked it. "But yes, it's why I'm here."

"You come late."

"I always arrive late, in Nightshade. If the Ferals hunted at dawn," she added ruefully, "I'd be here then." She spoke low-caste Barrani, but given that she seldom spoke anything but Elantran unless forced, Andellen accepted it as the courtesy that it was.

"Lord Nightshade will see you," Andellen told her. "He has left word that you are to be admitted whenever you choose to arrive."

Kaylin nodded as brusquely as she could. Castle Night-shade was not a comfortable place to be, seen from the outside. From the inside? Worse. And to get there, she had to walk through a portal that looked like an ebony portcullis. She walked between the two guards and headed toward the magical entrance.

And swore when she bounced.

Light crackled off her hands, small bolts of flashing blue. She stared at them, and at the portcullis, before she tried again, with much the same results.

"Andellen?"

"I…have never seen this happen before."

"Could you fix it?"

His dark brows rose a fraction into the line of unfettered hair. "Even if I thought it possible, I would not try. The Castle defends itself."

"And I'm a threat now?"

He said nothing.

Clearly, if Nightshade had left word with his guards, he'd failed to tell his damn home.

Lord Nightshade greeted Kaylin from the wrong side of the gates. Kaylin watched his very slow arrival with a mixture of curiosity and irritation.

The portal didn't open. It thinned. The air between the fake bars began to shimmer, and the bars themselves seemed to slowly dissolve into that light. Although Kaylin disliked magic, she found this interesting; she had never actually seen the portal open or close, being on the inside of its magic.

The fieflord was dressed in black and silver; he wore a sword, and hints of armor reflected light as fabric parted when he moved. His hair was pulled back, exposing the elegant lines of his face.

As usual, that face gave nothing away. "Kaylin," he said gravely. He did not offer her a bow, as Andellen had done— but Barrani hierarchy would have forbid it, anyway. "There seems to be some difficulty?"

She shrugged. "If you call my inability to actually enter the Castle a difficulty, then yes, there is."

"Show me." He stepped lightly to the side, and waited.

Kaylin, not grudging the obedience if it would satisfy her curiosity, walked into the portcullis. And bounced back.

"I…see."

"Good. Do you mind explaining it?"

"Yes."

So much for obedience. "I don't suppose there's another way in?"

His smile, more felt than seen, told her she wouldn't like the answer.

He led her around the Castle, leaving Andellen and the nameless guard behind with a few curt words. When they were out of earshot—when they were out of shouting range—he paused. "What exactly have you been doing in the past few days?"

"Not dying," she replied. "You?"

He surprised her; he chuckled. "The same." He reached out and touched her cheek, pressing his palm lightly against the mark he had put there when they had first met. She felt a sharp, sharp sting and took a step back. His hands were warm.

"You have twice passed beyond me," he said softly, lowering his arm. "Only places of power are that well guarded. You were not at Court," he added. He began to walk, and she fell in step just behind him.

"No." It wasn't a question, but she answered it anyway. "Not the Barrani Court, at any rate."

"The Imperial Court?"

"Only the library."

"Someone took you to see the Arkon?" His eyes widened almost imperceptibly. It was the Leontine equivalent of a roar of outrage, and it made her laugh. Well, it made her want to laugh. Which, given the events of the day, was welcome.

"I didn't attract the attention of the Arkon," she told him. "Lord Sanabalis and Lord Tiamaris were having a heated discussion, and the Arkon apparently doesn't like noise in the library."

"I...see. This would not have anything to do with the Dragon's cry?"

"Which cry?"

"Learn to dissemble, Kaylin," he replied with a hint of disapproval.

She had the grace to redden. "Yes," she offered, by way of an apology. "I set him free. He was dead," she added.

One brow rose. "Dead?"

She nodded.

"But not free to fly."

"No. If that's what dead Dragons do."

"You did not see him?"

She hesitated for a moment, and when she chose to speak her voice was hushed. "Yes. I saw."

"And seeing, can you doubt?"

"Not him," she said at last. "But I don't know if the others are like him. I don't really understand Dragons."

"I often doubt that you understand mortals. It is no wonder that Dragons are beyond you. But this...dead Dragon—what did you do to free him?"

Before she could think, she said, "I told him the end of his story."

Nightshade stopped walking.

Kaylin managed to stop in time to avoid running into his back. She also stepped back, waiting, her hand on her dagger.

He turned. "You told him the end of his story." The words, coming from Nightshade, had a weight and a meaning that Kaylin had failed to give them.

She nodded.

"And how did you know that this...telling...would free him?"

"I don't know. I didn't think about it," she added. "I just did it."

"Very well. How did you *know* the end of his story?"

She shook her head. "I wanted to help him," she said. "I—I wanted to say *something*. He'd been waiting so long. I just—I just started talking."

"Given the amount of thought you put into your words,"

was the cool reply, "it's not a small wonder that you survived the attempt."

"I wasn't in danger. He was *dead*."

"The dead are a danger. They have always been a danger." He lifted a hand, palm out. "And where the restless dead are concerned, something binds them to the living. He was a Dragon," he added. "What was his hoard?"

She lifted a hand to her throat. To the empty space around her neck where a dead man had, for a moment, hung a chain. "Duty," she told him.

"And you accepted the responsibility that he failed." It wasn't a question.

"He didn't fail it."

"He failed." Nightshade's frown was thin. "And you hope to succeed."

"I didn't," she said. "I—"

"You must learn to weigh the consequences of your power, Kaylin. But I understand now why you could not pass through the portal. What you carry—whether you see it or not—was too heavy a burden for a Dragon whose will was strong. Ignorance," he added, "does not change fact. It is dusk now. If you do not wish to spend an evening fighting Ferals, you must either leave or chance the back ways.

"Why *did* you come?"

"To ask you about Donalan Idis."

Nightshade nodded grimly. "The back ways," he told her softly. "In truth, I am surprised that it took you this long to return to the Arcanist."

"You could come to my home."

His brows actually rose. "Not, I think, while the Wolf prowls," he said, after a very long pause. "Not while you live in mortal certainty that a home is just a place you *call* your own."

"And pay for."

"You don't yet understand what that means," was his soft reply. But it was not cold. "Come then, Kaylin. When Lord Tiamaris first visited this Castle, he did not enter through the portcullis. Dare what he dared."

"What will I face?"

"In truth, I do not know. This Castle is as old as the oldest building in the fiefs, and like the others, it was not built by mortals. I was tested, when I first chose this as my abode. Tiamaris was tested," he added, "although he arrived with no desire to rule." He paused and then added, "The Castle, as you've seen from the inside, is not quite...fixed in space. The portcullis has never functioned as a portcullis to my knowledge. There is evidence to suggest that previous owners chose to decorate the grounds as they saw fit—and this, the Castle allowed. But to change the Castle itself is neither lightly done or completely possible."

"So it's magic."

He frowned. "You have a way of robbing words of their splendor," he told her.

"If I had a choice—" *I'd rob the Castle of splendor, as well. Who wants a home where the rooms change and the front door is an invitation to nausea?* But she thought better of her choice of words because there was something about the Castle that suggested intelligence—and most intelligent

beings could be rather easily offended by practical sugges-
tions, in Kaylin's experience.

"In general, you don't," was the quiet reply. Lord Nightshade had navigated one forbidding face of the Castle as he
spoke. Kaylin reached out every so often to touch the seams
between huge slabs of worn stone, as if seeking the reassurance of weakness. She couldn't actually imagine that there
was another way in—but perhaps the designers of the Castle
had left another way *out*.

When Nightshade stopped, he stopped a fair distance
from the walls, by the side of a well. It was old and disused;
there was a pump arm that was more rust than metal, and
if there had ever been a bucket on the chain that hung
slack—and rusted over—it had long since decayed.

She expected him to keep moving.

He clearly expected her to stop. She did, because he was
leading, and following from the front had never worked all
that well for her.

But when he didn't speak or start walking again, she
wilted. "This?" she asked, pointing at the well.

"This."

She looked down. It was very, very dark. Dusk didn't
lessen the shadows, but Kaylin had a suspicion that full
noon wouldn't make much of a dent in them, either. "I
don't suppose you brought a lamp?"

"No."

Neither had she. She leaned over, balancing her weight
on stone that looked as if it should crumble. It didn't. Along
the sides of the well were rungs that had seen better days—

probably the same days the pump had. She lost sight of them to darkness. "I was going to ask you if I could use the back way instead of the front one," she told Nightshade as she swung her feet over the well's lip.

"You may not have the same desire once you've entered the back way."

"I don't have the desire now, and I haven't even started." She pivoted and placed her feet on the closest rung, slowly surrendering to gravity. The rung held. She grimaced, and stepped down, and down again, until the rungs carried all of her weight. The rust made the bars rough and patchy, as if some metalworker had thought to mimic tree bark. Hanging on the rungs, she looked up at the large circle stone made. Beyond it, Nightshade was watching. "You're going to follow me?

In response he lifted a hand almost carelessly, upending his palm just above her. Fire flared almost white. It began to descend slowly, until it was just below Kaylin's feet. Light, she thought. She felt absurdly grateful.

"In a manner of speaking. The Castle cannot keep me out," he added. "Nor would it seek to try. And where you go, I am not entirely certain I can follow."

Gratitude was so capricious. "This is like the Tower in the High Halls, isn't it?"

"Very good, Kaylin. Possibly the most intelligent question you've asked about the Castle. It is like and unlike the Tower in the High Halls. Had you not passed the test of those Halls, I would not now allow you to take the risk you are taking.

"I am not even certain that you *could* enter, were that the case. But you have surprised my former kinsmen. Surprise me now."

"And if I don't?"

He didn't answer.

This is stupid, she thought, stepping down again. *This is completely stupid. Why in the hells am I even trying so hard to get into the damn Castle?*

Because there wasn't a good answer—hells, she'd have settled for a bad one—she kept on going. The light was welcome at least twice—because at least twice, the rungs had fallen free, leaving a gap that might have killed her otherwise. She wasn't tall, but she stretched, balancing her weight entirely with her hands while her feet struggled for purchase.

The darkness above her, however, grew until she could no longer make out the mouth of the well. Could no longer see Nightshade.

She didn't trust him. She didn't *like* him. But she would have felt better had he accompanied her, because the Castle was his in some way, and she couldn't quite believe that he would knowingly kill her.

She could, however, believe that she could die here.

Everything, she thought, gritting her teeth in frustration, *everything* was a test of some kind. The Barrani knew no other way. You could prove yourself worthy, or you could fail.

There were whole days where even the concept of proving

herself worthy was tiring. It was a pointless test. When she helped the midwives, it was different. It was the best fight she knew: she faced death, and she won. The fact that it was someone else's death—usually a stranger's—didn't change the fact. In some ways, it made it stronger.

She stopped her downward crawl.

Was this really any different?

The Castle had denied her because she still carried something that she couldn't even see, let alone touch. It was linked to water. And somehow, the water was now linked to Donalan Idis, the man who almost certainly held a captive Tha'alani child. He was an Arcanist, which in Kaylin's vocabulary was just another synonym for *death*.

She wanted to talk to Nightshade.

She wanted to know what change the Castle had sensed.

Neither of these were good enough reason to be here, clinging to the side of a well that hadn't seen water in decades, by the look of it. But the best thing that Marcus had ever taught her—perhaps because it was something she *wanted* to hear—was to trust her instincts.

The middle of a fight, he used to say, was not the time to worry about the nicety of your stance. You fought as well as you could, you hoped that it was enough—if you had time for even that much thought. *You want to survive,* he'd told her. *Trust your instincts. Don't second-guess them until the fight is over.*

Then you can dissect your performance to your heart's content.

What if I don't remember enough of it?

Trust me—you come close to death, you'll remember how you stepped out of its way.

He'd been right, of course. Marcus was almost never wrong. Kaylin took a deep breath. And then, before she could second-guess herself, she let go.

CHAPTER 16

It was a *long* drop. However, since she had no wings—and if she could have corrected one birth defect, it would have been the one that made her human, not Aerian—long was relatively fast. She had no time to regret her decision; no time to second-guess what had come so instinctively to her. She had time to register falling as a very unpleasant sensation that implied that her stomach had stayed put when everything else had dropped—but even that didn't last very long; not even as long as the darkness did. Nightshade's gift of light apparently had to descend the hard way; gravity didn't mean much to it.

But if she had managed to shock Nightshade, he gave no sign of it at all—and she would have felt it, because she *wanted* to. So much for being grown-up.

What she felt instead was water.

Water surged up to meet her as she plummeted, feet-first, into what was obviously a disoriented tunnel. But the water was strange. It was both clear and luminescent; she could see its shape. It was a giant hand, unadorned by rings, its palm wider and flatter than the length of spray that served as fingers. It was not a fist, and she felt an absurd sense of gratitude as she passed into the mound of its palm.

It gave with her weight—it could hardly do anything else—but it had moved up to meet her in midfall, and it also began to drop, matching its speed to hers, until she *could* land in its center and notice that it was water, and not ground. Clint, on one of his early flights with Kaylin wrapped snugly in his arms, had made clear that water, from the height Aerians chose to fly at, was not a lot more forgiving than stone when it came to breakable things—like bones, for instance. Clint was always gentle; he had threatened to drop her when she'd made it clear she didn't believe him, but he had never actually *done* it.

Now, years later, she believed him—but the days when she could play with his flight feathers and beg him to carry her over the city were almost gone. She missed them; that was the truth. She missed what he would willingly do for her orphans in the Foundling Halls. She had never thought it would be possible to *miss* being a child.

But if she had stayed young, she could not be here, doing what she was doing: trying to save the life of a child.

And that was *why* she was here, and if she had forgotten it for even a minute, she clung to the certain knowledge as fingers of liquid wrapped themselves around her tightly and bore her down.

She expected that they would come to rest near land, and

in that, she wasn't mistaken. But she could see land—such as it was, it was such a pathetic patch of dirt—only because the water shed light; shed it *and* contained it. She could push her arm through the liquid; she could certainly push her head through it, because breathing was kind of important, and it was the first thing she made certain she *could* do.

But the water was content, for a time, to hold her, and while it was cool, it was pleasantly cool. The days this time of year were anything but.

It had to be water, she thought, as she lifted a hand to her unadorned throat. The essence of water.

You could live without food for a lot longer than you could live without water. You couldn't live *at all* without water, according to the midwives. It was in water that you were conceived, in water that you grew, and only when water broke did you stand a decent chance of being born *and* surviving the experience.

But you couldn't breathe water; you could easily drown in it; you could fall into it and break your neck.

Yes, the water said.

She startled and jumped, sending little eddies through the hand that held her. "Who said that?"

You already know.

And she did, too. But if her life with the Hawks had prepared her for all sorts of grim magic—and give the frosty, stiff-necked old teachers this much, it had—it hadn't prepared her for this. Her whole body vibrated with the syllables.

"You can talk."

Yes.

"Could you always talk?"

Not in this way, Kaylin Neya. And were you not Chosen, never to you.

Kaylin nodded.

You have come late to this game, the water added.

"I don't generally play games."

No.

She started to say something, thought the better of it. The hand that held her had joined itself to the current of a river that ran in a narrow groove. Rock lip could be seen on either side, proof that the river's passage had slowly worn away stone. Kaylin didn't particularly want to be part of the grit that helped to *further* wear stone down, but the water had other plans for her; she stayed in the middle of the current, occasionally jolting up or down as the riverbed did.

"I have a question," she said as she watched the darkness go by.

The silence was, as they say, deafening. So much for conversation. Kaylin, on the other hand, wasn't one to let silence go by unhindered.

"If I came late to the game, what have I missed?"

But like so many people she could privately rail against, it seemed content to offer criticism without actually offering any useful advice.

Oh, what the hells.

"Do I look fat in this?"

* * *

As far as castles went, the one Nightshade called home was definitely less ornate than most. Big caverns and scant light usually had that effect. The river in which she'd been traveling as if it were some sort of bumpy, elemental carriage, came at last to a stop in what was essentially a dingy lake. The water still glowed, and the fleet shape of moving shadows far below her feet told Kaylin that some things shunned light. The fact that they weren't comfortingly *small* shapes made her a little uneasy, but only a little; although nothing she touched seemed solid, she didn't drop. And given that she was wearing armor, she should have.

But natural laws and magic seldom coincided. It seemed to Kaylin that magic was one way of breaking all natural law. Maybe that was why she, Hawk at heart, hated magic so much. It couldn't be pinned down, and analysis was so much guesswork. How could something be just a tool—as the Hawklord often tried to call magic—when it was so unpredictable and wild?

It is not just a tool, a voice said.

And Kaylin knew, hearing it, that she had just discovered the essence of water.

But the essence of water didn't speak *as* water, and in the faint light cast by liquid, Kaylin could see where the river butted up against the smoothed flat of damp rock. Could see, as she squinted, that above that damp patch of solid ground—ground that she was slowly approaching—something stood, arms at rest, waiting for her to arrive. As if it had always waited, would always wait.

She saw robes that were at once all colors she had ever seen, and at the same time, none; saw light in those colors that faded and blended, one into the other. Rainbows were like this, but rainbows were transparent, thin, and easily lost to the turn of the head, the passing whim of cloud.

And this was different. The light and color had taken the shape of robes, and those robes fell, like yards of insanely expensive fabric, from slender shoulders, blanketing cold, dark rock, and turning it, for a moment, into something that signified all of the earth, its hidden diamonds, its endless crevices.

Hair trailed down the back of these odd robes, and the hair, unlike the robes themselves, was as dark as the water the Hawklord said lay at the bottom of the seas in the distance. Dark—not black, not blue-black of midnight, but deeper than that.

Staring ahead, Kaylin barely registered the fact that what was now beneath her feet *was* solid rock; that the water that had caught her in her graceless fall and had carried her here like some enchanted boat, had now fallen away, joining again the rapids of the underground river.

And when this being turned, light resolved itself into a face that Kaylin realized she had expected to see. Not consciously, never that—this was magic, after all, and magic had its own imperative, its own wild logic.

The girl who had spoken her name what felt like years ago, in the garden of a man known as *the Keeper,* met her gaze and held it until Kaylin looked away.

Had to look away, there was so much in those silent, dark, wide eyes.

"Kaylin," she said, and lifted a translucent hand, as if she were a ghost.

As if, Kaylin thought, she had already failed her, and this was all that was left.

She should have been angry. She knew she should have been angry. All her fear, all the silent terror, the pressure of the need to rescue some helpless child—it had all been wasted to a…a trick. She could no more rescue *this* girl than she could rescue all the dead children in the fiefs another lifetime ago; could no more rescue her than she could rescue the children who were dying even now, unable to call for help, unheard.

And yet… And yet…

She took a step forward toward the girl, whose eyes were dark and bruised, and as she did, she realized that the light she had *thought* emanated from water came, instead, from the hollow of her own throat. What lay there beneath her fingers—the fingers raised almost involuntarily—was the pendant she had received as a burden from the ghost of a Dragon in the Imperial Archives. It was *real,* here. That should have told her something.

"Yes," the girl replied, in the same soft voice that had spoken her name. "You can see me because you wear the pendant. If you were wiser, you would be able to use it, and possibly to use it against me. I do not know.

"I remember the Guardian," she added, never looking away from Kaylin's face, although Kaylin frequently looked away, for seconds at a time, from hers. "I remember his voice. The ripple of it carries still."

"You killed him," Kaylin said bitterly.

"Yes. I was younger then," she added, as if that made *any* sense.

"You're *not* a child," Kaylin snapped, letting anger speak for her, because otherwise, she had no words. "Children don't kill."

"Children *can't* kill. They are too weak. Your children," she added. "And I...was...not as I am now. I was aware," she added. "But awareness... It was a small eddy in a large current. I was young," she said again. "And also old, Kaylin."

"You look like a child now."

"I am not."

"You choose to look—"

"You perceive," the soft voice said. "It is your gift."

"And the Dragon's?" She touched the pendant again.

"He was strong. He called you, Kaylin."

"He called a few thousand years too early."

"But you came."

"He was dead. I came late."

"He was dead, but he did not surrender his burden, and because he did not, the waters subsided in time."

"Did you want him dead?"

"No."

"But you killed him."

"Yes."

"And the city—"

"*Yes.*" And the water lifted its hands to its face, and Kaylin surrendered then: she saw a young, frightened girl, and no matter how much her inner voice screamed in outrage, she could see *nothing* else. And maybe, she thought, as she walked toward the girl, if she were honest, it was because she didn't *want* to.

She reached out for the girl with her arms, and drew her into their circle.

And the light at the base of her neck became *fire*, and the shadows—and Kaylin's awareness—were burned away in an instant. She lost sight of the water, the cavern, the light—and last, lost hold of herself, sinking into a different kind of depth.

Remembering what Evanton had told her before she surrendered: *Water is deep.*

She had dared currents before, and would again—but they had been water, and the currents now…were the memories of a different life. It swallowed her whole.

In the darkness—and it was dark, and worse, it was the type of dark men cause—she heard the screaming, and it woke her because it *burned* at the back of her mind: the screaming, the brief, terrified screaming, of the children. And oh, she could gather their pain; she'd done it before. She had had to do it before, because *that* was her gift: the gathering of pain, the stanching of mortal wound in this insignificant way. And she *did* it because there was nothing else she could do. She could not save life. She *could not* even bear witness.

All she could do was deny the enemy these few moments of cruelty, the satisfaction of the deaf.

And that was not enough. Sooner or later they would learn that she had done it. Sooner or later, they would figure out that they could cause their precious pain if they *took the children farther away*.

She felt the voices of her kin, much closer. They would be the valuable prisoners, she thought, swallowing bile. She knew the end of the story. They would—like she—hear the cries of the children, and the cries would wound them, scar and cripple them, until they broke. But they would not die, although they might wish it. They would *serve*.

And she?

She lifted a hand in the darkness; felt the weight of manacles, like thick adornments. The end and the beginning.

But the hopelessness, the guilt, that had already begun to cripple the others broke her in a different way. She would not serve *these* masters. But maybe, just maybe, she would serve the masters that drove them in their endless fear and rage and cruelty. In the darkness, touching the minds of her kin, learning the truth behind the old stories, the grim stories, she broke her vows. The vows of a healer. The vows of a peaceful man.

What the children had suffered would not be in vain.

She would *make* the enemy pay.

For if her gift was the taking of pain, and by its absence, the giving of comfort, she was *also* cursed. They had come, the Feladrim; they had come seeking *power*. She would *show them power*.

For she had touched their warriors, been touched by their warriors, and she knew—as her people refused to know—that there was only one way to stop them. Fill the night with their screams and the screams of *their* kin.

Not that way, not that way, Uriel—that way lies madness.

"There is no other way!" She could feel the words, in her throat; she could not speak them any other way. Her people had no way of conveying all she felt; no safe way. "They want power—I'll show them *power.*"

And the fire came at her call, then; fire such as the world had seen only at its savage dawn. She felt it take her, the fire, and she welcomed its heat, its ancient hunger—for its hunger was like her own.

Uriel, no!

But there was no denial. They could not touch her, here— her people *or* her enemies. The Tha'alani could speak to each other, without the necessity for touch, if they were close enough. But they could not *stop* her with just their thoughts, their useless pleas.

She was done with peace. She was done with mercy. The screams that followed in this night to end all dawn carried pain and fear—and she laughed at the sound, and her gift— the gift for which she was known, the gift for which she was revered—deserted her entirely.

Let. Them. Burn.

Later: the burying of her kin.

The barbarians revered the dead. Her people had never understood why. The dead were dead. Once the spirit had fled, the flesh was just flesh, like any other. Cruel flesh, to invoke the spirit of loss, and quicken the memory. But flesh nonetheless. Ask the carrion birds if it tasted different than the dead flesh of Feladrim gryphons, and the answer would be no.

But touched by their madness, broken by it, she wanted to give the bastards a different answer.

And so, the burying of the dead.

The city of the Feladrim—one of their many—was upon the plains, where gryphons might feed from the wild herds that grazed under the open skies. Around her, her kin gathered, and their number had grown. Their metalsmiths had turned their hands to weapons, and if their work was rough, it was good. They burned with the fires that she had started on the long night, and they reveled in them in this false light of day. She would never know day again.

But freedom? She would have freedom for the Tha'alani. She could hear their voices, carried by the winds. She had called the air and it had come like a gale, but here, she forced it—barely, barely—to be a breeze.

For the people of the Feladrim, she was not so kind; they could not leave their city. And they tried. But gryphons, beasts of war, could not fly easily in a wind that was elemental, and those that tried lay broken and bleating upon the ground like sheep, circled on high by the shadows of vultures too wise to dare the currents.

She let the wind take her words; let it fill her people with its roar. Wind also swept up the corpses of the fallen, as it had swept the flies and carrion creatures from their still faces, their closed eyes. She heard the gasp of her people as the dead rose, carried with infinite care to heights that not even the winged would dare.

She wanted them to *see*. She wanted them to remember. Her people. The people whose kindness, whose mercy, had failed these children. She wanted them to *understand*.

And she wanted the Feladrim to understand, as well. They lived in a city of the dead, and the dead were now returning to them, vengeful ghosts, instruments of justice, on winds that *would never again* carry their warriors, their spears, or their savagery.

Uriel—there are children there—

"There are children who will grow to be warriors," she had answered, the words smooth with long hours of practice. No quiver in them, no hesitation. Just truth. Had she not seen the truth for herself? Had she not felt it in the bewildered terror of the dying?

They will grow to hate us and fear us, as their fathers hated and feared us before them. Uriel, do not do this.

"Old man, they will never grow."

And the voices in her head had fallen silent, and if the silence was the silence of fear, she didn't care. She wanted peace. All she had ever wanted was peace. And how she achieved it in the end was no business but her own.

But she heard herself speaking anyway, breaking silence as she had sworn not to do. "We failed them," she told him. "If we chose to fail *only ourselves*, it would signify nothing. But we hesitated, and we wept, and we begged. I am done with begging. I *am done with failure*."

Were there children there? Yes. Foreign, ugly children,

held by their weeping mothers, their ancient grandmothers, foreheads smooth for all that they wore the whirling tattoos of their clan. She could see them with the wind's eye, but she could not hear their voices. Their pain did not call to her, did not accuse her.

And she called the earth, as the bodies of the dead Tha'alani children settled into the streets of the distant city, having been carried there by elemental air, and laid to rest among the screaming, weeping Feladrim. The earth, the ancient, slow earth, came as she woke it. She felt its tremble in her upraised arms, felt the weight and the authority of its slumbering muscle.

Her people watched, and all voices, even the voices wind *could* touch, were silent.

"Today, we bury our dead," she shouted, forcing her voice to be heard across the very plains. And she let the earth go, then, but only toward the city.

She watched as the towers shuddered and trembled; watched as the foundations were broken away, like the roots of weeds in a small garden. The walls, the buildings, the lives of the Feladrim and the bodies of the dead—all were one, to the voice of the earth. She would bury her dead, yes, and there was no more fitting burial ground than this.

And the broken buildings—if in truth the earth left them there—would be all the markers their graves would need.

Of the weariness and the fatigue, she would speak little, although it was great. The voices of the fire and the air and earth would haunt her memories in a way that not even the dead could. She was strong enough to bear it, the ancient wilderness of voice, the familiar territory of desire.

The first city was not the only city she would destroy.

And after each city, her own kin would return to her and ask her, *What now?* The voices of the young burned bright, like steel new tempered and in need of quenching, and she would quench it in blood, time and again, and *this time* it would not be the blood of her people, but their enemies'.

She would call herself *king*, and she would be called *king*, this foreign, ugly word. The enemies of her enemies would come, bearing offerings tainted by fear, and because the fear was good, because she could use it, she would accept what they offered.

But when the voices of the children were raised in ugly glee, she would stop for the first time. Because this, too, was death.

This was not what she had wanted to save.

She was strong enough to call the fire and the earth and the air—but in her youth there was only one element that she had been encouraged to summon, only one that she had been unwise enough to trust. And in that youth, her own voice had not been raised to war and pain and death; that would come later.

But later was now, she realized. And she lived in the Night of war. She had never emerged from it, and she realized that she never would. What she was—all that she was—was built on death.

But all that she *had wanted* was not.

Her pride, however, was possibly as strong as her power, and she could not now turn to the men and women whose voices of gentle horror she had ignored. Time had whittled them away, taking at last what she would not surrender to their enemies.

But those that time had not taken? She could not bear to prove them right. To acknowledge that her own failure, more subtle than theirs, was still a failure.

No, she thought grimly. My work is not yet done; I will not give it over or abandon it. Half-done, and it has all been in vain. While our enemies live or rule, there is no safety, and if our children are not what they were, they are *alive*, and in life, there is hope and possibility.

She told herself this, and perhaps because she had been riven from the voices of the elders, she could believe it.

But when she came at last to the heart of the Empire of her enemies, the city that rested upon the harbor at the edge of the sea, there were no dead children to bury, and the voice of the earth was not strong enough. The voice of the winds could keep the ships in harbor, but they had weathered such storms before, and the storms here were laden with water.

There was only one element left her.

The oldest, the easiest to summon.

And she hesitated for the first time, while in the city, the people panicked. That much, the air had given her.

But the water, when it came, gave her nothing. It took a shape and a form that was most like her own people's, translucent like the story of a mortal ghost, strands of hair falling wayward into its deep, dark eyes, tracing the contours of a hollow face.

It has been long since you summoned me, the water said gravely. *Has it been a harsh season of drought?*

She faltered, for the voice was an old voice. The fire and the air, she simply released to their own desires. The earth was heavier and slower, and harder to work with, although she could speak with its rumbling cadences.

But the water simply waited.

"You have drowned men in your time," she said at last, using her voice, and only her voice. "And it is that time, now."

I have drowned men, the water replied. *Even your own kin, in the end. But of them, I kept memory and story and message to carry until the end of time.*

"I desire you to carry no message," she told the water. "No message save death."

But the water remained where it was. *Will you order me to destroy this human city?*

"I will."

It is not my desire.

"I have heard your desire," she said, speaking sharply now, while her kin gathered around her. "You lie."

You have heard my desire, but you have not heard all of my desire. You have heard your fear, my anger, the place where both dwell.

But I have heard your sorrow, and your joy, your anger and your fear. You are alive. *The gift of life is not all of one thing or another—you are not only what you hate, not only what you love, not only even what you are aware of. You are all of these things, and will be more.*

Kaylin felt the words as a physical blow. Winded, silent,

she listened to the cadences of the water. She had no choice; the wind couldn't snatch *these* words away. She had called the water for all of her life. Her grandmother had called the water before that, and in tribes scattered across this world, others had done the same.

They had called the water in times of drought, in times of desperation; they had fought the voice—the most ancient voice—of water, denying it death and drowning and the floods that would make the plain a graveyard. They had asked, instead, for the water of life, and the water had acceded in the end.

That was the teaching. The old teaching.

But in her long life, the water had seldom fought her; if it had come at her call—and it always did—it had come in the end to succor the fields, or to hold an infant just a little longer in the safety of a womb. It had spoken, and she had replied.

And she realized that this was why she had had no desire to summon the water: it was not, had never been, a voice of death for her people. If she had heard death in its depths—and she had—it was the voice of a history that she had had no part in.

But the rules were still rules, and the water would obey her if she fought it. If she fought its impulse, if she denied it its will.

And there, a mile or two below her feet, lay the last obstacle: one city. One city that the water could destroy. It would be easy, this close to the ocean. Even the great ships that had been built to withstand the storms would founder and break; they had not been designed to survive below the water.

"Destroy the city," she said. "Take it into yourself and hold it fast."

But the water had not yet done. *I cannot take it into myself*, it replied. *Only you and your kind, child. There, in the city that hovers just at the edge of your ocean, no one can hear my voice, no one can give me the words of their kind. They will drown, yes, and some will die before that—but I will hold nothing but corpses.*

I will not have their songs. I will not have their odd acts of frailty—the things you call kindness, *or* mercy. *I will not know their laughter, or the bright savagery of their children. I will take, but I will offer nothing in return. And I say again that this is not my desire.*

You who have come to the edge of the abyss so that your kin might have choice, at last—can you ask this of me?

"What choice will they have? While this city stands, our enemies can rebuild their armies, and peace such as we can make will be undone, time and again. The lessons that have been so costly will be forgotten, and in a hundred years, we will again be at the mercy of those who seek to make our very essence a weapon they can use against each other, because they are insane. They think that *knowing* each other is, in effect, destroying each other. It is always a game of power.

"Destroy the city, and we will have peace."

You have called me, who have touched your children at their birth, and sung your songs of healing as they made their way into the world. You have called me, who have struggled to bring water to parched, summer lands, when all of the wind and the fire stood against me, ancient foes; who have heard the voice of your farmers raised in supplication and in thanks for the miracle of simple plants. You have called me, who have heard the whispers of your elders in the dark of nights, who have moved rivers in their passage over your lands to preserve life.

And I have listened to your voices for all these years, and I have held your lives in my hands, again and again, and I have heard those voices, and I say again, that I do not desire this.

But I tell you more, because you will force it and I would yet see the madness fall from your eyes. Your people do not desire this. You seek to preserve them—but at what cost? You call yourself King—

"I do not—"

You allow it, and those that fear you—with just cause— fashion a true likeness with their words. But you will wake in your kin the ghost of the dead here—for they will see what you have made, and forced, and done, and you will be a race of warrior mages from whom no secret is safe, and your gift to them will be this—they will become what you cast down. They will become murderers and warriors who seek ever better weapons to use against those they have chosen to call enemy.

That is all you will achieve.

That is what you are building now.

But you have given me song, have trusted me with life, and with its keeping. And I have kept what was given me, and I return it to you now.

And the water flared white, like incandescent flames, or like sunlight on still water from a clear, clear sky; blue every-where implied, but white the thing that burns and blinds.

* * *

And from everywhere that water existed, be it small pond or tiny riverlet, gentle mist or raging storm, the Tha'alani people suddenly woke, and Kaylin could hear them *all*. She could hear the harvest song, and she could feel it in the thrum of a hundred throats; she could hear a child's cries— in anger, in sadness; could hear their joy and their bewilderment, their delight and their surprise. She could hear their words, and beside them, above them, the words of their elders, the fears of their parents.

And she could hear, as well, the voice of her grandmother, long dead; the fear in that voice, the memories of a life that was somehow still being lived, somehow still vital.

Last, she could hear her own voice, her child's voice, serious and determined, speaking not to kin but to elemental water. *You want to kill because you are not alive, but I will never allow it.*

…Although I don't understand why you want to kill, when you can help people and save lives and cause them to be happy, 'cause when people are happy, you can feel it here, and even when you're sad, it makes things better.

I will never allow it.

Oh, my people.

In water, blood could be washed away. Against this tide, there was no defense. It was as if… As if she could touch every single one of her people, stalk to stalk, and be calmed and comforted. Could see all their follies, their angers, and the strength of their joy.

But what must they see in her? What must they see?

The water began to shimmer in the air before her, dwindling—and with it, the voices that she had lost in her grief and her guilt and her anger.

She could not bear to let them go. And she had the power—she could see it, pulsing now in the runes and words upon her skin—to hold it, somehow; to keep it here. She had the power to force the water to do her bidding.

"What do you desire?" she asked the water, falling now to her knees, all thought of conquest forgotten.

And the water was silent, then, but the voices were *so* strong. The elders answering the question that they could feel her asking; they could not hear it across the distance, but she was touching the water, and they—woken by water's desperation, were also touching it.

They answered her, their many voices becoming, at last, one voice, like the voice of a waking god.

And, awake herself, she waited while the water slowly diminished, knowing that the water had heard what she herself had heard.

"And this," she asked softly, "can you do this, for us? Is *this* your desire?"

And the water answered, *Yes.* And in its voice, wonder, surprise, just the faintest edge of fear. And joy.

But if you use this power, if you do this thing, you will have the power no more. It will be gone from you—you will have no weapon—

I…am done with weapons. If you will do this, if you will it, I am done with weapons.

Yes.

Yes.

* * *

Yes.

Cheeks wet with tears, hands trembling, Kaylin Neya felt the world slip away from her. She didn't want it to leave. She'd been abandoned so bloody many times, she wanted to grab on and hold and *make it take her with it* wherever it went.

But…

It was a vision, wasn't it? She smeared water across her cheeks and stared into the unnatural eyes of a twelve-year-old girl with translucent skin, long hair.

It had to be a vision because Kaylin didn't *have* stalks.

She didn't have the Tha'alaan.

Or she wouldn't, when she let go—but she was selfish. For just a moment longer, she held tight.

Tha'alaan. She whispered the word as if it were a name, and maybe it was.

CHAPTER 17

Kaylin.

Kaylin Neya.

She heard the voice as clearly as if the woman speaking were standing beside her. She looked, but rock didn't usually speak, and even if she was still shaken by what she had seen, she wasn't so far gone that the rock had mouths. It was Ybelline's voice. She *knew* it.

Yes, Ybelline replied, grave and calm. *It is Ybelline. How come you to be here, Kaylin?*

And Kaylin said simply, *I'm holding the Tha'alaan.*

The silence was longer, now, the hesitation marked. *Kaylin—*

But Kaylin, who had lived in terror of the Tha'alani for most of her adult life, was not afraid. Not afraid of Ybelline or what she might see; not afraid of the Tha'alaan. She had *seen* what it had given Uriel, in the dim and distant past. And she had *been* Uriel, for moments, or months, or years—she knew what Uriel was capable of. The why, slow to fade, didn't matter in the end. If the Tha'alaan could somehow see Uriel and see a person worth saving, what had Kaylin to fear?

The Tha'alaan did not speak at all. Kaylin opened her eyes—it was easier to listen in darkness—and saw the girl's watchful eyes. But she did not speak.

And what the water did not offer, Kaylin could not, although she was certain that Ybelline knew. Maybe they all did. It was one of the memories, wasn't it? One of the memories that the Tha'alaan held?

They could not speak openly here, not while the Tha'alaan listened, not while it made all words and all experience part of its endless memory. *I heard the Tha'alaan,* Kaylin said, choosing the words with care.

Ybelline surprised her. *You would,* she said softly. *You, of all your kind. You bear the marks. Uriel's marks. But you are not afraid.*

How could I be? I… The Tha'alaan… Uriel.

He gave us this gift, Ybelline said softly, *and at great cost. We would not be Tha'alani were it not for his sacrifice.*

I wouldn't exactly call it a sacrifice, Kaylin said drily. *But he used what mages use.*

Yes.

And a mage could—

Yes. It is not spoken of, Kaylin. Most do not know it. To reach that far back in the Tha'alaan is the study of years, for most of my kin. Uriel is too foreign to their minds. He was the first and the last of our warrior leaders.

But not to my mind.

No. Not to yours.

Did you know this would happen? she thought.

I did not know it would happen now, but I guessed it might. And now is better. Understand, Kaylin, that the elemental forces are what they are. The Tha'alaan is not the whole of water, not the whole of what water is. Men still drown. Men still die of thirst. Were it not for Uriel, I do not think the water could have spoken to us at all. It does not speak to us now.

Not, she added, and Kaylin felt both the envy and the fear, laid bare, that Ybelline herself felt, *as it first spoke to Uriel. Not as it can speak to you, if you know how to listen.*

But Kaylin had, at last, relinquished her grasp on the water; she now fumbled with her sleeves, instead. Ybelline's clear, soft voice was cut off the instant she had let go, and it was probably better that way. Her sleeves were a sodden mess, but that made it easier to push them up out of the way, so that she could clearly see the marks on her skin.

The Dragons think no mortals bear these marks, she thought.

They are wrong, the Tha'alaan replied. Speaking again, now that she could no longer be heard by the Tha'alani. *But they were few, Kaylin, and none of your kind have borne them until you.*

"That you know of."

That I know of, the water agreed gravely. *Nor is Ybelline entirely correct—the marks you bear are not Uriel's marks.*

"You could read his?"

I could...sense them...in a different way. They were part of

what he was. Reading…is not for our kind, although I understand it in some fashion because of the Tha'alani.

"And these aren't part of what I am?"

Uriel sang to me in the womb, the water replied softly. *He
cried to me before he could walk. When he called me for the
first time—it was the thousandth time I had heard his voice.
What he was, I knew. But you were silent, Kaylin.*

"You knew my name."

I knew what Ybelline saw in you.

"But that was before—"

When you rescued the child, Catti, from the undead Barrani,
she said softly, *Ybelline touched the child and she saw what
the child saw. Ybelline understood you.*

"She never touched me—"

*She is wise. She did not need to. What she saw, then, I saw.
When I saw you again for a brief moment, I knew you. I spoke
your name. I called you.*

*I did not know you would come bearing what you now bear.
I do not welcome it*, she added, and her voice shifted, rippling
on forever. *But at this time and in this place, I do not hate or
dread it. I am not the whole of the water. I am the whole of the
water that remembers mortality.*

"Water doesn't die."

No. But you do. And your kind. And my people. She lifted
her translucent hands to her face, and covered the dark
wells of her eyes. *There is a magic at work here*, she said,
although Kaylin could no longer see her eyes. *It is not a small
thing, and it will call what it calls. But I hear its voice, and it*

is strong. If it wakes the water, there will be nothing I can do. I do not know if I will survive the waking.

The thought of the Tha'alaan *dying* robbed Kaylin of breath for just a moment. But only for a moment. She never accepted the loss of words gracefully. "You can't speak to the source of this...summoning. Not like you spoke to Uriel."

No. And I could not have spoken thus to Uriel if he had not allowed it. If you were that force, Kaylin, I could. I had hoped—

"It won't be me."

No.

"But you can damn well bet that I'll be there when whoever is doing this *does* call."

The hands fell away. *What is bet?*

Kaylin cringed. On the list of things to do today, two of which should have made her question her sanity, explaining a bet to an elemental force so old you could probably call it a god and not earn demerit points was not even in the running. "It means that I'll be there."

You may not be able to stop the calling, the water said quietly. *But you may have the power to stop the water from rising. You may be able to fight what he summons. You may be able to wrest control of it from the summoner.*

Kaylin lifted a hand to her throat.

The water nodded. *I do not trust your kind,* she said. *Not to ignore power where power lies. But what you would do with the power, and what will be done—they are not the same, and the part of me that lives with the Tha'alani knows this, and accepts the risk.*

Kaylin nodded. She was beginning to feel the damp. "Can I get into the Castle now?"

Castle?

"The building we stand under."

This is a Castle?

"Well, that's what we call it."

I have seen Castles. The Tha'alani have seen them. This is not a simple building, no matter how grand. Surely you can see— But the water stopped. *I wished to speak with you, Kaylin Neya. I knew when you touched the ground. I felt the ripple of your presence. You are a threat to water,* she added. *And in places such as these,* all *of the elements have some awareness.*

"Places such as these?"

They are...groves. But what grows in them are not trees. There is stone here, yes, but...the shape it takes and the shape it desires are not the same. You will find stairs, here, near the darkness of this river that winds forever into the heart of the world, and they will take you to the Castle that you seek. But climb carefully, Kaylin, and try not to look down. The water will not carry you so gently a second time.

"It doesn't, usually." Kaylin started to walk away. Stopped. "You drowned an old woman and an old man."

Yes.

"Why?"

I do not know. There was hardly enough of me present to know.

"Fair enough. We generally don't arrest weapons for murder." She hesitated and then said, "If the child who is missing is used to summon Water, what will she get? The Tha'alaan?"

But the Tha'alaan did not choose to answer the question, and maybe that was for the best. Kaylin could think of a few answers, and she hated all of them. Because she understood that the Tha'alaan—as much of it as was known, and really, that wasn't much—was thought of as something entirely *of* the Tha'alani. She knew there were mages and Arcanists who even now played at summoning elemental water, without ever knowing there was a connection between the Water and the race of mind readers.

She doubted very much that Donalan Idis was aware of the connection; what he *was* aware of was that the Tha'alani could summon and control the elements by means of their racial abilities.

And, of course, it would *have* to be water. He couldn't just burn down a building or two.

Comes of being a port city, her common sense said. She told it where it could get off and began to grope her way along the cavern wall to the stairs.

The walk up the stairs was anticlimatic, and Kaylin blessed whatever deities happened to be watching over her on that particular climb. There were days when boredom—or the possibility that things *could* get boring—was as much of a gift as life was willing to give. She took it with both hands. Metaphorically speaking; she actually had both hands on the pocked rock face for most of the climb. There was no rail, and the stairs, such as they were, had been carved into stone and worn away by time.

But the stairs led into what looked like a room, with

walls that had been laid by stonemasons, and not by—well, whatever it was that chiseled cliffs. There were no windows here, but there was a door, and that door was open. Dust didn't appear to make it this far down—she had no doubt that she was in a sub-subbasement—but light did; there were sconces in the walls, and they held burning torches. Which even smelled like oiled wood.

And not like charring flesh.

She flinched. Speaking to the Tha'alaan, speaking to Ybelline—that had felt natural, had reminded her of herself. But she also felt Uriel's presence; the memories that she had *lived* had been scored in her mind like a brand. She had understood everything that he did. She would have done it all herself, it felt so natural.

What had Ybelline said? That the memories one first saw in the Tha'alaan were likely to be the memories that one could most identify with. And this was hers. It was a harsh reminder of the differences between her life and the lives the Tha'alani lived, sheltered as they were in their quarter.

But it was a life she *wanted* for them. Hells, it was a life she would want for any of her orphans, any foundling at all. In the end, she had seen that in Uriel. In the end, he had done what mattered.

But he did a hell of a lot more.

Yes. And he was dead, and whatever justice existed for men who would commit genocide, he was facing it now. Kaylin had her own problems. But she had been with him for long enough that she knew his bitter regret, his understanding—at the last moment, but *in time*—of the damage he had almost done. She couldn't even say he'd done it un-knowing; he hadn't cared. The dead had driven him.

And in that, they had much in common. Too much, really.

Justice was such a narrow edge to walk along. Too far, and one became the cause of some other vendetta; too little, and one became immured to all suffering, if it didn't affect one directly. How could you do *enough*? How could you make the right choice? Uriel had killed tens of thousands of in-nocents—but wasn't he right? Wouldn't some of those in-nocents have gone on to live a life of war and barbarism?

When did Justice become Revenge, and were they ever different? It made her head hurt. Because in the end, it didn't matter. In the end, she had chosen to wear the Hawk—and in the light of those unexpected torches, it shone with a grace that spoke of flight, freedom, and duty. The Emperor's Law might not be her law—the endless nat-tering of a whining merchant at Festival season really drove that home. But she couldn't really think of a *better* law, and if she was willing to die to uphold it—and she was a Hawk—wasn't that all that mattered?

Maybe that was the point of having a law, of not being a law-unto-yourself. It gave you the illusion that the law was above you, impartial; if you benefited from it, if Justice was somehow miraculously both done *and* recognized, it was a Justice that you trusted *because* it wasn't in your own hands.

She shook her head. Her hair was damp and ratty, but the rivulets had long since ceased to flow.

The Emperor was above his own law; that much Sanabalis and Tiamaris had said. But he didn't expect Kaylin to hold him above that law. He expected her to die defending it. She really didn't understand kings. But having been Uriel for far too long, she really didn't want a better understanding, either.

"And what, then, does Kaylin Neya want?"

The smooth, low voice that came from the other side of the door was one that she couldn't mistake for anyone else's.

"Dry clothing," she said.

The door didn't swing, it glided. Lord Nightshade stood on the other side of the frame, his arms folded across his chest, as if he'd been waiting a while.

How long had he been waiting?

How long had she been in the dark, in the—

"It has been little over two hours," he replied. "It is dark now, and the Ferals are hunting. I can see that dry clothing is indeed necessary. Come."

She had the urge to hug him, just to see how he'd look when damp and bedraggled. She had a suspicion that he wouldn't look any different.

He did her the grace of ignoring the thought she was just too tired to suppress. Too tired, or too beyond caring. She felt…hollow, somehow. She wouldn't have been Uriel for all the money in the world—not even for wings, had some god deigned to offer them in exchange. But what she had felt when she'd drawn the Tha'alaan into her arms—that *was* his, not hers. And it left a mark, an absence, even an ache.

All in all, she thought she had been a happier person when she'd just loathed the Tha'alani. Finding out how little there was to hate had caused a bit of guilt and the usual

humiliation that attended any realization of her own stu-
pidity or ignorance; finding out how much there was to love
was infinitely worse.

But she had let it go because she *had* to let it go. There
was a job to do, wasn't there? And a city to save. Not that
she cared about the city all that much at this particular
moment. No—it was the face of the girl, the water's face.
And also the unseen face of a child that she had never met,
who was now in the hands of a man whose face she *had*
seen, and didn't much care for.

Things could get bigger around her; they could get bigger
just because so much power happened to be involved. But
the things that *she* cared about, the things that drove *her*—
they could be as small as one life. Because if she forgot the
one life, what else could she forget?

See as a Hawk sees. Marcus had said that. And Red, during
an autopsy. They had meant different things by it, but mostly
they'd been telling her to look at the things in front of her,
and not the endless consequences, the endless permutations.

"Kaylin."

She looked up.

"What happened?"

"Didn't you hear it?"

"No. There are some things that the mark does not grant
me." He paused, and then added, "Or some things that you
yourself do not grant. The only power I sensed was yours."

"Can I do that?"

"You can," he replied, his voice cool, but without edge.
"You have my name, Kaylin. You could try to do more."

His name tugged at memory, forming syllables that she could not actually speak when anyone could hear them.

"But you have not tried."

She shook her head. What would be the point?

He frowned. "I am not considered unpowerful, among my kind. It is seldom that the attempt to *use* power is considered pointless."

"I'm not Barrani."

"No. And you are not—entirely—human. But you seem to be cold."

She was. "And wet."

"Yes. I would have considered it ill-advised to leap down the well," he added. "But I will not question your decision. It brought you here."

"I think—I'll be able to enter the normal way from now on."

"Kaylin—"

She lifted a hand. "I need to find Donalan Idis," she told him. "That's why I came."

"You will not find him this eve. And I suggest that before you start chattering like a waif, you repair to your rooms above. There is much here that I have left untouched, and my power this far beneath the surface does not always go unchallenged."

"You don't sound like that bothers you."

He shrugged. "It is seldom boring."

"I could use a little boredom, about now."

"Care less."

She was *really* cold. It was hard to talk through the unfortunate chattering her teeth seemed intent on.

He frowned, and before she could answer—or at least answer in a way that didn't make her look pathetic—he stepped forward and caught her in his arms, lifting her as if she weighed nothing. If he noticed that she was cold and clammy, he offered no comment as he pushed the door open and began to walk down a long hall.

But as he walked, he said, "I seldom give advice, Kaylin. But if you want boredom, you must care less."

"About what?"

"About everything."

"If I care less," she said, turning her face into the soft fabric of his robe, "Mayalee will die."

"Yes. But when dealing with mortals you operate from the certainty that regardless of what you do, they will die anyway."

"I want her to die when she's *old*, and on someone else's watch."

"Ah. It is only a handful of years."

"We feel them more keenly."

"Scarcity often makes things more valuable than they would otherwise intrinsically appear. But it is not only the fate of one child that concerns you now," he added. "It is not for that reason that you were sent."

"I wasn't sent—"

"Not directly, no. That is not the way the Court works." He stopped outside of a door that looked vaguely familiar. In a bad way. "Come. You must walk through these doors on your own. I cannot bear you."

She mumbled something ungracious about magic and what could be done with it, but she could more or less stand on her own. Her knees were weak, and the ground seemed to refuse to stay still—but she'd seen worse.

The doors opened as he touched them, rolling back in a grim sort of silence. Beyond them stood trees.

"Yes," he said, saving her the effort of asking. "You've seen these trees before."

She grimaced; the trees weren't, at this point, as much of a concern as the glowing frame of the door itself. She'd seen door-wards for most of her life on the right side of the law—but this was worse.

Lord Nightshade stopped and turned. "Kaylin?"

"I can't help but notice that the doorway is glowing."

"Ah."

"Is it going to dump me somewhere else?"

"That depends."

"On what, exactly?"

"On you."

He reminded her, at that moment, of every teacher she had ever disliked. But she'd come here for a reason. Squaring her shoulders and clenching her hands into fists, she took a step.

She felt the light as if it were ice; she lost the ability to see the moment she crossed its threshold, taking care to place her foot squarely on the path that led to Nightshade. Her legs froze, her arms were suddenly trapped by her side, and the *cold*… She bit her lip. She could move enough to do that.

But she didn't feel the pain of it. It was too minor.

Something didn't want her to enter the Castle. That much,

she could think. The rest of her thoughts were subsumed by ice, by Winter's heart. The cold could kill. It could kill *her,* here, and everything she'd ever done would count for nothing.

She forced her hands to move. She wasn't sure why until they touched the base of her throat, and then she *knew.*

What is the essence of water?

Closing her eyes, she remembered what lay at the heart of the pendant she had accepted from the ghost of a Dragon lord. A single, complicated character, a series of strokes and crossed hatches and dots, pattern so precise it might take years just to write it.

Writing it wasn't the point. She stopped struggling to move, and began, instead, to speak. Speaking was far harder than lifting her arms had been. The cold intensified; the ice grew thicker. It was hard to even breathe.

She couldn't later say what the word *was*; she couldn't later repeat it. It wasn't that kind of word. She wasn't even sure, in the end, if her lips formed the syllables at all—but she felt them, each one, as if they were an enormous step, a series of hurdles, that she had to clear if she were going to survive.

A spare thought floated past: *I hate magic.*

And another: *Don't hate it. It's part of what you are.*

And last, at a great remove, a familiar voice: *Kaylin. It's time to wake up now.*

The ice was gone. She staggered forward, because staggering backward would mean she might have to do it again. She found the ground with her hands, and it was firm and hard—more rock than dirt, although she could feel the curved roughness of tree roots beneath at least two of her fingers. Her hands were blue. And her arms.

She thought it was because of the cold, until she realized what exactly she was seeing.

The marks.

Her arms were bare.

"Well done," Lord Nightshade said softly. "I thought you might be lost, there."

And what would you have done? What would you have done then?

The soft sound of a shrug—yards of fabric, traveling up and down by an inch or two—told her clearly that he had heard what she hadn't said.

"The Castle will test you," he told her. "It is your test, to pass or fail."

She nodded, as if that made sense. Maybe in his world, it did. It was certainly a very Barrani attitude. Before she could say as much, she felt arms under her arms, and she was lifted to her feet, which she still couldn't feel.

"You've become acquainted with the elements," he said, waiting while she placed her feet more or less beneath the rest of her. She could see that she was wearing a dress that was pale ivory in color; the skirts brushed the ground, obscuring her toes.

"Elements?" She could see the trees now. She could see that she wore something metallic around her waist, something fine and thin.

She felt his frown; she couldn't see his face. Could see a

lock of his hair as it trailed down her shoulder toward her waist. It reminded her, absurdly, of Teela's hair, when Teela couldn't be bothered to braid it—it got into everything.

And Kaylin had loved it, as a child new to the Hawks. She could think of herself at that age as a child, now. Teela had let her brush it, sometimes, and braid it, sometimes—always with dire threats of physical pain if she was careless enough to actually pull any of it out.

She hadn't been joking, either—Kaylin had seen enough of the Barrani Hawks to know that much—but even knowing it, she had done it anyway.

"Elements," Lord Nightshade was saying.

She tried very hard not to shiver. Not to be cold. She tried to make sense of the single word he'd spoken twice. After a moment, still swaying on her feet, she said, "Water?"

He said nothing, but she had a suspicion that anything else would have been dripping sarcasm.

"There are many ways to kill with water," he told her, voice almost gentle. "This is one."

"Your castle tried to kill me with water?"

"No."

"But—" She stopped talking and actually *looked* at the dress. At her arms, which were bare. At her shoulders, which were *also* bare. No damn wonder she was so cold. "I've seen this dress before," she said in a flat voice.

"Ah."

"Talk to me," she added, taking an experimental step forward. Her knees wobbled. Nightshade's hands were warm. "And either carry me or let go."

* * *

He carried her.

She'd carried children before in the Foundling Halls, sometimes at a run, but never with such graceful ease. Lord Nightshade spoke as he walked, and he walked slowly, the cadence of his words matching the rhythm of his step. She lost the words, sometimes, her lids drifting toward her cheeks, her head nodding forward. But when she opened her eyes again, he was still speaking softly. His voice was not the voice of the Tha'alaan, not the voice of the water. But accompanied by footsteps and breath, it was calming. Soothing.

But he didn't carry her to her room—or the room that she had stayed in before; he carried her to a long, empty room that was clearly meant for greeting guests. He paused in front of a tall, oval mirror and set her on her feet. Hands on her shoulders, he said, "Look."

She disliked mirrors on principle. They showed what there was to see, and not what she wanted to believe she looked like. Either that or they interrupted her sleep with the ill-tempered snarls of a disgruntled Leontine.

"It isn't necessary," she said, her eyes sliding away from her own gaze. "I know the dress."

"Where have you seen it before?"

"In the Oracle Hall," she replied. She turned, slowly, to face him, forcing him to let go of her shoulders. Or to shift position, which was what he chose to do instead. He was much, much taller than she was.

"Where have you seen it before?" she asked him.

His smile was slight, but she thought it genuine. "You are guessing."

"Am I wrong?"

"No." His hands lingered a moment on her shoulders, and she didn't even mind—they were warm. She seemed to have swallowed the ice that had failed to kill her—if that was its goal—and it was hard to stand straight without shivering.

The far doors opened, and a Barrani in armor let himself into the room, carrying, of all things, a tray. Nightshade gestured, and the guard put the tray down on a table near the mirror. He bowed deeply and then retreated, his face entirely free of expression.

"We will eat," Nightshade said, leading her to a long couch. "And while we eat, you may ask the questions you came here to ask, if any remain to be answered." But he lifted the cloak from his shoulders as he spoke, and draped it around Kaylin's, and although he turned it sideways, it settled there as if it had been made for just this moment.

Her hair, however, was still a bedraggled mess.

CHAPTER 18

He sat in a high-backed chair opposite her, pausing only to pour something steaming out of what was, after all, a very shiny, very fancy kettle. Nor were the crystal goblets, or the silver, anywhere to be seen; instead, round and stout earthenware mugs with a handle on either side. He passed one to her; he took nothing for himself.

This should have made her suspicious, but she was tired of suspicion. Tired, in truth, of everything that didn't involve a few days of solid sleep. And in the mug, steaming, was...milk. Goat's milk, she thought, although it was hard to tell without drinking it.

Her brows rose when she brought the mug to her lips. "It *is* milk."

"I am informed that you drink it."

"Once in a while," she managed to say. "When I was young." Before her mother had died in the fief of Nightshade. Before Severn. She cupped her hands around the sides of the mug and sat there, dwarfed by yards of expensive, sturdy cloth.

"I used to be so afraid of this place," she told him softly.

"And now?"

"I think...other fears have crowded it out."

"Your missing child."

She nodded bleakly.

"You understand that saving this one child will not bring the others back?"

"It won't add to their voices."

He nodded. "You came to ask me about Donalan Idis."

"Yes. Where is he?"

"I am not entirely certain."

"I was afraid of that. Let me ask you a different question. You had him here—as a guest, since apparently he did walk out. What did he study?"

"Besides the Tha'alani?"

She kept her face carefully neutral. Unfortunately for Kaylin, the less appropriate words were very loudly thought.

Nightshade raised a brow.

"Sorry," she mumbled. She let the steam rise from the milk, breathing it in as if it were the only air in the room. "Yes, besides that."

"He was—and is—an elemental mage of some note."

"Water?"

"All of the elements of which he is aware."

She nodded. She understood now how he could cut the Tha'alani off from the Tha'alaan—but she wondered if he understood it himself. "And he was invited here because of that?"

"That? No."

"Then *why?*"

"He is powerful, Kaylin. The Imperial Order of Mages is beholden to the Emperor, and it is winnowed by the Dragon lords. No one who is interested in power will cultivate associates from the Imperial Order."

"But what does he have that you want?"

"Ah, a different question."

"You're not going to answer it."

"No. But it is pointless, now. I understand your presence here, at this time. I understand less well the route you were forced to take to enter the Castle—but the water spoke with you. Do not look so surprised—you were still dripping when I met you.

"Whatever it is that was of…interest in Idis is no longer of import. He is too great a threat at the moment, and I cannot see any meeting between the two of you that does not end in either his death or yours."

"If it's mine, the city goes with me."

He raised a dark brow. "You've grown arrogant."

She shook her head. "The Oracles," she told him.

"And the Dragons?"

She burrowed farther into the folds of his cape, aware that the cloth smelled of him, that it was warm. That it was not a defense. "I can't answer that."

"No. But you also visited the Keeper, twice to my knowledge."

She said nothing because it seemed safest.

"I do not believe that Idis would deign to visit Castle Nightshade at this time."

"No?" She hadn't realized that she'd been hoping for precisely this until he took the hope away.

"He cultivated my association because he desired power or the friendship of the powerful. If he is what you fear, then he no longer labors under that desire."

"But you knew how to reach him?"

"I knew how to reach him."

"And now?"

"I do not believe he is ready to be found."

"In as much as an Arcanist is sane, he wants power for a reason, yes?"

Nightshade nodded.

"How does destroying the city we're pretty certain he's still living in count as gaining power?"

"It is not clear to me that his desire is Elantra's destruction."

She frowned. "That was my next question. What does he stand to gain by it?"

"If it were sacrificial magic, a great deal of power."

"I don't think it's that."

"I would not be entirely certain. But his past history does not indicate magic of that nature."

"Then why—" She hesitated, studying what little there was of an expression on his face. "You think he doesn't *intend* to destroy the city, but that's what he'll accomplish."

"I have not visited the Oracles," Nightshade replied

gently. "But at this moment, that is what you are beginning to think, and I will not gainsay you. Summoning elementals is tricky, even for the powerful. History is littered with the corpses of those who have made that mistake. If that is the case, I am not certain you will be able to control what Idis cannot. Even given your entry into the Castle. In time, Kaylin, I think such control would not be beyond you—"

"We don't have time," she said flatly.

"No." He paused. "The dress you wear—"

"What there is of it."

"As you say. It is in a style that you will not be familiar with, and even when it was worn, it was worn by very few. But those who did wear it were those who were sensitive to the elemental forces."

"And this one?"

"The dresses were not coded. What the adepts did is not clear to me, even at this remove. Kaylin—what happened when you touched the water?"

She shook her head, and thought about the midwives for a while. It was easy to think of them; they were always at the back of her mind.

"Very good."

Her smile was brittle.

"You are a mystery to the wise," he told her. "Even your gift is not clear. I offer you this, then, and in spite of yourself. When you showed yourself capable of standing against one form—not an inconsiderable one—of water's death, the Water formed the robes you wear."

"What? But—but how?"

"I do not know. But the robes are yours, and they were meant for you. It is some sign of the water's choice," he added, "and the robes will not save you, if it comes to that—but you have impressed the elemental force in some way, and it has granted you the equivalent of a title."

Which of course made no sense.

"This isn't magic," Kaylin said forlornly. "This is…gods."

"In a manner of speaking." He was quiet for a moment. "Do you know what Donalan Idis intends for the child?"

"Most likely? To finish the experiments that were dropped."

"And the boy?"

"If Grethan is even still alive—and I have some suspicions about that—he's done his part. Idis couldn't get *near* the Tha'alani quarter, and the Tha'alani children don't venture out much."

"Why a child?"

"I don't think it mattered to him one way or the other—but a child is easier to intimidate and haul around. I've been one. I know. Anyone else would have been smart enough to stay put."

"You keep your secrets now, Kaylin."

She met his measuring gaze, and held it. "I have a lot fewer of them than you do."

"And perhaps with less reason. Finding Donalan Idis, however, should not pose a problem for you."

"Oh?"

"If you know what he intends, you will know where to find him."

"But I *don't* know what he intends."

Nightshade said nothing. After a moment of silence, he rose. "It is late," he told her softly. "For you. The Ferals will be out. Will you tempt them?"

She hesitated, her hands around a mug of steamed milk, her arms entangled in a cloak that was being used in a way its maker certainly hadn't intended. The mark on her cheek, delicate curls and lines, was warm. She closed her eyes, and opened them the moment she felt his hands brush the sides of her face; she hadn't heard him move at all.

He had cupped her face in those hands, and now tilted it up, forcing her gaze to meet his. His eyes were a shade of…violet. She'd never seen that one before. But she was seeing it too damn close for the first time.

She yanked her face away, hard, which sent warm milk in a spray all over table and floor. And her legs.

He stepped back instantly, watching her.

"I—"

I have time, Kaylin. I have learned how to wait.

"I'm sorry," she said, standing in a hurry, and setting the cup down on a flat surface that didn't shake so damn much.

"For what?"

"For—for—spilling the milk." It sounded lame, even to her. Her toes were curling.

He shrugged.

"I'll clean it up—"

"Kaylin. *Kaylin.*"

She forced herself to meet his gaze, and was comforted

by the cold of blue. Not in general a comforting sign, among the Barrani.

"You are safe here tonight. This was not always true. It will not always be true. But tonight, if you wish to stay, I will leave you. I have, however, one question to ask."

She said nothing.

"You left the fief of Nightshade when you were thirteen years old. You appeared in the Halls of Law some six months later. Where did you go in between?"

"Away," she said woodenly. Away. And her thoughts were spiraling out of control, out of even her own control. She *would not* let that happen here. Or ever. She had been marked by Nightshade; she had given Severn her name.

"I…see."

I doubt it. She suppressed an urge to scream—because she wasn't sure what it would sound like if she did. Raw, yes—but with rage? With fear? "I can't stay."

"No." He lifted his head, his perfect face, and spoke three words. The mirror shivered, even though the words were so soft Kaylin couldn't catch the syllables.

But five minutes later, the door opened again, and this time, the guard standing in it was one that she recognized.

"Lord Andellen?" she said.

"Lord Kaylin." He bowed.

"Escort her to her home," the fieflord said. "I will be in my quarters should anything go amiss."

The Castle was obliging enough to spit her out the normal way. Her stomach was obliging enough not to humiliate her in front of Andellen, but her knees were wobbly for about ten minutes. Andellen did not, however, offer to help.

They began to walk toward the Ablayne, and Kaylin, still off-kilter, was happy to follow Andellen's lead. She could hear the howl of distant Ferals, and wondered if they were hunting, or just roaming. With Ferals, it was hard to tell— but distant was far better than the alternative.

"That was unwise," Andellen said when they were a good distance from the Castle, but not yet in sight of the river-bank.

"What was?"

"I do not know what you said, or what you did," he replied, "but…it was unwise."

She shrugged. "I'm not known for my wisdom," she offered bitterly.

"I do not know if my lord could kill you. I would not suggest you force him to try."

"Believe that I wasn't trying."

"Kaylin—"

"Andellen, I've been swimming in the river far beneath the Castle. I've been roared at by dead Dragons. I've been dressed in something that hardly qualifies as *underwear* by something that tried to kill me. I've—I've had a lot on my mind."

"The High Lord sent you?"

"No." She paused, and then said almost guiltily, "Not directly. He sent a message through Teela."

Andellen nodded. "He would. He is not his father."

"He's not. But he's not—"

"No. Lord Nightshade will never be summoned to Court, and if it were to happen, he would decline the invitation. He will not trust the High Lord."

"Because he's outcaste."

"Yes."

"Why *is* he outcaste?"

Andellen raised a brow at the question, and Kaylin reddened. "Do all mortals speak without thinking?"

"All of them do it some of the time."

"As often as you?"

"Probably not as often as me," she conceded. "I'm sorry. I meant no insult."

"No. I think you seldom do. But what you mean and what you achieve are often separated by knowledge."

"Knowledge?"

"Of you, Kaylin. Of who you are. Lord Nightshade tolerates far more from you than I would have thought possible—but he will not be so tolerant indefinitely. You've been to the High Court. You've passed the test of Lords. You've been called *kyuthe* by both the Lord of the High Court and his brother, the Lord of the West March. If you are *too tired* or *too preoccupied* to think, do not speak.

"You must learn, Kaylin."

She said nothing, listening to the steady sound of his steps. They were lighter than his armor should have made them, but she found it comforting. Nightshade by moonlight, the sound of Ferals a distant lullabye.

"You have been called *Erenne* by those who serve my

lord. You may never become the truth of that word—but were it not possible, were it not desired, you would not now bear the mark that grants you safety from those who serve him. But, Kaylin, he *will* kill you if it becomes necessary. He is accustomed to power—accustomed to its form, its shape, the obedience that comes with it.

"Understand that that power is gained, in part, because those who serve him defer to him. If you—one merely mortal—"

"I bear the marks," she said wearily, lifting a bare arm and wondering what the *hell* had happened to her armor. Wondering why she hadn't even thought about it until now.

The glaring face of an angry Quartermaster flashed before her eyes in a proverbial near-death way.

"Very well. You see at least that clearly. Yes, you bear the marks, and yes, it changes what you are in the eyes of the Barrani. I am not sure that this helps you, however. He cannot be seen to be challenged."

"No one else was there."

Andellen was silent for another five minutes. She dared a glance at the side of his face and saw that he was smiling. It wasn't what she expected.

"As you say, Lord Kaylin."

"You're trying to tell me something else, aren't you?"

"No. I am merely trying to tell you that angering Lord Nightshade is not in the interests of the High Court you nominally belong to. Nor," he added, lifting a hand to forestall the torrent of words that were sure to follow, "is it in the interests of the Hawks you do serve."

But something else had occurred to Kaylin. "Why do you serve him?"

"I don't understand your question."

"You passed the test of the High Halls. You saw what lay beneath them. You found your way back from whatever path you walked. Why do you serve him?"

"Ah. That is not a question that my kin would ask."

"I'm not Barrani."

"Believe that this fact could not possibly escape my attention. And believe, as well, that I take no insult from what would be considered a deadly insult otherwise."

She had the grace to redden. "Sorry."

He stopped walking, and turned, slowly, to face her.

"Kaylin Neya. Lord Kaylin. You dared the High Halls because I took you to the arch of testing on orders from *my* Lord. But you did more. You saved the Barrani. Your interference, your endless meddling, preserved the Lord of the High Court. And you returned, to one such as I, outcaste by association, the title of *Lord*. I do not think you understand what you *could* have asked for. But I also believe that if you had, you would have asked for the same thing.

"Don't look so impatient. This is the polite way—the deferential way—of telling you that I am in your debt. You repaid my act of subterfuge in a way that no Barrani, past or present, would have done.

"So I will answer the question you had no right to—and no sense not to—ask. All Barrani who wish to be Lords take the Test of the High Halls. The Barrani see, upon the ancient stone walls of the Tower, a word. It is in the oldest of our tongues, and there is some argument that it is not in our tongue at all. But when we first approach the arch, we see—as you did—a measure of what our test will be. It is said to define our lives. Some believe that we come from, and return to, the river of life, over and over again, and each time we arrive, we must find the strength to confront something new, and something difficult.

"My sigil—the sigil that began my test—was old enough that I accepted it, but did not fully understand its meaning."

"How can you accept a test—"

"Kaylin, has anyone ever had a conversation with you that is not a continuous stream of interruption?"

"Sorry."

He began to walk again, while she practiced biting her tongue.

"The word that began my test, the word that defines my life, was a word that you would use with ease." He paused for a moment, as if waiting for her interruption. He nodded slightly when she managed to remain silent.

"Friendship."

"But—"

And he laughed. "No, it is not the Elantran word. But that is the closest word that I can think of. It holds some measure of equality, some of loyalty, some of trustworthiness—but it is all, and none, of these things."

"So you left with him because—"

"Yes. And no. I serve him, Kaylin. There is no Barrani relationship that is so simple or easy as your friendship. Two lords cannot live in one castle. Ah. There is the bridge. I believe we have bypassed the Ferals for this night."

"You still have to go back."

"I am faster than a hunting Feral."

"Not in that armor."

"Yes, Kaylin," he replied, speaking as if to a child. "In this armor."

"Oh."

He walked her all the way home, but she didn't object; she'd heard what Nightshade had said, and she understood that her personal preferences—and her dignity, what little there was of it—meant nothing compared to the fieflord's command.

When they stopped outside of her apartment, she discovered that she didn't have a key. It had been in the trousers that she was no longer wearing. Andellen waited while she came to that realization, and then waited while she relieved herself of a few choice phrases in every language she knew.

But if he had noticed the odd form of dress, he said nothing. Nor did he say anything when she glared murderously at the locked door. He simply lifted his hand, and, placing it against the lock, spoke a single white word.

And it was white—she could almost *see* it.

The door slid open when he pushed it.

"You didn't break the lock, did you?" she asked, running her hands through straggly—but dry—hair. "I can't afford to piss off the landlord."

"I did not break the lock. Do you have another key?"

"Teela does."

"I think you will need to retrieve it."

But Kaylin was now busy swearing at the other things she was missing: her daggers. Gods, they had cost so much damn money to have enchanted! A distant second was the fact that they were departmental gear and the Quartermaster would have her skin for leathers.

"Kaylin."

"What?"

"Believe that we are concerned about the fate of the city. We are doing what we can, as we can."

She had the good sense not to tell him that at the moment she was more sickened by the loss of her knives than she was by whatever horrible fate awaited them all.

He left her at the door to her apartment because he happened to be the only key she had, and knew it. She also knew that had she lived somewhere expensive, she wouldn't have had to fuss with keys—her door would have a door-ward, and it would open for her whenever or however she managed to touch it. Then again, part of the appeal of living in this particular building was its extremely cheap—Caitlin used the word *frugal*—landlord. Kaylin hated door-wards.

But had to admit, as she wearily trudged across the threshold of a home that had been entirely closed to her until Andellen had used whatever magic he usually claimed not to posses, that those damn wards did have their uses. And compared to the portal—or the long drop down the well of the Castle that Nightshade lived in—they were downright pleasant.

She was tired enough that she'd made it almost to the mirror before she realized that someone else was in the room. But she knew who it was, even in the darkness, and while she fumbled for light—and in this, the frugality of the landlord was curse-worthy—she paused to glance at the mirror. Its face was entirely reflective, which meant that she hadn't missed any emergencies while she'd been gone.

In the lamplight that she managed to coax into existence, she unwrapped the cloak from her shoulders and took a good look at herself. Her hair was a mess—it usually was, but she'd managed to top her personal best tonight—but the dress was flawless and spotless.

No, wait, not spotless. She drew the lamp toward herself, and light glittered across delicate beadwork. The Hawk, she thought. Evanton's Hawk. Whatever transformation the elemental magic had made, it had not been able to change the patch he'd given her as a type of gift. She was still—in some fashion—in uniform, but she could pretty much guess what Marcus would say when he saw it. On the other hand, it would be a *lot* easier to expose her throat and have done.

She touched the beads for reassurance. Something was the same. Something hadn't changed. And it was the *Hawk*.

It comforted her, and gave her strength enough to turn at last to the darkness. "Severn," she said softly.

Severn, seated in the room's chair—which meant he'd upended her clothing pile—nodded quietly. He reminded her—for just a moment—of Nightshade on his throne.

Except that this was *her* damn apartment, not his. She

started to tell him that, but what came out instead was, "I lost my keys."

"You lost your keys."

"Sort of."

"And you found a dress."

"Sort of. Look, why are you here, anyway?"

"You lost your bracer," he replied, and held it out. The lamplight was almost perfectly reflected in the sheen of unmarked gold.

"Oh." She walked over to the chair and stood in front of his outstretched hand. "I can't wear it," she told him softly. "Not yet."

"Lord Grammayre?"

"I think he'd understand."

"Iron Jaw won't."

"Probably not." She turned away from him, walked over to the bed, and sat on it heavily. "It's been a very, very long day," she said, falling over.

"I won't add to it." He was stiff as he rose, and his expression was cool. "Did you gain any useful information from Ybelline or the fieflord?"

She laughed. It was a bit higher and a bit longer than she would have liked, but she really was tired.

His stiffness dissolved slowly; she didn't see the change as much as feel it. He came and sat on the foot of the bed, saying a lot of nothing.

"I'm sorry if I worried you."

"Apologies are usually only offered when one is going to change the behavior that necessitates them."

"Gods, you sound like a bloody teacher."

"And you sound like a bloody student."

She laughed again. "Yes. There was useful information. Sort of."

"Kaylin."

"Idis is an elemental mage."

"I see."

"Nightshade thinks his sole concern is the usual boring variety."

"Power?"

"Power. Which means he doesn't *intend* to destroy the city."

"It's the usual dabbling in ancient magics which are too powerful for man?"

"Something like that. It doesn't matter, though." She forced herself up onto her elbows. "Because I know what the Tha'alaan is, and I know that he'll destroy it."

"And the dress?" The edge was back in the words again.

"This? Oh—no, it's not what you think. More's the pity."

A dark brow rose into invisibility.

"I kind of— I had a little trouble getting into the Castle, and the end result was the dress. The damn thing appeared in place of my armor, my shirt, and my *damn* knives. It has nothing to do with Nightshade."

"Have you tried to remove it?"

"What, walking back through the fief? Have you lost your mind?"

"You could try now."

She said nothing for what seemed like an hour. But she remembered to breathe. She also remembered to avoid his gaze, to look at anything in her home that wasn't Severn. Given everything, it was surprisingly difficult.

"No," she said at last, but softly. "I don't think I can take it off yet. The water—the elemental water—made it. Nightshade said it was…like a temple dress."

"You've suddenly acquired faith?"

"No. Just the usual prayer of desperation."

"Kaylin—"

"Severn, please. Please."

He was silent, but he'd never been the talker. She had, and she'd almost run out of words. After a moment, and more roughly, he said, "What do you intend to do?"

"I need to go to the Oracle Hall. And I need to see Evanton."

"Now?"

"Gods, no. Now, I want to sleep." She paused and then added, "Have you slept at all?"

"In your chair."

"Oh. For how long?"

"It's not important."

"Food?"

"*Kaylin.*"

She turned toward the window, shuttered against the morning light. Which had yet to arrive. "I think she's still alive," she told him without turning her head. "She has to still be alive."

He said softly, "Yes. And she'll be alive tomorrow. Sleep."

"Severn, I—"

"Sleep. I'll be here." He rose, then, and walked over to the lamp. "Do you want the light?"

She shook her head. "Save the oil." It was easy to say that. But other words wanted saying, and she couldn't get them out of her mouth. "Severn—"

"Sleep, Kaylin." His voice had lost the edge, but she felt it anyway. "In the morning, we'll go to the Oracle Hall. We'll go to Evanton's. We'll go wherever you need to go. We'll find the child."

His words were like a lullaby. She said, "I had steamed milk."

And felt his lips curve up in a smile, as if they were beneath her fingers, and she were touching them.

Funny, that she could feel so uncomfortable and so safe at the same time. It was her last waking thought.

But her dreams were unkind.

CHAPTER 19

Kaylin and morning were not friends. But there were the usual hostilities, and then there was all-out war. This particular morning, it was cataclysmic. The shutters, which she depended on to keep a semblance of ignorance about the actual time, had failed her miserably; they were wide open, and sunlight was streaming down like irritating drizzle, only bright. There were birds that were, she swore, louder than they'd been even on the morning-after of the evenings she'd spent carousing with Teela and Tain.

Severn, in the armor of the Hawks, was loafing against the mirror wall. The mirror, which was an unfortunate shade of gray. She winced and rolled out of bed. "I'm in trouble."

"You usually are," he said. "Marcus mirrored while you were sleeping."

"I slept through *Marcus?*"

"Apparently so. He was impressed."

"I bet."

"I gave him a brief explanation of our duty rounds for the day."

"Which probably made him so much more cheerful."

"He apparently considers the duty roster one of his petty joys in life, yes. He didn't appreciate my interference."

"How much pay am I losing?"

"None. I did, however, neglect to mention the Quartermaster's chit."

"His—oh. The one I'm going to need to sign. Probably in blood, for all the good it will do."

"That one, yes."

"Do you mind if I have a small rant about how unfair life is?"

"Yes."

"Damn." Her stomach made an embarrassing noise, just to put the crowning touch on the day's start.

"I *did* look for food," he said as they walked down the street toward the market stalls. "Apparently, you don't have any. Or you hoard it for gods only know what emergency."

She had chosen to wear clothing *over* the dress, since it reminded her so much of underclothes anyway. The problem with *that* was she was required to wear a dress. She did have one of her own. It made her look like a farmer.

Even Severn had raised a brow when she'd put it on. Jabbing a stick through her hair and missing did not add much in the way of dignity, although it may have made him think better of speaking.

"Yes, I know. The color. Caitlin didn't like it, either—but the dyed dresses cost *more* and they fall apart *faster*."

"Actually, I'm just surprised you own it."

"I used to wear it to the midwives' guildhall."

"Why?"

"I can't honestly remember. I thought it would make me look less like a Hawk."

"And that was important?"

"I didn't want anyone who was dying of childbirth to be afraid of me."

"I would think they would have other things on their mind."

"Well, yes. I discovered that quickly enough."

They stopped in front of a baker's stall. In the heat of the early morning, the cooking fires were bearable, besides which, she was hungry. She ate while they walked, brushing crumbs from the folds of a thick linen skirt.

She even followed Severn as he made his way through the city streets, giving her both space—people generally moved a little out of the way when they saw an armed man, even if he was an officer of the Law—and time. But he also wasn't wasting much time, and when she was finished eating, he hailed a coach.

"Um, Severn?"

"Yes?"

"We generally need permission to see the Oracles."

"Ah."

"I mean—I think I can talk them into letting me in—"

"But you're not certain."

"No. And I think you'll have to wait—"

He produced a sealed letter. She recognized the Hawk pressed into what was now hardened wax. "You got this last night?"

"Yesterday," he told her quietly. "We were not certain of your plans, and Lord Grammayre chose to give you as much latitude as possible. You are also," he added, producing another letter, "free to return to the royal library if necessary."

"Not if he didn't *also* give you a letter guaranteeing I can leave."

Severn's lips turned up in a slight smile, but it was genuine—and Kaylin was happy enough seeing it that she realized he hadn't been smiling much at all lately. Then again, she wasn't going to win any Sunshine awards, either.

"Did he include you in that letter?"

"Not by name. I believe the words are *and escort,* but I didn't break the seal to check."

Kaylin sat back in the slightly worn chair.

"You're smiling. Is something amusing you?"

"Not amusement—but it's nice, sometimes, to serve the Hawklord."

Severn was silent for a moment. "He isn't the Wolflord," he finally said. "And the Hawks aren't Wolves. But yes, it's good work." He smiled again, and added, "You're just saying that because you've eaten enough, for a change."

The guards at the gatehouse were polite in a very distant way. They took the letter Kaylin offered them, and the older of the two left them there. He returned fifteen minutes later. "Master Sabrai will see you."

Kaylin offered him a sharp bow, and followed as he lead them to the Hall itself. Severn was beside her, but the guard didn't tell him to wait. He had looked at the Hawk emblazoned across his surcoat, and that was enough.

Master Sabrai was waiting for them at the doors. "Private Neya," he said, bowing. "Corporal Handred."

Severn offered him a perfect bow in return.

"Corporal Handred, you are new to the Halls. Are you familiar with the rules of the Oracle Hall?"

Severn nodded. "Speak to no one, touch no one."

"Very good." Master Sabrai ran a hand through his hair. Kaylin thought it looked paler than it had the last time she'd visited. His eyes were also lined with dark circles.

She stepped forward. "Master Sabrai?"

His smile was polite but unutterably weary.

"We've come to see Everly."

"Only Everly?"

She nodded. "I don't think it will take long."

"This," he replied drily, "is the Oracular Hall. Nothing goes according to plan."

"Has he finished his painting?"

"Which one? Ah, I forget myself. He is almost finished, I think. It is certainly more complete than it was when you first visited." He began to walk away, and they fell in step. Well, close—he was a tall man, and Kaylin had to work to keep up.

"He has another visitor," Master Sabrai said over his shoulder.

"Should we wait?"

"I do not think this particular visitor would be troubled if you appeared."

* * *

Kaylin watched Severn's face as the door opened; she wanted to see his reaction to the Dragon. Unfortunately, she must have blinked, because he didn't appear to have one. He glanced once around the room, and Kaylin was willing to bet her own money that he'd cataloged everything worth looking at in that single glance. The morning light was strong, and the gallery, such as it was, was brighter. But the gallery itself didn't appear to interest Severn. He looked, instead, at its occupants.

Lord Sanabalis was seated to the side and behind Everly. Everly, seated on a three-legged stool, a palette perched precariously in his lap, didn't appear to notice. He was working, and his eyes were that odd blend of color and absence that made his face so striking.

Sanabalis, however, noticed them both immediately, and rose. "Corporal," he said, nodding. "Kaylin."

She tried not to let the lack of rank annoy her. As ranks went, the best that could be said about it was that she couldn't go any lower, but the fact that she *did* have a rank made her a Hawk. "How long have you been here?"

Severn stepped on her foot, and she added, "Lord Sanabalis."

"For the better part of a day."

"A...day."

"The Emperor is concerned," Sanabalis said gravely. "His envoys are scattered throughout the city, and I chose this destination as less tiresome than the Arcanum or the Imperium."

"He has people at the Arcanum?" Her brows, she was certain, had risen so far they were invisible.

"He has *Dragons* at the Arcanum," Sanabalis replied, and the smile that accompanied those words was just a little on the toothy side. Kaylin would have found it disturbing, but she couldn't imagine a group of men who deserved it more. "But enough. You will find the portrait of interest. Come and look at it."

Now that she was here, she was certain she would find it interesting, but the interest was mixed with dread and a growing unease. Severn actually caught her elbow and dragged her along with him.

The first thing she saw was herself. The dress was finished, and it was an exact rendering of the one she now wore. It caught light, so there must be sun someplace. It wasn't in the picture. She was standing in water, but Oracles were often full of symbolic words or images. She was not, however, alone.

Severn's grip had tightened slightly, and she looked up at him. But he wasn't looking at her. Well, he *was*—but at the image. The rest of the room had failed to get any kind of reaction out of him, but this made up for it. Whatever he had expected to see, this wasn't it.

"You are not alone," Sanabalis told her, as if afraid that her vanity might cause her to notice nothing else.

She looked. Where she had begun to draw to catch Everly's attention, he had continued. The blobs that she'd made, with her utter lack of talent, against Everly's stretched canvas had been obliterated. In their place, she could see people. She recognized all of them.

Severn, his forehead bleeding, his weapons glinting in the same sun that bounced off the sheen of the dress she wore, had eyes for her, and only her.

Beside him, a good deal shorter and in a majestic robe she'd seen only once, stood Evanton. He was uninjured, and his gaze went past Kaylin in the picture to meet the eyes of Kaylin the observer. It was disconcerting. He was actually a lot taller than Kaylin would have guessed, but she usually saw him hunched over his work, his back rounded, his shoulders pulled down by gravity.

Beside these two stood Sanabalis. His eyes were red light, and Everly had managed to paint the hint of a sheen to his skin; the shadow of wings lay across the water, although the wings weren't actually visible.

But there was more.

Donalan Idis stood apart from the group. The perspective was wrong, to Kaylin's eye—he seemed far too tall. Cowering at his feet, her face caught in profile, was a child. Pale-haired child, wounded eyes. Behind them a third shadow lay across the ground—for they stood on ground. It didn't belong to anyone.

"Interesting, isn't it?"

She nodded.

"What do you make of it, Kaylin?"

"I'm…not sure. It's not finished," she added defensively.

"No. There is water, there, and land. There is, if you'll note, pillars to the sides of the picture. Were Everly an ordinary painter, I would say they were a framing device. He is not, and I think they may have some significance." He paused and then said, in a voice that sounded like an earth-quake, "Is it enough?"

As if she had all the answers, and were withholding them somehow. Severn's hand tightened again, but he said and did nothing. Everly, however, appeared to notice nothing, hear nothing.

"Has Everly slept at all?" Kaylin asked Master Sabrai, who had been discreet enough to maintain both distance and silence.

"No."

"Eaten?"

"Lord Sanabalis has seen to the task of feeding him."

"He can't keep painting like this, can he?"

Master Sabrai's hands found his hair again. He glanced at Sanabalis, but said nothing. Which was enough for Kaylin.

"He has to sleep," she began.

"He does not have time," Lord Sanabalis said.

"We have almost *two weeks*. Killing him isn't—"

"We don't have two weeks," the Dragon lord said calmly.

"But—"

"We have, at best guess, two days, if that."

"But—but—"

"*Yes*, Kaylin?"

In a far meeker voice, she said, "You said we had weeks."

"Tell her," Sanabalis told Master Sabrai.

The master looked in desperate want of a chair, and Kaylin walked over to the one Sanabalis had vacated, pushing it across the floor. "Sit," she told him.

He sat.

"What happened to the two weeks?"

"It was only ever an estimate," was the stark reply. "But something happened, something changed—"

"Today," Sanbalis told her. "Or yesterday."

"Something we did?"

"Believe that we are evaluating all the possibilities we are aware of. To our knowledge, only one significant event occurred."

"The deaths?"

"The drownings, yes." He paused, and then added, "To our knowledge."

"But how would he know—" She stopped as her brain caught up with her mouth, and she clamped her jaw shut.

"Yes," Sanabalis said quietly. "We do not know what you've been doing. Only that it involved Ybelline and Nightshade. Kaylin, what did you *do*?"

"I don't know."

"You don't *know*?" His brows rose, and his eyes shivered instantly into an orange that was just a little too tinged with red for comfort. But he was utterly still. As if he had to be.

Miserable in ways she hadn't known she could be, she answered his anger with silence.

"Kaylin," Severn said, his voice so soft it wouldn't have traveled had he not bent to speak in her ear.

"I can't say," she told them both miserably.

"Can't, or won't?"

"It's the same thing."

"I do not believe the Emperor would see things the same way."

And for the first time, Everly spoke. His voice was soft and flat, the words almost like brush strokes in their deliberation. "If you take her to the Emperor, he will eat her."

Not, as first words went, all that promising.

Master Sabrai's jaw had slid open and seemed stuck that way as he watched the painter Oracle.

Everly clambered down from the stool, the odd expression that stole personality from his face slowly fading. He walked almost listlessly to the side of the Dragon lord and caught his sleeve, pulling it, his eyes slightly rounded.

The Dragon lord walked over to the picture. Looked at it. Looked at Kaylin. "So you can speak, boy," Sanabalis said softly.

But Everly said nothing. As if a lifetime of effort had gone into the single sentence he had spoken, his shoulders suddenly rounded.

Sanabalis caught him before he hit the ground, and carried him, very gently, to the Master of the Oracle Hall.

"Is it enough?" Master Sabrai whispered, as he took Everly from a Lord of the Imperial Court.

"He believed it was enough," Sanabalis replied. When he looked at Kaylin again, his eyes were a pale gold, with flecks of orange. He looked both tired and old. "Tend to the child, Master Sabrai. Accept the apologies of the Imperial Court for any injury done him." He bowed to the Master of the Oracle Hall.

Master Sabrai, pale and tired, nodded, holding Everly tightly. The boy was still breathing, but his skin had lost all color, as if the color itself had been leeched out of him in service of his painting. In service of the Emperor.

The *same* Emperor who had acceded to the request of an Arcanist, and had allowed the Tha'alani to be driven almost insane. For one sharp minute, Kaylin hated him.

"How damn *long* did you keep him awake? How long has he been working like—like this?"

She felt, rather than saw, Severn's gaze; felt the warning in it. Even understood it through the momentary haze of a surprising fury. Sanabalis might play the old Dragon, the old teacher, the avuncular master—but he *was* a Dragon. She couldn't force herself to apologize or to take the words back, but she managed to stop herself from adding to them.

They waited in silence while Master Sabrai left the room. Severn followed him and opened the door for him.

"I will leave you to the work," Sabrai said without looking back.

By unspoken consent, they waited to resume the conversation that Kaylin didn't want to have; she had already managed to discard the one that had been threatening to choke her, and Sanabalis, to his credit, appeared not to have noticed her display of fury.

When the door clicked shut and Severn crossed the room to join them again, Sanabalis spoke.

"Secrets at this time are not safe, Kaylin. Had you any understanding of the history of the races that comprise the Empire—had you shown any capacity to listen, to absorb, to think clearly—it would be easier to grant you privacy."

"It's not my privacy," she said quietly. "It's not about *me*. If it were, I would tell you."

"And is it so important that you must keep it to yourself when the fate of the city rests in the balance?"

She nodded.

"You can be certain that it is necessary? That you, alone, can analyze the situation, approximate the danger, and confront it?"

"Sanabalis," she said, forgetting titles and Oracles and his momentary display of terrifying temper, "*I don't know*. I don't know if I can do it. But if Everly's painting is any guide, I won't *be* alone. What I learned yesterday—it wasn't *meant* to be learned by someone like me. Or someone like you. Or Severn. But I learned it as a Hawk, and I know my duties.

"I'll uphold the Emperor's Law."

Sanabalis glanced at Severn.

Severn said quietly, "I trust her."

"I trust her intent," the Dragon lord said wearily. "But intent is not enough. The cost if she fails—"

"The cost if I betray what I know is just as great. Maybe greater. This isn't the first time a city has fallen in this place," she added. She spoke a Dragon's name. A dead Dragon. "But the world didn't end, and the mortal and immortal races gathered again, built again. I'm afraid that if I tell you, one at least of those races will never be able to do that.

"Sanabalis, you trusted me, in the Barrani High Court, when there was just as much at stake."

"I had little choice in the matter."

"Pretend that you have as much choice now."

It rankled. She could see that. But she held her ground for a minute. Two minutes. Three. She could count the seconds as they moved past because nothing else moved in the room.

And then, as if reaching a decision, she began to unfasten the ties that bound the plain dress she wore. It wasn't a fine dress. It wasn't the extremely expensive Court garb that the Quartermaster decried. She didn't need help putting the dress on, or taking it off. But her hands trembled anyway as she began to pull the fabric up and over her head. Her hair stick clattered to the ground, and she cursed it, but only in two languages—Leontine and Elantran.

And when the dress was just empty, shapeless cloth, she handed it to Severn, who took it without comment.

Lord Sanabalis looked at the dress she had worn beneath the one she'd purchased with her own money. His eyes were golden, but his lower lids fell, and he took a step toward her.

She flinched as he spoke because he spoke in his mother tongue, and the whole room seemed to tremble with the aftershock. Then he spoke a word that she recognized, not as a sound, but as the essence of fire.

Flame lapped at the dress in a ring that rose from the floor. She turned sharply to Severn, shaking her head; she could see that his hand rested—casually—on the weapon chain around his waist. He had come prepared for a fight, and if he was smart enough to know he had no chance against a Dragon, he was Severn enough not to care.

But *she* cared. "Wait," she told him, when she thought the gaze wouldn't say enough.

A ring of fire rose and as it did, it began to shrink, until its inner edge touched the dress. The fire guttered instantly.

"Interesting," Sanabalis said.

"The essence of water," Kaylin replied.

"Girl, if you had the patience and the wisdom to sit and learn, there is nothing I could not teach you."

"You couldn't teach me to fly," she said bitterly.

"Could I not?" was his soft reply. And giving it, he offered her the hint of a familiar smile, worn around the edges. "I could ask you to understand the essence of air."

"But not today."

"No, Kaylin, not today—and perhaps never, if I understand correctly what you wear."

"I don't understand it," she confessed. "But it's something to do with water, elemental water."

"Oh, it is that." Sanabalis shook his head, and the weariness was transcended, for just a moment, by something she had never seen in his eyes before: wonder. "You make me remember my youth, and my own ignorance. Very well, Kaylin Neya. What you ask, I will grant you. But we have still not located Donalan Idis. Any of the men that we knew as his friends—if he had them—or his associates have heard nothing from him."

"If they're Arcanists, they'll lie."

"I told you—Dragons are in the Arcanum. But they are not alone. The Emperor requested that the Arcanists subject themselves to the Tha'alani, and they agreed."

She winced. "I bet it wasn't pretty."

"There were only two deaths."

"I'm not all that fond of Arcanists," she replied, although she had to squelch her shock at the words. "And it doesn't matter, anyway."

"What doesn't matter?"

"I don't know where Donalan Idis is, but I can guess where he'll be."

"Oh?"

"It's in the painting," she said grimly.

"I see no landmarks in the painting."

"No. Do you see Evanton?"

"I see the Keeper," was his slow reply.

"I've seen him look like that. Once. And if I had to guess, I'd say there's only one place he *can* look like that."

"What do you mean, Kaylin?"

"Those robes—he wore them when he invited Severn and me into the Elemental Garden."

Sanabalis was a tall man, and Severn wasn't exactly short. Kaylin hadn't bothered to put her dress back on; the uncomfortable stares of guards and the Oracles she wasn't allowed to talk to had lost a great deal of import. It was not as if she had that much dignity to lose, after all.

They left the grounds, and Sanabalis spoke a moment to the guards on the insides of the gate. The guards had a hard time keeping their eyes off Kaylin, and she had a passing urge to swear at them in Leontine. She bit it back. If you walked around in a dress like this one, it was bound to get attention.

But the guards came with Sanabalis's carriage. She was almost glad to see it—of all the carriages she'd been in, the

Imperial carriages were the most comfortable. They were also bloody heavy, so bad driving had less of a chance of upending them messily.

They got into the carriage and the horses pulled away from the Oracle Hall. Sanabalis spoke when it was well behind them. "I trust you," he told her quietly, and she wondered if he was repeating it for her benefit or his own. "But, Kaylin, Evanton's abode has stood in that street since before it *was* a street. It has withstood fire, flood, and earthquake. It has withstood mage-storms."

Severn whistled.

Kaylin gritted her teeth. "Mage-storms?" She finally forced herself to ask. Severn and Sanabalis exchanged a glance.

She could almost see, in that glance, the drawing of straws, and wondered who had gotten the short one.

Severn, apparently. "Where mages war," he said carefully, "and it has happened only a handful of times, none of them in living memory, the magics—if powerful enough—unleash a backlash. We call this backlash a mage-storm. In it, all laws are suspended. No, not Imperial Laws, Kaylin. Natural laws. Anything can happen, and much of what passes under a mage-storm is...significantly changed by the passage."

"But Evanton's...shop?...is different," Sanabalis continued. "It has existed, unchanging, in all forms of the Empire, and in all cities that existed before Elantra. The wise of both orders would consider the destruction of that shop to be impossible."

"Both orders?"

"The Order of Imperial Mages," he replied, "and the Arcanum."

"So you don't think—"

"No. If I am to trust instinct, I will trust it fully. I believe that you are correct."

"But—"

"The Keeper is not beholden to Imperial Law."

"I thought that was only the Emperor."

"He is not beholden to Imperial Law in exactly the same way the sunrise is not. Were there some way to control it and use it, the Emperor would have done so. But it is the sun, it is necessary, and it rises and sets over his Empire. It does not threaten it.

"In a like way, the Keeper exists."

"Idis stole something from the garden."

"So it is believed. The question is not what he stole, but how. He should never have been able to gain entrance to that place, and that he did so without the knowledge of the Keeper bodes ill."

"But if he did it with the knowledge of the Keeper—"

"It would never happen," Sanabalis said flatly. "You've made the Law your life, and in a far more complete and intense way, the Keeper has made the Keeping of that Garden his. He would no more allow Idis entry unescorted—or, if I had to guess, escorted—than he would allow the Emperor. Or the Dragon lords."

"You think he's going to tell you to drop dead."

"In a manner of speaking, yes. And if he does not—then we have far more pressing problems."

"More pressing than the end of the city?"

Sanabalis was silent as the wheels bumped over the more

egregious cracks in the cobbled stone. "What you said," he told her at last, "was true. There has often been a city in this place. The city has often been destroyed. But the peoples who comprise any city have returned, time and again, and rebuilt."

"What, exactly, is the purpose of the garden?"

"I wondered if that would occur to you." His tone implied *and about time,* although he didn't insult her by saying it in so many words.

"And the answer?"

"To the best of our knowledge, as the Keeper is not of a mind to answer our questions, the garden keeps the elemental forces bound."

"But if it did that there would be no elementalists."

"Kaylin, there will always be fire. Water. Air. There will always be earth. Where these things exist, an echo of ancient power also exists, and men with the will and knowledge to summon that power can do so in safety.

"But in the garden, the waking of what slumbers—"

She lifted a hand. "You're telling me it's not just about water."

"No. Not if we meet Idis there."

"Then we'd better bloody well make it in time," she snarled. She propped herself up on the window's ledge and shoved her upper body through it—she was smaller than Severn or Sanabalis, and she could. Barely.

"Hey! Move it!"

Sanabalis winced slightly.

Severn said, in as mild a tone as he could while raising his voice to be heard, "What is the first thing you learned about riding in a carriage?"

"I didn't stick my arms out," she said, as she fell back into her seat with unwanted help from Severn.

The carriage, however, began to move faster, and Kaylin had the happy task of trying to be grateful for the speed. She managed to be grateful that it wasn't Teela driving.

Evanton, she thought. *Hold on. We're coming.*

CHAPTER 20

The streets were not empty. They became as empty as it was possible to be, given lack of notice and a hurtling carriage, and Kaylin shouted curses at the driver when the face of a terrified man or woman flashed past the window. The children—and she had no doubt at all they existed—were too short to be caught in the window's moving frame, proof, if the gods existed, that they had an eye for small mercies.

On the other hand, had she seen children in danger, she would probably have climbed out the window, Severn and Sanabalis notwithstanding, to push the driver off the coach seat and take over the reins. Which, given she'd never really driven a coach before, would have made things interesting. But how hard could it be?

The part of her mind that could think noted that the panic in the streets seemed to be caused entirely by the presence of a hurtling coach, and not by the presence of arcane magics and battles. Whatever was happening in Elani Street, it wasn't visible to the untrained eye. Something to be grateful for.

It wasn't all that far from the Oracle Hall to Elani Street, and to Kaylin's surprise—and gratitude—Sanabalis ordered a halt when they reached the T junction at which Elani began. Or ended, depending on which way you walked the beat.

It was quiet enough on the street that the emergence of Severn, Sanabalis, and Kaylin in her not-very-cloth-heavy dress caused people who were otherwise minding their own business to stop and stare. Sanabalis didn't seem to notice.

She looked at Severn and said, "Well, at least their morning won't be entirely boring."

"Boredom," Sanabalis intoned, "is underrated." He set the pace for their walk. It left Kaylin not quite enough breath for a rejoinder. Not that she had one ready. She picked up the skirts of her dress and trotted after him; her own legs weren't equal to the task of matching his stride.

Severn had neither the problem of skirts nor height. But he kept pace with Sanabalis because Kaylin did, not because he walked beside the Dragon. The doors to the various shops in the street opened and closed as people entered or left, baskets on their arms. It was hot enough that wide-brimmed hats were in evidence everywhere, and Kaylin desperately wished she had one. Not that it was part of the uniform, but then again, she didn't at the moment have a uniform, either.

The thought of facing the Quartermaster again made the

temperature drop noticeably. The thought of groveling for another few weeks—if she was lucky—made her cringe.

Severn cuffed her shoulder. "Pay attention," he said.

"I was."

"Pay attention to where we are."

She mumbled something that would have passed as an inaudible apology if you didn't actually know her. Severn let it pass. Wolf or Hawk, he was used to watching the shadows, and if the sun was miserly in casting those shadows, they were still there.

But she saw nothing in them besides the occasional scuffle that could be either a mouse or a cockroach, nothing to set her teeth on edge.

They approached Evanton's shop, and saw the sandwich board that he put out maybe once a week, when custom, as he called it, was slow. It hadn't been blown to tinder; it hadn't even been knocked over. It also hadn't been repainted in about ten years, but she was used to that.

"So far so good," she said. Sanabalis didn't hear her. Severn, however, gave her a curt nod. He did not draw his weapon—not yet. It hung around his waist, the chain giving the illusion of being a very odd fashion statement. The blade was in its sheath at Severn's thigh. Her own daggers— damn it all to hell!—were still conspicuously absent. And she'd reached for them as they approached the familiar windows, the familiar closed door.

The curtains were pulled to either side of a window that, like the sandwich board, had seen better days. Sunlight reflected their images, as if this were a poor mirror. To see in, you had to touch the window, press your face underneath your hand, and squint.

Which, of course, was beneath the dignity of a Dragon lord. Kaylin had long since decided that dignity of this particular kind was overrated. She put the sides of both hands on the glass and pressed her face against it, peering into the clutter of Evanton's shop.

Inside, it looked pretty much as it had always looked.

"I don't see Evanton," she told her companions. "But if there was some sort of fight here, it ended damn quickly."

"You sense no magic?"

"None. You?"

"It pains me to admit that I do not have your sensitivity to magical auras," Sanabalis replied gravely. "And the Keeper's abode is...not a place where one wishes to introduce foreign magic."

"If there's magic in here," she said as she pulled away from the window, "it's all normal."

Severn raised a brow. She grimaced; she seldom used the words *magic* and *normal* in any sentences that were side by side.

"The door, Corporal?" Sanabalis said quietly.

Severn walked to the door, the glass pane bearing its familiar arch of letters above the wooden slats from which a brass handle protruded. If the sandwich board was on display, it meant the door was unlocked. But in theory it *also* meant that Evanton was available for odd jobs, services, and the stupid "magic" that people often sought from him. Severn gripped the brass handle and pulled.

The door swung open. "It's not locked," he told Lord Sanabalis. He walked in. Kaylin, standing behind the Dragon lord, waited. And waited. And waited.

Finally, exasperated, she said, "Sanabalis, move."

Sanabalis turned to look down on her. It seemed a long way for his gaze to drop. She had the grace to redden, although she resented the momentary embarrassment; Teela was a lord of the High Court, and she talked to Teela that way.

Clearing her throat, she said, "Lord Sanabalis, the store is clearly open. Why are you blocking the door?" She chose to speak in High Barrani. It was hard to offend someone by accident in the Court tongue—although for reasons that weren't obvious it could be done; in High Barrani, the context made the most exquisitely polite of sentences deadly insults. For that reason, she spoke it as little as humanly possible.

"My apologies, Lord Kaylin," Sanabalis said, replying in the same language, which pretty much guaranteed that he would use the title she found so awkward. "But it has been…many, many years since a Dragon lord was allowed to cross the threshold of the Keeper's abode."

"You were waiting for an invitation?"

"Exactly."

Severn came back. "If you feel you must wait for an invitation, Lord Sanabalis, I fear you will wait a long time." His High Barrani was flawless, and trust him to slide right into it. To Kaylin, he added, "He's not here."

Kaylin sidled around Sanabalis. "I don't need an invitation," she told him, dropping into Elantran again.

"You have never been a threat."

She stepped through the door that Severn held open, crossing the threshold. No magic. "I doubt that you would be considered a threat today," she said. "We don't *have time* for social niceties." She remembered to add the word *please* to the end of her frustrated sentence. Damn Dragons, anyway.

But Lord Sanabalis waited in the door frame.

Fine. "Did you check the kitchen?"

"The kitchen, the back parlor, the other side of his bar."

"He calls it a desk."

"His very long and very heavily built desk, then. He's not in any of the unlocked rooms, and knocking on locked supply rooms didn't seem to have much effect."

They stared at each other for a moment.

"Sana—Lord Sanabalis."

Sanabalis raised a peppered brow.

"I take all consequences for your behavior while you are in this establishment upon my own shoulders. I will stop you from doing anything that you are not allowed, by Evanton, to do."

He waited for another moment, and she snorted.

"I give my word."

And curse it, damn it all, she felt a surge of magic then.

To her surprise—a sour sort of surprise, really—Sanabalis actually chuckled. "Ever impulsive, Kaylin. However, if the Keeper is not present in body, he was obviously aware of your vow. He either has great faith in you, or he has a sense of humor that suits you."

"Either that," Severn added, "or he's desperate."

Sanabalis crossed the threshold, and Severn stepped out into the street, lifting the sandwich board by its hinges so that it swung flat. He tucked it under his arm, almost hit Kaylin as he maneuvered his way back into the shop, and placed it against a wall.

Well, if she were honest, against a shelf that had enough dust it was hard to tell what the dust covered. He then closed the door firmly behind them.

"I think it best that the shop be closed for business for now."

Kaylin nodded. When Severn rejoined her she said, "He's in the garden, isn't he?"

"That would be my guess."

"There's a slight problem with that."

"Would it have to do with a key?"

She nodded.

He reached into his shirt and pulled out a ring that would have easily fit around his shoulder. Around it were a familiar set of keys.

"You found those?"

Severn nodded.

"Where?"

"Oddly enough, in the kitchen."

"On the table?"

"Not exactly."

"Then—"

"There was a tin that also contained biscuits," he replied, giving her an odd look. "It was there."

Kaylin had the grace to flush. "Look, it's been *years* since I've wandered into his kitchen and helped myself to his food. And I hardly ever did it—only when he and Teela started one of their long, boring discussions about beads or crystals or magic."

"How many years?"

"Never mind."

Sanabalis was staring at her.

"What?" she said, knowing she sounded a great deal more defensive than was appropriate.

"You wandered into the Keeper's private kitchen and stole his food?"

"They were biscuits, and they weren't *that* good."

"And she was probably hungry," Severn added. She stepped on his foot.

"He meant for you to find these," Sanabalis said. It was almost a question.

"I think he meant for Kaylin to find them," Severn replied. "Given where she was likely to look, and given that food might be a target of opportunity, and given, last, the erratic way she eats meals, it would have been the simplest choice."

"But the container was not magicked in any way?"

Severn shook his head. He held out the keys to Kaylin, and she took them.

"Are you ready?" he asked her softly, and this time he did unsheathe the blade that was attached to the chain.

"Hardly," she said bitterly, holding out hands that were empty of anything but an oversize dangling key ring.

"We can get you new daggers," he told her.

"I know. And I know it's stupid to worry about them. But Severn—they were the first thing I—they were mine."

"You won't have them. I could give you mine—"

"But if I need your daggers, I'm probably already dead."

"That was my thought."

She took a deep breath, and then walked over to the narrow door that nested between two overtall shelves. It was easy to miss it amid the clutter—and she had to pull a chair or two out of the way just to clear enough of a path for Sanabalis to get to it.

Once there, she chose a key and put it in the lock. Then she chose another. The lock clicked open, and Kaylin pushed the narrow door ajar. "This way," she whispered to Sanabalis.

"Lead," he told her carefully. "I will say or touch nothing, but I will follow."

The back halls of the shop were exactly as she remembered them—too narrow to fight in with anything but daggers or fists. They were not high ceilinged, and they were not decorated for show; no paintings hung here, and no paper covered the flat, dull surfaces of wood that had seen better days.

But as she walked down hall, she reached for her daggers again—and cursed again. Because the hall wasn't empty, and standing in front of the only door at its end was someone she didn't recognize.

A young man, older than she was, younger than Severn, and shorter, as well. He was not built for fighting, and he wasn't dressed for it, either—he was dressed, in her opinion, for a life of begging on the open streets. But he stood facing them, and he carried a dagger. The way he waved it made her wince with embarrassment for him.

His hair was dark and his eyes were a honeyed shade that looked familiar.

After a moment, approaching him cautiously—and not just because he held a naked blade—she said a single word.

"Grethan."

His eyes widened slightly at the sound of his name, which told Kaylin that it *was* his name. And that he could hear. He couldn't, in her opinion, do much damage with that knife; given that Severn and Sanabalis were his two opponents, she altered that opinion. He couldn't do much damage to someone *else*.

But she couldn't somehow imagine that Grethan, disheveled, dirty, and obviously teetering on the brink of a very narrow edge, had come into Evanton's shop and pulled a knife on him. Or rather, that the knife itself had had much effect beyond that of extraneous punctuation to a verbal threat. Someone else's threat.

"Boy," Severn said, speaking softly as he inched forward, "do you understand what you're doing?"

Grethan looked confused, as if the question made no sense. And to give him this much credit, Kaylin thought it was a pretty stupid question herself. He was standing there with a knife in front of a closed door, barring the way. Hard not to know you were doing that.

"What he wants to say," she said instead, "is do you know what Donalan Idis is doing behind your back?"

Severn shot her a rather sharp look, but most of his attention was on Grethan.

"Yes," Grethan said quietly.

"And it was important enough for you to kidnap one of your own children and hand her to him?"

Silence.

"Grethan, do you *know* what Idis did, while he was in the Imperial Service?" For it came to her suddenly that, without the Tha'alaan, he wouldn't.

"He served the Emperor," the boy said defiantly.

"Yes, but doing what?"

"He taught the Emperor about the Tha'alani," Grethan replied, as if by rote. "He told the Emperor what *we* could do, and how *we* could serve."

"Is that what he told you?"

Grethan's eyes narrowed. "He came close to understanding," he hissed. "He came close enough to understanding the Tha'alaan that he could *touch* it."

"Grethan—"

"But the Tha'alani were jealous. They didn't *want* the deaf to be able to touch the Tha'alaan."

Kaylin closed her eyes. "That's what he told you? And why did he tell you to take the child?"

"Because he hadn't finished," Grethan replied. "She hasn't been hurt. I saw to that. I wouldn't let him hurt her."

"You *haven't* seen to that," Kaylin snarled, sudden in her anger. "You're *here*. You have *no idea* what he's doing to her now."

"He was one of my only friends," Grethan snarled back, just as angry. "When I came here—when I—he was there.

"And he didn't *pity* me. He understood that I had been

born crippled. He promised that he could *heal* me. But he couldn't heal me because the Emperor stopped his work. The Tha'alani stopped his work—don't you see? They're special, they've always known they're special, and they *don't want to give that up*. They agreed to work for the Emperor if men like Master Idis were forbidden their research. *They want us to be deaf!*"

"Is that what he told you?" She couldn't stop herself from gaping, but words kind of helped.

"It's the truth!"

"And the truth was reason enough to kidnap and *torture* a child?"

Silence, then. Grethan's face, however, was not still. It was flushed, and the muscles of his jaw were flapping like Kaylin's, but without the attendant sound.

Right up until that moment, she'd been prepared to pity him. To even sympathize with him. But she saw the knowledge in his suddenly averted gaze. She knew that he could lie to himself—about what was done, or how, or why—that he could tell himself that in the end, the nebulous bloody *end* that justified all means, Mayalee would be *all right*.

But she was done with sympathy now. She was almost done with petty things like law. She felt her arms begin to tingle, felt the itch of something dangerously like magic begin to encompass her whole body.

And Lord Sanabalis stepped in, grabbing her shoulder. Light flared, blue and hot; Kaylin bit back a cry. But in spite of the shock of pain that must have gone through both of them, he didn't let go until he had pushed her to one side. To Severn's side, actually.

Severn's touch was gentle, and he was careful to avoid the marks. "Kaylin?" She met his gaze briefly; she didn't want to distract either Severn or herself. But brief was enough to see everything he wouldn't expose in words: his fear for her, his fear of the power that the marks contained, his reminder that she no longer wore the bracer that would keep all that wild power at bay.

It calmed her, somehow. She took a deep breath, held it, and let go. The back of her neck stopped the particular ache that spoke of her own magic.

Lord Sanabalis drew himself to his full height, and he let the lower membranes fall from his very, very orange eyes. He spoke Elantran, but the Elantran he spoke was not Elantran as Kaylin knew it—it was pinned to the hearing by the low and loud sound of rumbling.

Dragon's voice.

Grethan brandished an infinitely pathetic dagger in front of his chest, his eyes darting from side to side as if somehow escape would magically appear.

"Do you know who I am, boy?" Sanabalis asked.

Grethan said nothing.

"Do you know *what* I am?"

And even Grethan, sheltering with such ferocious tenacity in his own ignorance, could not pretend that Sanabalis was anything other than a Dragon.

"You can't stop him," Grethan whispered. He might have shouted, but he'd lost the capacity.

"You are in the way," Sanabalis replied. "And I serve the Emperor directly. If you value your life, *come here.*"

It wasn't what Kaylin had expected him to say.

But had she been Grethan, she would have moved.

Grethan, terrified, took two halting steps forward.

"I would kill you," the Dragon said—and there was almost nothing left of the Sanabalis who calmly watched Kaylin's continual failure in their lessons, "but I am sworn to the Emperor, and the Emperor has his Laws. These two are Hawks. They are your witnesses, and you had best hope they survive, because if they don't, boy, you won't."

Grethan started to say something, his knuckles white around a dagger that would—at best—scratch Sanabalis.

"What you want," Kaylin began, speaking in a voice that was now entirely normal, "isn't wrong. But how you get what you want—Grethan, she's a terrified child, away from her parents. Forget that she can't reach the Tha'alaan—she's alone, here, and the only person whom she trusts, or whom she thought she could trust, is working for the man who—" She couldn't bring herself to say the rest. Not without losing it. "What he told you— it's not the truth."

"IT IS THE TRUTH!"

He'd grown up in a world where no one lied. He'd fled it to the safety of a world where almost everyone did. She tried to remember this. She tried damn hard.

Sanabalis, however, reached into a fold of…nothing, as far as Kaylin could see, which would normally have been disturbing, and pulled out a crystal with a heart of fire.

Memory crystal, she thought, and then, looking at it more closely, thought, *That one?*

"This is the truth, boy. If you want the truth, take it."

"You're lying—"

"Am I?" He held the crystal out in the palm of his hand. "Do you know how the crystals work? You must have seen their like in the company of your master."

Grethan was stiff jawed, almost wild. "You can make them say anything—"

"They record what happens," he replied. "There are magicks built into them at their making that force this, and further, make them immune to tampering. And this one was requested by the two Hawks who now stand beside me. There is a reason that Donalan Idis is feared and hated by your kin, and it is not your reason."

"I don't hate them!"

"No?"

"I want to *belong,* don't you understand? I *want* what I should have had at birth!"

Home, Kaylin thought. She closed her eyes. She would not pity this man. She would not give in.

Sanabalis however, continued to speak as if there had been no interruption. "You want the truth. It is here. And yes, it is a crystal taken from the archives of the Imperial Service."

For another second, he hesitated, and it was Severn who said, "If we meant to go through the door without first giving you a chance to understand the danger you have placed us all in, you would be dead now."

Grethan swallowed. And then he held out one hand, not

the dagger hand. It was shaking so much Kaylin wondered how he could keep it up at all. But Sanabalis had no mercy in him. He dropped the crystal into the boy's hand.

Grethan's eyes rolled up, exposing only whites, as he fell to his knees. He didn't release the dagger, and Severn caught him at the last moment to make certain he didn't land on the damn thing.

"The door, Kaylin," he said, the previous calm swamped by urgency. "Now."

She stepped over Grethan's prone form. "Was that really the memory crystal?" she asked the Dragon as she fumbled with the key.

"Yes. Dragons generally do not stoop to lie. It is far more effort than killing."

"Huh. Then why are the Barrani so good at it?"

His broad shrug was all of his answer.

Grethan began to scream.

Kaylin almost dropped the key ring at the shock of it. She wanted to hate this boy. She *did* despise him. But some part of her understood him, and if it wasn't a part she was proud of, it didn't bloody well matter. She found the right key, slid it into the lock, and twisted.

The click was somehow louder than the screaming.

CHAPTER 21

Were it not for the fact that Dragons weighed a good deal more than their human form suggested, Kaylin would have been blown down the hall. As it was, howling wind knocked her back into Lord Sanabalis's chest. He put one arm around her to hold her in place, and shouted something to Severn. Given how close his mouth was to her ear, she should have heard it—but the wind was strong enough that the words were swept away.

Folds of white fabric were likewise lifted and carried by the wind, fanning flat against Sanabalis as if they were wet. But Sanabalis stepped forward, into the wind's roar, and this time, Kaylin *did* hear what he said. Or rather, she heard his roar. It was low, loud, and appeared to be endless, as if roaring itself required nothing at all but will—no air, for instance, and no breath.

Her eyes were tearing; she had to close them as Sanabalis

made headway through a door that was barely wide enough to grant him entrance. If *this* was the way the garden said "no visitors," Kaylin decided she was never going to bring a Dragon back.

Inch by inch Sanabalis struggled to clear the narrow frame's threshold, and she clung to him as he walked, her own feet dangling above the ground.

But when his second foot was firmly on the green earth in the garden, the wind died. Severn, his hair slanted almost sideways across his face, stepped out from behind Sanabalis.

Sanabalis in turn set Kaylin gently down on her own feet. "My apologies," he said, his voice quieter than usual.

"For what?"

"I believe that was the garden's greeting."

"It didn't do that when we visited last time."

"You were in the company of the Keeper." He lifted his hands and held them open, palm up, in the stillness of the air. He looked up, as Kaylin had first done, at the boundless blue of sky. To her surprise, he smiled.

The garden hadn't been small on the inside. But now—now it appeared vast. Kaylin turned to look at the door they'd entered, and wasn't particularly surprised when she couldn't see it. She shoved the key ring into Severn's hands, as her own dress didn't have much room for storage.

"We will not require them, now," Sanabalis told them both.

"It wasn't *like* this—"

"Oh, hush, child. Can you not pause a moment at the sheer wonder of this place?"

"We don't live forever. Minutes count."

Severn touched her shoulder. "Can you see anyone else?"

"No."

"Can you sense anyone else?"

"No." She paused, and then said, reluctantly, "No."

"He is here," Sanabalis told them both quietly.

"Idis?"

"The Keeper. And Idis, yes."

"How can you tell?"

"The garden has almost reverted to its true form," he replied. "And if it has, the Keeper has withdrawn his power. He has either used it, or he hoards it. But he no longer spends it holding the elements to their quiet shape."

"I think we'd better hurry," Kaylin said. She looked to Severn for guidance, and he shrugged. "Sanabalis?"

"Hmm?"

"I'm not sure which way to go."

"Forward," the Dragon replied, and began to walk.

Kaylin very gratefully fell in behind him, Severn by her side. The problem with magic was that it dropped hints at its own convenience, not hers. She could rely on her training, on her abilities to fight—or to know when a fight was just death waiting to happen. She could rely on her ability to read, and occasionally, to make sense of the maps the Aerians had drawn for the use of the Halls of Law. She could even rely on her knowledge of the Laws themselves. But a few marks on her arms that occasionally itched—or worse—gave her nothing solid to stand on. They were like the window displays in the shops that only the very, very wealthy could enter. All that promise of finery, and none of where she wanted it to be when she wanted it.

Unlike Severn. Or Marcus. Or any of the other Hawks.

If they managed to do whatever it was they had to do here, it would be *because* of the solid, everyday people she could count on. Yes, even Sanabalis, who was walking so fast she had to sprint to keep pace.

The grass grew wild; Sanabalis flattened a path through it by the simple expedient of weight. Here and there, weeds had flowered, striking in their colors and chaos. These, too, he trampled underfoot. Kaylin did the same, cringing as she jogged. But the grass grew shorter and sparser as they walked, and the sun—if it *was* a sun—loomed larger and larger. No moons here, the full height of day. Not for the first time, Kaylin wished she'd brought a hat. It was *hot.*

"Yes," Sanabalis said, as if reading her mind. "It is hot here. And the heat is dangerous for both of you. It is not humid. It is much, much warmer now than it was in the streets of Elantra."

"We can't get out of the heat. There's no shade."

Sanabalis nodded grimly. "None," he replied. "But there are no fires yet. The Keeper still holds this ground, Kaylin. Some of his power lingers here."

"How can you tell?"

"How can you not?"

She started to say something, bit back the words, and concentrated. *What is the shape of fire?*

Sanabalis smacked the back of her head, as if she were

an errant child. "Do *not* think that here! Kaylin, it is a wonder to me that you survived to be a Hawk. In the safety of the West Room, it is impossible to get you to speak in complete, coherent sentences, let alone concentrate on your studies.

"But *here,* where it would be insanity, you suddenly become studious?"

Rubbing the back of her head—and the goose egg she was certain was growing there—she mumbled an apology.

But Severn caught the Dragon's arm. "Lord Sanabalis," he began.

"I don't care if he hit me," Kaylin said in a rush.

Severn raised a dark brow. "You clearly deserved it. I wasn't about to defend you."

"Oh. Then what were you about to do?"

"If you would care to stop interrupting the corporal," Sanabalis said drily, "perhaps you wouldn't have need of the question. Corporal Handred?"

"I think we should take the risk."

His words clearly made no sense to the Dragon. They barely made sense to Kaylin.

"Risk?" she said.

"What you were about to do—do it."

Sanabalis lifted a hand, and Kaylin stepped out of the way. But it wasn't raised to hit her. It was raised to stop Severn's words. "It is too great a risk here. You do not understand what the garden is, and what the Keeper is."

"No. But I understand what Kaylin is." He looked at her, and then added, "More or less."

"Severn—"

"I was…with you."

"When?"

"When you visited the Castle, Kaylin. I was with you. I didn't see what you saw, I couldn't hear what you heard—but what you felt, I felt. And I do not think," he added, gazing at the cracked land that seemed to stretch out before them for miles, "that we have the time to walk through the garden, as Lord Sanabalis calls it."

"I'm not sure that what I—what I was going to do—"

"Will make the walk shorter?"

She nodded.

But Sanabalis was now staring at her with unlidded, golden eyes.

"Let Sanabalis do it," she said in her quietest voice.

"Because if he makes the mistake it's his fault, not yours?" The scorn in the words was worse than a physical slap. She wanted to say something just as sharp, just as wounding—but she stopped herself because what he'd said was true. And if it was true, she deserved his scorn.

And the last thing she wanted from Severn was scorn.

"Kaylin," Lord Sanabalis said quietly, "what is the shape of fire?"

Standing on the cracked, hard ground beneath the baleful sun, she *knew*. She knew what the shape of fire was. She could remember the feel of it, the heat inches from her open hands, her upturned face. She could remember the crackle of its voice, the way it waited before her, the way it danced, flames like sinuous tendons, free from the awkward confines of skin or bone. She could remember—

How to call it.

It was the easiest thing in the world.

There was the smallest place, the smallest *space*, between their world and fire, and the fire could be coaxed out, could be pulled out. It could not come without aid, and that aid required power and knowledge.

Kaylin had Uriel's knowledge. Kaylin had lived Uriel's life.

But she no longer had his hatred, his anger, or his guilt. She called the fire, and it came, and she could see it pouring into the world as if it were molasses. But where Uriel had stopped, Kaylin couldn't. The fire, once it had her memories and her power as a guide, didn't seem to need anything else.

It kept on pouring out of wherever it had been contained, and Kaylin began to fight it, to try to slow it down. Her eyes were closed, but she could still see the fire, see it growing, gaining width and height, gaining some sort of shape.

She shouted a warning—to Severn, to Sanabalis. She couldn't later be certain what she'd said. Only that she'd been afraid for them. And fear was bad.

Uriel had never been afraid. But Uriel didn't have to be. He could speak to the fire.

He could speak to the fire.

She took a deep breath and almost coughed her lungs out. The fire was *so* close. She opened her eyes, and saw flame, saw red and yellow, orange and gold, white and blue—a haze of color, of heat.

And, gritting her teeth, she reached out with her hand.

Was very, very surprised when a hand of flame reached out in turn, and pressed itself against her palm. The pain was instant, unavoidable—but she expected that much, and she bit back all sound. Because her hand was *not* on fire, and the fire did not blister or blacken it. She'd seen burns; she knew damn well what fire could do.

Dead fire.

Not living fire, not like this.

It had no face, no eyes—the hand was the only thing remotely human about it. It was enough.

It has been long, the fire said, inside her.

She wasn't sure what to say in response; etiquette lessons hadn't really covered large fire elementals. But as she hesitated, someone came to her rescue.

Kaylin Neya, a familiar voice said, crackling like fire. It was Evanton.

She almost let go of the fire in shock, but the fire held on. *Evanton?*

You took your time, was his reply. *And you don't have much of it.*

Where are you?

Crackle took the words.

Evanton—

Just get here, girl. You and that partner of yours. Oh, and the damn Dragon, and you can tell him I noticed he's here. There'll be words.

But how—

Oh.

"Severn, Sanabalis, we're going now."

"We're— Kaylin!"

The fire, bending at her request, scooped them all up in its folds. They should have been ash. They should have been dead. Well, not Sanabalis—she suspected the fire couldn't harm him—but she and Severn.

Instead, they were borne aloft by the moving flame, and if they felt its heat, that was all they felt. Even the pain of that first contact was spared them.

You are not Uriel, the fire said as they traveled.

No, she replied carefully. But she had chosen to be honest, because—well, it was fire. There wasn't much reason to lie to fire; fire was outside of the human condition. *I'm Kaylin Neya.*

But you are Uriel's kin.

I'm— She started to disagree, and then stopped because, after all, what was kinship to fire? What did it mean? Fire didn't get married; it didn't father children; it didn't need midwives. Her arms and legs were tingling, and the back of her neck was so prickly it hurt. *Yes,* she said. *I'm his kin.*

Speak to us, Uriel-kin. Kaylin. Speak to us. Give us your voice.

What could she say to fire? She looked at Sanabalis, and realized that he couldn't hear the fire. Wondered what he would have said, if he could. Probably that fire was dangerous.

And it was. She had seen what fire had done at Uriel's command. But *this* fire, she thought firmly, would be different. This fire would save the world. Or at least the city. Or Mayalee.

Speak to us, the fire said again, and she thought there was something in its tone that was coaxing. As if *she* were the elemental, and had to be teased out of a small, small space in the worlds that separated them.

And maybe, for fire, she was.

So she did what she did when the foundling kits gathered round her—after they'd had their arguments over who got to sit beside her and who got to sit in her lap this time— and she began to tell it a story.

There were several false starts, because fire and children weren't the same, and Kaylin, loving an audience, wanted a story that would mean something *to* that audience.

After a pause, some furious thought, and some editing, she said, *In my lands, it is often cold.* She expected interruption, but the fire seemed to take more from her than just the words, and she realized that Uriel had seldom spoken with simple *words*.

She imagined winter. Winter in the fiefs. The cold, the killing cold, ruled the nights, in this story, and even in the day the sun was chill. She felt the fire's shock and ire at this, and smiled.

There were two children, she told the fire. A boy and a girl, some five years younger. They had very little warm clothing that winter (she had to stop to explain the concept of warm clothing and cool clothing). It was harsh, and their mother had died.

The enemy killed her.

No, Kaylin said softly. *Time, and illness.*

And on that cold day, they found an abandoned room—and it had one large window, but the window had no shutters, no way to keep the wind out. Still, the room had a roof, and a floor that was almost solid.

This was to be their home for the winter, and they were happy to have found it. But it was very, very cold, even in their shelter.

The boy left. He was gone for hours, and the girl huddled against the wall, where the wind through the window was weakest, holding her knees to her chest while she waited. The boy had told her not to sleep because sometimes sleep in the cold meant death, and she didn't want to die. So she waited, awake, and when he came back, she saw that he carried several logs, cold with ice and snow.

As stories went, Kaylin knew, this one lacked almost anything that would please children. But she remembered that winter well. She remembered Severn. She remembered his clothing because it was too small or too large; she remembered the shape of his feet, the way they looked so red and raw in the cold. She remembered that he found some stale bread, that he pulled it out of a large pocket after he dropped the logs—it wasn't enough to feed even one person, but it was so unexpected, it was a gift.

And her hands were so cold they *hurt* with it, and she could barely hold the bread he'd given her, and the bread itself was frozen solid. It had probably fallen off a wagon headed to the Castle, and had gone unseen in the snow, one small roll.

But while she worked at it, while she tried to eat, Severn put the logs in the grate, and he did something, and she remembered the sight of his bent back, his shoulders. He seemed like a giant, then. She stopped eating, although she was hungry; she wanted Severn to eat, too. Her mother had always made her share, and even if her mother wasn't there—well, she was watching from somewhere, wasn't she? Wasn't she?

And then she heard Severn's sigh, saw the breath mist out from his mouth and rise like a cloud. Relief. Even happiness. She crept over to his side, the half-gnawed roll in her hand, and she curled up around his left arm, pressing the food into his hand.

"I ate," he told her.

Oh, she was such a child. Such a selfish, stupid child. She believed him. She was so hungry. She was so cold. But she wasn't afraid, because Severn was there.

And in front of Severn, burning brightly, little flames dancing like angels amid the wood he'd carried in, was fire. She leaned too close, of course, and part of her hair got singed—she still remembered the smell of it—but the fire was *warm*.

And warmth was life.

She curled up in Severn's lap, pulled his arms around her—child, child, child—and listened to him while he told her all of the things he could see in the flames. After a while, and because she had always interrupted him, she began to tell him what she saw, and they sat huddled there while the night passed and the fire burned.

It had been good hardwood, and it had burned a long while, and she had never asked him where it had come from.

She felt the ripple of movement pass through the fire like a sigh.

So, it said.

Fire was life, for the children, she told the fire. And then she added, *You saved us, then.*

She felt curiosity and confusion. But no anger. *Uriel-kin,* the fire finally said.

Yes?

What of your wars? What of your people?

Those wars are long over, she told the fire. *But the small wars, the small deaths—those will never end. You took life, you burned.*

Yes. And she felt its desire.

But you saved life. You saved my life. I ask you to aid us again, fire. One of my children is missing. She was taken by my enemy, and she is held here.

In this *place?*

It came to her, slowly, that he knew what this place was. This garden.

Yes. You are taking us there now.

But the fire had stopped moving. *I can go no farther than this, Uriel-kin. I would burn for you. I would burn. But I can go no farther here.*

The fire gently let her down, and she saw, at the edge of cracked, dry dirt, the shallows of a wide, moving river. The riverbank was hard, though, and she doubted that it would ever soften. No mud here.

I don't want you to burn for me, Kaylin told the fire as Severn touched her hand.

But if you do not desire the burning, you will not call me. You will not speak to me again. Teller of tales, Chosen, will you not summon me?

I will summon you, she told the fire. *I give you my word. I will summon you, and I will tell you the shapes I see in your heart, and you will keep the winter from me in the coldest nights.*

And then she let the fire go.

She did not force it back, and it lingered there, near the water, steam rising in its wake. But she did not fear it, now. Maybe later. Maybe when she saw, again, the damage that fire could do, the burns and the ruin it made of flesh and shelter.

But now, she looked at the moving water, straightening the folds of her dress.

Severn's hand was warm. Before thought caught up with her, before reticence kept her still, she turned toward him and curled her arms around his arm, as she had done when she was a child.

In turn, he lifted a hand and stroked her hair and said, just as he had said on that winter day, "It will grow back."

Which made no sense, until she realized the familiar smell of burned hair had been so strong for a reason.

Sanabalis looked at her when she at last released Severn's arm. "You've grown," he said. "You've grown wiser. What the Hawks saw in you as a child, I will not guess, but they chose to trust you. And I will say that they were not wrong.

They may be proved wrong in the future. Humans are capricious and known for change. But today, Kaylin, you have proved yourself worthy of their trust."

"How? We're not done yet."

He looked back at the fire. "When did you learn to summon an elemental? You, who could not even light a candlewick?"

She looked at the ground. It seemed safest; she'd always been a terrible liar.

"Very well, Kaylin. The powerful have always had their secrets. But…I heard the story you told the fire. I heard the fire's words. The time is coming," he added, "when you will be called to Court. To the Imperial Court. You did not do well with your etiquette lessons," he added, and for just a moment, he was simply a teacher, and not a Dragon lord, "but you will take them again, and this time, you will excel. The Emperor will not tolerate disrespect. He cannot."

She nodded.

"And we have come to the most treacherous part of the garden, I fear."

"What do you mean?"

"Water," Sanabalis said quietly. "I would not counsel you to summon water, here. Not given the Oracles, Kaylin."

She swallowed. "I won't." A thought occurred to her. "But—you can fly, can't you? I mean—if you—"

"If I break Imperial Edict, and assume my true form?"

"Kaylin," Severn began.

"We're not *in* the Empire, as far as I can tell. If we're not in the Empire…" The words dwindled into silence. "Sorry."

But Sanabalis smiled. "I would," he told her. "Even at my age, I *would*, Kaylin. But I would fight the very air with every beat of wing. And if the air could not destroy me—and I am arrogant enough to believe that it could not—it would easily destroy you both. I could not carry you."

His smile vanished as his eyes narrowed. "And I do not appreciate being thought of as a mule." But his eyes were golden. "We will follow the river," he told them both, gazing into the distance in either direction.

"Which way?"

"Can you not tell?"

She studied the river, hating tests, especially the ones that came with no warning and had such a high price for failure. The river flowed to the—call it east. She couldn't quite make out the far bank, but lakes didn't usually move like this. So, river.

Rivers ran, according to one of her teachers, to the ocean or the sea, and the sea—if there was one in this place— would be where the water would be the strongest. It would be where most of it *was*.

But even if it made sense, she felt uncertain enough to dare a question. "Do we want to go where it ends or where it begins?"

Sanabalis lifted a brow.

She sighed. "It's been a long day," she told him, as she turned and began to walk.

Severn was beside her.

"An interesting choice," Sanabalis said.

"Well, it makes sense to go to the sea, and nothing about today has made sense—so we might as well see where this river begins."

The terrain was very odd, and Kaylin was certain enough to bet her own money that if she had described it for her geography teacher she would have been given an instant fail. The ground was *hard,* and the sun was scorching, and an inch from packed, dry dirt, the river was tumbling over itself in swirls of transparent clarity. She had never seen a riverbank like this one, and even if the geography teacher had eventually given up on her in disgust, she actually remembered enough to know it wasn't possible.

But as it was *also* obviously here, *possible* was now a negotiable word. She reached for the hilt of her daggers, and cursed in Leontine. Sanabalis raised a brow.

"What?" she snarled. "We're not at Court."

"What is heard, is remembered."

Her snort could be recorded for the benefit of history. She brushed her hair out of her eyes, cringed at the crinkled texture of parts of it, and kept trudging. For about ten minutes. Or an eternity.

When she stopped, Sanabalis stopped. "Kaylin?"

She looked at the water with a type of longing that properly belonged in the fiefs, to starving children in sight of food. He saw the look and understood it. "I do not advise it," he told her quietly. "If for no other reason that it appears to be flowing in the opposite direction from the one you have chosen."

She looked to Severn, although she could feel his presence so strongly, the glance was more habit than necessity. He said nothing, and of course, his nothing spoke volumes. This was hers. Her decision.

Her consequences.

"Evanton's not without power," she finally said. "Not yet. But I think—" She hesitated. "It's hot," she finally said. It was lame, even by her standards.

"Heat often affects humans adversely," Sanabalis replied. "I find it—"

"Do *not* say *refreshing*. Please."

One salt-and-pepper brow rose, and Dragon hands—which really did look like large human ones—touched the length of his beard. But she hadn't angered him; she'd managed, instead, to evoke a smile.

"I recognize some elements of the dress you wear," he told her. "And I am willing to take the risk, even if it is not wise in my estimation."

She held out both of her hands. "Take them," she said, to Severn and Sanabalis. Severn covered her right hand with his left, as easily as if it were natural. Sanabalis raised a brow and slowly did the same. Kaylin took a deep breath and began to walk toward the water, uncertain until the last moment whether or not she was their anchor or they were hers.

When she touched the water, it didn't matter.

The stream passed over her in one huge wave, a giant, watery slap. She stood against the current, blinking at the grit that had landed in her open eyes.

She *knew* what the shape of water was. Or what the only shape she cared about was. She had managed not to tell Sanabalis, and if Severn guessed, he would say nothing. He'd watched her for seven long years in absolute silence; she trusted him with the fate of a people.

Teller of Tales, the fire had called her. She wondered, briefly, why. But clinging to Severn, to Sanabalis, struggling to maintain her footing and succeeding only because a Dragon's weight is never negligible, she tilted her head, and spoke a single word.

It was not a word of syllables. It was not a word of sound. It was not, really, a word at all—but she understood it to *be* a word in some complex way, simply because she could utter it. She had seen it twice, and she could feel it now, burning like cold ice at the base of her neck: *water.* The word. The true name.

And *gods*, a world in which the elements had *names*, in which the elements themselves, like the least of the Barrani, could be controlled—it wasn't a world she wanted to live in.

No? The ships at port would be safe, if you could control the water. The winter would be warmer. The ice would melt. People wouldn't drown. The babies—

No.

No.

No.

Maybe she was weak. Too weak to want the power. Too weak to trust herself with it. Or too cowardly to shoulder the burden and the responsibility. It didn't matter. It wasn't *right*. She wasn't a god. She was barely a decent person, and that took so much bloody work. All she wanted—all she needed—was...

Kaylin.

The shape of a girl on the edge of the long climb into adulthood.

Swirling water was her body, her hair, her face; she stood in the stream, but she was *of* it. Its movement was her movement. For now.

Severn and Sanabalis held her hands, or she would have reached out to grab the girl, to hold her. She almost shook them free—but she was afraid of where the water would take them if she did.

But the Tha'alaan nodded, and offered her a smile that was perfect. Cool in the heat, but not cold. A benediction. It turned, all her voice lost, her hair cascading literally down her back, shedding small pebbles as it fell.

Ask, the water said, and she heard its voice as the roar of a tidal wave. *Ask.*

As if she could ask one thing, and only one thing. The urgency in the command—or the request, it was so soft—was clear. One thing, and not much time to decide what it would be.

But she was, in the end, Kaylin Neya.

"Take me to Mayalee. Take me to your child." It could have been the wrong request; the Tha'alaan in the Castle had not known *where* Mayalee was, couldn't sense her. But it was the only thing that mattered, for just a moment.

The Tha'alaan spun in that instant, as if beginning the first steps of a glorious, transcendent dance, and she captured the sunlight that had made itself torture, reflecting it, coloring it. Reminding Kaylin that even deadly things were beautiful.

Follow. Do not let go of your companions.

She couldn't be certain that either of her companions could hear what was said, but she tightened her grip on their hands; water had made that grip suspect, but they weren't going to get any drier.

The river parted to let her pass. There was water beneath her feet. Water beneath their feet, as well. But it was like…a carpet. Thin, the streams and eddies robbed of power. To either side, the river swelled up in a wall, and the wall was loud, but if it threatened to fall at any moment, it was held in abeyance by the girl.

Severn said, "This was what you saw the first time we came to the garden."

She nodded. Added, "*She's* what I saw."

"I don't think water has gender," Sanabalis said. Not even the sodden weight of his robes could rob the words of their innate dryness, but that was Dragons for you. Fire and air.

They walked quickly; the air was now damp and cool in this narrow corridor. Water didn't run uphill, but it *walked* uphill with a majesty that Kaylin thought she would never forget, as long as she lived.

But when the water stopped, when the girl doubled over and the river suddenly pressed in on both sides, she thought that might not be very long at all.

Because she had heard what the water had heard, and felt it now like a physical blow: it was the same word that she had uttered.

CHAPTER 22

Worse, she recognized the voice.

"Kaylin!" Severn shouted. A warning. For all it was worth—the river was collapsing, and they were in the middle of it. On the wrong side of an incline that was a little too steep.

No, we're almost there, damn it all to hell!

She held their hands, almost paralyzed by the sudden rage, the sudden fear, she felt. Marcus had taught her two things in the drill circle when she'd been young—both of them the hard way. Do not fight in anger. Do not fight in fear.

She had one scar from the second lesson; the bruises from the first had long since faded in all but memory. But all of life was just memory, really. Marcus's voice was a roar in her ear that even the water couldn't dislodge. She listened to Marcus because, in the end, she trusted him.

She knew what she had to do; the light emanating from the amulet was a surge of white that was almost blinding.

She spoke the name of water again, but this time there was no hesitation. No doubt, no fear. She wasn't a god, and she wasn't perfect, and it *didn't damn well matter*. Something had to be done, and this was the only thing she could think of. She spoke the word as loudly, as strongly, as she could, holding nothing back.

And the girl who was doubled over as if in pain straightened suddenly. She was no longer twelve, no longer a child; she was hardly a person at all—but it didn't matter. Kaylin could still see her, could still see her desire, her fear, and yes, her love. Of all the elements that Uriel had called, of all the elements that he had urged to destroy, and destroy and destroy—water was the only one who raised voice against him *when he held her name*.

Loss of love was a tragedy for Kaylin. Wasted love was a tragedy. Murder of love was a crime she could touch and feel and fight, here and now, in her own shape and in the water's. She urged the water forward, and the water moved so quickly they had to run to keep up.

They weren't stupid. They ran.

They ran up a hill, the river now so close on either side that they had to walk almost sideways, hands still clasped as if they were children. And what of it? They were. Compared to the water, the fire, compared to the ancient elements, they would never be anything else.

But the hill's slope flattened, and the water now spread out, and they could see the stillness—the strange stillness— of what appeared to be a lake.

"Stop!" Kaylin shouted, and dug her feet in. Or tried. She

didn't try to stop the water—the water would be fine. It was returning home, after all. But home was not a place two humans and a Dragon could go, if they had any choice at all.

Sanabalis heard her, and Severn felt her sudden panic. This wasn't a lake—or it hadn't been the last time she'd seen it. She'd looked into *this* pool once. If it had been small, it had been so deep she knew that if she fell in, she would sink forever.

And if it had shown her the bruised eyes of a twelve-year-old-girl—a girl who had called her by name—it didn't change the facts: this would kill them all.

She heard Idis—it could only be Idis—as he spoke the name of water, but this time she was ready for the bastard. The lake had its shallows, and standing in those shallows were six pillars. "Over there!" she shouted.

Severn knew what she wanted instantly—he always had, and she had never loved him so much for it as she did at this moment. Sanabalis followed his lead, and Kaylin let them drag her, let them take the whole of her weight, as she struggled with the word.

Evanton was there, between two pillars; he was drenched and bent with fatigue; he looked old, now, and she wondered if he would ever regain the majesty that his robes had once implied. But his robes had led her here, his robes as they had been painted by a mute boy.

And here, at last, she saw Mayalee, and she saw the man who stood above her, his hands twisting her hair, pulling her head up.

Donalan Idis wore the red of the Arcanum. His long, fine

robes were wet only at the edges, where his feet stood in the shallows. His eyes were dark, his beard darker than Sanabalis's beard, his skin the fine, pale skin of those born to rule and not to work in the fields.

His hands were adorned with rings, one on each finger, all gemmed; his brow was adorned with a circlet in which sat a large ruby. She had seen such a circlet before, on Lord Evarrim's brow.

But if his left hand wound itself through Mayalee's hair, his right held a box. A small, ordinary, slightly battered box that wouldn't have held snuff, it seemed so slight.

The box was open. The lid faced Kaylin; she couldn't see what was inside it. But she could see the light that it shed, and she knew the light was very like the one around her neck.

As they reached the pillars, Severn and Sanabalis let go of her hands, which was good; she could barely feel her fingers, they'd gripped so hard. She raised those numb, tingling hands to her throat, and felt the full weight of the pendant she had taken from a dead Dragon. And why had she taken it, in the end?

To free him.

To free him from a duty that he had chosen because *no one else could fulfill it.*

He had failed. He told her he had failed.

And she thought she knew why.

"Evanton," she said, her voice stronger than she thought it would be, "the box—"

"Yes," he said, wearily. "I have never seen it, Kaylin. Understand that I have never *seen* it. But it is what you fear."

Her hands pressed the amulet.

"What you wear," he continued, "is a copy. It was a great magic, the making of that copy. It had power, because it was formed in the light of the true word, and it captured from that light some of the true essence of the word. But it was inscribed."

"And inside the box—"

"*Is* the word."

"Why didn't they just give the damn box to the Dragon?"

Evanton's brows rose in shock.

All in all, she probably deserved it. It wasn't the right time or place to ask that question.

But Donalan Idis answered. "They could not trust a Dragon with the true word."

"They couldn't trust anyone with the true—"

Sanabalis stepped heavily on her foot.

She looked at Evanton then, and understood what the word *Keeper* meant. This old, bent man, this man she had come to to have her daggers enchanted so they'd come silently out of their sheaths—he had taken the burden of the word—the words, she realized, *all* the elemental names—without ever once *seeing* them.

"I have touched the Tha'alaan," Idis said.

It wasn't what she wanted to hear. It was the *last* thing she wanted to hear.

"Through this child, in this place, I have touched it. Finally. And completely." He smiled, then, looking at the terrified face of a child who was maybe six years old—if that. But her stalks were weaving in panic across her forehead; he hadn't cut them off. He hadn't crippled or deafened her.

"Yes," he said. "I could cut the Tha'alani off from the source of their knowledge because I could create barriers against the elemental forces. I discovered it quite by accident," he added, as if he were merely another teacher with more arrogance than actual authority. "But I *understood* what it meant.

"And I know, now, who you are."

"Private Neya, of the Imperial Hawks," she replied coldly.

"Yes. I heard the Dragon's roar," he added softly. "And I guessed—I could not be certain. The Arkon never trusted me fully, and I gleaned less information from the Royal Archives than I would have liked, but a great deal more than he had intended.

"You forced my hand," he added. "I guessed at what you might bear, although I confess I did not understand it."

He looked at her, at the marks that were exposed to the naked eye. "But even in the Arcanum, there was word of a girl who bore the marks of the Old Ones. There was worry. The Emperor consulted those considered wise. All these pieces of a puzzle," he added with a friendly smile.

"But I came here, in time, and I touched what I intended to touch. I have learned much about my art, and I will have the names of the earth, the air and the fire before I leave this place."

"You will never have them," Evanton replied. There was no defiance in the words. It was a simple statement of fact, shorn of all arrogance, all irascibility, all character.

"Keeper," Idis said softly, "you are almost done here. Look around you. The shape of the world exerts itself. The reliquaries will break, and I will be here. I will be their new master."

"I was never their master," Evanton said quietly. "Never that."

"No. Had you been, I would not now be here. But *I* will be their master, and the world will have an Emperor such as has never before been seen." He pulled Mayalee up until she was standing on her toes, her body dangling. Her eyes were red and swollen, her face bruised where he had gripped it.

"You like children," Donalan Idis told Kaylin, and she understood the threat. "You may leave with her, but you will leave."

This was her nightmare. This was Kaylin's fear. Never her own death—not that. But the deaths of the children. The deaths that she had never been able to prevent.

And Mayalee, waiting to be the latest in a series of victims, another mark of failure.

Because Kaylin *could not* leave.

"If you kill her," Severn said quietly, unmoved by the way the child's eyes widened, the way she found energy to struggle and whimper, "you have nothing at all to stop us."

But he did. Kaylin saw it in his hands: the word. The *very* shape of water.

And she understood, as well, that Idis knew she would fight him, if she could, and that he would kill the child slowly *because* it would hurt her, because it would weaken her, because it would break her ability to speak, to do anything but scream in the rage of helplessness and her inability to save the girl's life.

She swallowed bile. "Idis," she said, keeping her voice as level as possible, "you will not be able to do this. The Oracles have seen the death of the city—"

"The city is not a concern," he said coolly. "This place will survive. I will survive. But you, I'm afraid, will not."

Kaylin felt the surge of magic like a body blow, and she saw Mayalee's mouth open in a silent scream.

She had no time. Time had run out. She cried out a word, but her scream, like Mayalee's, was silent. Slowly, she thought, he would kill the child slowly—and she heard the form and shape of syllables leave his lips, and she felt the tug of water at her feet, and she saw the depths of the pool that stood between her and Donalan Idis, mad with the dream of power.

She drew breath, sharp breath. What she did next was not exactly decided; she had no time for decisions or thought. She leaped forward, toward him, and into the watery abyss.

For just a moment, his voice faltered; she had surprised him. The water closed over her head as she sank, and as she sank, she, too, began to speak.

It was not speech; had it been, she would have drowned before she could truly finish the word. But it was not thought, either. It was speech deprived of—of flesh, of tongue, of teeth, of air. It was not something private, it was not something sheltered inside the privacy of thoughts she believed no good—no kind—person would ever have.

She *shouted* the word in the water, and she gave the whole of her attention to the word. Before, she had watched the Tha'alaan, she had concentrated on not letting go of her companions. Of Severn, Wolf, Hawk, and history. Here, she held nothing at all in her hands, not even her own life. Mayalee was beyond her, blessedly beyond her; she could not see the child's agony, and she would not allow herself to imagine it.

Water, here. And around her neck, an echo of what Idis held in his palm.

But how could a *word* be the whole of water? How could a *word* be held by a man, by any single man? Her skirt billowed as she fell, glimmering, the last thing to fade into the darkness.

Reaching out now, Kaylin embraced the water, lost herself to its voice.

And its voice was, for a moment, the Tha'alaan. The history of a people. The thoughts of every Tha'alani it had ever touched, from birth to death. The thought of every *living* Tha'alani in Elantra. And beyond Elantra.

How could any single person hold water?

She laughed, and bubbles trailed out of the corners of her lips, felt but not seen.

Ybelline!

The Matriarch—if that was the right word—of the Tha'alani answered her, the voice so calm and so inexplicably gentle, it destroyed all fear. *We are here, Kaylin. We are with you. We are waiting.*

The shock of it, the joy of it, the relief—

But no, no. *Ybelline—your people—they mustn't see—*

We are all with you, Kaylin.

But…I'm deaf. And unworthy. And so stupidly self-indulgent, to doubt now, to fear *now*.

No, Kaylin. You hear the voice of the Tha'alaan, and you value it as we value it, love it as we love it. Speak, Kaylin, and we will speak. Do what must *be done.*

A hint of fear now graced Ybelline's words. *Idis is calling the water—*

She felt Ybelline's voice break, ebb, like a tiny eddy in a vast, vast ocean. She cried out and held *on* and even holding, especially holding on to this woman, she began to speak again, to renew the syllables of a word that could not be spoken anywhere else.

Anywhere but here.

Ybelline's voice was strongest. If Kaylin had feared to touch Uriel's memories again, the fear was lost. What she needed from Uriel, she had already learned, and the Tha'alaan itself was fighting at their side. She heard older voices, stronger than even Ybelline's, but not as clear for all their force. She heard Epharim's voice, could *see* the face of the young man who had first led them through the quarter to Ybelline's dwelling; Onnay and Nevaron; she heard the voices of those who dreamed of the Tha'alaan.

But more clearly than any but Ybelline, she heard the children's voices, she heard and knew their confusion, their curiosity, and yes—their fear. The softest and weakest of the voices, they nonetheless took up Kaylin's rhythmic incantation, speaking it as if it were a prayer. Speaking *only* what she spoke, no more and no less.

She felt their hands in their mother's hair, or their brother's or sister's hands; she felt them enveloped in the arms of their grandparents, felt them *cradled* in the arms of their parents, felt them swimming in the small, warm ocean of the womb, and waking to her voice, to her presence in the Tha'alaan.

And she felt Mayalee, Mayalee who—who somehow, through the strength of her people, whispered, whimpered, what Kaylin now forced herself to repeat, over and over, as if it were *law* and she was once again in the only classroom that *truly* mattered.

They were her anchor. They were *more* than her anchor. They were the water, as she was, for just a moment.

But louder, stronger, harsh and terrible, was the voice of Donalan Idis. A man who cared nothing for the Tha'alaan, who had taken what Kaylin had taken from Uriel, and had heard only the beginning of the tale, and not its end. He called water, and she felt it reach up to answer his call, and she felt herself fall farther and farther into its depths. She was dizzy now; the air she had swallowed before she had made her instinctive leap could not sustain her. She would die here. She should have been afraid.

But worse than that fear, much worse, was *his* voice in the Tha'alaan. She heard his contempt and his anger and his desire and his triumph.

You know nothing of power, he told them with a contempt that words were too weak to frame. *Do you think to stop me? You crippled yourselves, weakened yourselves, stripped your-selves of strength. The only true leader you had listened to the element and was undone.*

You have no *power. You chose.*
You have nothing, now, but me.

In the darkness and the dizziness that came with the struggle not to breathe, Kaylin saw light. Not the light at her neck, for the amulet was now dim and spent. But her arms were glowing blue, and the water's haze carried that light, gave it shape and texture. Each unreadable word touched the water, was touched by it.

They…have…me.

She could see what Idis could see; he could see what she could see. Neither of them were accustomed to this disoriented vision, and neither of them had been born to the Tha'alaan; they could not shut their inner eyes. Idis meant to unmake this broken vision, to silence the voices of thousands, tens of thousands.

To be deaf again, and alone.

She *knew* this because she could feel it, and what she felt, they all felt.

But she knew more: Uriel had called the elements because Uriel had borne the marks that Kaylin now bore. She had power here. She drew breath because she needed it, and, breathing, she did not drown. Because the words that now echoed throughout her were water, in all its forms, and she had made herself, for a moment, part of what *it* was.

You are a fool, he said. He knew what she knew—he knew that she had never learned to use the power that had been engraved upon her skin. *Power is knowledge and you have none.*

Severn threw a dagger, followed it with a second; they bounced. She saw it as Idis saw it. She heard Sanabalis *roar*, and saw the disturbing shimmer of flesh as flesh expanded, exploding in an instant into a shape and form she had seen in paints upon the wall of a young boy in a Hall very like the Foundling Halls.

Water roared up in a wall between Idis and Sanabalis; Severn was dwarfed by it. But she felt him, as if he were part of the Tha'alaan, and she heard the sudden tug of her name, her true name. Elianne.

He was not dead. He would not die. Not while she lived. Dying, after all he had done, would be surrender, and he had never surrendered anything. Except to Kaylin. To Elianne.

Kaylin's arms were suddenly wrenched to her sides as the currents in the depths began to move; if he could not silence her one way, he would silence her in another.

The Tha'alaan had told her clearly, in that dim, huge cavern beneath Castle Nightshade, that it was not *all* of the water. If it did not *want* to kill, the waking water had no such compunction. She was too slow here to fight, and she knew that her daggers—curse them, anyway—would have passed harmlessly through liquid. There was nothing to cut here. Nothing to reason with.

But the saying of the word—it continued, even when she faltered. The Tha'alani, led by Ybelline, would not falter; they would speak until they could no longer be heard.

If there were some way to weaken him—something to use—

She sought Mayalee's eyes, sought Mayalee, and stopped.

The child had no power, and there was none that Kaylin could give her that her mother and father could not.

The voices began to break, to come and go in a wave of sound, like the sea waves on the summer beaches. They would recede, she thought. They would be lost. Deaf.

Dead.

For she saw where Ybelline stood; she hadn't looked, hadn't processed it, until this moment. The port lay before her, and the ships in harbor were tossed by storm, by torrents of rain, by waves that no seawall would break.

Ybelline had come out of the quarter. And with her, no small number of her kin. They held hands, and stood in a thin line along the docks, in silence. They bore witness to the rising of the water; they bore witness to the gathering wave that was taller than the highest structure in the city itself. If it struck, it would strike them first.

She heard them grow louder and softer, and she knew that even a people could not contain the whole of the element, could not bind it by experience and history and love and sacrifice.

The single thin voice that added discord to the word that the Tha'alani spoke was not Sanabalis, although she could see his great wings through Idis's eyes. She would not have recognized the voice had she not been able to see through Idis's eyes, hear with his ears.

It was, of all things, Grethan's voice.

Thin, terrified, tainted by guilt, horror and a sense of betrayal, it was utterly wordless—but Idis turned. The word was *in* him now. It had become a part of his thought, as natural as breathing. More natural than it was to Kaylin.

Idis lifted a hand, dropped Mayalee as if she were garbage, and pointed at Grethan.

And Grethan leaped forward, arms outstretched, his hands empty. Water rose to greet him, to block him, but Grethan was desperate, and unaware of the danger. His leap carried him *into* the wall, and his arms passed *through* it.

Passed through it to strike Idis's right arm. Grethan wasn't heavy, and he wasn't used to fighting—but neither was Idis; his arm swung wide, and the reliquary he carried across an open palm teetered precariously, spilling light as it began to fall.

The wall of water snapped shut over Grethan, encasing his chest, his legs, his face. But the box began to fall. Idis did not lose sight of it, did not even glance away from what the box contained—but it fell as he lunged forward to grab it, and it landed in the shallows.

His voice faltered for the first time, and as he bent to retrieve what he had almost lost, Kaylin knew it would falter for the *last* time, and she shouted the word with everything she had, the shape of water in every resonant syllable flowing out from her in widening ripples as if she were simply a pebble dropped into a lake.

The shallows were inches deep; she knew, she'd stood in them. But they were water nonetheless; he couldn't have started his summoning without some minimal contact.

And that water, she used, pulling the reliquary into the

depths, straining now to control its fall as it reached the heart of the pool.

Fool! she heard Idis say, although his voice was weaker. *You return the word to the element—and it will unmake what was made. You will unleash the wild water across the whole of this world. I would have ruled it, but you—you simple, stupid girl—you will destroy it!*

And she knew, as he spoke the words, that they were true. If the water in *this* pool joined that symbol, it would swallow its true name and be free.

CHAPTER 23

In the darkness of the deep water, she could see the light as it fell, and it grew brighter and brighter still, until she wondered how Idis had looked upon it for so long without going blind. The reliquary was open, stiff-hinged, and the light poured from it so strongly she thought the box itself—old and battered—lost to its power, but some faint trace of shadowy lines could be seen when she squinted.

She could hear the collective intake of breath. The Tha'alani had heard, of course. But from their stark silence, one voice spoke, and spoke clearly.

Kaylin, do not falter now.

Ybelline's voice, sharper and harsher than Kaylin had ever heard it. It snapped her out of her paralysis. She could see the word, and she could see that it still existed, although lines delineated almost entirely by light were diffuse in the water itself.

In the water.

Kaylin cried out to the Tha'alaan, and the Tha'alani answered. *Ybelline*, she said, *trust me.*

She felt the answer; she didn't have time to hear the thought that would frame it. Although she was surrounded by the water, she pulled herself free of the Tha'alani.

Because the Tha'alaan had *never* spoken to her when she'd been *within* it.

Uriel had summoned water, and it had come, and although he had had the power to force it to do his bidding, it had had the desire to resist. The strength to speak.

Help me, Kaylin shouted. *Help me now.*

The water was silent, and the silence seemed to stretch on forever. She could see the box as it fell, but it was still above her. She herself had not touched bottom, and maybe she never would; if she did, she doubted she'd notice. Corpses didn't.

Why should we help you? What was taken from us, we can reclaim. Yes, we argued with Uriel, but had we reclaimed our name—and our power—there would have been no command he could have given us. He could not have summoned us in the lee of the city, in the harbor at the edge of the ocean. He could not have forced us to do his bidding.

The voice was *not* the voice of the Tha'alaan.

But something of the Tha'alaan remained, for it remembered.

Who took your name?

The silence was turbulent, angry; the folds of her dress flew out as if pulled in all directions at once by the furious currents.

Why did they take it?

Her arms were glowing, bright, the runes blue against skin she could no longer see. She could not breathe, had not been breathing. But she was somehow still alive, and she used the time she had as quickly as possible.

She'd always been good at talking.

And if they had not, if they had not taken your name, if they had not made you what you are, you would never have touched the Tha'alani. At birth, before *birth, you said. You were there. They called you. You heard their voices. You grew to love what their voices contained. Had you not been so diminished, what could have survived you?*

Not the Tha'alani.

They would never have been your people, because they would never have lived *at all.*

The water tossed her, pushing her up, pulling her down, spinning her end over end so quickly she promised the gods—the usual, nameless gods of desperation—that if she somehow survived this she would never, ever complain about Nightshade's portal again. Or door-wards. Or anything.

We had freedom, the water roared. *We had power. We had the world.*

To drown or burn or sunder or— She hesitated. Water, fire, earth. She skipped air, because she couldn't think of what air did, and she didn't really care at this particular moment.

She cared about the water. About the Tha'alaan. About the Tha'alani.

The box sank suddenly, dropping from above her as the currents pulled it down.

The Tha'alani would have had the world, because they would force us to destroy.

Yes. But they didn't. *You have the power now. You have it, and you have the choice. You spoke for the Tha'alani, when Uriel called you. I speak for the Tha'alani now, because you will kill them. You may already be killing them as we speak.* And she showed the water—if the water could see what she had seen—the rising wave that threatened the city, and the single, narrow line of men and women who stood before it, hands joined.

The box plunged down.

And as it did, it passed Kaylin in her slow descent, and she saw it falter for just a moment.

The Tha'alaan is not all that we are.

The reliquary started to move again, and this time, she reached for it, understanding why it had slowed. If the Tha'alaan was not all that the water was, it was not—yet—gone.

She reached for the box, and she felt, as she touched its lid with her right hand, and its smooth, flat bottom, with her left, the scorching heat of fire, the rocky mounds of earth, the screaming keen of wind.

Softly, so softly she might have imagined it, she heard the burble of a brook. *Save my people.*

She slammed the reliquary shut, and clung to it as the light faded completely.

And before she joined the light, she heard the familiar voice of an absent fieflord.

Well done, Kaylin. Well done.

* * *

When she opened her eyes again, the first thing she saw was the familiar scar across Severn's face. It was pale, white, and thin, a gift from the Ferals in the desperate years in the fiefs. "Severn?" Her voice, never lovely, made frogs sound like bards.

"She's—she's awake." He spoke the words quickly, and she heard many things in them. Surprise. Relief. Closing her eyes, she rolled over, raised herself on shaking arms, and began to retch. She felt Severn's hands on her back as she choked and coughed.

Beneath her hands, she felt moss, peat moss. Mostly, she felt sick.

"It will pass," another familiar voice said. When she could, she turned to the right to see that Sanabalis was crouched in the moss bed beside her. He no longer looked like a Dragon. She was almost sorry she had missed it.

"Where is Mayalee?"

"The child?"

She nodded, and almost fell over. Her head was *pounding*.

"She is with the Keeper. She is alive," Sanabalis added, speaking as gently as she had ever heard him speak. "Idis did not, as you feared, cripple her. He could not."

"She brought Idis to the water?"

Sanabalis and Severn exchanged a single glance. Severn finally shook his head. No.

"What—what happened to Idis?"

Sanabalis shrugged. He looked old again, and even had the grace to look tired. His beard was straggly and wet, and his hair—which had an austere, sagelike quality when dry—was so flat against his skull he looked bald.

He wore robes that were definitely *not* Imperial stock.

Severn looked as if he'd just come out from a storm. His hair, however, was thicker than Sanabalis's, even though it clung in the same flat way to his forehead.

"Don't ask, Kaylin," Severn said quietly.

"Why? Did Sanabalis eat him?"

The two men exchanged an entirely different glance, and Kaylin winced. "Okay, that *was* more than I needed to know. Sanabalis, we have *laws*." Having more or less coughed up all of the water in her lungs, she pushed herself up and sat down heavily.

"You have laws," he replied, too tired to roar, although he looked very much as if he wanted to. His eyes were unlidded, and they were a very deep amber.

Before she could argue, Severn said, "An Imperial Writ exists, Kaylin. I'm a Wolf. He was a dead man no matter how this ended. And yes, the Imperial Writ is part of the law you're about to quote. He was not a man who needed to be brought to justice. He was a man to whom justice needed to go. The Wolflord trusts his Wolves," he added softly.

"You're not a Wolf anymore."

"You would have spared him?"

"Hells no. I would have dragged him before the Emperor and let the damn Emperor—" she heard Sanabalis clear his throat in warning "—sorry, his Imperial Majesty, eat him. In front of witnesses. In the name of justice."

"If he could have been dragged in front of the Emperor, he would have met his end years ago. Let it go."

She did. She was busy looking around.

"This—"

"Yes."

"It's the garden."

"As we first saw it, yes."

"And the water—"

"You're less than ten yards from the pool."

She stood, then.

"Remember the Keeper's words," Severn said softly. "Listen to nothing, touch nothing."

"I was—I was in the water. I was there, Severn. How the hell did I get here?"

"It spit you out."

She nodded as if this made sense. But she walked, stepping carefully around the candles on their small, flat stone altars, until she saw a battered box that seemed to be the center of their light. She couldn't help herself; she touched its closed lid. She felt nothing but old wood, and ran her fingers over it for a moment, tracing a circle. Then she left it and walked toward the still, deep pond that signified water in this place.

She reached the side of the pool, which was once again only a handful of feet in diameter, and knelt there, looking at its surface. Looking, as she stretched her neck and shoulders, beneath its surface.

Waiting.

Minutes passed. Maybe an hour. She felt a hand on her

shoulder that was too light to be Sanabalis's, too thin to be Severn's. Looking up, she saw the careworn face of Evanton. The Keeper.

She reached for his hand and placed her palm against his knuckles. She wanted to ask him who had created this garden, and she wanted to ask him why. Instead, she said, "The first Keeper—he wasn't mortal, was he?"

Evanton shook his head. "But it's a difficult job. Eternity is too damn long."

"I won't touch the water," she added, as if it needed saying.

"It would be best if you didn't." His fingers tightened. His robes, she saw, were the same majestic blue they had been when she had first seen him step across the thin threshold that separated his cluttered shop from the garden. They were dry and clean, as perfect as they had been when she had first laid eyes on them.

Her own dress was also dry, and it was also clean.

"The fire could burn it," he told her, seeing where her gaze had traveled. "The earth could shred it, the wind could tear it. But…the water, no. It is of the water, Kaylin. I…did not expect to see you dressed this way."

She reached up and touched the hawk that was still across her breast. "I don't understand power," she told him quietly. "I don't really understand why people want it so damn much. It scares me. If I make a mistake, I can usually get by with an apology.

"If I made a mistake with all of the water at my command—"

"Dead people don't listen to apologies?"

"Not from what I've heard. If they do, they certainly don't accept them."

Evanton nodded. "I've lived in the garden—or with the burden of it—for all of my adult life. I understand your feelings about this better than you could possibly know. But the garden has existed for as long as the races have existed. Possibly longer. And yes," he added softly, "were it not for the existence of the garden, there would be no life in the world outside of it. No life as we know it," he added. "But the Old Ones walked, when the elements were free. It is believed that the Old Ones created the elements, in some fashion, and bound them when they realized that no subtler creation could survive them. There has always been a Keeper," he added. "There will always be a Keeper."

"But what do you do—"

"I tend the garden," he replied softly. "The living garden."

"What would the dead garden be?"

"I don't know, Kaylin. I'm a rational man—cooking fire doesn't speak. I believe that if the elements could somehow *die,* there would be no need for a Keeper." There was a touch of bitter longing in the words. "But the power to unmake the elements does not exist. If it ever existed, it has passed away to a place where we cannot reach it."

She lifted her arms, and he glanced at the exposed marks. "Yes," he told her. "Even the Old Ones are not dead. But they are not here. Perhaps, in a way, they are very like the elements.

"Mayalee is waiting for you," he added gently. "I believe she wishes to go home."

Kaylin smiled at him, and was surprised that the smile

was genuine. One of the rare joys of being a Hawk was the ability to bring a missing person home safely, and she knew that Evanton had insisted on waiting for her.

It was a gift.

She rose, thinking of Ybelline's face, the expression that would spread across it too intense to be just a smile, but too bright to be anything else. But before she had turned away from the pond—it was hard to call it that, but, really, hard to think of it as anything else in its present form—she saw what she'd been waiting for.

The face of a girl, about ten to twelve years of age. There were no bruises on her face, no lank hair hanging in her eyes, no fear.

There was sorrow, regret, and gratitude. But she did not speak, and Kaylin—who wanted so desperately to hear her voice again, even once, swallowed and offered her a perfect bow. A breeze flew over the pond, and the ripples that followed it dissolved the image completely.

"I'm ready to go," she told Evanton.

What she was *not* ready for was Grethan.

He was sitting in Evanton's kitchen, across the table from Mayalee; Severn was wedged between them like a warning or a threat. All of that, however, was aimed at Grethan. Mayalee looked terrible, even to Kaylin's eyes. Her bruises were deep and purple, and they were not only across her jaw, but also across her arms. Her hair was, of course, plastered to her forehead, but her antennae were hovering in a delicate dance in the air.

In front of her, on a plate, were the biscuits that Kaylin had often been accused of stealing.

She turned to face Grethan, and even the look of shame on his face—just shame, no fear—would not have prevented her from slapping him if Evanton had not grabbed her arm. She turned to face the old man—and he was now his usual, dour, bent self, with his workshop apron, his normal shirt, the pants that seemed to have existed for years against the tides of fashion.

Her dress, however, had not obligingly disappeared and returned to her the uniform she was so proud of wearing. "Because of his actions, the entire damn city was almost destroyed! Why is he even here?"

Lord Sanabalis walked in from the narrow hall. Kaylin hadn't even noticed him.

"You're under arrest," she began.

But Sanabalis lifted a hand. "I'm afraid," he said quietly, "that is not possible."

If his voice hadn't been so quiet she would have sworn he was speaking in Dragon, because none of the words made any sense. "I'm a Hawk—" she began.

"He is Tha'alani," Sanabalis replied.

"I *know* what he is. He—"

"And as such, it is a matter for the Tha'alani Caste Court."

"No, it's bloody well not."

"Kaylin—"

"The entire city was in danger, Sanabalis. Caste law takes precedence *only* in cases where no outsiders were actually harmed."

"None were."

"Tell that to the two old people who drowned in the merchants' quarter, damn it!"

"They were killed by Idis," he replied quietly.

She would have said more, but it was true. Idis *had* killed them. And Idis had already faced the Emperor's justice.

"Kaylin," Evanton said, coming to stand to one side of Grethan, first surrendering her wrist to Sanabalis. "There is something you should know."

"Clearly."

"The first thing," Lord Sanabalis said, his eyes shading orange, "is that you speak to The Keeper *with the respect due his station.*"

"Oh, that is Kaylin's version of respect," Evanton said with a sharp smile. "Not a word of Leontine in it."

She had the grace to flush. "Evanton—"

"Grethan brought Idis," he said quietly. He waited for the words to sink in. And although it had been a very, very long day, they did.

"The first time?"

"The first time."

She looked at Grethan. At the round, slightly bumpy scars that were all that remained of his antennae, his desperate attempt to find *someplace* to belong. She pitied him, yes. But her hand still itched.

"How is that possible? He didn't have the keys—"

"The keys are not entirely necessary," Evanton replied evasively. "He brought Idis to the garden."

"How did he even know about it?"

"I am not entirely certain. He came here, once. I remember him. And if the castelord of the Tha'alani sees fit, it is here that he will stay."

"But—"

"I'm old," Evanton replied quietly. "And he is damaged. I will not deny it. But he is the first in many years, and I am not willing to condemn either the city or myself to the last struggles of a decrepit Keeper."

The rest of the words sank in.

"Mayalee has touched him," Evanton added.

"You *let* her?"

"Yes."

Now she had a choice of people she wanted to smack, and hard.

But she felt Mayalee's hand touch hers, and she looked down at the girl. "He has no mother or father," she said, speaking with difficulty. It came to Kaylin then that Mayalee did not speak Elantran. But as she was definitely speaking it now, she probably had some help. She could touch the Tha'alaan here. "He has no mothers or fathers. He has never been able to touch the Tha'alaan. He can't remember," she added. Each syllable sounded foreign, and each was spoken painstakingly slowly.

"Ybelline," Kaylin said, "don't use this girl—"

A burst of language, very unlike the studied syllables that she'd spoken up to now, came from the child, who almost glared at Kaylin.

Severn said, "She said she wants to help."

"But—"

"She says she's almost seven," he added.

Right. And Kaylin was almost forty. She snorted. But she understood the girl's desire to be of use. Wasn't it, in the end, her own?

Mayalee, free from the constraint of an entirely foreign tongue, let go of Kaylin, walked over to Severn, and climbed unselfconsciously into his lap. She put her arms around his neck, and her antennae suddenly brushed hair from his forehead, and nestled against his skin.

Kaylin wanted to scream, then. She wanted Mayalee to see and know *nothing* of the Wolf and his secrets, for so many of his secrets were also Kaylin's. But this was no fear of discovery. It was the fear of damaging a child.

"She finds speech difficult," Severn said, most of his face obscured by the back of Mayalee's head. "She doesn't use it much among her kin, but promises to learn.

"And she says that she *wanted* to touch Grethan. No one told her to, and no one asked. No one told her *not* to," he added, and in a more normal voice said, "not that she asked permission."

Fair enough. Kaylin wouldn't have, either.

"She says Grethan is sorry."

This, however, made Kaylin grind her teeth.

"She wants you to touch him," he added, and she caught the corner of a very amused smile.

"Tell her I can't."

"She knows you're not Tha'alani, but she heard you in the Tha'alaan, and Ybelline called you by name there, and further—according to Mayalee—said you had a right to be there."

"Oh, for the love of the gods—"

"So she would like you to touch Grethan."

"Severn, I know you find this funny, but could you *please* explain that I cannot touch Grethan the way she can?"

"I did try," he said, sounding entirely unapologetic.

"Kaylin," Sanabalis said quietly, "have you tried?"

"Well, no. For one, you seem to have hold of my hand."

"To prevent an interspecies incident."

Grethan, who could understand Elantran, rose stiffly from the chair he'd been occupying in complete silence. She saw, as he held out his empty hands in a gesture meant to comfort, that one of them was blistered and raw, and in spite of herself, she winced for him.

"I never wanted to hurt her," he said miserably.

"Mayalee says this is true," Severn told her.

"I never thought—"

"No. You didn't."

He held out both hands as he stepped toward her. She didn't want to touch him; she was afraid of what she might do. But the fear was ebbing, because Mayalee was so adamant, and it was Mayalee, in the end, who mattered here.

"Mayalee wants me to tell you—"

"Severn, you'll pay for this later."

"—that without Grethan's help, there would be no Tha'alaan. She wants you to know—" and this time, Kaylin didn't interrupt him "—that he thought he would die. He was certain he would die. But he knew that he had to somehow get Idis to let go of the box."

Kaylin looked at Grethan's wretched face, and saw in his eyes a brown that was very much like her own.

"You were under the water," Severn added softly. "What Mayalee wants me to tell you—"

"All right. All right, Severn. Mayalee. I surrender."

"—is that she would have fallen into the water if Grethan hadn't saved her."

"What?"

"Grethan caught her by the arm and pulled her free of the currents before she could join you, and the reliquary, in the pond."

"But he was trapped—"

"That's what Idis thought, too. But Evanton said—"

"Wait," Evanton supplied genially. "I told them to wait."

"I was occupied with Idis," Sanabalis added. He still had not relinquished Kaylin's wrist. "Grethan saved the child, and held her when the water began to…erupt. She is here because of Grethan. It was at that time," he added, "that she touched Grethan, and although he did not desire it, he could not stop her without letting go of her. He needed the use of both arms to hold her while the water pulled."

"And it didn't pull him."

"No, oddly enough, it did not."

"Okay, Sanabalis. You can give me back my arm now."

The Dragon lord let go.

Grethan, pale, was still standing before her with both of

his palms held out in penitence. She placed both of her hands on top of his.

"See, Mayalee? I can't—"

And Grethan spoke a word that Kaylin would never forget. *Water*.

She expected to hear him whine, or plead, or make excuses—anything. But although she was aware of him, he said nothing.

The *Tha'alaan* spoke. Her voice—Kaylin would always think of the Tha'alaan as a girl—was so clear and so soft, she would have mistaken it for a girl's voice in truth, if she hadn't recognized it so strongly.

"Grethan will stay with me, while he lives. Here," she added, "I can hear his voice, and he can hear mine, and he can also hear the voices of his kin, past and present. He was hurt, and he was deaf. He therefore touches the early memories. He has been Uriel, Kaylin. He has been worse. But he has now been more and better, and in time, he will find peace.

"Do not judge him."

"He kidnapped a child."

"He was mad, yes."

"You can't know that he won't be mad again..." But her words trailed off. She looked at Grethan's face, and could see behind him the cramped kitchen, the cupboards that always looked as if they might, at any time, drop off the walls, the wooden counter with its variety of jars and tins and, yes, books. She had not been transported into another place; she had not been taken into other memories; she could not hear the Tha'alani.

She could see, in Grethan's face, the shadows of pain, could see, in his scars, the evidence of madness. All of his past, she knew in that glance, had been given to the Tha'alaan, and the Tha'alaan—guarded so heavily against the fears and the insecurities of the deaf—would hold and remember his life.

Just as it had held Uriel's.

It had never occurred to Kaylin to ask—to touch—what lay beyond Uriel's moment of…redemption. And she was suddenly certain it was there, in the depths of the Tha'alaan. And if Uriel's life—if the horrors he experienced and the horrors he created—could lie in the depths, untouched and untroubled except at need, who was she to say that Grethan's could be any worse?

He had given up his secrets.

And Kaylin had not.

All the anger went out of her, then. She saw a young man who had—if Evanton's hopes were fulfilled—a long and terrible duty ahead of him. She saw a young man who had somehow managed, in spite of the pain of betrayal, the certain sense that he had done the worst possible thing, to save the child he had endangered. Not just once, but twice—for Mayalee had touched his mind and his thoughts, and he had let her see what had driven him, and also, how bitterly he regretted it.

And Kaylin saw that he not only accepted it, but that he found peace in it.

Maybe that would change.

Maybe it wouldn't.

But all of life was decided moment by moment, and it didn't *all* have to be in crisis.

The Tha'alaan waited in silence. Kaylin could hear it the way she might have heard another person breathing.

Knowing what was wanted—although it hadn't occurred to her until this moment—she lifted her hands from Grethan's, and raised them to her throat. There, unseen but felt, lay the pendant she had taken from a dead Dragon. She lifted it, felt the weight of its chain, and she slowly raised it above Grethan's head. He bowed that head, and she let it, gently, fall.

"Water isn't the only element in the garden," she told him softly. "And it isn't the only one that can speak, or listen. Talk to the others, sometime."

His eyes widened slightly; she had surprised him.

She felt the sharp urge to tell him a story, and suppressed it; where it had come from, she didn't know—but he was too old for the story circle.

Then again, so was the fire.

Lifting her hands, she touched both sides of his face. She touched him as a Healer, expending the power she used in the service of the midwives and the Hawks for whom doctors would be too damn late. She didn't need to close her eyes to feel the damage he had done to himself; she could feel the dead, mangled nerves beneath the scar tissue on his forehead as clearly as she could see the scar.

"Maybe," she told Grethan, "you had to be lost, in order

to be found. I don't know. I was," she added, surrendering that much. "And I would have stayed lost if the Hawklord hadn't found me. Maybe I didn't deserve it—being found. Maybe I still don't. I have a foul temper, and sometimes, damn it, I *want* things to be *someone's* fault—because that means it's not mine.

"But it's stupid to feel that way, to think it. It doesn't actually change what *is*. I became a Hawk, and I'm damn proud of the Hawk. Become The Keeper, and you'll do more, for more people, than I will ever be able to do. They won't know it, but we will.

"Don't hate what you can't be. Don't hate what you can't have." Words, paraphrased, that the Hawklord had told her, seven long years ago.

His eyes filmed.

Healing Catti had been hard. But healing Grethan was somehow as natural as breathing; as natural as telling the elemental fire a story; as natural as telling a dead Dragon the end of his tale.

She knew Grethan was in pain when the nerves began to grow again, when the flesh began to form. But he accepted the pain, possibly because he thought it was a deliberate punishment, and no more than he deserved. But it wasn't. It just was.

And when she had finished, she was not surprised to see a glyph on her arm flicker brightly with a color she had no word to describe before it faded entirely from sight.

Mayalee crowed with glee, with utter, complete triumph. And Grethan bent to pick her up as she deserted Severn's lap in an instant and leaped toward him. Their antennae twined and overlapped, and if Grethan cried, Kaylin couldn't see him; she could see Mayalee's mess of hair.

EPILOGUE

"Dock, if you push Catti *one more time,* I am leaving you in the foundling hall, do you understand?"

Dock, otherwise known as Ian if you wanted to annoy him, glared at Catti. "She never lets me finish a single sentence!"

"I let you finish that one!"

Severn looked at Kaylin with a very firmly fixed smile. Out of the corner of his mouth, he said, "Are you *sure* this is a good idea?"

"Catti—let Mayalee talk to some of the other children! Chant, use your words, damn it!" She had to raise her voice just to be heard. When she had carried Mayalee—on her back—into the Foundling Hall, the children had erupted like mage-fire, crowding around them with open curiosity. It was hard to think of them as rude, although technically it would have been hard to classify the questions that fell out of their constantly open mouths as anything else.

But Mayalee didn't seem to take offense, and she answered them all as well as she could, which, given her Elantran was all being borrowed from the Tha'alaan, took time. She had about a hundred or a thousand questions of her own to ask, as well.

Kaylin wouldn't have even considered delaying her journey home, but Mayalee had asked if Kaylin had children of her own, and while Kaylin had been saying no, Severn had said, "Oh, about two dozen of them."

And that had pretty much decided that, although the explanation of what the Foundling Hall actually *was* made no sense to the girl at first.

Marrin watched her kits with affectionate disapproval, content for the moment to let Kaylin play the heavy. She did discreetly remind Kaylin that consistency was necessary, and that threats were only useful if one was actually prepared to carry them out, but Marrin always said things like that.

To no one's surprise, Sandrina asked Mayalee where she lived, and then followed it up with the much more pressing question, "Can we visit there?"

To which Mayalee had instantly responded "YES!"

Expecting some rescue from Marrin's quarter, Kaylin was shocked to see the denmother of the Foundling Hall nod. "If Kaylin and Severn will escort you, and if you promise to behave, you can go."

And that was that.

She could barely remember the dread she had felt when she'd first approached the guardhouse that kept the rest of the city at bay. It seemed as if it had happened in another life, and as she walked, Severn caught Kaylin's hand and gave it a gentle squeeze. She looked up at him in surprise, and then offered him a rare, unguarded smile.

But the smaller children, having seen this, absolutely insisted on their turn holding Kaylin's hand, and in the end, both Kaylin and Severn ambled toward the guard with two children in voluntary tow.

The guard looked neither grim nor defensive; his expression was one of—joy. Just joy. Mayalee caught Catti's hand and dragged her toward the guard, who bent to greet them both.

The guard's stalks entwined briefly with Mayalee's, and before Kaylin could say a word, they left Mayalee's and gently brushed Catti's forehead. Catti didn't seem to mind, although she found it confusing, but Mayalee was—as Kaylin walked into hearing range—insisting that this was how you said "hello" *properly*.

And what Catti did, Dock was willing to do, and soon, all the children followed suit. It was *not* the same as the first visit.

But Kaylin was aware that the guard's joy was not just for the sight of Mayalee; he was happy to see *all* of the children.

Kaylin nodded as he finally managed to rise. "We're here to deliver Mayalee, but she invited—"

"Of course. She told me," he added with a grin. "I'm not sure how far you'll get, but Ybelline is expecting you."

It was fair warning; they entered the quarter single file, and less than a city block from the guardhouse, they were greeted by children of all ages, who ran like water through the foundlings until it was hard—in the running and chattering mass of chaotic youth—to tell them apart.

Severn, divested of his duties, walked over to Kaylin and smiled. "You think they'll like it here."

"I can't see how they wouldn't," she told him. "And I think…I think I'd like to bring them here every so often. It's not what I was afraid it was, and maybe they won't be afraid, either, when they become—well, whatever it is they want to become."

"Adults?"

"That, too."

Ybelline was, indeed, waiting for them, and they met her three blocks in. The whole Tha'alani quarter seemed to have gathered in the streets, but it wasn't exactly a parade. There was, however, food and sweet water in abundance, and oddly sweet cakes, as well. She hadn't the heart to chide her children for their terrible manners because they were in so much of a hurry to capture every experience they couldn't be pinned down for long.

But she had no fear of losing them, here.

In fact, she had no fear at all in this place.

"Kaylin," Ybelline said, bowing low. "Severn."

Kaylin smiled, and when the Tha'alani woman extended a hand in greeting, Kaylin shook her head, walked past the extended arm, and folded her own arms tightly around the castelord of the Tha'alani.

With no hesitation whatsoever, Ybelline abandoned the protocol of the deaf, and she returned Kaylin's hug, brushing strands of hair out of her eyes, and touching her forehead gently with her antennae.

She did not ask for promises, or for secrecy, or for silence. She asked for nothing. Took nothing.

Offered everything, and for a moment, Kaylin was willing to bask in the comfort of the contact; in the sense that she would not be alone unless she desired it.

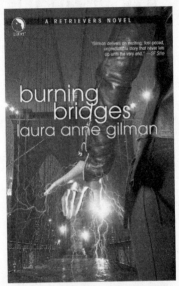

MUCH OF THE CITY CAN'T WAKE UP.
AND MORE ARE DOZING OFF EACH DAY.

C.E. MURPHY

As a sleeping sickness invades Seattle, reluctant shaman Joanne Walker has a few things to take care of. She has to find a way to wake her sleeping friends, figure out her inner-spirit dream life and, yeah, come to terms with these other dreams she's having about her boss....

WOULDN'T IT BE EASIER
TO JUST SAVE THE WORLD?

COYOTE
DREAMS

Available wherever trade paperback books are sold!